VOICE
of the
ANCIENT

THE KING'S MEN

VOICE
of the
ANCIENT

CONNILYN
COSSETTE

BETHANYHOUSE
a division of Baker Publishing Group
Minneapolis, Minnesota

Published by Bethany House Publishers
Minneapolis, Minnesota
www.bethanyhouse.com

Bethany House Publishers is a division of
Baker Publishing Group, Grand Rapids, Michigan

Printed in the United States of America

Library of Congress Cataloging-in-Publication Data
Names: Cossette, Connilyn, author.
Title: Voice of the ancient / Connilyn Cossette.
Description: Minneapolis : Bethany House Publishers, a division of Baker
    Publishing Group, [2023] | Series: The King's Men ; 1
Identifiers: LCCN 2023008924 | ISBN 9780764238918 (paper) | ISBN 9780764241314
    (casebound) | ISBN 9781493440627 (ebook)
Subjects: LCGFT: Bible fiction. | Novels.
Classification: LCC PS3603.O8655 V65 2023 | DDC 813/.6—dc23/eng/20230303
LC record available at https://lccn.loc.gov/2023008924

This is a work of historical reconstruction; the appearances of certain historical figures are therefore inevitable. All other characters, however, are products of the author's imagination, and any resemblance to actual persons, living or dead, is coincidental.

Author is represented by The Steve Laube Agency.

Baker Publishing Group publications use paper produced from sustainable forestry practices and post-consumer waste whenever possible.

23 24 25 26 27 28 29   7 6 5 4 3 2

For all those who walked beside me through the valley of cancer. You know who you are. You sent notes of encouragement, helpful items, gorgeous flowers, and handmade gifts. You fed my family and drove my kids all over town. You cheered me with your visits and folded my laundry. You gave of your time and your finances. You were my doctors, my nurses, my surgeons, and the ones to welcome me to treatments with an ever-present smile. You were patient with two years of upheaval in my writing process, chemo-brain drafts, major rewrites, and multiple pushed-back deadlines. You kept me going on the toughest days with your calls and texts and unwavering support. You tended to my basic needs when I was too sick to move. And most of all, you did not sit on the sidelines but instead battled alongside me with your prayers, lifting me up to the Great Healer and pleading on my behalf. You heeded the sacred call to fight at my side and on your knees. For all the suffering I endured over these past couple of years, I was gifted with a far greater abundance of love, joy, and peace—because of you.

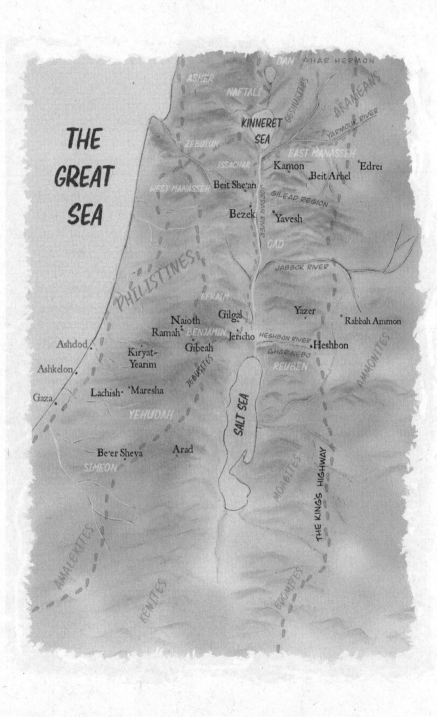

So Samuel told all the words of the LORD to the people who were asking for a king from him. He said, "These will be the ways of the king who will reign over you: he will take your sons and appoint them to his chariots and to be his horsemen and to run before his chariots. And he will appoint for himself commanders of thousands and commanders of fifties, and some to plow his ground and to reap his harvest, and to make his implements of war and the equipment of his chariots. He will take your daughters to be perfumers and cooks and bakers. He will take the best of your fields and vineyards and olive orchards and give them to his servants. He will take the tenth of your grain and of your vineyards and give it to his officers and to his servants. He will take your male servants and female servants and the best of your young men and your donkeys, and put them to his work. He will take the tenth of your flocks, and you shall be his slaves. And in that day you will cry out because of your king, whom you have chosen for yourselves, but the LORD will not answer you in that day." But the people refused to obey the voice of Samuel. And they said, "No! But there shall be a king over us, that we also may be like all the nations, and that our king may judge us and go out before us and fight our battles." And when Samuel had heard all the words of the people, he repeated them in the ears of the LORD. And the LORD said to Samuel, "Obey their voice and make them a king."

1 Samuel 8:10–22a ESV

A Psalm of Ronen ben Avidan

The anointed one shall abide by the counsel of the
    Most High,
The voice of the Ancient One to light his every step.

A shield to both the humble and the valiant,
His mighty fortress offers refuge to all who call on the
    Name.

From ashes and dust shall his glory arise,
a diadem of splendor to grace the head of the lowly.

His scepter lifted high shines justice across the Land,
Heavenly righteousness, like a river of gladness, flows
    from his throne.

Selah.

PROLOGUE

Avidan

1043 BC
MITZPAH, ISRAEL

Today, the first king of Israel would be chosen. And I would
see it happen with my own eyes.

"Heads down!" rasped my cousin Zevi from beside me
on the ground. My other cousin, Gavriel, and I plastered ourselves
to the dirt. The thick grasses atop the ridge hid us well from the
gathering of tribal leaders in the valley below, but we could not
take any chances.

My heartbeat drummed hard against my ribs as I held my
breath, praying the three of us hadn't been spotted. If we were
caught spying on the proceedings, my father would have me hauling water for the women thrice daily for a month. But such a
punishment would be worth enduring to bear witness to such a
pivotal event.

"What did you—" Gavriel began, but Zevi slapped a palm

across his mouth and gave a solemn shake of his head. The eldest among us at eighteen, Zevi's word usually held sway in situations like these. Even though he was older than me by only a year and Gavriel by nearly two, the horrors he'd witnessed as a child gave him the bearing of someone far older. Gavriel obeyed the silent command but not without rolling his eyes at Zevi's dramatic delivery. However, a scuffle behind us in the brush proved his caution worthwhile.

I sucked in a breath, lifting my eyes only far enough to search the stand of acacia trees that shaded our hiding place. I could almost feel the weight of the shoulder yoke across my back and the sun on my head as I imagined the next few weeks of walking back and forth from the stream. But instead of meeting my father's furious glare, it was our younger cousin Shalem's honey-brown eyes that peered around the trunk of the largest tree.

Gavriel huffed out a low laugh, shaking his head as he muttered, "Of course he followed."

"Shalem, what are you doing?" Zevi hissed. "We said we'd tell you the outcome as soon as it was over."

Shalem's black brows drew together. "It's not the same as being here. Why do you all get to watch and I don't?"

It was a valid question, and one he'd posed many times before. He hated whenever we left him behind. Hated being the youngest of us. But when we were boys running through the woods in Kiryat-Yearim with Zevi's giant dog loping alongside us, Shalem had paid the price for our negligence. The scar that bisected his right eyebrow, where a sharp branch had very nearly taken out his eye, was a constant reminder of that mistake.

None of us would ever forget the gush of blood streaming down his face, nor the tongue-lashing we'd received from his mother for not being more careful with her precious youngest child. Although Hodiya adored all of her children, she favored Shalem above the rest. Perhaps because with his black curls, bronze skin, and light-colored eyes he favored her—and her distant Egyptian heritage—the most.

So, for as frustrated as our young cousin was with our overprotectiveness, there were simply places we did not take him and times we did not invite him along. Sneaking up to the ridge overlooking an exclusive gathering of Israel's tribal elders was one of them. Even my own father, one of the most prominent musicians among the Levites, had not been invited to this meeting. It would be no small thing to be caught spying today.

However, like most people, I had a hard time denying Shalem anything. The boy was as charming as he was brilliant. He was also well aware of our weakness where he was concerned and rarely hesitated to use it to his advantage.

"Let him stay," I said with resignation. "What harm will it do now that he is already here? And someone could see him leaving."

Zevi frowned, forehead pinching as he searched for a reason to refute me. Shalem pressed his palms together beneath his chin, begging unashamedly. The small silver patch of hair he'd been born with, just above that scarred eyebrow, glimmered in the sunlight. Somehow the oddity only made his already-too-handsome appearance more intriguing. His mother called it the brush of Yahweh's finger and, much to the consternation of his older siblings, she insisted it proved Shalem was inordinately blessed.

"All right," grumbled Zevi, running his fingers through his mussed hair in frustration. "But keep down and say nothing."

Shalem's smile was a beam of light on this overcast day. Crouching, he scuttled through the grass, then wedged between Gavriel and me on the ground. "What did I miss?"

"Mostly arguing," I said in a breathy tone that even Zevi wouldn't chastise. "They are preparing now to cast the lots, but there were heated words over which set of priests—those who live here in Naioth or those from down in Hebron—had the authority to do so."

From what my father had told me over the years, there was ongoing dispute about who exactly held the divine blessing when it came to the priesthood—something about a shift in power over the lineage in long-dead ancestors. But since Samuel had been the judge over most matters among the tribes for decades now, and since it was he who'd called this meeting in the first place, he'd ended the argument by announcing that he would be the one to cast the lots.

"This decision will go as Yahweh wills, not men," he'd declared, ending the argument.

Although both groups acquiesced to his authority, it was obvious that the delegation from the southern tribes were less than pleased. My father thought the rifts between the sons of Yaakov were just too deep to mend after all this time, even when this new king was installed, but surely this gathering of all the tribes proved him wrong. Even delegations from across the Jordan River—Gad, Eastern Manasseh, and Reuben—had come to witness this moment. Although their clothing was odd and their accents strangely tilted after so many years of separation from the tribes on the west side of the Jordan, their presence here today would signify to the nations that Yaakov's sons were still one beneath the banner of Israel after all this time.

It was impossible not to feel the gravity of these proceedings, even for the four of us hiding in the brush like a pack of thieves. When Gavriel had come up with the idea to climb the ridge well before dawn so we could witness this decision, I'd been surprised Zevi had gone along with it. Instead of shrugging off the idea, a strange light had sparked in our cousin's eyes and he'd been insistent we get as close as we could so we would not miss a word. To my delight, the rocky cliffs around the gathering ushered the voices upward and straight to our curious ears.

Samuel and a few priests stood at the center of the congregation, and one gray-headed leader from each tribe was called to gather around in a tight circle to oversee the lots. I itched to be among them, wishing I knew exactly what the stones looked like and how the priests determined the answers given by Yahweh. I'd always wondered if it was like when my uncle Natan tossed his sheep-knuckle dice during games. But as I'd been born a Levite, like generations of men before me, we were not of Aharon's lineage and therefore not privy to the secret inner workings of the high priesthood.

With his official priestly garb and his silvery Nazirite braid trailing nearly to the back of his knees, Samuel's special status as a mouthpiece of Yahweh was never more apparent. He raised both hands in the air, a hush falling over the crowd as he supplicated loudly to the Most High before beginning his sacred task.

As Samuel began casting the lots, it seemed as if the entire valley held its collective breath. Even the birds in the trees above us were silent and the breeze went still. When the announcement was made that Naftali was the first tribe to be eliminated, the tension grew even more fraught.

One by one, tribes were ruled out by the stones, those representatives who remained pulling in closer and those who'd been rejected sidling back to rejoin their brethren. Soon, only the elders from Yehudah, Benjamin, and Efraim stood before Samuel. Again, the lots were cast, and Efraim was excused, the leader not looking at all surprised by the decision as he retreated to stand with his delegation.

However, when the tribe of Benjamin was announced to be the winner of the next toss, the men from the tribe of Yehudah exploded, their displeasure with the decision tinging the air with loud accusations that Samuel had somehow influenced the outcome. A few left the meeting altogether, heads shaking and expressions thunderous as they turned their backs on the assembly. And truly, I too was astounded that the wolves of Benjamin had been chosen over the lions of Yehudah. One of the smallest tribes, Benjamin had nearly destroyed themselves by instigating civil war decades ago and there was plenty of resentment left over for their foolishness, even after all this time. And even more than that, it was Yehudah who'd received the royal blessing from his father Yaakov. What could possibly have shifted in the mind of Yahweh?

A shofar sounded somewhere down in the chaos, startling everyone into relative quiet. Samuel stood unmoved in the center, arms folded across his barrel chest, and a stern look on his face. He waited until all eyes were on him before speaking.

"We've come here today to determine the will of Yahweh, my *brothers.*" He leaned into the word—a reminder that despite our tribal differences, the familial bond between the descendants of Avraham remained. "And if Adonai has chosen Benjamin for this honor, that is his right, as king and creator of the universe."

The revered prophet paused, gaze roving over the leaders standing before him. "And may I remind you that this is what *you* asked for? What you begged me for, even though I have warned you of the consequences? You may question my wisdom, as I am only a man, but do *not* question that of the Most High."

Satisfied order had been restored, Samuel continued his task, calling forth leaders from the major clans among the tribes of Benjamin and, just as with the tribes, eliminated them one by one, until the elder of the Matrites stood alone. I knew nothing of the family, but Gavriel, whose father was a Benjamite himself, whispered they were a small family but had a reputation for fierceness in battle.

From among them, the family of Kish was chosen by the lots, and I wondered if the man with iron-gray hair and broad shoulders was the one we'd been waiting for all this time. But another flurry of activity brought forth the man's sons.

"Which do you think it will be?" whispered Shalem as we surveyed the candidates who ranged in age from just a couple of years older than Zevi to one who, like his father, sported a dark gray beard and a regal posture.

To my surprise, the firstborn was the first to be eliminated. And in fact, when after a few more rounds of lots, Samuel called out the name *Saul*, everyone looked around in confusion, while the rest of the brothers appeared stunned.

"I saw him down near our campsite," replied one of the younger sons of Kish. "Hiding among the baggage."

Nervous laughter skittered through the crowd, but someone offered to go fetch him. Samuel's expression was a blank mask as the congregation below waited while shifting their feet and murmuring to one another.

Who was this man chosen by Yahweh to be king? His entire life had suddenly been redefined, transforming whatever mundane purpose he'd had before into something extraordinary, and I could not help but envy him. Not the weight of his coming responsibilities, or even the glory of such an exalted position, but that his life would not merely be the expected continuation of his father's legacy. My own path had been set in stone by the happenstance of my birth into a particular Levitical line, and into a family whose musical abilities were lauded all the way back to our sojourn in Egypt. What would it be like to have everything flipped upside down with one flick of a wrist?

While I was still knee-deep in my musings, a commotion near the back of the crowd snagged my attention. It seemed Saul ben Kish had been found.

A shiver tingled across my shoulders as I glanced over at my cousins, who were held in rapt attention. Gavriel and I had always been close, and Shalem naturally gravitated toward us older boys since all the cousins his own age were girls. But when Zevi had been adopted by my uncle Natan and his wife, Shoshana, our little pack solidified. We all wore a crosswise scar at the base of our thumbs as evidence of a blood-brother pact we took as children, testifying to our lifelong commitment to one another. I was grateful that all four of us, including Shalem, were here to witness this moment.

The crowd finally parted, and a man came forward, one who stood nearly a head above anyone around him. I'd thought Natan was the tallest man I'd ever seen, but Saul at least matched him, if not exceeded him by a couple of fingers. With dark brown hair, a thick beard along a strong jaw, skin bronzed from the sun, and his shoulders broad and hard-muscled, he looked like a man used to labor in the fields. Now that I saw him, I no longer doubted why he'd been selected above even his eldest brother. He would be impressive on and off the battlefield. Our enemies would think twice before going up against such a man.

A surge of hope swelled in me. Perhaps now our nation would no longer be so vulnerable to the others around us. I could almost see it all unfold in my mind: an army to make knees around us shake; a leader whose might was respected and feared among the nations; and tribes that would finally band together to claim what was ours by divine right.

All eyes followed Saul as he came forward to stand before Samuel. Perhaps it was only shock, but I could not help but think that the man's expression was strangely troubled for someone who'd been suddenly whisked from obscurity to glory, and whose name would be permanently inscribed in our nation's history as the first king of Israel.

As for Samuel, the prophet appeared unaffected by the man's impressive appearance, like he'd already known whose lot would fall before him today. He commanded Saul to turn and face both the tribal elders and the *nassim*, the princes of Israel whose born headship was now subject to a man of Benjamin appointed by Yahweh.

Samuel lifted his voice, the echo of it rolling over the expectant crowd. "Do you see the man Adonai has chosen?" His words rang with authority as he gestured toward Saul, whose strong stance belied none of the fleeting trepidation I'd glimpsed on his face moments before. "Do you see that there is no one like him among all the people?"

The men of Benjamin were the first to shout, but one by one the rest followed suit—even the men of Yehudah who'd been so angry at the unexpected cast of the lots.

"Long live the king!" came the cry from every corner of the valley of Mitzpah, from my own lips, and from my cousins on the ground beside me. "Long live King Saul!"

Avidan

NAIOTH, ISRAEL
1042 BC

The enemy grinned at me, tipping his chin upward as he slapped a flat palm to his chest, daring me to attack again. Although my muscles screamed, I took the bait, barreling forward with my sword raised.

We clashed, weapons tangling, both of us grunting and sweating and determined not to give the other the smallest measure of ground. Sword to sword, we circled each other, taking whatever hits we could but neither able to claim victory. I may have been taller and broader, but he was well-honed and relentless.

I swung again and missed, and he took the opportunity to taunt me, so I dug into whatever reserve of strength remained and slashed, the edge of my sword meeting the top of his shoulder where bone met bone.

He cursed, dark eyes flaring as he lost any hint of civility. He dropped his weapon and charged me, his body coming at me like a rampaging bull. The breath was knocked clear from my body as he took me down and we landed in a heap in the dirt. I blinked hard, trying to clear the haze from my head, and found a knife at my throat.

"You're dead," said my enemy. Then a slow grin spread over his face. "Again."

"Perhaps, if you'd actually unsheathed your knife." My gaze was pulled upward where Gavriel and Shalem were leaning over the two of us, smirking. I called them both a foul name and then pushed at Zevi with a snarl. "Get off me."

My cousin rolled away. "At least it was better than last time. It took me twice the effort to fend you off than it used to. You should never let your guard down."

For as long as I could remember, the four of us had played war games, sparring with sticks or pine cones or whatever makeshift weapon we could find on the forest floor. But Zevi was nearing the age of twenty, when he would be allowed to stand with his Yehudite brethren. So along the way, our games had transformed into casual training exercises, and we took turns trying to best him by whatever means necessary. I'd even spent extra time lately running the hills and lifting heavier and heavier stones in preparation for his arrival in Naioth, where our families had gathered to celebrate the Pesach holidays in the Levitical community built by Samuel the Seer. Yet, no matter how hard I had pushed myself these past weeks, Zevi was still victorious.

Perhaps it was simply that he spent most of his time in Kiryat-Yearim cutting down trees with his father and hauling timber to help support his family, or because any spare moments he had were spent in training himself for what he considered his life's purpose. Perhaps it was that he was simply a born soldier whose every thought was vengeance. I was certain that when he finally had the opportunity to join the fight Saul's men would take immediate notice of his skill.

His father had told him he must wait until after the fall festivals to take up arms against the Philistines, an obvious attempt to stall the inevitable. And because of Zevi's great respect for my uncle, he'd submitted. But he was like a stallion champing at the bit, huffing and stamping as he awaited the moment he was finally cut loose.

It had been a decade since he'd been swept up in the destruction of the town of Zanoah and taken into slavery by the Philistines. And while I was glad that he would finally have the chance to stand against our enemies like he could not as a child, it was difficult to quash the envy that had lately dug its claws into me. The next time the enemy reared its head, Zevi would have the freedom to march into battle while I would be stuck here, making pretty instruments.

Frustration boiling over, I sprang to my feet to charge at Zevi again. Thrown off-balance by my surprise attack, my cousin went down with a thud, my forearm locked on his throat. I may not be as skilled with weapons as Zevi or Gavriel, but my uncle had showed me a thing or two from his time as the bare-knuckled champion of Ashdod.

Zevi's eyes were wide as he blinked up at me in shock, but then he began to laugh. Shaking his head, he lifted his large square palm and splayed it over my face, pushing me backward. "Get off me, you big sweaty ox."

"You should never let your guard down," I mocked and then began laughing too. Gavriel and Shalem joined in, the four of us making enough ruckus to set a bevy of blackbirds darting into the sky.

Zevi grinned as he stood, brushing crushed leaves and dirt from his tunic. "That, I should not. Especially against the Philistine half of you."

I grabbed for him again, pulling him into a headlock and scrubbing at his forehead with my knuckles. "You'd best not forget it either."

He pushed me away with a playful growl. It had always astounded me that he never held a grudge against me for my mother's heritage, even after what he'd endured.

"My turn!" shouted Shalem, swinging the wooden sword I'd tossed aside during my altercation with Zevi. Gavriel had made the practice weapon from some sturdy terebinth a couple of years ago and the thing was thicker around than both of Shalem's slender wrists combined. He'd not yet grown into his gangly limbs, and no matter that he ate nearly as much as Gavriel and I combined, he never seemed to gain even a spoonful of bulk. And much to his chagrin, his face remained as smooth as the day he'd been born.

But whatever our younger cousin lacked in build or physical maturity, he made up for in heart and astounding intelligence. He might not ever be a warrior like Zevi or Gavriel, since he too was of the Levitical lineage, but I had no doubt that someday he would be a force to be reckoned with in one way or another.

Accepting our younger cousin's challenge, Zevi snatched up his own practice sword and met Shalem in the center of the clearing. Of course, he used little of the force he'd employed against me during our match, yet preserved Shalem's honor by making a believable pretense of effort.

"Are you really going to let a boy with no beard beat you up, Zev?" Gavriel called out when Shalem got in a surprise hit to Zevi's shoulder, then hooted in victory. Zevi called the two of us a name for our laughter but also congratulated Shalem for the strike.

"Uncle Natan will never be comfortable with Zevi's choice to fight," Gavriel said from beside me, "but he has to be impressed with how he's prepared himself."

It was true. Zevi was more than ready to be a soldier, even if his father himself had vowed to never lift a hand in violence for anything other than immediate defense of his loved ones. The two of them had had many arguments over Zevi's determination to go to war, but Natan could not debate Zevi's origins. Zevi may call Natan and Shoshana his parents, but they never insisted he forget his heritage among the sons of Yehudah. And neither did they forbid him from pursuing what he felt was his purpose—to avenge those he'd watched suffer all those years before.

"If only I didn't have to wait to follow him," Gavriel said under his breath.

Even though Gavriel was nearly two years from military age, he was almost as restless as Zevi, eager to do his part for our people and even more anxious to be out of his stepfather's home.

Although my aunt Miri's husband was nothing like his drunken abuser of a brother, who'd fathered Gavriel and then died an ignominious death, the man who'd stepped in to marry his brother's widow was far too absorbed in building his business contracts and amassing wealth to care what her son did, or to fulfill his own responsibilities to his tribal brethren.

Instead, the wealthy Benjamite employed a cadre of mercenaries to protect his large home down in neighboring Ramah and trusted that his connections with others—be they Canaanite, Israelite, or even Philistine—would keep him and his family safe, no matter who was in power. He'd even found favor with our new king over the past year, but Gavriel was determined to prove himself in battle, not by filling the royal coffers with silver.

"At least you'll *have* a chance to go," I said. "When the time comes, you'll be gaining glory on the battlefield with your Benjamite brethren and I'll be here strumming a harp."

"True. But just remember"—his brow furrowed as he clapped a hand to my shoulder, his expression solemn—"that means you'll have plenty of time for all the women in town while we are off fighting."

I swung at him, laughing. "As if any of them would look twice at your ugly face, even if you were here."

He dodged my halfhearted punch. "Don't worry, I'm sure Uncle Ronen will beg a few fathers to force their daughters to consider you while we are gone."

"Have you forgotten who I resemble most?" I replied with a smug grin. "My mother said her brother was the most sought-after man in all of Ashdod. They used to scream and faint at his feet like he was a god."

He shrugged. "Well, I've heard Philistines also bow down to snakes and rodents, so . . ."

I growled, grabbing him by the shoulders and yanking him to the ground. We wrestled, pinching and taking easy shots at each other while Zevi and Shalem ignored our antics and continued sparring.

21

A distant ram's horn broke through our noise, the sound emanating from the direction of Ramah. We paused our scuffling to listen, the hair rising on my neck as the haunting echo of the rapid bleats died away.

When the shofar sounded again, this time with an even more urgent pitch to the call, the four of us looked at one another for a breathless moment before we were on the move, racing out of the clearing in silent accord to the valley below. We'd be late to the evening meal and the celebration to follow, but I'd apologize later. I had to find out why all able-bodied men had just been summoned to the city gates.

2

We pushed through the teeming crowd gathered in front of the city gates, Zevi in the lead and Shalem between Gavi and me so he'd not be separated from us in the confusion. It had only been a quarter of an hour, if that, since the shofar had screeched out its command, but already there was a horde of men gathered near the entrance of the city.

From the swarm of conjectures going up around us, everyone else was just as clueless as we were. A few believed the Philistines were on the move again, and others wondered if perhaps the new king of Israel had already been deposed; no one had heard much of Saul over the last year since he'd been crowned, after all. All we knew was that he'd retreated to Gibeah to begin building his council and learning his new role as sovereign. There had been a few small incursions of our coastal enemies over the past months and the tribal militias had handled it on their own, thus far. But judging by the fraught tension in the air, something had changed.

The crowd jostled, pressing the four of us together as Ramah's elders came into view. Shalem stood on the balls of his feet, neck stretching in an attempt to see the proceedings. Although he'd grown a good handspan in the last few months, he still was head and shoulders shorter than me.

"I can't see anything, Avi," he groused. "What is happening?"

I put my hands on his slender shoulders. "Nothing yet. The

elders are taking their seats up on the dais. It won't be long until order is called."

Once the silver-headed men were perched on the stone seats where they mediated arguments, meted out judgments, and discussed issues with the town, a short trumpet blast cut through the furor and brought every curious eye to the front, where Zavdiel, the head of the council and a close associate of Gavi's stepfather, stood to address the throng.

"Good men of Ramah, thank you for your swift answer to our summons. A group of King Saul's men has arrived from Gibeah with an urgent message from the throne." He gestured off to the side, where four men stood, hair windblown and tunics dusty from what looked to have been a swift ride on horseback. "They tell us their message is an urgent one that every man of Benjamin, and those who live among us, must hear and obey. It comes directly from Saul's mouth to your ears. So give them your full attention."

How odd that the elders seemed just as stymied by these strange events as the rest of us, their usual solemn faces lined with curiosity as the four men came forward, one of them leading a thick-muscled horse by the reins.

I shared a glance of confusion with Zevi and Gavi. For our entire lives, these tribal elders controlled the region, their seats passed down through ancient bloodlines. Only the nassim, the princes of the tribes who'd inherited their power from the sons of Yaakov, stood above them, in accordance with Mosheh's ancient division of responsibilities.

But once Saul had been crowned, the line of authority had shuffled downward, and the elders now answered to both the princes and the king of Israel, along with anyone else Saul appointed to offices of power. For the first time, we were witness to the new order of things. This message was being delivered directly from the king to the people of Israel, not filtered through the council, and they had no choice but to comply.

"Avi," said Shalem, his tone desperate, "what is going on?"

"Hush," I whispered. "One of Saul's messengers just stepped forward to speak."

The man waited until the murmurs of the anxious crowd melted away before he spoke. "Men of Ramah and the surrounding region, descendants of Benjamin and brothers of our king, we bring you a missive from the lips of our sovereign. We are only one group of many sent to every corner of Israel's territories with the same news."

Gavi leaned into my shoulder. "It's war," he said, his voice pitched with excitement. "It has to be. There could be no other reason for Saul to send so many messengers all at once."

On my other side, Zevi had gone stiff, his gaze locked on Saul's men. Two of them were working together to untie some sort of parcel from the back of the horse. Whatever was wrapped in black wool must be heavy, since it took both men to heft the burden between them.

"Here is the word of our king, Saul ben Kish, anointed of Adonai," said the first messenger, with a gesture toward his companions. One jerk of the leather tie that held the wool-wrapped parcel together and it unrolled like an enormous scroll. For a hazy moment, my eyes could not quite reconcile what I was seeing. I didn't know what I'd expected, but it was not the raw and bloody limb of some sort of hoofed animal. One that had not been butchered with skillful precision but instead appeared to have been hacked from the carcass in haste. Shoulder to hoof, the foreleg still dripped with deep crimson lifeblood.

The throng burst into horrified chatter as the messengers stood silent, allowing panic to take hold of the crowd.

"What?" demanded Shalem. "What is it?"

"The foreleg of an animal," I said. "A bull or an ox by the appearance of the hide."

Shalem's nose wrinkled with disgust. He'd never been one to tolerate gore. "What sort of message is that?"

I shrugged, just as bewildered. I looked to Zevi to see if he had any insight, but my older cousin's eyes were focused on the gruesome scene, his jaw ticking as he ground his teeth.

The messenger lifted both palms in the air, a silent command for quiet. When the tumult calmed, he pointed to the morbid offering. "Hear the words of King Saul, men of Benjamin. This is one of twelve pieces of our king's own oxen. One portion sent to each of the tribes."

"What does it mean?" called one brave soul from somewhere in the crowd.

"It means," replied the messenger, "that your king needs you. The Ammonites under Nahash, King of Rabbah, have attacked our brethren on the other side of the river. Not only have they razed a path of destruction through the territories of Gad, Reuben, and Manasseh, but they also have besieged the city of Yavesh in Gilead."

Something familiar niggled in the back of my mind at the name of the Gaddite city, some fleeting memory I could not quite grasp.

"Nahash has promised to put out the right eye of every man within the walls of Yavesh," continued the messenger, "to both humiliate Israel and keep them from raising arms against him in the future. We have less than a week to come to their aid."

He pointed to the disgusting heap of flesh and bone in the dirt. "Anyone who does not follow Saul, and with him Samuel the Seer, this is what will be done to *his* oxen." He slid a menacing gaze over the crowd, a deeper threat underlying his words. "You have two days to gather at Bezek, from where we will march on Yavesh and defeat the dog who dares bare his teeth against our brethren."

Our families were gathered beneath the canopy of two ancient terebinth trees, chattering on blithely by the flicker of torchlight, when Zevi, Shalem, and I returned after sunset. Gavriel had stayed behind to share the news with his family, but I knew my cousin would not be long in joining us. He was far too stirred up to stay down in the valley for long. He'd want to discuss the upcoming battle and talk about all the weapons the men would be taking with them.

My father was the first to spot us, searching the dark treeline for our arrival. He popped up from the blanket he'd been sitting on with my mother and my two youngest sisters and headed for us with a deep furrow between his brows. Not far behind him was Natan, his long legs eating up the distance. My uncle was built like one of the trees he spent his days chopping down in the forest, and although he'd left behind the fighting grounds long ago, he still looked every bit the champion of Ashdod, especially with the glare he leveled at Zevi.

"Where have you been?" demanded both my father and Natan, nearly in tandem.

"Everyone has been looking for you boys," my father added.

I bristled, stretching to my full height, which was nearly within reach of Natan's. "We weren't gone all that long."

"You missed most of the meal. Your mothers have been worried sick."

I bit my tongue against the urge to remind him that I was no longer a boy. "We were up on the ridge when we heard a shofar down in the valley, so we went to find out what was happening."

They glanced at each other, their expressions befuddled.

"I heard nothing," said my father. "Did you?"

Natan shook his head. "I've been negotiating with the elders of Naioth all day over a delivery of timber for the roof of the assembly building."

Natan's skill at finding the best lumber and providing it for building projects was well known in this region. He led a crew of nearly fifty men who supplied the finest timber south of Tyre. Most, if not all, of the riches he'd walked away from in Ashdod had been replaced, even though he'd merely set about to provide for his wife and children. Yet they still lived in the small four-room house he'd rebuilt with his own hands ten years before, and no one in Kiryat-Yearim ever went hungry or without necessary supplies due to his generosity—even if many of those same people had called him Demon Eyes and reviled him when he was a boy.

"What was this shofar call about?" said my father, just as Iyov, Shalem's father and my mother's second-eldest brother, joined us.

Iyov placed his hands on his son's shoulders. "Where did these mischief-makers take you now, son?"

"I was safe, Abba. I promise. We went down to Ramah to hear the king call us to war!" Shay was practically bouncing on his heels.

My father's eyes went wide. "War? With the Philistines?"

Natan flinched, but Zevi shook his head. "No. This threat isn't from the west, but the east. We are heading out to rescue the people of Yavesh in Gilead from a siege by the Ammonites."

"We?" Natan's gaze narrowed on his son.

Zevi's chin went up, his expression like granite. He may not be anywhere near his father's height or breadth, but he was nothing if not determined. "I am in my twentieth year. A few months means nothing."

My uncle's mismatched brown and green eyes seemed to darken. "That will be a discussion for later."

"There's nothing to discuss, Abba. Our king has called—no, *commanded*—us to join together against an enemy of Israel. In fact, he threatened anyone who refused to heed the call."

"Threatened?" Iyov pulled Shalem a bit closer to himself.

"Tell them, Avidan," said Zevi, knowing the news was burning a hole in my tongue. His words were usually sparse and carefully chosen, but he knew there was nothing I loved more than describing events in detail. And what we'd witnessed today was like nothing I'd ever seen before. Every moment was etched in my mind like on a tablet of stone. Even as I relayed what we'd witnessed at the gates of Ramah, I could feel the pulse of zeal from the men as they discussed preparations for the battle.

"Why would the king send pieces of an ox to the tribes instead of simply asking for help?" asked Natan.

"It's a warning," replied my father. "A reminder of something that happened decades ago, when the Mishkan was still standing at Shiloh. I will not go into all the grisly details, but suffice it to say that it drove the sons of Yaakov to civil war and nearly brought the tribe of Benjamin to extinction. Only rather than pieces of an ox being sent out as a warning, it was pieces of an innocent woman who died at the hands of repugnant men."

Of course. That was the reason Saul's message had seemed so familiar to me. The gang of Benjamites had been so entangled with the Canaanites that they'd taken on their vile ways, raped and murdered the poor woman, and their brethren did not repudiate that behavior. It was a tale of woe meant to warn against assimilation with the various foreigners who still lived among us and a grim reminder that rebellion against Yahweh's commands would tear our nation apart at its very foundations. I'd been both fascinated and scandalized by the disturbing story when I first heard it as a boy.

"What does that have to do with the town of Yavesh?" asked my uncle, who was still learning our histories even after two decades among Hebrews.

"There were so few men left among Benjamin after the tribal civil war, and even fewer women, that a campaign was made to find wives for the survivors. The people of Yavesh were among those who refused to raise swords against Benjamin during the conflict. A group was sent to punish them for condoning the abhorrent and rebellious behavior against the Most High, and they returned with four hundred of their young women as brides for the remaining Benjamites. Saul himself would be a descendent of one of those women."

"So the tie between Benjamin and Yavesh is a familial one," mused Natan. "No wonder Saul is so determined to go to their rescue."

"As he should," said Zevi. "We should be one united nation beneath the king's banner. If we do not come to the rescue of our brothers, then our nation will be torn apart like that ox. The time is now to show the enemies who surround us that our new king will not tolerate invasion."

29

"We should be united beneath the banner of the Most High," said my father. "Not merely Saul."

"Saul is the anointed of the Most High, is he not?" Zevi said. "And the messenger made it clear that Samuel was involved as well."

My father tipped his head slightly, but something about his posture made me think he was not quite convinced. From what he'd told me over the years about the power struggles between Levitical leaders and priests, and how his own father and brothers had perished due to weak leadership, I suspected he might always be skeptical of any man in a place of power, even one anointed by his own teacher and mentor.

"And what else did this messenger say?" Natan asked.

As I told them of Nahash's threat to take the right eye of each man in Yavesh, I wondered if perhaps I would prefer death to such a dishonor. A lifelong reminder of such humiliating defeat would be difficult to bear. "Saul's messenger said that we could not allow the Ammonites to humiliate our brethren or we might as well gouge out our own eyes."

This was why a king had been crowned in Israel. To unite us in purpose against those who dared go against the people of Yahweh. The people of Yavesh were our kin; of course we should come together for our brothers, even if we'd been separated from them for centuries. As Zevi said, it was far past time when the tribes should march beneath one banner, no matter which side of the river we called home. King Saul's command was like a shofar call reverberating in my chest, and I ached to answer the summons.

From beneath the terebinths, Zevi's mother, Shoshana, called out to us, announcing that we should come eat before all the food was gone.

With only a quiet nod of his head to the rest of us, Iyov led Shalem over to their family. I watched as Hodiya pulled her son close with a frown, likely chastising him for disappearing with us yet again. However, within only a few moments, she was smiling and kissing his forehead. The boy had a tongue fashioned from silver that matched the streak in his hair. No one could stay angry with him for long.

"I'm going," said Zevi, without a hint of vacillation. "First thing tomorrow when the rest of the men leave. I'll meet up with my Yehudite brethren at Bezek."

Natan stiffened as he stared down the boy he'd rescued from slavery. I knew for certain that my uncle loved Zevi more than his every breath and considered him no different from the rest of his and Shoshana's children. But he also acknowledged Zevi still felt a strong loyalty to the tribe he'd been born into.

"You told me I should use my hands to defend the weak, Abba," said my oldest cousin. "The people of Yavesh need us."

Natan closed his eyes, arms folded over his broad chest, looking pained and nearly as unsteady as one of the trees he felled on a daily basis. I often wondered how my uncle reconciled the two halves of himself: the Philistine blood that ran in his veins with the fierce allegiance he'd chosen to offer the tribes of Israel a decade ago. If only I, like the uncle I so resembled in face and form, had the luxury to choose whether to go out and fight for our people, instead of being born into a life of Levitical duty and therefore banned from military service.

Dropping his shoulders with a shake of his head, Natan sighed in resignation. "Your mother will kill me for not forbidding you. But I also know you have trained hard for this day, and I have every confidence in your ability to defend yourself and others."

Zevi's shoulders straightened as he locked eyes with the man who was nothing less than a savior in his eyes. Natan's large palm squeezed Zevi's shoulder, which nearly rivaled his own for muscle after years of working together in the forest. "Come, let's eat now. You can tell her after the meal."

Zevi blanched. "Why can't you?"

Natan shook his head. "I went up against some of the fiercest fighters in this area of the world, but Shoshana could terrify the best of them. If you really want to go up against the Ammonites, you'll have to face your mother first."

I remained in place as everyone walked away, not ready to join a carefree celebration with the image of that bloody foreleg rolling across the ground in my head and frustration with my lot swirling in my gut. The men around us today at the city gates had immediately begun making plans for their departure, talking about which weapons they could scrape together and what provisions to gather—and I had nothing to add to the conversation.

"And so it all begins," said my father from beside me. I startled at his unexpected presence.

"What begins?"

"Samuel told us any king we lifted up would demand the best of our young men to fight for him."

"Are we not to defend ourselves? Shall we let the Ammonites oppress our brothers?"

"Of course not," he said. "The eastern tribes left behind their families to fight for us during our conquest of this Land before returning across the river. We should absolutely stand beside them against any enemy."

"Then what is the issue?"

"The method," said my father, on a sigh. "To come here not with a call for volunteers who choose to serve their brethren out of love and loyalty but with a bloody threat of violence against those who do not heed his demand. To me, it alludes to what sort of king Saul will be. A truly great leader will inspire his people to unite, not threaten them into submission."

"He hasn't had enough time on the throne to build such loyalty," I said. "Persuading all of us to come together as one through more gentle means would take too long. The people of Yavesh need us now."

He nodded, contemplating. "True. And time will tell what kind of king Saul will be. There is a reason Yahweh chose him, after all, and a reason Samuel anointed him. We can only pray that he will inspire the tribes to put aside long-held differences and embrace the Torah as the tie that binds us. There are some tribes up north and to the east that barely speak the same language we do. And some in the south who have no interest in bowing their knees to a Benjamite. If he thinks he can force them all to do so with threats alone, then our union will be a difficult endeavor at the least."

"Perhaps he knows that many of the tribes will not bother to go unless it's demanded of them."

"Even under threat, many will not," said my father. "The harvest has barely begun. Those who heed the call will have to lay down their sickles in ripe fields and with fruit still on the vine. For some, feeding their own families is far more important than going to the aid of people they've never met, in a far-distant region they've never seen, even if those people are our brothers."

"And yet some who actually want to go, who are ready and willing and have nothing tying them down, are barred from it."

My father's brows pitched high. "And you are among the willing?"

Perhaps I should have let the question go unanswered, brushed it aside as an off-handed remark. But somehow I found the words spilling over anyhow. "Zevi has trained me."

He tilted his chin up to look me in the eye. "For what?"

"For battle. You know that Gavriel, Zevi, and I have spent years sparring together whenever possible. But these last couple of weeks while Zevi's been here, we've been helping him ready himself for battle. In doing so, we've prepared ourselves as well."

My father paused, his gaze intent on mine. "So you think you are ready for war?"

I shrugged.

"And tell me, son. Are you prepared for what war actually is? For the brutality?"

I folded my arms over my chest. "As much as any other young man who has not marched into battle."

"Coming against an enemy on the battlefield is not playing at swords with your cousins, Avidan."

33

I huffed a laugh. "I'm fully aware."

"I don't think you are. You've lived in Naioth your entire life, a priestly community insulated from many of the issues common to other towns. You've never traveled farther than Kiryat-Yearim. You, along with the rest of our family, were hidden here during that last battle with the Philistines at Mitzpah, so you have no clue what such a thing is actually like. There is no glory in war, only destruction."

"I'm not ignorant to the horrors of war, Abba. I've listened to the stories all my life."

"But have you ever seen a man's entrails spilled on the ground? Or a slew of arrows pierce armor and limbs? Watched slingstones knock a hole in a man's skull? Have you witnessed enough gore and blood and filth around you to fill a cistern? Or heard the shrieks of men pleading with the heavens for their own deaths? What about the crows picking away the carnage once the entire horrific battle comes to an end?"

"No," I said, exasperated with his long-winded argument. "But neither have you."

"Because I am a Levite, Avidan. As are you."

My teeth snapped together, my blood surging hot. "Like I needed a reminder."

"Apparently you do."

I shook my head, a thousand retorts ready to spout from my lips. But none of that would sway him, so why bother?

"Listen, Avi. I was your age once. And I was disillusioned, restless, and full of bitterness. I nearly stole the Ark of the Covenant, son, because I listened to the wrong men and did not wait for Yahweh's direction before choosing my path. I understand—"

"No. You don't. Because yes, perhaps you walked the wrong path for a while, but you've never doubted your role as a Levite, as a musician. You've never—"

"Of course I did! There were many years when I did nothing but go through the motions, when my heart was not in the least engaged in what I'd been created to do. When all I could think of was avenging my father and brothers. Music was a mere after-thought."

"But you never hated it!"

He flinched, taken aback by my acidic tone. A tendril of guilt unfurled in me, but I ruthlessly cut it off.

"You've never dreaded picking up another instrument or wished you were anywhere else but in the middle of one more lesson on how to play songs that some ancient person wrote about things that have nothing to do with today. We aren't in slavery anymore, so why are we still lamenting being trapped in Egypt? We know the history of where we came from. It's time to look to the future."

"Those songs don't teach us about ourselves, son. They teach us about the God who freed us. Because if we forget who Yahweh is, if we let ourselves slide down that slippery slope, then we are no different from the nations around us."

I knew the stories of the ancients. Loved them. I could recite them backward and forward, inside out and upside down in my sleep. Many of them I'd learned from the prophet Samuel himself during Levitical training sessions in Naioth.

"This is a new day, Abba. We have a king now. One who is strong enough to demand that we gather and fight. If we don't protect the Land, there will be no one left to sing your songs to. And nothing will ever make me want to sing those songs anyhow. I'd rather be doing much of anything else than playing music."

"I know you aren't as eager as some of your siblings when it comes to performing, but you've always taken part. Why haven't you said anything before now?"

I sighed. Because more than anything, I hated disappointing my father. How many times had he told me that as the firstborn I would inherit the priceless lyre made by his ancient ancestor back during the flight from Egypt? That the legacy passed down from father to son for countless generations would one day be mine?

"And what would be the point? Being a Levite isn't something I chose to be. I can no more stop being one than I can cease being the son of a musician heralded by everyone in this region."

"There is more to being a Levite than music, Avidan—"

"Not in this family." I gestured to my sisters, Noa and Shiron, who were singing a blessing to conclude the meal I had now missed entirely while everyone sat in awe of their perfectly balanced harmony.

My father ran both hands down his face. "I know you may not believe me, but I do understand your frustration."

I opened my mouth to refute him, but he lifted a staying palm.

"It may feel wrong to stand back and let others go to war, but the duties that we Levites have been given are a blessing. A unique service to the Eternal One and his people that we have the privilege of devoting our lives to. And besides, if you have forgotten, you are named for a man who died on the battlefield. A man who followed misguided leaders and perished for it."

I knew well the story of my grandfather's end. I'd heard it so many times that I could practically feel the weight of the Ark on my own shoulders as I imagined him and my uncles striding across the battlefield toward the Philistines, toward their deaths.

"But at least he did *something*, even if the battle was lost. He did not hide in the hills with the women and children like a frightened jackrabbit. And if he and the other Levites would have been armed in that fight, known how to defend themselves better instead of being lambs sent into a pack of wolves, perhaps I would not be named after a dead man."

The moment the words passed my lips, I knew I'd gone too far. I'd never once heard my father even raise his voice in anger, but I had the distinct impression that he would gladly hit me right now without remorse. And I almost welcomed his wrath. My fists were clenched tight, my chest heaving, and my blood on fire.

His voice came out low. "I think it best we reserve this discussion for another day, son."

I scoffed. "What is there to discuss? I know what is expected of me, even if I think sitting here singing songs in safety while our brothers risk their lives is the coward's way."

"That is enough," he said, a sharper edge to his tone than I'd ever heard before. "We are finished with this subject for now. Go join the family."

As furious as I was, I'd never flagrantly disrespected my father before. Anything more that came out of my mouth would be something to regret later. Besides, no matter what I said or did, I could not escape who I was destined to become: a Levitical musician and instrument maker, just like Ronan ben Avidan and his father before him.

Therefore, I submitted to his authority, accepting with quiet thanks the bowl of food and cup of wine my mother had saved for me, even though the words of Saul's messenger continued to ring in my ears.

The threat of being cut to pieces was nothing to someone who already felt torn in half by his own heritage, and I would gladly answer the king's call to fight for the people of Yavesh if I were allowed to do so.

Instead, I was shackled by a nearly five-hundred-year-old mandate made at the foot of Mount Sinai, one that was meant to be a blessing to my ancestors and those born into the Levitical bloodline. But to me, it felt far more like a curse hanging around my neck like a millstone.

3

Keziah

KAMON, ISRAEL

S arru's hooves thundered over the plain, the rhythm a soothing drumbeat as I let my body move in perfect rhythm with
his large one. There was no distinction between him and me
when we ran like this—wild, abandoned, nothing but the sky above
us and the earth below. I gave him the freedom to lose himself in
speed and gave myself permission to flee the thoughts that had
kept me tossing and turning on my bed all night.

Mine was a horse meant for flying, his solid body a perfect
sculpture from forelock to heel. Bred from the bloodlines of the
famous warhorses of the Zagros region, he knew he was meant
to carry kings. Every toss of his black head was a demand that all
take heed of his beauty and strength. It was only with me that the
arrogant head tosses and dismissive snorts were nothing but a ruse.

His line came from a trio of warhorses gifted to my great-
great-grandfather long ago for heroics during a battle that saw
the Hebrews chasing the king of Aram and his forces all the way
back across the Euphrates River. The issue of those horses, which
had been taken as spoils during that battle, were known far and

wide as some of the fastest and strongest within the Land. They'd afforded our family great wealth and status among the tribe of Manasseh, making my father one of the most powerful clan chiefs in the region.

Sarru's dam had gone sickly during the pregnancy and was unable to nurse once she delivered. My father hadn't thought the foal would survive that first night, let alone the days that followed, with as weak and frail as he was. He counted the little horse a loss, but I could not fathom the idea of letting such a beautiful animal die. With my stomach roiling like a thunderstorm, I screwed together enough courage to approach my father, even though he'd not spoken to me in the six months since my mother had passed, and begged that the foal not be destroyed. To my great surprise, he'd said the horse was mine to do with as I wished but not to come weeping to him when it died. Then he'd walked away without another word.

Although I'd only been nine years old, I'd spent weeks sleeping in the stable and feeding him with my own hands until the foal came through the worst of whatever illness his dam had passed to him. By the time my father realized that Sarru would live, the horse followed me everywhere and answered only to my voice. Sarru had been the only gift my father had ever given me since my mother's death, and I made certain to never give him reason to take him back. I kept to myself within our home, never venturing outside the gates unless it was to exercise Sarru out in the country-side, and I maintained a placid and complaisant demeanor at all times—especially in my father's presence. And my horse, my only friend, was worth it all.

Even though Sarru had sired many masterpieces of his own now, he still preferred me over anyone and grew fiercely agitated if I went longer than a day without visiting him or letting him stretch his long legs with a run like we were doing now.

I slowed Sarru to a walk and then led him to a bluff overlooking the valley. The Yarmouk River lay below, sparkling silver and gold in the morning sunlight as it made haste toward the Sea of

Kinneret in the west. Across the divide, the hills of Bashan arose, their fertile peaks and valleys hiding the three snowy heads of Har Hermon in the northern distance.

I breathed deeply of the sweetly scented air, detecting a hint of apple blossom on the breeze that made my mouth water as I leaned against Sarru's twitching side. The thickly forested hills and lush valleys around Kamon were blessed by the gods.

"Keziah!" called a voice I knew as well as my own.

I turned to find my maid, Imati, a few paces away, her yellow turban bright in the sunlight. For all the years I'd known her, I'd never once seen her hair undone, nor her veiled face uncovered.

"We've been looking for you all over the valley," she said as she approached. "Your father asked us to fetch you."

I frowned, stroking Sarru's neck when he twitched his ears back nervously. "I've not yet finished my ride."

"He is adamant, mistress. We must make haste." With a pinch in her brow, she gestured up to the ridge, where a chariot sat waiting. Beside it was Nabal, my father's cousin and right-hand man, watching me with a blank expression.

It had been years since my father had directly called me into his presence. In fact, unless he needed to trot me out like one of his prized mares, dressed in finery and my mother's jewels, like he had last night when a group of visitors had arrived from nearby Beit Arbel, he barely seemed to notice my existence.

Stomach twisting, I touched the amulet of Asherah I wore, one that had always been around my mother's neck and now never left mine, and lifted a silent prayer to my goddess for favor. I had a good idea why I'd been summoned today, and the conflict it stirred in me made me consider jamming my heels into Sarru's sides and steering him for the hills.

But there was little use prolonging the inevitable. Where would I go? I had no friends other than the one huffing and stamping his hooves beneath me and had never even left this valley. I'd be lost on my own. All I could do was obey my father and accept my fate. Even though it meant leaving the only home I'd ever known.

Resigned, I slid off Sarru's back and gathered his reins, then followed Imati up the ridge, where Nabal waited with arms folded. The man very rarely spoke to me other than to relay commands from my father in a condescending tone. But more than a few times over the past several years, I'd caught his deep-set gray eyes following me from across the room. I had the distinct feeling that he hated me for some reason I could not fathom, so I steered clear of him whenever possible.

I would much rather ride Sarru back to Kamon just to avoid riding in the chariot with him, but I knew it would profit none of us if I arrived before Nabal in my haste to discover what my father had decided about my future.

So I submitted to having my stallion tied to the back of the chariot and then mounted beside Imati. The entire way back to town, I clutched my mother's amulet and prayed that if I was to be handed off to a man from the visiting clan and sent away from everything I knew, like I feared, it would be to one who treated me like more than a pretty but useless vase to be placed high on a shelf.

I knocked on the door to my father's chambers, pulse hammering and my gut in knots. With her usual skill, Imati had swiftly removed all traces of my morning ride, taming my windblown black curls into something more fitting of a clan leader's daughter and ensuring my skirts were no longer covered in dust. My father might not bar me from riding Sarru whenever I pleased, but I was certain he would not tolerate me dishonoring him by appearing before him smelling of horseflesh. And certainly not on a day when he was entertaining distinguished guests and a betrothal may be at stake.

However, when he called me into his receiving room, I found him sitting alone at a table, examining a set of papyri. No potential bridegroom in sight. He did not even look up at my arrival as he silently continued reading the official-looking document in front of him.

I well-remembered admiring my father when I was a little girl, begging to ride in front of him when he exercised his own favorite mount and soaking up his knowledge of horses as he recounted to my mother his plans for breeding certain pairs. He'd indulged me back then, doting on me just as much as he had my mother, bringing me trinkets or sweet treats from his travels.

All of that had ended, right here in this room, when he told me my mother—my whole world—had died. Two days before, a standing oil lamp had tipped over during a meal and lit her long fringed skirts aflame, which scorched the entire left side of her body and caused a swift-moving fatal infection.

His voice had not even wavered as he'd informed me of the death of his favorite wife, even though he'd refused to meet my gaze. When I'd wailed and collapsed into a heap of tear-soaked grief at his feet, he'd told my eldest brother to remove me from his sight and did not speak to me again until the day I'd begged him for Sarru's life—and very rarely since then. He'd neatly cut me out of his life, leaving me confused and alone. Even my brothers kept their distance after that, acting as though I was little more than a fellow occupant of their home.

Their mothers were even worse. My father's first and third wives treated me with barely disguised contempt—although never in the presence of my father. Around him, they simply ignored me with the same air of indifference that he did. I spent my days alone in my room, or haunting the stables, or on Sarru's back, doing my best to keep myself out of my father's sight as he'd requested.

Coming before him alone now was unnerving, especially when it was far past the time I should have been married. My one hope was that my father had made the right decision about who took me off his hands.

Because last night, when I'd escaped to hide behind a tree and to take a breath away from the noise and chatter of the feast in honor of our guests, someone had followed me.

His name was Lotan, the son of the clan leader in Beit Arbel. Although he'd at first startled me, we found a commonality in our love of horses. We spoke only for a short while, but I'd decided that the idea of marriage to a stranger was not nearly as frightening if it was to be with an attentive young man like Lotan. If anything, at least I would not be so alone anymore.

I could still feel the soft kisses he'd left on both of my cheeks before he'd walked away with a promise to seek me out again. Later on, I'd seen him speaking intensely with his father off to the side of the courtyard and felt certain it was me they were discussing.

As if he'd just remembered my presence, my father abruptly put down the papyrus and fixed his eyes on me. "We are under attack, Keziah."

"Attack?" I echoed, looking around the room, half-expecting to see enemies advancing from the corners.

"Our region is under attack—not Kamon, just yet. Nahash, a particularly aggressive and vicious Ammonite king, has been pushing westward for weeks, burning Hebrew towns and taking slaves. I received word days ago that he has besieged Yavesh, just to the south of us. The city walls are holding fast for now, but they cannot withstand the siege for any length of time. Their resources are limited and dwindling."

"What can be done?"

He gestured to the missive on his table. "Messengers have been sent to King Saul in Gibeah across the river. But there is little hope that he will do anything. He was crowned over a year ago, and yet our enemies are still as brazen as ever. What does he care for Hebrews on this side of the Jordan?"

I'd never heard of this king and wished I could ask more, but my father continued. "If Yavesh falls, Kamon will be vulnerable. I cannot let us be overrun."

Fear slithered around the base of my spine. From what I understood, my father had always trusted that his lucrative trade of horseflesh with the Arameans to the northeast of us would ensure our safety. He had men around our home, of course, and men who took turns guarding the city gates, but as far as I knew, there were few with the training necessary to stave off an invasion. My father's resources were focused on horse breeding and trade, not building an army. He'd not even bothered to have the city walls fixed after a heavy rain washed three large sections of it down the hill years before. I'd overheard a couple of stable hands muttering that my father cared more about horseflesh than his own people, letting Kamon crumble while his herds flourished.

My stomach lurched as my mind called up images of all the innocent lives in our city who were vulnerable to an attack by this Ammonite horde.

"But what can you do?" I asked, stymied by his reasons for sharing all of this with me. "How can we protect Kamon?"

Instead of answering my question, his gaze tracked over my face as if he'd never seen me before today. "You are just as beautiful as your mother."

My cheeks flushed hot. It had been seven years since she'd been gone, and although I remembered how much she loved me, her face was little more than a familiar blur in my mind. But I did recall the way my father stared at her with unabashed admiration. Did my features remind him so much of her? Is that why he'd barely looked at me until now?

"Which is why you are to be married within the week."

My knees wobbled, my head feeling as though it was spinning in circles. "You've accepted an offer?"

"Indeed I have. And truly, there is no better choice. An alliance with Beit Arbel will ensure we have all the protection we need. Their clan is large enough that should the Ammonites come north, we will have hundreds, perhaps thousands, of well-armed men to come to our aid."

A surge of relief swept over me. Lotan himself had told me all about Beit Arbel last night, describing its vast resources, his father's standing army, and the lucrative trade the city's prime position along the King's Highway afforded. Perhaps I *was* worth a little more to my father than one of his broodmares after all.

However, a terrible thought swiftly swept away my gratitude. "Will I be allowed to take Sarru with me?"

He paused for a moment, his gaze assessing, and then nodded. "Sarru and five of our best breeding mares will be part of your dowry."

I let out a sigh of relief. "Thank you, Abba."

"This is the right decision, Keziah. Your marriage will ensure that Kamon is safe."

"I am happy to be of service to our people."

"That is good to hear. Are you ready to meet your bridegroom?"

I did not bother to tell him that I already had and that I approved of his choice as a rapid flutter took wing in my stomach.

"Nabal," he said, "bring them in, will you? And call for refreshments."

I turned, surprised to find my father's cousin behind me, his back pressed to the plaster wall. I flinched, unnerved that he'd been present for the entire conversation with my father. Yet there was no reason to be surprised; wherever my father went, so did Nabal. There was no one he trusted more. From what I knew, they'd been close since childhood, even though my father was a few years younger than his cousin.

With his usual bland expression, Nabal gave an obligatory dip of his head and left the room to fulfill my father's command.

In the meantime, my father returned to his documents, his brows furrowed as he read. And I waited without speaking, used to silence between us. I moved off to the side when servants arrived to lay out a spread of refreshments—kibbeh meat pies, sweet dates stuffed with goat cheese and fig jam, and the strong infusion of herbs and citrus rind that my father preferred. None of the servants bothered to meet my eye as they bustled about, accepting of our mutual roles.

"Chava would be so glad to see you wed," my father said, not looking up from his documents. "She always told me you were worth any cost."

Before I could react to the first time he'd uttered my mother's name in my presence since the day she died, the doors opened and Lotan's father entered, followed by his men. I stood still, a smile fixed on my face as my father offered greetings, and I waited for my bridegroom to appear. However, Nabal closed the doors behind the group.

Confused, I waited for him to announce that Lotan was on his way, but Nabal moved in front of the doors, hands clasped behind his back like a soldier at attention. My father took me by the arm and led me to stand in front of Lotan's father.

The clan leader made no apology for the way his eyes roved over me slowly, from head to foot. I stifled a flinch at the blatant perusal, feeling like a mare up for auction all over again.

"She'll do nicely, Menachem. I am more than pleased to make this connection between our two clans." He made a gesture toward one of his men, who brought forward an ornate cedar box. The clan leader opened it in front of me, revealing an array of bracelets, bronze rings, copper cuffs, a large golden nose ring, and strings and strings of colorful beads made from costly stones.

"Your bridal gifts," he said.

There seemed to be something lodged in my throat. I opened my mouth to thank him, as was expected, but no sound came out.

Lotan's father frowned at me. "Are you not pleased?"

"She is merely overwhelmed," my father replied, his tone far too jovial for such a strange and confusing moment. He squeezed my arm, a silent demand to not humiliate him.

"I am very grateful, my lord," I pressed out quickly, my mouth as dry as a wadi. "But should not Lotan be the one to present such gifts?"

My father's brow wrinkled. "Vadim's youngest son? Why would he be involved in your betrothal?"

"But . . . isn't he . . . ? Isn't he who I am to marry?"

A bark of laughter came from Vadim's lips. "Lotan? He's far too young to be considering a wife. Not for at least another five or six years. If, that is, I can get him to stop chasing after every pretty smile that tilts his way."

A flush of sticky embarrassment washed through me. Had Lotan been toying with me last night? Feigning interest for his own entertainment? Sickness rolled through my middle as reality settled into my bones.

Knees trembling, I took in the man before me as I had not done before. He was at least ten years past my father's age. Perhaps he'd once been handsome but the years had not been kind to him—as evidenced by the generous paunch and the deep lines around his mouth and eyes.

My father's smile was tense as he proclaimed my fate in one succinct declaration. "Daughter, you are betrothed to Vadim. The *ketubah* has been signed and your dowry accepted. Since Vadim is eager for you to join his household, in one week's time you will be given in marriage and go to Beit Arbel with him."

It was fortunate my father was holding my arm, because as I met the gaze of my betrothed, who I'd learned from Lotan was in possession of no less than four wives already and numerous grandchildren, my knees went watery.

Vadim reached into the box to select the most ostentatious of the rings and placed it on my trembling finger. Then he leaned to kiss both of my cheeks, his lips hot and wet on my chilled skin. "Smile, my beautiful young bride," he whispered in my ear, in a faintly ominous tone that sent gooseflesh spreading up my neck and over my scalp. "Or I might think you are displeased with this honor."

The smug expression in his brown eyes made my stomach roll as I obeyed his command, even as I fought every instinct within me to spin away from this horror and flee to the stables. To Sarru.

"I look forward to the union of our families," said Vadim, all threat wiped from his voice as he leaned back and gestured for one of his men to hand my father the marriage contract that would bind me to him for life. "The continuation of my line through your daughter will benefit us all. And once we are joined, your people will be my people, so Kamon will be safe."

"And we are ever so grateful, Vadim," my father said, bowing low with the expected deference. But all I could see was my father halfway to licking the soles of another man's sandals. From the day my mother died, I'd known he cared little for me, but I'd not realized what a coward he was until this very moment.

The men ignored me as they discussed the details of the wedding, the Ammonite threat, and how to best merge their resources for mutual benefit. Instead of listening, I sank down into a nearby chair, staring at a brightly patterned rug beneath my feet that was far too cheerful for this day and waiting to be excused. It seemed my part in these negotiations was over.

Avidan

The ox leg landed in front of me again, blood pooling on the ground and its wool wrappings stained beyond use.

"What was done to this animal will be done to you if you do not stand up for your people." As the ominous words vibrated my bones, I began to shake, my body jerking sharply.

"Avi!" the messenger rasped, pushing at my shoulder. "Avi, wake up!"

My eyes snapped open, taking in the blackness above me. My mind shifted slowly from the valley of Ramah to the upstairs chamber I shared with two of my younger brothers, Elidor and Koli. Again, a sharp poke pressed into my shoulder, and I blinked the sleep out of my eyes to find a shadowy figure hovering over me.

Suddenly alert, I grabbed the hand that gripped me and twisted hard.

"Avi! Let go! It's me, Gavi."

I yanked even harder. "I know."

"Then why are you twisting my arm?"

"Because you woke me, fool. What are you up to?" I could not see his face in the dark, but I knew my cousin better than most anyone in the world. He had some plot in mind, especially since he'd never returned to Naioth to join the family gathering, leaving me alone to endure a seemingly endless night of singing and dancing while Zevi left early to prepare for his journey to Bezek in the morning.

"I'm going with Zevi." Gavi's revelation sucked the air from the room, leaving behind only the soft breaths of my brothers and the sound of my own thundering heart.

"You aren't old enough yet."

"Makes no difference," he replied. "I can pass for twenty. I'm going to fight for our people. They are *desperate* for swords to raise against this enemy. Who will question which hands lift those weapons?"

A flash of jealousy struck me like lightning. Gavi was nearly a full year younger than me, but yes, he absolutely could pass for a man of military age. His beard was even thicker than Zevi's, and although he was not as tall as we were, there was a weightiness to his frame and countenance that aged him, something I guessed had to do with what he'd endured when his father was alive. It would take very little to convince the king's men that he was old enough to fight, especially if Zevi backed his story.

I sat up on my bed, thankful that my brothers slept so deeply that they did not even stir. "What about your family? Your mother?"

Gavi hissed a sharp breath through his teeth. "She knows who I am. Knows all I've ever wanted to be is a warrior for Israel. She has to let me go sometime, whether it's now or in three years. I choose now."

My *doda* Miri was my favorite of my mother's sisters. Gavi's disappearance would bring her pain for certain, but it was true that he made no secret of his ambitions. And just like myself, my cousin was, by any measure of our traditions, a man. Yet, unlike me, his heritage was not a limitation but a strength, since Miri had married into Benjamin and King Saul himself was of the same tribe.

"And what of your uncle?"

He huffed a laugh. "He is too much a coward to fight. I'll go in his stead. Besides, he is not my father. What can he say?"

That was true. Hanan fulfilled the levirate law when Gavi's father had succumbed to his own drunken folly, perishing beneath the wheels of an ox-drawn wagon, by marrying Gavi's mother. But he and my cousin were constantly at odds. Gavi refused to call him anything other than uncle.

It did not surprise me that Gavi would refuse to take Hanan's opinion of his decision into account, but Miri? My cousin adored his *ima* like none other. Any woman who truly caught and captured Gavi's wandering eye would have much to live up to. He was fiercely protective of his mother and sisters. The fact that he would leave them all behind to chase the glory of battle said much for how determined he was. And no matter that he was not yet of military age, his skill with every sort of weapon was undeniable. I had no doubt he would excel on the battlefield.

If only I too could lie about my age and my bloodline and join the fight—

My mind stumbled over the rebellious thought. I sifted through different possibilities, examining them from a number of directions. There was no one better than me at crafting stories. Surely I could convince the commanders that I was eligible to fight. And with my cousins to vouch for me . . .

"Grab my cloak," I whispered as I slid from beneath the blanket, careful not to wake my brothers. Thankfully, I knew every inch of this chamber by heart, even in the dark, and I knelt on the floor, groping under the bed for my leather pack.

"What are you doing?"

"Coming with you, of course."

"But you—"

"We'll talk on the way," I said with a tone that brooked no argument. To his credit, Gavi kept his mouth closed as I pressed some essentials into the small satchel.

Before I left the room, I paused beside the bed. I hated to leave my brothers without any notion of why I'd left. And my parents—much as they would not understand why I'd made this choice—at least deserved to know I'd not simply vanished.

Even though I'd been a boy when my uncle returned after going missing for ten years, I well remembered the anguish my ima endured during his long and unexplained absence. Therefore, I knelt down by the bed and gently shook Elidor awake.

He peered up at me with bleary eyes. "Avi?" He attempted to sit up, blinking eyes the same brilliant green as our mother's, and my own, but I pressed him back down onto his pillow.

"I need you to do something for me. All right?"

He scrubbed his face and nodded his dimpled chin.

"Tell Abba and Ima that I am going with Zevi and Gavriel. Tell them not to worry and that I will return soon. Can you do that?"

"Where are you going?"

"I'll tell you all about it when I return. But I need you to wait until later this afternoon, perhaps even until nightfall, to say anything. Can you remember that?" I could only pray that by the time anyone discovered that the three of us were gone, we would be halfway to Bezek.

I smoothed my hand over Elidor's brown curls, and he smiled up at me sleepily, his adoration filling me with a mixture of both pride and guilt. "When you come back, can we go jump off the rocks again?"

"Of course." One day when I'd taken him with me to deliver a message for one of the Levites who lived north of town, we'd come across a pool formed by a frigid mountain spring, deep and clear enough to jump into from the boulder above. I'd taught him to swim there and then together we'd tossed ourselves into the water below over and over until our limbs were numb and our bellies aching from laughter.

"Just you and me?"

"Just you and me." I kissed his forehead and stood to go. "Now, go back to sleep. And remember, don't say anything until much, much later today. It'll be our secret, like the spring."

His eyes drifted shut as he nodded, his words slurring. "See you soon," he murmured, already back in the arms of slumber.

I closed the door and padded outside to find Gavi waiting for me on the roof.

"The sun will be up any minute," he said. "We need to go if we are going to intercept Zevi." Adept at sneaking out of this house, since we'd done it so many times before, we carefully made our way down the staircase and into the courtyard of our home. Hopefully, after the late night of celebration, most everyone would sleep past sunrise and our flight would go unnoticed.

However, much to my chagrin, Liba, my mother's favorite goat, caught sight of us. With a fluttering bleat, she jogged toward the object of her relentless obsession—my cousin— her full bag swinging. Gavi cursed, fending off the little black-and-brown goat's affections, while I pressed my lips together to keep my laughter from waking the entire household.

"Stop your smirking and help me," rasped Gavi as he yanked the hem of his tunic from Liba's insistent teeth and attempted to push her away with his knee.

It took some wrangling to free my cousin from the amorous goat, but I managed to maneuver the side gate between the two of them and latch it closed behind us. I could only hope that Liba's noise, along with our ungraceful exit, had not awakened anyone within.

"There is something wrong with that animal," Gavi grumbled, brushing hair and dirt from his tunic.

"You should be glad that at least one female finds you attractive." I dodged his halfhearted punch with a laugh.

He glared at me, but his mouth twitched with barely disguised humor. "Watch yourself, cousin. I spent all night sharpening my weapons."

I grinned at him, used to his empty threats. "Let's get moving. My mother never sleeps past dawn, even after a feast."

A pang of guilt hit me. She would be heartbroken when she found me missing. But I could not let this one chance—*my only chance*—to fight slip away, no matter how hurt she would be. Just as Gavi had said, his mother had to let him go so he could become the man he was destined to be. And mine did too. It would simply be sooner than she expected.

Gavi had left a couple large packs full of supplies in the bushes near the path down to Ramah. I was embarrassed to realize that I'd been so fixated on getting out of the house that I'd not even considered packing something to eat. Already, my empty stomach protested the neglect.

Gavi reached into one of his packs and tossed me a loaf of bread and a handful of dried meat. "I only have enough for today, so enjoy. We'll be expected to find our own food once we meet up with the others."

It was no surprise that Israel could not provide for a standing army like the mighty and well-fed ones in Egypt and Aram. Those nations had been building up their military apparatus for hundreds, even thousands, of years. Our nation was young, ill-equipped, and made up of mostly farmers and shepherds, not finely trained soldiers bred from ancient warrior bloodlines.

However, we Hebrews had spent hundreds of years fending off the enemy nations around us, so we were not unaccustomed to warfare. Those same men who spent their days plowing fields to put food in the mouths of their families would now use their combined efforts to defend our brethren—even if the only weapons they had at their disposal were the tools they used to plow and harvest those same fields. Besides, the great Mosheh who'd brought us from Egypt had once been one of those valorous generals within the house of Pharaoh, and his knowledge of warfare had been passed down via our own generations.

So, let our enemies underestimate us and our God, as they had always done. We would show them that a well-crafted sword alone does not make a warrior but a heart of fierce devotion to his king and country can transform the humblest of men into legend.

A stirring quickened in my soul. In a few days, *I* would be counted among those courageously marching into battle. Would see our enemies vanquished with my own eyes and then return with the mantle of victory spread across my shoulders—something no one could ever take away from me. Perhaps if I was successful at Yavesh, I could even be named one of Saul's armor bearers, an honor given only to the most loyal of men.

Footsteps crunched on the path, breaking into my thoughts of the future. Gavi and I ducked down in the brush to wait. And when Zevi came around the corner, unaccompanied by his father, I breathed a sigh of relief. Our uncle would not in any way give his blessing to our plans, and I was glad not to have to lie to a man I held in such esteem.

Zevi startled when Gavi and I emerged from hiding, his hand flying to his sword. His father had procured the weapon as part of a trade for lumber, and it was made of the finest Philistine iron—a rarity in Hebrew territory, since our enemies dominated the trade and had a stranglehold on the supply of metal in the region. With so few well-made swords among us, Zevi would be at a great advantage during the battle.

Our older cousin furrowed his dark brows. "What are the two of you doing?"

Gavi gestured to the leather armor he wore, similar to Zevi's own. "What does it look like?"

"It looks like you are being foolish," replied our cousin, peering at us in the intense manner he'd had since childhood, unsmiling and severe.

Undeterred, Gavi grinned. "No more than you. And I've seen you do some fairly foolish things."

"You aren't old enough. Go home."

Gavi's stance shifted, and the jovial veneer he usually maintained so well slipped, replaced by a countenance of stone. "I am plenty old enough to fight for my people. And I'm just as prepared as you are."

"I don't question your skill, Gav. But you have nearly three full years before you are permitted to join the army."

"And who will know? Or care? They need swords, bows, slings, and spears, and I excel at all four." His voice went hard, his jaw set like iron. "I can go with you, or I can walk to Bezek alone. Matters little to me."

Zevi scowled but then turned to me. "And you think you are going as well?"

"This is my only chance, Zev. The moment I turn twenty, I'll be chained to Levitical service for the rest of my life. I cannot waste this opportunity."

"Ronen will be furious."

"I'll deal with that when I return."

"And your mother will be gutted after what my father did to her."

I could not help but flinch at the thought of my ima's tears. "I'll be gone a week or two. Not a decade like he was."

"It could be far longer than a couple of weeks," he said. "Sieges can last months when the enemy is well supplied."

"Isn't that the reason we are going? To end the siege of Yavesh and free our brothers?"

"Battles never go to plan, Avi." He pinned me with a searching gaze. "War is nothing to take lightly."

Whatever he'd experienced at the hands of the Philistines haunted him, and I had no doubt he wanted to protect me from similar torment. But I was not a child like he'd been at the time. And I would not be swayed.

"I am well aware. And I am going." With my heart thumping unevenly, I stood tall, making a show of my superior height.

After a long moment of staring at me, Zevi shook his head in defeat and his attention went back to Gavi. "What weapons did you bring?"

"Practically everything I have collected or made," Gavi replied, his smile full of pride. He'd been scavenging spare bits of metal since he was about eight years old and had learned forging from a metalsmith down in Ramah, much to his uncle's consternation. If he was not reluctantly running errands for his uncle or passing time with me, he was building weapons. By the looks of the scaled armor on his body, greaves on his shins, and the thick bracers on his forearms, he'd even figured out how to sew leather into durable protection.

He fetched one of the packs he'd hidden in the brush and then rooted around, laying out two bronze daggers, four slings, six pouches full of sharpened stones, a javelin, and two vicious-looking clubs inset with bone spikes.

"Get the other pack, Avidan," he said over his shoulder. "There's another set of armor in there."

With a rush of excitement, I did as he asked, finding a sturdy shirt of heavy leather scales that covered my front, back, and sides, with thick straps that spread over my shoulders and a pair of greaves for my legs. Although the armor was a bit short in the waist and snug about the chest, once I latched it onto my body it would at least give me some measure of protection during the battle, which would be more than most Israelites would have.

"Oh! I nearly forgot!" Gavi rushed over to retrieve three round shields from behind another bush. Fashioned from sturdy oak and hardened hide, the shields would be invaluable during the fight and looked like they'd been constructed by a master, not an unproven youth.

Grinning at our shocked expressions, Gavi handed one to me and the other to Zevi. As he did, realization hit me like a bolt of lightning. "Three?"

He huffed a laugh. "Like you'd let us leave you behind."

Warmth filled my chest. "You knew I'd come."

"It's always been the three of us, together," Gavi said with a shrug. "Well, and Shalem. But he wouldn't pass for twenty, no matter what he does. That boy's face is smoother than a baby's backside."

Even Zevi laughed at the truth of it.

Shay would be hurt to be left behind, for certain, but I would console him with stories from the battle. There was nothing he liked better than my tales. I'd have an abundance of stories to share with him and my younger brothers when I returned. Elidor and Koli always begged me to trade stories in exchange for doing some of my more tedious chores, and I was usually more than happy to indulge them.

Someday I would tell my grandchildren those same stories and of the very moment Zevi, Gavriel, and I left behind Naioth and set our sandals on the road eastward and toward the faceless enemy that awaited us on the other side of the Jordan River.

I would have much to apologize for when I returned, but for now there was nothing more important than the call to go to war for my people, with my cousins by my side.

Keziah

M y cheeks hurt from maintaining a false smile all evening, but I had no choice other than to graciously
accept the repeated blessings of well-wishers for my
betrothal. Regardless of how uneasy I was at the center of the
boisterous celebration, or how repugnant my bridegroom, I could
not risk shaming my father by revealing my true thoughts about
how he'd traded his only daughter away to save his own skin. My
family members, who were gathered here now to toast my upcoming marriage, already hated me enough as it was.

I would not even have the luxury of a long betrothal period to
adjust to the idea of being swept away from my home by a stranger
before the union was solidified. And the satisfaction on my father's
face as he accepted all the felicitations made it clear that any hopes
for a change of his heart were pointless.

Already, Vadim had called in reinforcements to bolster our meager defenses. Unlike my father, who had little more than untrained
farmers to call up in the case of attack, Vadim had built his own
loyal force of men and now offered enough resources to stand by
at all times. I could almost see the relief emanating from my father

as a group of at least thirty well-armed soldiers took up stations around the city.

So I kept my smile in place, knowing that without those reinforcements from Beit Arbel, the valley I loved so much, and all the innocent people who lived within its boundaries, would be vulnerable to attack. And I would be to blame.

Besides, what did I have to complain about? After my marriage, I would want for nothing. The shimmering crimson robe I wore tonight, the soft calfskin sandals, and the alluring Babylonian perfume that graced my neck spoke to the way Vadim's wives were indulged. If it was my lot to be one of those pampered wives, then I must make the most of it.

Though my father had invited the most skilled musicians in the region to play for us and the most talented storytellers to unfurl tales of the gods, it was little more than a clash of jangling sistra and muddled words in my head. If only I could be with Sarru instead, his broad back and solid warmth beneath me as his hooves pounded the earth, taking me far, far away from here.

Vadim's large body leaned into me, his rasping voice in my ear again. "Are you not hungry, my lovely bride?"

I looked down at the low table, where every sort of delicacy had been laid out before me. Bowls of fruit in thick syrup, hearty stews, plates overflowing with meats and cheeses, herbed salads made with the freshest produce the farms around Kamon had to offer, along with wine my father had claimed was a gift from a very satisfied royal customer in Damascus. It was a meal fit for any king, or queen. And yet my ungrateful stomach turned at the sight. The bites I'd forced myself to take earlier had tasted like dirt in my mouth.

"It all looks delicious," I said, pulling my smile even tighter and offering my prettiest lie for the sake of my people. "I have simply been so excited that it seems I've lost my appetite."

He grinned, pleased with my answer, and reached to twirl one of my waist-length curls around a thick finger. "I think we will get on very well, my dear." His gaze tracked over my kohl-darkened eyes and the gaudy gold ring in my nose—a mark of his ownership—and landed on my hennaed lips. His own eyes, reddened from the copious amounts of drink he'd guzzled, seemed to darken. "Yes, very well indeed, my beautiful, clever girl."

Nausea flamed up my throat. Even if I was fairly ignorant to some things in the way of marriage, some I was not—I'd been raised by a man who bred horses, after all.

Thankfully, before Vadim could move in closer, one of his men tapped his shoulder and whispered something in his ear. My betrothed stood without apology or excuse and accompanied the man out of the courtyard, giving me a few moments to breathe deeply and loosen the white-knuckled grip I'd had on my skirts beneath the table.

Gathering the courage to cast my gaze over the guests, most of whom I'd never seen before, I met eyes with my oldest brother, Bram. Since he was nearly fifteen years my senior, I'd had very limited interactions with him—with any of my brothers, really. Although we'd grown up in the very same household, my siblings were little more than strangers to me.

At the moment, my father's heir was scowling at me from across the table, most likely annoyed that I had the audacity to meet his gaze. I dropped my eyes back to my lap, planning a late-night visit to the stables the moment this farce was complete.

Startling when I felt someone sit down beside me, I braced myself for more unnerving conversation with my future husband, but instead of his gravelly voice, a familiar one met my ears. I flinched in surprise. Lotan had taken his father's place, his profile illuminated by the firelight as he kept his face forward and his eyes off me.

"My congratulations," he said, although his tone was more akin to an offer of condolence.

I mumbled my acknowledgment but could think of nothing more to say. Only days before, the two of us had shared a pleasant conversation that gave me a small measure of hope. Now there was nothing but fraught silence between us. I stared at my useless hands.

"I did not know," he said, his low words for my ears alone. "I hope you understand. I thought he wanted me to speak to you for my sake, not his . . ."

My head snapped up. "He told you to speak to me?"

His gaze flicked from one side to the other, making certain no one was watching before he finally met my stare. "He wanted me to find out what sort of a woman you are."

My stomach lurched. "And what did you tell him?"

"That you were meek and lovely and would undoubtedly make a good wife." He pressed his lips together, shaking his head.

"It seems as though he agreed."

"I'm sorry," he said, his eyes again darting to the side. "I thought . . . well, it does not matter now. I wish I'd said nothing."

As do I. "It would not have mattered. This was likely the plan for some time."

"Still, it was not my intention to deceive you. I only wish . . ."

My heart clenched tight as he let his words die out, both of us knowing there was no use dreaming things were different. I was already betrothed to his father, the ketubah signed by both parties and bridal gifts exchanged.

"I should go." He surged to his feet, then looked down on me with a distinctive shadow of regret in his lovely brown eyes. Even now, the young man seemed sincere and kind, nothing like his brash and arrogant father.

Just as I thought he would walk away, he took one more swift look around and then leaned down to whisper in my ear. "For your own safety, do not cross him, Keziah. Ever."

Every hair on the back of my neck rose to attention, but before I could respond to the cryptic warning, he was gone, leaving me with a thousand questions and a gut roiling with fear. How would I face a lifetime of marriage with a man whose own son seemed afraid of him?

Imati appeared at my side, crouching beside me with a deep pinch between her brows. She must have witnessed the panic on my face. "What can I get for you, my lady? More food or drink?"

In a haze, I blinked at her, then down at the food I'd not touched. If only she could whisk me away from this sham of a celebration. But Imati was helpless to change anything about her own circumstances, let alone mine.

She'd been my mother's maid long before she'd attended me and had always been patient and kind. But as I considered the distress in her dark eyes, and the obvious concern for me in her low voice, I realized that this maid—who'd been enslaved by my family for most of her life —loved me more than my own father did.

Before I could respond to her gentle question, Vadim reappeared. Knowing her place with such a powerful man, Imati stood abruptly and dropped her eyes to the ground. He leaned to speak into her ear. She flinched at his proximity but nodded and left to attend whatever command he'd given without a word.

My betrothed sat down with a grunt next to me, arranging his striped robes around his thick legs, and then reached across me to pick up the wine cup I'd not bothered to sip from. He tipped it back and drained it in one long, noisy draft.

Curious about why he'd rushed away during our betrothal feast, I chanced a question but chose my words carefully. "I trust all is well?"

He let out an unapologetic belch. "Yavesh in Gilead is near to falling. The king of Ammon has offered terms of surrender."

I'd never been to the stronghold of Yavesh but guessed its fertile resources, proximity to trade routes, and lush forests would be coveted by the Ammonites. Kamon's only precious resource was the priceless herd of horses my father had bred from Sarru's famous ancestors.

"What terms?" I dared ask.

"They surrender and the king of Ammon will spare their lives. However, each male will lose one eye as a reminder of their defeat."

I gasped. I'd heard the Ammonites were ruthless, but taking the eye of every man was horrific.

"Is anyone coming to their aid?"

"They are Gadites. Let them rescue their own." He shrugged,

unperturbed that our not-so-distant neighbors were under attack. Deep unease shifted in my chest. If he was so unconcerned with the fate of Hebrews from another tribe, why did he care about this town? We were all of Manasseh's tribe but not related in any meaningful way that I knew of. The region around this town was little more than a collection of small farms far from major trade roads and inhabited only by humble people, goats, and sheep. *How did coming to the aid of Kamon benefit my bridegroom, anyhow?*

"What did my son have to say?" I went very still as Vadim leaned in close, his wine-and-onion-laden breath wafting across my face. "I told you before that he enjoys toying with women. Do not be taken in. He only wants you because you are mine."

I caught my breath, clammy hands trembling beneath the table where they again twisted into my skirts. Lotan's warning blared loudly in my head. "He only gave his best wishes for our marriage."

He chuckled, the sound nowhere near jovial, and then slid his own hand beneath the table where he took my wrist in his grip, even as he continued smiling down at me like a doting bridegroom. "Stay away from him. From any man." His fingers squeezed until I felt the bones in my wrist grind against each other. "I do *not* share my property."

Tears burned my eyes, and I pressed my lips hard against a sob of pain and fear. Vadim might be older than my father was, but he was a warrior. His powerful hand could easily snap my wrist if he tightened his hold much more.

"Do you hear me?" he said through gritted teeth.

Pain radiated up my arm and the back of my throat was on fire as I nodded. To my dismay, one lone tear broke free with the movement, trickling down over my chin and dripping off my jaw. His terrible smile grew even wider at my reluctant display of emotion.

"Excellent." He leaned to kiss my cheek, brushing away the evidence of my fear with his lips, even as my entire body vibrated with terror. "If you obey, you will be treated well. Clothes. Jewels. The best food and drink. We will both have what we want."

Finally releasing his crushing grip on my wrist, Vadim turned aside, leaving me in excruciating pain and powerless to do anything but swallow down scalding tears and pray that this horrible night would come to a swift end.

However, those prayers went unheeded when Imati returned a short while later and offered my betrothed the linen veil he'd obviously ordered her to retrieve. Vadim took the fabric from her and stood, making a show of waiting for all eyes to be on him before he spoke.

"I must offer my most humble thanks to Menachem for accepting my suit of his daughter." He bowed his head in my father's direction, then turned his gaze upon me with a semblance of adoration. "I could not be more pleased with my bride. She is a treasure that I look forward to bringing into my household, where she will be highly valued for both her glorious beauty and abundant meekness."

All eyes turned to me, and my face flamed at the attention.

"Therefore, I will give her the same honor due one of the royal woman of Aram and Babylon," he said as he lifted the cream-colored linen high. "This will be a reminder to all that this cherished woman will soon be permanently delivered into my protection."

I held my breath as he draped the linen atop my head with a flourish, another visible declaration of his ownership settling around me like a death shroud. "And so it will be with great joy that I *alone* will lift this veil from her face when I come to receive my bride into my tent."

No wonder Vadim held such power among the people of Manasseh. He was a persuasive speaker, his voice commanding and his convincing lies smooth as glass. As he returned to his seat beside me and began a boisterous conversation with someone nearby, I sat in isolation beneath the fabric, listening to the resurgence of free-flowing laughter and gossip around me. Holding my still-throbbing wrist in my lap, I swallowed against the searing despair in my throat, fighting the rising sob that threatened to break free.

I'd always been ostracized within my own household, isolated from my brothers, and edged to the side by my father's wives. But somehow, with one thin piece of finely woven flax, my betrothed had made me completely disappear.

6

I blinked hard against the sudden brilliance of lamplight in my chamber as Imati removed my veil. While my vision cleared, Imati's ebony eyes skimmed a frowning gaze over the mess on my face.

As humiliated as I'd been by the way Vadim had veiled me, it had given me permission to let my tears flow. The neckline of my priceless gown was stained black from kohl that had trailed down from my decorated eyes and dripped off my jaw. Without a word, Imati retrieved a small vial of olive oil and a soft cloth and began to clean my ash-streaked face.

Her soft touch, as usual, was reassuring, and her expression full of worry, even if I could not see most of her face. How strange that I'd always known her and yet had never seen more than her large almond-shaped eyes and the strong brows that rose over them.

Once my face was cleansed of tears, sweat, and kohl, Imati removed the ring from my nose. The large and gaudy disk had pulled at the new hole in my right nostril all day, leaving it sore. I was glad to be rid of it and grateful that it would be replaced with only a small copper hoop to keep the hole from closing.

Imati paused for a moment, staring at the disk in her palm. The piece must have been crafted by a skilled artisan, the tiny details within the gold displaying extraordinary craftsmanship. From the complicated pattern of granulated circles dotting one side to a stamped image of a kingfisher on the other, it was a truly striking piece of jewelry. But nothing about it should cause the maid's eyes to well with tears.

She blinked, likely to clear away some image from her mind, and then answered my silent question. "My mother wore a similar ring in her nose."

My brows flew high. In all the many years I'd known her, she'd never once spoken of her past.

"I have not allowed myself to think of her in so long. I cannot even see her face anymore, but I do remember her wearing something similar to this." She tenderly stroked the gold with her finger.

My curiosity raged. I knew nothing of where she came from before she served my mother. "How were you separated from your family?"

She took a long inhale. "I've dreamed about it many times. Sometimes I am not certain which memories are true and which are images my nightmares have conjured."

A flash of guilt overtook me. "You need not tell me any more. I do not mean to upset you."

"You have done no such thing. It has merely been so long since I've spoken of my home and of that terrible night. I was just twelve years old. A woman in body, perhaps, but not yet at heart. In fact, I'd just been told that I would be betrothed to a boy from one of our sister clans. I forget his name. . . ." She paused, her gaze going unfocused, peering back through those hazy memories, uncertain of which were solid and which were shadow. "I do, however, remember my village. I can still hear the sound of the nearby spring gushing down into the pool below and feel the coolness of the wide stream that came from it. Our village was not large—only a few homes constructed on either side of that stream, since many of the people still lived in tents like our nomadic ancestors—but it was beautiful. And it was home to the people of the Rehavite clan. My family."

The ache of loneliness in her voice echoed in my chest.

"When the visitors came to our village, they sought out my father, who was the chief of our clan. I remember my mother being unsure of them. She'd just had a baby and was concerned about inviting strangers of unknown origin into our dwelling. But my father insisted, saying he would not dishonor our people by refusing hospitality to anyone. It was our way. If anyone sought shelter with us, be they friend or foe, we would offer protection, food, and water. It was a point of great pride for my father, because he spoke of it often." She shook her head sadly. "However, these men did not have the same respect for the traditions of hospitality as we did. My father invited the four of them in, kissed them, gave them food and drink, and after offering a salt covenant, insisted that they take shelter with us until they were ready to move on."

To break such a covenant—one in which two people ate of bread dipped in the same salt and oil— was the height of insult. Whoever took Imati from her home had no honor. It was as good as an act of war to partake of someone's food and then betray them.

Horror passed through Imati's eyes, and I could only imagine what she might have seen that night. My stomach curled in on itself. I'd lived in perfect safety all my life atop this hill, in a beautiful home where I was afforded every luxury. Why had I never even considered before what this woman had endured as a child?

"You don't have to continue—"

"It's all right. I think you should know." Her dark eyes swam. "All I remember is waking up in a man's arms. His hand was over my mouth. It was a moonless night, so I could not see much, but I could hear . . ." She paused, her hand going to her throat as she swallowed hard. "I could hear screaming. I don't know who else was taken captive. I think I saw my older brothers fighting for a moment before the men put a blindfold and gag on me."

"And your parents?"

"Were likely first to be murdered."

No wonder just a glimpse of a nose ring would stir despair in her heart. Tears formed in my own eyes. We both knew the loss of a mother.

"But I am much more fortunate than other slaves," Imati said. "I was given to your mother as a wedding gift soon after I was snatched away. And I was grateful to serve her until the hour she died. It could have been worse. Far, far worse."

Although I wasn't certain what she meant by that, I could guess by the hollow look in her eyes that she'd been witness to terrible things. But I'd already pushed her enough today. I would not ask her to clarify.

"Enough of sadness," she said, laying the nose ring aside. "Let's prepare you for sleep, my lady." She gestured for me to stand and reached for the hem of my gown.

"We certainly never had anything so fine as this beautiful dress," she said as she pulled the water-smooth fabric over my head. "But I do remember my mother weaving me a striped tunic that—"

Her words cut off abruptly. Startled, I followed the direction of her gaze to my forearm, where a large bruise wrapped completely around my wrist in deep shades of purple and red.

"What is this?" She took my arm gently in her hands.

Shame flooded me, and I jerked my hand away, tucking it behind my back. "It's nothing."

"Let me look, Keziah." Imati always spoke with a low and gentle tone, her manner submissive at all times. But these words were close to a demand. Startled by the shift and shocked by her boldness, I allowed her to reach for my arm so she could examine the bruise my betrothed had inflicted.

After a moment, she lifted her eyes to mine, the ebony depths of them swimming in concern. "Vadim did this."

Naked in all ways before my maid, I dropped my eyes to the floor. She must have sensed my unease with such vulnerability because she dressed me without another word and then began to braid my hair, just as she did every night.

"What happened?" she asked as she wrangled my abundant curls into a long queue. Although it made my skin crawl to say it aloud, Imati would keep my confidence, I had no doubt.

"His son came to speak with me. Vadim was furious. Perhaps I should not have responded."

"I was watching the entire time, and there was nothing untoward in your manner."

"My betrothed did not agree, and as I am now bound to him, I am obligated to obey him in all things."

The truth of that had yet to settle into the deep places in my heart, but it did so now, causing the question I'd been pushing away all evening to rise to the surface. If Vadim was so quick to hurt me for something so slight, and in the presence of everyone during our betrothal feast, what might he do when no one else was around?

I began to tremble, and she placed her warm hands on my shoulders, squeezing gently. "You must speak to your father, my lady. Show him what the man did to you."

What would I say? That Kamon should be left vulnerable because of one bruise and some veiled threats? No. I could not claim to be more important than everyone else.

I shook my head. "He believes this marriage is an answer from the heavens to protect the town."

"But you must—"

I put up a hand to stop her argument, straightening my spine with a measure of bravery I did not feel. "Vadim said I will be treated well if I obey him, and I am determined to do so, for everyone's sake." I would heed Lotan's warning, remaining quiet and submissive. "Please, snuff out the lamps. I am beyond weary."

She pressed her lips into a hard line but complied, then situated herself on the pallet beside my bed, where she'd slept for as long as I could remember. Just as I was on the very cusp of sleep, I heard her whisper into the darkness.

"I will always be with you, Keziah. In one way or another."

And I was glad for it, because although I was used to being ignored, I'd never felt so alone in all my life.

7

Avidan

Coated with a thick layer of dust and sweat, my tunic was plastered to my back. Although we'd been walking since dawn, Zevi was as relentless as the sun overhead, not only refusing to join the groups of soldiers we'd passed on the way but never slowing his stride. And after we emerged into the Jordan River Valley, passed Jericho, then turned north on the well-traveled trade road, he stepped up his punishing pace even more.

More than once, I'd seen Gavi glaring at Zevi's back as we pressed forward without rest. Our older cousin had some sort of drumbeat in his head that urged him on at a clip that would tire Pharaoh's stallions. But even the king of Egypt fed his chariot teams once in a while. We'd had little more than a few bites of bread from Gavi's pack as we raced northward, and the waterskins slung over our shoulders were nearly dry. My stomach protested the neglect, and my tongue clung to the roof of my mouth.

"It'll be dark soon, Zev," I said. "Should we make camp?"

He shook his head. "We have hours to go."

Gavi's jaw gaped. "Are we walking all night?"

"You can rest when we get to Bezek."

"What use will we be on the battlefield if we are half-dead already?"

"We should really take a break," I said, slowing my pace a little. "Gavi has a point. What use are exhausted soldiers?"

"Fine," Zevi answered, speeding up even more. "Then turn your lazy carcasses around and go back home."

Shocked by his vehemence, I met Gavi's eyes. We both grimaced and scrambled to catch up without another word, and I vowed to keep my complaints to myself from now on. The sun set behind the western hills, but we continued our twilight march along the rugged trade road, the ancient and sacred town of Gilgal up on the shadowy ridge to our left and the rushing river glimmering under the moonlight to our right.

To take my mind off the blister forming beneath the pad of one foot, I let my thoughts wander ahead of us, considering how we might deal with questions about our origins and our ages. The three of us may be cousins, but there was no resemblance between us. It shouldn't be too difficult to claim Benjamite heritage, since I'd lived in their territory most of my life, but there was always the chance someone might look at my unusual height and lighter skin and press into my lies. I certainly could not tell them I was half Philistine, or age would be the least of my issues. My mother's allegiance to the Hebrews was without question among those who knew her, but I doubted men who'd fought my vicious ancestors for decades would care. They would see me only as a child of an enemy, not the son of a tenderhearted woman who'd joined herself to Israel through covenant and marriage.

I wondered whether Elidor had obeyed me and waited until the evening meal to tell her where I'd gone or if he'd not been able to contain the secret beyond the rise of the sun. The question I'd been pushing down since this morning suddenly elbowed its way to the surface.

What if I did not return? I'd left on a bitter note with my father. My mother would be racked with anguish. And the youngest of my siblings would be left with nothing but faint memories of the brother who'd vanished one morning without even a good-bye . . .

With a jolt, I shut down that line of thinking. Of course I would return. I would make my apologies to my family when I arrived home, triumphant after our victory, and I would vow not go against my father again. I'd made my decision, and I could not turn back. I refused to look like a coward to my cousins or let this one chance to grasp glory slip through my fingers.

Without warning, Zevi came to a standstill, one fist held up in silent command for us to halt.

Confused, Gavi and I both stumbled to a stop, looking around to determine why he'd ceased his furious pace. Darkness had fully fallen, and the nearly full moon shone bright enough that the road ahead was illuminated. I glanced over my shoulder. The path behind us was empty as far as I could see, and all was silent except for the whirring of night insects and the murmur of the river in the distance.

"What is it?" rasped Gavi, knife in hand and stance defensive.

The intense expression on Zevi's face as he gave one small shake of his head in warning lifted the hair on the back of my neck. My hand moved to rest on the pommel of my own weapon. We were deep in Hebrew territory, but bandits were common on busy trade roads like this one. Especially at night.

However, instead of drawing his own weapon, our older cousin responded in a voice that did not match Gavi's hushed tone. "I'm going to find a tree to water. Wait here."

Bewildered, Gavi and I stared at each other. Zevi hadn't once paused to allow Gavi and I to relieve ourselves all day, forcing us to catch up when we had. And yet in the middle of the night he insists we wait while he wanders into the brush?

"What is he up to?" I breathed out.

Gavi shook his head, his features barely visible in the dim light. "Don't know. But keep up your guard."

I let my gaze slide along the dark tree line beside us, searching the black shadows. My scalp prickled as I imagined a thousand pairs of eyes peering back at me, and unease slithered up my spine as Zevi remained gone far longer than if he were only relieving himself.

A muffled cry spun me around. I jerked the bronze dagger Gavi had given me from the sheath at my belt. Zevi's form emerged from the shadows about twenty paces back and moved into a bright patch of moonlight, dragging another figure behind him. The stranger struggled, flailing and squawking in protest. Gavi and I jogged forward, weapons at the ready.

"He's been trailing us since Ramah," said Zevi, his tone strangely relaxed for someone who'd just dragged an enemy from the woods.

"Let me go!" Zevi's prisoner shouted, the voice higher pitched than I'd expected. Whoever my cousin had apprehended was no more than a youth.

Zevi complied, releasing his quarry, who stumbled forward and fell at my feet. I peered down at the boy, whose features were obscured by more than just nighttime shadows. Mud, perhaps?

"You didn't have to drag me," said Zevi's captive, in a voice as familiar to me as my own.

"Shalem?" I barked, all the fear draining from my body in a rush. "What are you doing?"

"You left me behind," said our young cousin as he pushed to his feet, brushing debris from his tunic.

I let out a sigh. *Of course he followed us.* How he'd made it this far without us seeing him I didn't know, but it was no surprise that he'd tagged along. He'd done it many, many times before.

"We are joining the tribal armies, Shay," said Gavi. "You don't belong here."

Shalem's chin lifted, his muddied face displaying a rare show of defiance. "Neither do you or Avidan, but Zevi took you both with him."

Zevi groaned. "That's because they can at least pass for twenty. And they are able to fight grown men. Go back home before you are hurt."

"I want to come with you. I won't be in the way."

Zevi shook his head. "We are not playing at war with sticks. We are heading into a real battle against vicious enemies who torture their prisoners. You must go back to Naioth."

"He can't go alone, Zev," said Gavi. "Who knows what could happen along the way?"

"True." Zevi turned to me. "Avidan, you'll take him back."

I flinched at his command. "Me? No. We have to be at Bezek tomorrow. I'd have no time to catch up before the army crosses the river."

"I'm sorry," said Zevi, "but Shalem needs an escort."

"Why not Gavi?" I snapped. Regardless of the brief doubts I'd entertained earlier, I had no intention of going home. I'd come too far to turn back now.

"I'm not going anywhere," said Gavriel, arms folded over his chest.

"You are the youngest of the three of us," I said. "And you have plenty of battles ahead of you. This is my one chance."

"If I go, my weapons go with me," said Gavi, an edge of iron in his voice.

I narrowed my eyes at him, shocked by his pettiness. "You'd leave us without protection?"

"Stop!" Zevi's sharp warning echoed off the trees. "This is profiting no one. You are both acting like children. I'll go on alone. Take Shalem back together."

"No!" Gavi and I snapped at the same time.

"I'm fighting the Ammonites beside you," I said.

"As am I," said Gavi.

Zevi gritted his teeth, digging his fingers into the thick waves of his hair. "I never should have let myself be talked into this in the first place. I knew it was foolish."

"No one needs to go back," said Shalem. "I made it this far without being seen by any of you. I'll stay away from any danger, I promise."

His skill at following us since dawn without detection, while

76

keeping up with Zevi's punishing pace, certainly *was* impressive. My mind began to churn.

"That is not—" Zevi began.

I spoke over him. "Look. What's done is done. He cannot go back alone, and neither of us is willing to leave. And he did evade us quite easily, after all."

"Avi's right," said Gavi. "Shalem is here now. We need to make the best of it."

Zevi shook his head. "You want to bring a child with us into unknown territory while we go up against the Ammonites?"

"I'm not a child!" Shalem interjected. "I've been considered a man for two full years!"

I ignored the outburst that belied his argument. "We can find him a place to hide, far away from the fighting. Hours away from Yavesh, if need be. When the battle is over, the four of us will travel home together."

"The region of Gilead is mountainous and heavily forested from what I've heard," said Gavi. "I'm certain we can find a wadi or a cave for him to hide in."

"Yes!" Shalem said. "No one will even see me. And you know I climb trees like a cat."

"What about the journey there?" Zevi asked. "We have a river at the height of its flow to cross. How would we hide him during the march?"

"There will be so many soldiers, I doubt anyone will even take notice," Gavi said.

"And I'm a strong swimmer!" said Shalem. "Avidan taught me himself. I'm not afraid to cross the river!"

"He *is* a capable swimmer," I said. "He picked it up far faster than any of my siblings."

"See?" Shalem gestured to me with a splayed palm. "And if anyone does notice me, I'll just say I am delivering a message to one of the soldiers from another tribe."

"It will never work," said Zevi, although his tone had softened considerably. "And if we get caught dragging a boy with us, we may all be sent home."

"I'm *not* a boy! And it will work! Listen!" Shalem raised his brows, an innocent expression on his muddy face. "I'm only here to deliver a message," he said in a perfect imitation of a Yehudite. "I must tell my brother that his wife is sick."

Gavi and I glanced at each other in surprise. It was astounding how perfectly he'd mimicked the meandering drawl of our southern brothers, some of which Zevi himself still retained in his own speech after all these years.

"Why yes, my lord," he continued, now sounding just like Segal, one of the Jebusite traders who came through Ramah regularly. "My mother sent me with food for my father. He forgot his pack, and she's worried he might go hungry on the march to Yavesh."

I stifled a smile. Shalem had always been able to mimic voices, a trick that had given us plenty of amusement over the years. But I'd never considered the skill to be useful until now.

"And what of this?" Shalem said, obviously proud that he'd shocked Zevi into silence. He then launched into a long narrative in some language I could not interpret, leaving the three of us slack-jawed.

"What did you say?" Gavi asked.

"That I was a slave from Aram beyond the Euphrates and was here to find my master."

"Where did you learn the language of the Arameans?" Zevi asked.

Shalem shrugged. "One of Hanan's slaves taught me a few words in his language. I don't know all that much, but it's enough to fool people."

I laughed, squeezing Shalem's shoulder. "See, Zev, he'll be fine. He's sharp and resourceful. We'll make certain he is safe."

Zevi tipped his head back, his eyes dropping closed. "This is ridiculous. My father will kill me, as will Iyov, for even entertaining this."

"I'll do whatever you tell me to do, Zevi. I promise," Shalem said, with his right palm lifted, the scar of our brotherhood on full display.

Our elder cousin growled to himself. "I wish I'd come alone."

Gaze tracking off to the black tree line, he shook his head as if he were silently arguing within his own mind. The moment he let out a defeated huff through his nostrils, I knew we'd won the fight. Shalem grinned, his teeth gleaming in the moonlight.

"I'll probably regret this the rest of my life," Zevi muttered as he turned to stride away. "Step up the pace. We have at least a couple more hours to go."

8

The deep hum of myriad voices and the general din of activity greeted us long before we came out of the trees and into the valley of Bezek. I'd expected a large turnout of men heeding Saul's urgent call to arms, especially with how many we'd passed by on the road here, but the sheer numbers gathered in the sprawling army camp were staggering. The mass resembled a vast swarm of bees, the buzz of activity growing with the rise of the sun. My heart gave a thump of pride in my people. So many had answered the call. Victory would be ours.

Thankfully, Zevi had allowed us a couple of hours' respite before forcing us to finish the march toward the gathering place, finally giving in to our pleas since Shalem had been falling asleep on his feet. Even with the rest, I was more than tempted to join the sea of slumbering bodies blanketing the hillsides beneath the few stars that remained in the western sky. However, some men were already awake, sharpening their weapons, building cook fires, and preparing for the long march ahead.

Shalem climbed atop a boulder nearby to better view the far reaches of the crowd. "I've never seen so many people."

We'd wrapped my cloak around his body to hide his slender form and covered his distinctive hair with a long scarf that wrapped twice around his neck. With his smooth cheeks and dimpled chin hidden among its ample folds, along with the remains of his muddy camouflage and Gavi's pack on his shoulder, he looked much more like a servant than the pampered son of a Levite.

"Where do we even begin?" I wondered. The magnitude of this hastily assembled army was overwhelming. There had to be tens of thousands here—perhaps even hundreds of thousands.

Zevi joined Shalem on the rock to survey the chaos. After a moment, he pointed to one of the only tents pitched on the nearby hillside. A large square of yellow fabric flapped near its doorway, emblazoned with a crude charcoal rendering of a lion. "Yehudah's banner. We'll start there."

Gavi scowled, his gaze still searching the crowd. "Why not Benjamin?"

"I came to fight alongside my brethren," said Zevi.

I flinched at Zevi's brusque statement. He was eager to fight as a Yehudite, of course, but I'd never thought he would throw us off to do so.

Gavi spoke my thoughts aloud. "Are we not your brethren?"

"You know what I meant," said Zevi, hopping down from the boulder. "I need to rally under my tribal banner."

"And why not that of Benjamin?" Gavi lifted his chin, his stance widening. "You've spent the last ten years of your life living in our territory."

Zevi's jaw ticked as he met Gavi's eyes, the air between them practically shimmering with tension. "This is when I come into my purpose as a soldier, Gavriel. I've been training for this day most of my life, ever since the Philistines dragged me out of Zanoah into slavery. This is when I begin to build my reputation. Make my mark among the men of my tribe."

"Then perhaps we should split up," said Gavi, not swayed by Zevi's impassioned speech.

"No." I moved to stand between them, putting up my hands. "We stay together. We took an oath, the four of us, and we will stand by it. The time will come for us to take separate paths, but it is not today."

Zevi glared at Gavi before nodding. "I agree. We stand a better chance of survival together."

I gestured to the tent with the banner of Yehudah. "We are closest to Zevi's tribe, and it looks as though they outnumber any others by far. We have the greatest chance at anonymity with them. Gavi, there's a distinct possibility you'd be recognized by men from Ramah."

My younger cousin pressed his lips into a hard line but reluctantly agreed. "You're probably right. Most everyone knows my uncle. I guess we can take our chances with Yehudah. For now. But this will be the *only* time I fight under a banner that is not my own."

I let out a relieved sigh. The last thing we needed was the two of them brawling for the upper hand. "The most important thing is to find a group to join that doesn't question our age or origin."

We followed Zevi down the slope and toward the place where Yehudah's flag flapped in the cool breeze that swept across the river in the distance. Beyond the loose grouping of those gathered around tribal banners, there seemed to be little to no organization of the masses. This makeshift army was nothing like the well-organized companies I'd heard grizzled soldiers speak of with awe when reminiscing about skirmishes with the Philistines, and certainly nothing like the fearsome forces employed by Pharaoh, whose training regimen was legendary. There were many of us, to be certain, but most men looked like who they were—farmers or shepherds. More than a few were preparing crude spears tipped with stone arrowheads. Most had well-worn slings dangling from their belts, and perhaps one out of ten carried a sword, though none as fine as the one that Zevi wielded.

We likely had only two things in our favor: sheer numbers and the element of surprise. And I had no idea how Saul and his men thought this unruly, disorganized horde could take on the Ammonite army. For the first time since I'd seen that ox leg unfurled on the ground, I questioned whether this might be a fight we could not win.

The rich scent of roasting meat wafted across our path as we approached a sprawling oak tree, under which a group of about ten men were gathered around a fire. After having eaten nothing but the stale bread in Gavi's pack, my stomach roared to life. Also, by the looks of the scarred leather armor strapped to some of their bodies and the battered shields scattered about, this was far from the first battle most of these men had taken part in. These were exactly the sorts of people I'd been longing to talk to, men who'd looked Israel's enemies in the eye and lived to tell of their experiences. I was just as hungry for the meat that crackled over their fire as I was for their stories.

"What I would not do to dig my teeth into that," muttered Gavi, his gaze longing as we passed by.

Perhaps overhearing his covetous words, one of the men stood from his place near the fire and waved a hand. "Shalom, my friends! Come, join us!"

Anticipation kicked up in my chest, and my mouth watered. But before I'd managed to take more than three steps in their direction, Zevi snagged my arm and yanked me to a halt. "What are you doing?"

"Accepting their hospitality."

"No," he said. "We need to find a place to set up camp where no one will take notice of us and wait for instruction from the commanders."

Zevi had always been wary of strangers. Gavi, Shalem, and I were his only friends that I was aware of. Outside of working with his father in the woods or traveling on timber deliveries, he spent all of his time with his family in Kiryat-Yearim. But if there was anything I knew of war—and granted, it was only from scattered tales I'd heard from old men at the gates of Ramah—it was that the strongest of ties were forged in battle between brethren in arms. We might as well begin making those connections. If Zevi wanted to be a soldier of renown, he needed to get past whatever held him aloof.

I gestured toward the group. "They seem to have been here for a while. I'm sure they can tell us whatever we need to know."

"We need to eat, Zev," said Gavi. "If they are willing to share some of that meat, then I say we take it."

"I may have to eat one of my sandals if we go on much longer without a meal," said Shalem, his words muffled behind his disguise.

"They'll be looking closely," said Zevi. "They may see through our ruse."

"If we are going to pass as soldiers," I said, "now is as good a time as any to test our story."

Zevi's gaze skittered over the teeming mass of humanity around us, his jaw twitching. I could practically see the arguments forming on his lips, so I ignored my usual tendency to defer to Zevi in such matters and continued toward the oak tree, knowing my cousins would follow. Zevi would thank me when his belly was full.

The man who'd called out strode forward, greeting me with a kiss of welcome. "You men in need of some food?"

"That we are," I responded. "We'd be most grateful if you'd share whatever you have cooking over that fire."

The man gestured toward a butchered carcass hanging from one of the branches, its lifeblood still dripping into the dirt. "Came across a lame doe and couldn't let it go to waste. The meat is tough, but at least we'll not be running into battle half-starved. Come. Have a seat. There will be plenty." He told the others to make room, and the group shuffled, clearing a place for the four of us to sit.

Leaving our own shields and packs in a heap, we settled next to the fire, Shalem and Gavi finding places on either side of me and Zevi sitting near the man who'd extended the invitation. Someone handed us a skin of barley beer, and we all took a long draft. One of the men turned the meat on a hastily constructed spit, and the fat crackled in the flames below, the smell teasing my nostrils.

The older man introduced himself as Dorel and then listed off names for the rest gathered beneath the oak, none of which I would remember, since I was distracted by the scent of roasting venison.

Nothing had ever smelled so delicious. I licked the corner of my mouth to keep from drooling.

"So, tell us," Dorel asked Zevi, "where do you hail from?"

My cousin's discomfort was evident as he stared at his hands before responding. He rarely spoke of his life before Natan and Shoshana brought him into their family, and never of the Philistine raid that saw him enslaved in Ashdod. "Maresha."

With a nod of recognition, Dorel gestured toward one of his companions. "We're from Lachish, but my friend there has relatives up in Maresha, don't you, Rezev? Perhaps your families are acquainted."

Zevi shook his head. "I doubt that. The family of my birth died of fever when I was a young boy. I was sent to live elsewhere and then adopted into another family. I barely remember Maresha and have no recollection of anyone who lived there."

His tone made it clear he had no interest in revealing more and I guessed Dorel might continue to press, so I interjected. "Isn't Lachish on the edge of Philistine territory?"

"That it is. We have only the foothills between us."

"So does that mean you've engaged with them?" Gavi asked, his eyes lighting up.

Rezev gave a wry chuckle. "When are we *not* dealing with them? Those dog eaters refuse to leave us be. If we could drive them back to the sea where they belong, we would gladly do so." He spit on the ground.

I held my flinch in check. Living in Naioth with those who knew my mother and her Philistine background well, I'd never encountered such vitriol. But who could blame these men? Although the Philistines had been fairly quiet lately, they'd been relentless in their pursuit of our territory since Yehoshua's day, constantly raiding our border towns and taking slaves, lusting after the priceless trade routes we'd controlled for generations. It was only with the help of Yahweh that our place in the Land was as secure as it was, especially with all the friction between the tribes over power and land disputes.

"Well, now that we have a king, the Philistines won't be a threat much longer," I said.

To my shock, the entire group burst into laughter at my statement.

"Oh, if only that were true, my young friend," said Dorel, shaking his head.

I shifted in my seat, annoyed by his condescending tone.

"The Philistines have control of all the sea trade in this region of the world. They have the support of Egypt and friendly relations with the Phoenicians, with Tarshish, and with many other nations around the Great Sea. They've been sailing ships and establishing connections since long before Yehoshua stepped foot in the Land. Their cities are massive, well-fortified, and overflowing with wealth you cannot even imagine. What makes you think your little upstart king has any chance at besting them? No one has even heard from him until now, when he's so desperate for help that he had to threaten us to assemble the tribes."

"But he's the king chosen by Yahweh," I said, thrown by his obvious disdain. "Anointed by Samuel himself."

A smattering of laugher followed my ready defense.

"Says who?" said Rezev. "The so-called prophet who was born in Benjamite territory? Whose loyalties do you think he has in mind when he has his *revelations*?"

I'd known that there were those who did not believe Samuel was a prophet of the Most High, but I'd never met anyone who was so openly disdainful of the man who was considered nearly equal to Mosheh in Naioth. "The choice of kings was left up to lots, which were cast in full view of the priests and the elders of *all* the tribes."

Rezev gave a snort. "You think a couple of painted rocks should determine the leadership of a nation? We may as well simply choose a man at random."

Another spoke up, his mouth full of bread. "I heard Saul was hiding among the baggage while the entire selection process was happening, like some frightened woman!"

"Perhaps he'll carry our packs for us while we fight!" said another man. The rest of the group laughed, some saying that this was a plan they could support.

Another man raised his voice to add to the mockery. "Or maybe Samuel will show up and throw his little stones at the enemy!"

The Yehudites all laughed again, and my skin flushed with heat. I divided a glance between Gavriel and Zevi, who looked equally horrified at the way these men were dishonoring Samuel, a man of Yahweh we'd been taught to revere our entire lives, and with whom we'd all interacted, and Saul, the man we knew to be the rightful king.

"If you all have no intention of honoring Saul as king of Israel, then why are you here? Why join this fight at his request?" I said, attempting to keep my tone even.

"Spoils, of course!" said Dorel. "What other reason is there to go to war when it is nowhere near our borders?"

"But we are going to free the people of Yavesh, not plunder them," said Gavriel.

Rezev shrugged. "Nahash has already done the plundering. We'll just take back what he's stolen."

"So you plan to benefit from the looting of our own people?"

"They aren't *our* people, boy," said Rezev, his tone condescending. "They may have been at one time, long ago. But they've been across the river for centuries. They're more Aramean and who knows what else with all the intermarriage over that time. They barely even speak our language."

"But they are still our kin," I said, "sons of Yaakov, even if we've been separated for many years."

"They're no kin of mine," said Rezev. "They are no better than the rest of the heathens on that side of the Jordan. Yahweh is just one of the many gods they worship."

I had no ready answer for such an accusation, but it was clear these men would use any excuse to justify their behavior. Before I could conjure a response, Zevi startled us all by speaking.

"It does not matter who they worship or how long they've been separated from us. They are still Yaakov's sons. They are part of Israel, and we have an obligation to come to their aid."

Rezev peered at him, head tilted in curiosity. "And where does your allegiance lie? With your own kin? Or a horde of Benjamites and their coward king?"

Zevi bristled, his gaze traveling over the circle of men from the tribe he'd been born into. "My brothers are those who stand for our people, be they from Yehudah, Benjamin, Asher, or Gad."

"Do you know what the king has planned?" I interjected, attempting to steer this conversation away from the cliff it was careening toward. Zevi was not one to explode, but his heritage was a sore point, and I did not want to take any chances.

"The commanders announced last night that we are splitting into three divisions, since there are so many of us," said Dorel, with a swipe of his hand toward the tent with the yellow banner in the distance. "Each company will take a different route to Yavesh. We're to be ready to march before the sacrifices are offered at sunset."

"We're crossing the river at night?" I shaded my eyes to allow my gaze to travel along the Jordan in the distance, rushing along with a roiling swell of frigid runoff from the white-headed mountain range on the northern horizon. Between the cold, the current, and the thousands of men fording at the same time, it would be a treacherous endeavor.

"Indeed. Rumor is Saul plans to encircle the Ammonite camp before dawn."

The conversation around the fire veered away from us and toward the upcoming battle, dissipating the tension from before. As the venison roasted, becoming even more fragrant and mouthwatering, we learned that the tribes of Yehudah and Simeon were to gather near the river before dusk in one company; Benjamin, Manasseh, Ephraim, and Dan would rally together a little to the north of them; and the men from Naftali, Asher, Issachar, and Zebulon would make up the final company just south of this camp.

"That looks like a fine dagger," said Dorel, gesturing to the long knife at Gavi's belt. The pommel was carved from mahogany and inlaid with some type of bluish stone.

Never one to shy away from compliments on his craftsmanship, Gavi removed the weapon from its sheath and held it out for the man's inspection. "Made it myself."

The bronze blade flashed in the sunlight as Dorel accepted the dagger, his eyes rounding at the revelation. "You're a metalsmith?"

Gavi shrugged with false modesty. "I've learned a few things from a . . . friend. But I mean for my weapons to be in hands all over the region someday. In fact, I made most of the weapons we'll carry into battle tomorrow, along with the armor and shields."

Dorel leaned in to inspect the leather breastplate on Gavi's chest, humming his appreciation for the careful stitching. "You're a young man with many talents. I have no doubt you'll be famous one day."

My cousin did a very poor job of squelching the smug grin that quirked his lips as he accepted the dagger back from Dorel.

"Where did you say you are from again?" asked Rezev abruptly. His gaze slid from Gavi to Shalem, who'd thankfully remained silent with his eyes downcast and his smooth jaw tucked away in the folds of his scarf, and then moved to me. There was brewing suspicion in his dark eyes, and I wondered what exactly had sparked it. I took a measured breath before answering, hoping my tone would remain placid.

"Kiryat-Yearim," I answered, having decided that stretching the truth in a familiar direction was best. The fact that the town where Zevi lived and where much of our family remained was within Yehudite borders was a convenient prevarication.

Dorel's brows lifted. "Where the Ark is hidden?"

"That's what I was told when I was a boy," I responded with a shrug, as if the family we all belonged to had not been charged with guarding that sacred object for decades, in a hiding place so secret even I didn't know its location.

"Where are the rest of the men from your town?" Rezev asked, suspicion coloring his tone. "Your fathers and uncles? Surely you *boys* didn't come alone."

Cold dread skittered up the back of my neck at his emphasis on our youth. Having meat in our bellies was not worth being caught in our lies. My mind spun with ideas for how to nudge the conversation in a safer direction, but before I could untangle my tongue enough to spin one of my tales, Zevi beat me to it.

"We were sent ahead to scout out a good site for the rest of them to camp," he said as he surged to his feet. "Thank you for your offer of food, but we really should complete our task before they arrive." He picked up his pack and shield and walked away, leaving the men of his tribe and their questions behind. Stunned for only the span of three breaths, the rest of us jumped up to follow, Gavi and I muttering our own apologies as we darted after our cousin.

Although I'd expected Zevi to find a place to settle within Yehudah's camp, he veered in the opposite direction, down the hill and toward the river. I quickened my stride to catch up with him. "Where are you going, Zev?"

"To the river," he snapped.

"But don't we—"

"We need to get over before the rest of the army. I'm not taking any chances with Shay in that raging water. We will ford now, hunt something to eat before the horde scares all the game away, and then be ready to meet up with them on the other side after they rally. It will be much easier to blend in after the sun goes down."

"That's a good plan," I said. "I'd wondered about the chaos of crossing with so many. But why are you heading north?" I gestured toward the place Dorel had indicated Yehudah and Simeon had been commanded to gather.

"We're joining Benjamin," he stated.

"We are?" Gavi's confusion echoed my own. Zevi had been so adamant about fighting beside his tribal brethren before.

"There is too much of a risk that we will run into Dorel and his friends again. I'm not taking any more chances that the three of you will reveal yourselves. Between Avi's insistence on running his mouth, your strong Benjamite accent while you boast about your weapons, and Shalem's beardlessness, we might as well shout the truth at the center of camp."

"Fine with me," Gavi said. "I have no desire to fight alongside worthless men who don't respect a divinely appointed king and care only for the spoils of war."

Zevi's jaw ticked but he kept quiet, his pace quickening toward the rushing water.

"I don't care which company we join," I said, "only that we fight for our people."

"I wish I could fight too," said Shalem, his headscarf having fallen back to reveal that silver patch in his dark hair.

"We'll be in enough trouble having taken you with us," said Gavi. "Your ima would murder all three of us without remorse if her precious boy went anywhere near a battlefield."

"Don't worry, Shay," I said, slinging my arm around my young cousin's shoulders. "We'll have plenty of stories for you once we retrieve you from your hiding place."

He grinned up at me. "You'll tell me everything?"

"Every last detail," I said with a wink as we came to a stop beside the Jordan River. I'd been hoping to catch a glimpse of Samuel, or even King Saul, as they burnt offerings before the march and asked Yahweh's blessing over the battle ahead, but Zevi was right that crossing before everyone else was the safest decision.

The ample reeds that grew along the path of the river clogged the banks, swaying downstream with the force of the currents snaking beneath its dark surface. From what the Yehudites had said, the walk to Yavesh was only a few hours to the east. By the time the sun rose tomorrow, I'd already be counted among the warriors of Israel.

I checked that my dagger was secure in the sheath at my belt, my shield was tied securely across my back, and my satchel was snug across my chest. "Now let's get ready to swim."

9

Keziah

here have you been?" I asked as Imati entered my room late in the afternoon, a basket full of glimmering fabric in her arms. She'd slept beside me on the floor last night, as she'd done each night since the disastrous betrothal ceremony, but had slipped out the door at dawn without explanation, leaving me with only my fears to keep me company on my wedding day.

Not long after the sun went down this evening, Vadim would come for me and I would have no choice but to follow him to the guest quarters where he'd been living like a king at my father's expense and there become his property for the rest of my existence.

"My apologies," she said, not meeting my eyes as she set the basket on my bed. "There was much to do before your departure."

Although I meant to ask what sort of preparations she'd been attending, my attention snagged on the gown she pulled from the basket—the wedding garment I was meant to wear.

It was exquisite. A cacophony of colors had been woven into a brilliant floral design by the skilled hands of a weaver in Damascus, then trimmed with fringe the exact hue of a summer sky. The generous draping of the fabric would disguise the slimness of my figure, and Imati's skill with cosmetics would lend a mask of maturity to my face, making me appear far less the frightened girl I was and far more the enticing bride of a powerful tribal chieftain.

Thankfully, everything but my kohl-decorated eyes would be hidden behind layers of sheer veils, overlaid with a shimmering headpiece made from twelve embossed pieces of polished silver, the same one my mother had worn on her own wedding night.

She'd been gone for seven years now, and most of my memories of her had frayed heavily at the edges, but I did remember her gentle voice and her soft hands brushing hair from my face as she told me stories of the gods under the stars.

"Am I like my mother, Imati?"

Her head jerked up from the wedding gown, and she blinked at me, visibly startled by my abrupt question. "In some ways. She too was kind and generous."

"I wish she were here to tell me what comes next. How to be a wife. A mother."

"I do too, my lady." She cleared her throat and gestured to the stool nearby. "Now sit so I can braid your hair. Your betrothed will be here soon."

With a resigned sigh, I sat down on the stool and tilted my head back so Imati could begin braiding. Pulling a wide-toothed comb through my hair with sure strokes, she carefully untangled the wild strands and gathered the bulk of it into one thick tail near my crown. Her skilled fingers had twisted my curls into submission hundreds upon hundreds of times, and I always enjoyed the soothing ritual.

Grateful for the calming rhythm of her ministrations, I let my mind wander down more pleasant paths, bypassing the uncertainty of tonight and instead considering how I might explore the area around Beit Arbel on Sarru's back.

My head jerked forward as Imati released my hair and loose strands slid across my forehead. With a start, I realized that those strands were much shorter than before. A fringe of curls now lay over my eyes. Confused, I brushed them aside, my mind scrambling to comprehend what was happening. Had she trimmed some of my hair to accommodate a new hairstyle for my wedding?

"Imati? Why is my—" My words halted when I set my hand atop my crown and discovered that not only were the curls at the front of my head now short but the rest of the hair that had once flowed past my waist was missing as well.

With a gasp of horror, I turned around to find my maid standing behind me with the entire length of my thick braid clutched in one of her hands and a sharp knife gripped in the other.

I jolted from the stool and tripped backward a couple of steps until my calves collided with the bed. "What did you do?" My voice rose along with my panic.

"Hush," she demanded in a rasping whisper, her eyes darting to the door. "You must keep quiet or someone will come check on you."

My eyes were drawn to the sharp blade in her hand, and heat rushed through my body. Was she going to cut my *throat* next?

Seeming to sense my fear, she tossed the knife on the floor. "I will not hurt you, Keziah. You know I would never . . ."

Relief rushed in, but my confusion did not wane. "But why would you ruin my hair before my wedding?"

"Please," she said, speaking low as she slowly approached, palms lifted in a gesture of innocence. "Just listen to me—"

"How could you do this? Vadim will be furious." I remembered how he'd twirled one of my curls around his finger, his gaze greedy as he spoke of my beauty.

"I have a plan, Keziah. I'm sorry to force your hand by cutting your hair, but it's the only way."

"A plan for what?"

"Your escape."

My knees wobbled, so I lowered myself to sit on the edge of the bed. "You want me to run away?"

"You cannot marry that man. He is a monster."

"I told you I would submit to him. I won't give him any reason to hurt me."

She shook her head. "You don't understand, Keziah. After the night of your betrothal, I spoke with one of the slaves who traveled here with Vadim. Even though he put himself in danger to speak the truth to me, he revealed that not only are the male servants subjected to vicious beatings whenever mistakes are made, every female servant is terrified to be alone with him. More than a few have found themselves forced into his bed." Her dark tone caused shivers to race across my shoulders. "And it is not only his slaves who fear him. His first wife was murdered on her own childbed, hours after giving birth to her third daughter—the punishment for daring to deny him a son. He rules Beit Arbel and his own household with perverse brutality."

I could not say that any of this was a shock to me, not after Lotan's warning and the way Vadim had threatened me so blatantly during the feast. But to hear that he'd killed one of his own wives for something completely outside her control was horrifying.

My voice came out in a broken whisper. "I have no choice, Imati. Kamon will be overrun by the Ammonites if I do not submit to this. My father—"

She cut me off, the change in her demeanor truly shocking. A completely different person stood before me, fury flashing in her dark eyes. "Your father has made a grievous mistake, one he will come to regret. I will not stand by and watch you become a victim of his shortsightedness."

"What do you mean?"

"The man who told me these things also said that Vadim's agreement with your father is not what it seems. He could not tell me what exactly his master has planned, but he overheard Vadim talking with someone about you two nights ago, saying he has no need for another demanding female in his household. He said that once he was *finished* with you, the man could do with you whatever he liked."

I gasped, blood running cold. "Who was he speaking to?"

"The slave said he did not know the voice and was not in

a position to see a face. If he'd made an attempt to do so, he would have been caught and beaten for listening to a private conversation."

"My father could not have known how terrible Vadim is or he wouldn't have made this agreement. Surely, if I go to him, tell him what I know . . ."

Imati shook her head vehemently. "Your father is not ignorant, Keziah. He may not understand the extent of Vadim's wickedness, but he knows he is giving you to a man with a reputation for ruthless behavior with his enemies. It's why he made the pact with him in the first place. He sees it as the only way to protect this town. Your pleas will fall on deaf ears, believe me."

I searched her eyes, wondering how she could be so certain about my father's choices.

"We must flee," she continued. "*Before* Vadim comes for you. There is no other way to be safe from his violence. You will never appease such a man, no matter how carefully you choose your words and guard your actions."

Panic swelled in my gut, my breaths coming fast as I considered all the implications. "But what of Kamon? I cannot leave everyone at the mercy of the Ammonites."

"You are *not* responsible for this town, Keziah." Her words were edged with a surprising measure of venom. "It is your father's duty as clan leader to find a way to guard his people. One that does not involve sacrificing his daughter to a demon."

I flinched at her tone. "But where would we go?"

"South," she replied. "To the mountain where Mosheh died."

I blinked in bewilderment. "Har Nebo? But why?"

"There is a clan that lives there, just to the north of the mountain in a village beside a stream. They are the Rehavites, descendants of Mosheh's sons."

"But why would they give us refuge?"

She paused and took a long breath before speaking again. "Because you are one of them."

Something vibrated in my head, as if she'd struck me in the

skull with a heavy mallet. "But I . . . My father is of the tribe of Manasseh, as was my mother."

"You are, on your father's side. However, the woman who gave birth to you is not. She was taken from her family and sold into slavery." As I tried to reconcile her words, Imati reached up and began to unwind the turban from her head, which released long black curls and allowed her veil to flutter to the floor.

Stricken mute by the sight of my maid's visage fully uncovered for the first time in my life, it took a few moments before I understood the reason she'd done so—the hair, the shape of her face, even the curve of her lips was perfectly familiar. If it were not for the darker shade of her eyes and the longer slope of her nose, staring at Imati would be like looking in my own mirror.

"You . . . ? How . . . ?" I stuttered. "Why?"

Her mouth curved into a rueful smile. "There was a reason you were known as Chava's only child, Keziah. She was barren. For four long years she tried to become pregnant, watching Belah give birth to son after son. When your father told me to carry a baby for her, I had no choice but to comply."

"But why was it hidden? Why the veil?" It was common enough for female slaves to stand in for barren wives. The practice was as ancient as Avraham and Sarah, the ancestors of the Hebrew people.

"Your father refused to let Chava be shamed for her barrenness and made the subject of gossip. Belah, never one to hide her jealousy over the love your father had for his second wife, already publicly treated her as a broken vessel. So a story was concocted that the midwife had ordered Chava to stay abed for the duration of her pregnancy. She and I were closeted away until I gave birth to you. When you came forth, not only a girl but favoring my looks above your father's, the decision was made that I would hide my face to avoid rumors. And when Chava died, your father told me that if I ever showed my face, shaming her even in death, I would be sent away. And I could never purposefully do something that would separate me from you . . . my daughter."

My heart squeezed so tightly at the words that I nearly gasped from the pain of it. She'd remained hidden behind that piece of cloth just to be close to me. "How could my father be so cruel?"

"I don't think he *meant* to be cruel, Keziah. Only to protect the memory of the woman he worshipped. Just as it does now, fear ruled his heart and mind. Which is why we cannot wait any longer to go. There is nothing either one of us can say that will sway him."

"You never considered escaping? Returning to your people?"

"I would never have left you, even if I had to take my secret with me to the grave."

What a heavy burden Imati had labored under. I could not imagine the pain she must have endured after being forbidden to tell me who she was or how it must have bruised her heart to hear me lauding my mother as nearly divine for these past years. Now she was risking everything to reveal herself for my sake. I could not let her sacrifice be for nothing. She was right. We needed to flee.

"How would we find our way to your family?"

"It will be easy enough to follow the Way of the Kings and find the trade road that leads to Jericho, especially on the back of your swift-footed horse. Har Nebo lies just south of that route in the Abiram mountain range. I may have been twelve when I was taken, but I would recognize that peak anywhere."

"All right. How will we get out of this house and get to Sarru? Vadim's men are everywhere."

She let out a sigh of relief at my acquiescence, then pawed through the basket she'd brought with her, lifting out an oversized and threadbare tunic that had been hidden beneath my wedding garments. "With your slight figure and your hair so short, you'll easily pass for a young male slave dressed in this. I've even scrubbed dirt into the fabric so no one will even give you a second glance as you make your way to the stables."

I blinked, astounded at the lengths she'd gone to help me. "But what about you?"

"I'll need to cause a diversion. One large enough to ensure you can get away easily."

"That's too dangerous. We should escape together."

"We must flee separately, Keziah. The guards at the stables must be distracted enough that you can get away with Sarru."

"Where will we meet afterward?"

She paused, chewing on her lip as she considered. "The stream. At the same place I found you the other day during your ride."

"But you *will* come," I said, allowing a command to flow from my lips, regardless of who Imati was to me. "Because I cannot survive on my own."

She nodded. "I will come as soon as I can. However . . ." She came closer. "If something were to happen . . . If I do not make it to the stream by the time the moon reaches its high point, you must promise to go on without me, Keziah."

"But—"

She placed her hands on either side of my face. "There is no time to argue, my precious girl. Promise me. I must know you are away from here."

Icy panic streaked through my bones, but I nodded anyhow. How could I deny her anything after what she'd just told me?

Her shoulders relaxed, and she placed a kiss in the center of my forehead. "Good. Now, let's get you dressed."

10

An acrid smell lingered in the air and one of the cooks shouted at an underling for burning a batch of bread. Thankful for the commotion, I headed toward the gate across the courtyard, my eyes latched on the rough papyrus sandals Imati had removed from her own feet and insisted I wear.

She'd planned every detail so carefully, down to the little pot of soil tucked in the bottom of her basket. Instead of outlining my eyes and tinting my lips and cheeks with fine cosmetics meant to please my husband, Imati had smudged my face with dirt. Instead of weaving my long and shining black hair into intricate braids, she scrubbed filth into my shorn curls. And instead of decorating my hands and feet with lovely henna designs, she'd told me to dig around in the soil to dirty my fingernails and then swiped the rest over my arms and legs.

By the time she'd finished with me, the image in the mirror was unrecognizable. Unlike the wedding gown that would have added the illusion of curves to my slender body, the loose tunic obscured any hint of femininity. Imati said she was certain not even my own father would recognize me like this.

I could only pray she was right because the disguise I wore did nothing to conceal my shaking hands, and the courtyard teemed with cooks and servants preparing for tonight's festivities—the ones that I, the bride, would not be attending.

I kept to the shadows, making my pace steady and my steps light so as not to jostle the small leather pouch around my neck. The contents had faintly clinked with a metallic sound when Imati had slipped it over my head and tucked it beneath my tunic, but she'd told me not to ask any questions, so I'd been forced to set aside my raging curiosity.

Did it really matter, after all? If Imati had to steal for us to survive, then so be it.

When I reached the courtyard gate, which stood wide open, I breathed easier, but the moment I turned the corner to head toward the stables, I slammed into a large male body.

Two big hands grabbed me by the shoulders, and I startled, making the mistake of looking up, directly into the eyes of my second-oldest brother, Azan. Beside him stood Bram, the first-born of my father's sons, both of them looking windblown from riding. I dropped my gaze immediately, all the blood seeming to rush to my dirty toes. How could I have been so careless? These men, with whom I'd never even had a conversation outside of obligatory niceties, would no doubt drag me right back to my room and lock me inside until Vadim came for me. Throat burning, I braced for the inevitable question of why I was dressed like a servant instead of a bride.

"Where are you hurrying off to, boy?" Azan pressed, his fingers digging into my skin.

Shocked that he'd not seemed to recognize me or question the presence of a servant he'd never seen before, I scrambled for an explanation that would require me to speak as little as possible. "Fetching wood."

"Watch yourself next time," he snapped, giving me a shake.

I opened my mouth to apologize, stealing an upward glance, but found Bram peering at me. He looked so much like my father, except without the deep lines around his eyes and the weariness that seemed to cling to the leader of Kamon.

"Leave him be, Azan," Bram said, his tone dismissive. "He's only doing his job. There's much to do to prepare for the celebration."

"As if there is anything to celebrate," said Azan, with a scoff as he released me.

"Carry on," said Bram, as he gestured off into the gathering darkness outside the courtyard. "And forgive my brother's rudeness. He's a bit . . . on edge, this being our sister's wedding day, you know."

What an odd statement. Surely neither of these men cared whether I was married off to Vadim, did they?

The irrational urge to make myself known and reveal what Imati had learned about Vadim's intentions buzzed in my chest, but I could not bring myself to open my mouth. It was not only my safety at stake tonight, but Imati's as well, and whatever she planned to do was already in motion. I could not make either of us so vulnerable, not when I did not know my brothers well enough to trust they would not expose us.

Ignorant to the battle raging inside my head, Bram snagged my sleeve just as I took a step to hurry off to the stables. "Before you go . . ."

My heart stuttered, and my mouth went dry. Had he seen his only sister hiding behind the thin disguise after all? Would they send me back to my awful fate?

"Once you are finished fetching wood, bring me a fresh pot of water. I need to wash off the dust of my ride."

"Indeed," said Azan, elbowing him in the side with a grin. "Your wife will have your head if you show up at the wedding like that."

"Does she ever need a reason to complain?"

The two of them laughed as they walked away, leaving me in weak-kneed relief that they had not recognized me. For the rest of my flight down to the stables, I doubled my pace.

The sun flared its final rays of red and orange in the western sky, surrendering to twilight, as I came around the side of the large building where my father housed his prized stock of horses. Even if the rest of our home had recently begun to show signs of neglect, the stables were always well tended and his herd meticulously cared for. Pressing my back to the thick stone wall, I waited until the light had completely faded from the horizon before carefully peering around the corner to where the guard stood watch. If anyone would recognize me, it would be Yossi, since he greeted me every time I came to take my horse out to stretch his legs. Whatever Imati had planned to draw him away would have to be urgent, because I'd never seen him abandon his post.

To my surprise, Sarru was already hobbled in full view near the doorway, his coat thoroughly brushed and his saddle strapped to his back. Five mares stood by as well, prepared to be transferred to Vadim as part of my dowry. An involuntary shudder rippled through me as I realized I'd been foolish to think that Vadim would have ever allowed me to keep Sarru. Like me, the stallion was nothing more than payment for Vadim's promise of protection.

The question remained, however: if Vadim had already promised to slough me off to some nameless man after this wedding night, what did he have to gain by making such a show of marrying me?

I had no time to consider the possibilities because, just then, Imati's diversion became apparent. Behind the far end of the stables, where fragrant bundles of fresh hay were stacked in an enormous pile, a black plume of smoke billowed up against the dark sky. The horses stamped and huffed at the foreign smell, which made Yossi crane his neck to search out the source.

"Fire!" he yelled and then ran toward the orange glow. How Imati had known he'd be so careless, I did not know, but my father would probably have the poor man whipped for his rash actions. With no time to feel sorry for whatever consequence he would endure, I ran to Sarru, grateful that here on the eastern side of the building, shadows were already as thick as night.

Whispering assurances to my horse while my blood pounded in my ears, I untied him, then led him away from the stable with as much haste as I could possibly muster, all while keeping my ears open for any indication that Yossi had noticed Sarru's disappearance.

I passed by plenty of people as I descended the winding path through the center of town but forced a blank look on my face, hoping that no one would sense the urgency surging through my every limb and instead see only a beleaguered young stable boy doing his master's bidding by leading a stallion to some unknown destination. By the time I slipped through one of the gaping sections in the crumbling city walls, my chest hurt from the way my heart had been battering itself against my ribs.

Without hesitation, I slung myself onto Sarru's back, but before I urged him onward, I swept my gaze back to the top of the hill, where the large house I'd been born in perched atop Kamon like a crown. A shot of guilt pierced my heart at the sight. In thwarting my father's agreement with Vadim, I was leaving the town completely at the mercy of the enemy. But, as Imati had said, as the chief of his clan and the leader of the people who lived on this fertile hillside, it was my father's duty to protect them, not mine. And he would have to find another way than trading me to a brutal man whose intentions in Kamon were anything but clear.

Seeing that the glow near the stables was nearly extinguished, and with it my window to escape, I turned Sarru's head in the opposite direction of the stream and dug my heels into his sides, reveling in the power of his immediate response and the snap of wind in my ears as he burst into a furious gallop.

———

I woke at dawn, disoriented, with Sarru sniffing at my hair and my back aching from being propped against an oak tree all night. Blinking at the glare of sunlight filtering through the forest canopy, awareness slowly came over me. I was about fifteen paces away from the stream, dressed as a boy in filthy slave garments and the sandals Imati had given me. And she hadn't come.

After I'd fled the city, I'd made a wide loop around the far side of Kamon and then wound back to the place Imati had said she would meet me. And yet hour after hour went by and I remained alone in the dark, terrified and squeezing the amulet at my neck so tightly I could still feel the imprint of Asherah outlined on my palm.

And still she had not come.

Midnight had passed by, and the promise I'd made demanded I leave this place, run into the thick-forested hills to save myself from being caught by my father's men—or Vadim's—but I hadn't been able to make my feet move. *Just another hour*, I'd thought. *She'll be here soon.*

And yet, the sun had risen and I was still alone.

"*Boker tov*," said a voice from nearby. "Are you all right?"

I jolted to my feet, a rush of relief in my veins. However, it was not my maid regarding me curiously with an empty water jug in hand, but an unfamiliar young woman.

Panic streaked through me.

Would she recognize me? Run to alert the guards?

My first instinct was to throw myself onto Sarru's back and run, but the belief that Imati would appear any moment kept me from giving in. I'd just have to lean into my ruse and pray she did not see the daughter of Kamon's leader beneath the thin layer of dirt.

"I'm fine. Just . . . resting," I said, making an attempt to alter the pitch of my voice.

Her brow furrowed, her gaze tracking to Sarru for a moment, then back to me. "Are you from Kamon?"

I did my best not to flinch. "No. Passing through."

She watched me for a few quiet moments, and my pulse pounded with fear that she'd easily seen through my pretense. But then she smiled and lifted her jug.

"Just fetching water for my mother," she said. "She's usually the first to come to the stream each day, always up before the birds, but one of my sisters has been ill, so I offered to help so Ima could stay and watch over her. It's a beautiful morning, though, isn't it? I love being the one to see the sun come over the hills and hear the sound of all Yahweh's creatures stirring to life. It almost makes me feel like I am the only one awake in the world and that he is here walking beside me like he did with Adam in the garden, listening to me tell him about my concerns and showing me his goodness by pointing out the shifting colors of the morning sky and the dew on the leaves of all the wildflowers he designed." She sighed, kneeling by the stream to fill her jug. "It's truly the perfect way to begin a new day."

Thrown by her open and easy manner, I remained silent as she continued prattling away. I knew little of Yahweh, the deity my ancestors had worshipped exclusively, only that he was a god of judgment and wrath who'd ripped the sea in half to free the Hebrews from slavery in Egypt. Just as Chava had done, I'd always prayed to his consort Asherah instead, trusting that she would intercede between myself and her terrifying husband. To hear this girl speak of Yahweh as if he was some kindly father figure interested in the little details of her mundane life was confusing, to say the least.

"It was quite the ruckus," she was saying. "They were looking everywhere last night. From what I heard there was no trace—"

My gut clenched so tightly nausea rose in my throat. I'd been so lost in thoughts of Yahweh I'd missed the direction of her incessant chatter.

"Looking for what?"

She looked up, brows arched. "Looking for the chief's daughter. Didn't you hear me say she disappeared last night, in the middle of her wedding?"

Head feeling light and knees wobbly, I leaned back against the tree.

"What . . . what happened?"

"It was the strangest thing," she said. "My father heard all about it at the tavern last night, and I overheard him telling my mother when he returned. Apparently, the wedding feast had been going on for a while when there was a huge commotion."

The feast had proceeded without me? That made no sense. Surely when Vadim arrived to escort his bride out to the courtyard everything had gone awry. This girl must have misunderstood her parents' conversation.

"My father said that when the chief of Beit Arbel went to remove his bride's veil, he began shouting that he'd been tricked."

"Tricked?"

She nodded, her eyes wide. "It was not the daughter of Kamon's leader beneath the layers of fabric. It was a servant!"

The little gasp that flew from my mouth startled Sarru, and he danced backward a couple of steps. I patted his neck to reassure him while I tried to make sense of this revelation. There was only one explanation that made any sense, and I hated to even consider it.

Imati had to have taken my place. But why? She'd had plenty of time after setting the fire to escape. I could think of no other reason why she would disguise herself as me, other than to give me more time to run.

Regardless of what her reasoning had been, I could not let her take the blame for my disappearance. On Sarru's back, I could make it back to town before the sun had fully risen. I would go directly to Vadim and accept the consequences. I should never have agreed to go anywhere without Imati in the first place. It had been selfish and cowardly and now she was paying the price.

"I have to go," I said, already slipping my foot into the loop that hung from Sarru's saddle.

"If you mean to go to Kamon, it's probably not a good idea," she said, in a tone that sounded faintly like a warning. Once I was settled in my seat, I looked down at her.

"Why not?"

She tilted her head, gazing up at me with a little frown. "Because they are searching for the missing bride. And her horse."

I swallowed hard, realization buzzing under my skin. This young woman had not been fooled by my disguise at all, or perhaps she simply recognized Sarru. I'd probably passed her before during my many rides through this valley over the years.

"And what's more," she said, with a note of urgency in her voice, "from what my father said, a servant was killed in the confusion last night. Kamon is not . . . safe. It would probably be best to avoid the town for a while."

Her revelation slammed into me, and I slumped forward at the force of it, gripping Sarru's mane in my hands so I would not slide from his back.

Had Vadim actually *killed* Imati in retaliation for my flight?

Instead of insisting that she come with me, I had left her to suffer at his hands. Left her to die in my place.

Now I have lost everyone.

The girl was still watching me, brown eyes so full of compassion that the ache of loneliness flared hot in my throat. Perhaps, if things had been different, if I'd not been the daughter of Kamon's chief and therefore forbidden to mingle with the rest of the children in town, perhaps she and I could have been friends.

"What can I do to help?"

I shook my head. I had no answers for either of us. All I could think of was Imati's final plea before I left the room. *"You must promise to go on without me, Keziah. . . . I must know you are away from here."*

Imati had been so adamant that I not return if something happened, but how could I possibly go on alone? I might be dressed as a boy, but I was defenseless, and there was no guarantee Imati's people would even welcome me. And yet she had endured so much to be near me when she could have escaped at any time and returned to her village. So how could I possibly throw aside the one promise I'd made to her?

The sun had already risen too high, and I needed to go. I pressed a hand to the center of my chest, where the little pouch Imati had given me lay beside my mother's amulet of Asherah. The two items were all I had left in the world of the only two people who'd ever truly loved me. I blinked back the scalding tears the thought inspired. I had no time to grieve Imati in the manner befitting her sacrifice, but I would honor her by abiding her wishes. If she could find the courage to endure all these years, then so could I.

"I must go," I said. "Please do not tell anyone you saw us."

I could only hope that the false trail I'd laid away from Kamon would be followed and Sarru's hoofprints downstream had been washed away by the rushing water overnight. I had no other plans than to make my way to the trade road they called the King's Highway in the east.

The girl raised her hand in farewell. "Your secret will be safe with me. May Adonai go before you and behind you. May his steadfast love surround you with peace."

With the blessing made in the name of a god I did not know ringing in my ears, I honored the woman I'd only known as my mother for less than a day by guiding my horse toward the freedom she'd given up for me.

11

Avidan

This is the perfect hiding spot," I said to Shalem as I pushed the pack I'd carried from home into the dark recesses of the small cave I'd discovered not far from the trade road we'd been marching on. I shimmied backward on my belly out of the cleft in the rocky hillside and into the dim light of the makeshift torch Gavi had fashioned from a bulrush he'd cut from the stream we'd crossed.

The gentle flame illuminated a deep pinch between Shay's black brows as he peered at the cave entrance. "Are you certain I can fit?"

For the entirety of our march from Bezek, the boy had not once complained or questioned. He'd endured the frigid river crossing without hesitation, kept his head down and his face mostly covered once we met up with the army, and easily kept up with the swift pace our commanders set. But now that it was time to stow him in a safe place until we returned, trepidation was written all over his young face.

"Absolutely," I said, hoping my confidence would temper his fears. "Once you move past the opening, there is plenty of room for you in there. And it's fairly clean of debris, other than the remains of some sort of nest."

"A nest?" His voice pitched high, and he frowned, his fingers worrying one of the straps of the packs Gavi had told him to keep watch over during the battle. Shalem had an almost irrational fear of wild animals. It had taken him months to fully trust Zevi's huge dog, Igo, after the duo arrived in Kiryat-Yearim all those years ago.

"Whatever animal had been using it is long gone," I said. "There's no need to worry. You'll be perfectly safe here."

He looked back over his shoulder, where below the ridge and across the river, the seemingly eternal line of soldiers trudged along the trade road by the light of a nearly full moon and several scattered torches. "How long will you be?"

A knot tightened under my breastbone as his trembling voice reminded me just how young he was. When I'd defended his plea to come with us, I'd been so certain he could handle the uncertainties, but perhaps his bravery had been little more than a veneer. There was nothing to be done now, though. It was too late to change course.

"There's no way to tell," I replied. "With Yahweh's blessing, it will be over fairly quickly and I'll be back before sunset. But I need to go. Gavi and Zevi are waiting for me."

He shifted the weight of the pack on his shoulder, along with the waterskin we'd filled in the stream before we climbed up the ridge to the cave. "You'll remember how to get back here?"

I pointed to the sharp bend in the stream not far from the ridge. "That curve in the flow is very distinct, and you aren't far from the trade road. Don't worry, I would never leave you on your own."

He nodded, accepting my promise with trust born of the bond we'd shared since earliest childhood. I'd been nearly four years old when Shalem was born, and I'd always considered him more of a brother than a cousin.

I gripped his shoulder, giving it a reassuring squeeze. "I'll see you soon."

"Thank you, Avi," he said, brushing his fingers through his

black hair, that odd patch of silver standing out in the torchlight, "for standing up for me when Zevi wanted to send me home."

"You were pretty brave to follow us as far as you did, alone. Now, just prove me right by staying put here, all right?"

"I will," he vowed. His face looked a little pale, but he lifted his closed fist and give it a little shake. I knew that within it he held a small talisman, something that gave him a boost of courage whenever he was uncertain.

I waited as he disappeared inside the cave and his shuffling went quiet.

"You settled?"

"Yes," he replied, but his voice was small.

"We'll be back before you know it, cousin," I said as I snuffed out the bulrush torch. "Just stay hidden."

Once my eyes adjusted to the darkness, I headed back down to the stream. The heavens were brilliant with stars, giving me a clear view of the rocks Shalem and I had used to cross the water. Once back on the opposite side of the stream, I headed for the place I'd left my cousins, about twenty paces away near a trio of tall pines. They stood with their backs to me, their eyes on our fellow soldiers walking by, the parade eerily silent except for the sound of countless feet crunching over the stony ground of the well-packed trade road.

"Is he secure?" asked Zevi, without turning.

"There was a cave up on that ridge," I said, gesturing back over my shoulder. "I told him we'd be back before the sun goes down."

"From your mouth to the ears of the Mighty One," Gavi said, grinning as he slapped his shield with the flat of his palm. "Those Ammonites will regret ever setting foot in the Land when we are finished with them."

"Let's go," said Zevi, already moving to join the seemingly endless flow of bodies heading toward the rallying point. "It's not that long before sunrise, and we need to be in place to hear instructions before the attack."

Pressed in among the men of Benjamin in the valley where we'd been waiting for the tail end of the army to arrive, we watched as four men moved into position atop an outcropping not too far from our position. If the flashing bronze armor, sturdy helmets, and wickedly curved *khopesh* dangling from their belts were any indication, these were the high commanders of this army—one from each of the tribes that made up this vast company.

We'd already been briefed by designated tribal leaders about how the attack on the Ammonites would be carried out and warned that once we left this place we were to snuff our torches and be silent. Surrounding an enemy camp before dawn would be no easy feat for this multitude, but if we were successful, they would have no idea we'd encircled them until it was too late. The tactic reminded me of the story of Gideon, an ancient man of Manasseh, who rose from obscurity to become a *shofet* of Israel and successfully employed a similar offensive on an army of Midianites—although he'd had only three hundred men instead of tens of thousands. But hopefully we would be just as successful in surprising our enemies.

One of the commanders moved forward to address the crowd, his face illuminated by a torch. Something about the way he carried himself was familiar, but nothing distinguished him from the other leaders except his height, which was similar to my own. Perhaps I'd seen him before in Ramah?

"Brothers," he began, his voice bellowing out over our heads and echoing off the stony cliff behind us, "you have heeded the call to come against the enemies of our people, those who dare lift a hand against the descendants of Gad, Reuben, and Manasseh. May our actions today prove to the nations around us that the sons of Yaakov will not tolerate incursion on the Land of Promise. May they understand once and for all that not only was this territory given to us by divine decree from the mouth of Yahweh himself but also that our God is above all others. It is our sacred duty to protect this Land, to guard her against the enemy, and to proclaim the name of the Most High on every hilltop and in every valley."

The hair on my neck and arms stood on end as he shouted out this statement, and my veins rushed with anticipation.

"My father, Saul ben Kish, the King of Israel, adjures you to fight with all your strength in the name of Holy One and know that Yahweh's blessing is upon us as we uproot this evil from his Land."

A shock of understanding went through me. No wonder he'd looked so familiar. From our hidden perch on the ridge above the tribal assembly, we'd all seen Saul the day he was selected as king. This man must be his eldest son, Yonatan. He was the king's mirror image, tall and broad-shouldered, with a face that women would no doubt call handsome. He looked every bit the eventual successor to the throne of Israel.

"I've heard Yonatan is beyond brilliant," said Gavi, awe in his voice. "And absolutely fearless. A man to inspire those in his command like no other."

The sudden flare of five torches up on the hill behind the commanders diverted my attention from Gavi's hero worship. All around us men began to move, heeding the signal to march, since shofar blasts would only call attention to our stealthy predawn attack.

A thousand buzzing hornets began to loop about in my stomach. Thanks to Gavi's talents, the three of us were better armed than the vast majority of the men who surrounded us. The javelin he'd given me fit perfectly in my right palm, the shield in my left, and the bronze dagger was easily accessible at my belt.

"Stick close together," said Zevi, as the disorganized horde began to move forward. "But if we get separated during the battle, we meet at the banner of Benjamin once the dust settles."

I nodded, heart thundering and my javelin gripped with icy fingers. This was the moment my story as a soldier began, a story that would likely be over within only a few hours. Determined to leave any regret behind, I pushed aside fleeting images of my father's disappointed expression and my mother's tears, along with the lingering memory of Shalem's pale face as he entered the cave, and kept pace with Zevi on my left and Gavi to my right.

"And whatever you do," Zevi said, his tone commanding as he pierced me with a stern look, "stay alive."

One lone ram's horn sounded into the silence and then a hundred shofarim screeched all around us, the ear-piercing command setting our restless bodies into motion and sparking an overwhelming roar of Hebrew battle cries. My heart thundered along with the cadence of tens of thousands of feet pounding the ground alongside my own as we hurtled toward the slumbering enemy camp that lay not far from the thick walls of Yavesh.

Arrows and slingstones whizzed through the air over our heads as startled Ammonites poured from tents, most half-dressed, their wide eyes and startled expressions making it clear that we had indeed surprised Nahash's forces from their beds.

Pulse at a gallop, I followed Zevi as he pushed forward, ignoring the masses of Hebrews and Ammonites hacking at one another and the screams of those who had already fallen. My cousin seemed determined to get as close to the center of the camp as possible before engaging the enemy, but he was thwarted when an Ammonite surged toward him out of the chaos, sword uplifted and curses flowing from his lips. He swiped the wicked blade toward my cousin who, without slowing his pace, plunged his javelin into the man's neck. The man had barely crumpled to the ground as Zevi passed by, and I tripped along behind him, stunned at the ease in which he'd taken a life.

Behind me, Gavi let out a whoop. "One down! A hundred to go!"

I kept my eyes on Zevi's back, but a loud grunt behind me, paired with a thump and a metallic clash, made me swing around to find Gavi locked in a duel with another Ammonite, one similar in age to him and nearly as relentless. Yet Gavi met every one of his blows with almost gleeful enthusiasm. His double-edged sword was singing through the air and pushing the young man backward step by step. My cousin's blade glimmered in the sunlight that was just now spilling over the horizon to illuminate the brutality that surrounded us.

For as far as I could see, bodies littered the ground, some twitching, some still, and some wailing with agony as they beseeched the gods for death. Smoke and gore and the cacophony of war overwhelmed my senses as my cousins—my brothers—battled for their lives on either side of me.

And then, as I blinked the sting of sweat and ash from my eyes, my own enemy appeared. White-haired and stark naked, an Ammonite surged toward me, armed with the longest khopesh I'd ever seen. He screamed at me like a demon, his beard already tinged with what I guessed was Hebrew blood.

My mind scrambled as he barreled toward me, and I tightened my sweaty hold on both my javelin and my shield, pivoting just as he swung his sword. The jarring contact of his weapon against my shield rattled my teeth. It did not matter that I was a head taller than him, or that he was at least thirty years my senior. I reeled backward at the force of his blow, nearly thrown from my feet.

Bracing myself with my back leg, I blindly stabbed at the enemy with my javelin and was shocked to feel it thump against flesh. A sharp cry of pain burst from his mouth but transformed immediately into a sound of fury. I blinked hard to clear the sweat from my eyes as the Ammonite came at me again, his teeth bloodied from my haphazard but fortuitous blow.

Before I could retighten my grip on my javelin, he'd slashed downward with his iron sword and snapped the shaft in two. Stunned, I dropped the remaining half and grabbed for my dagger but had no time to lash out with it before the older man had kicked my leg out from beneath me and I went down to my knees. Pain shot up both thighs as I landed hard on the stony ground, my shield flying from my sweaty hand and spinning out of my reach. Desperate, and without a moment to plan, I lashed upward with the dagger, aiming for his gut. Yet somehow he easily anticipated my move and my blade swished by without connecting.

He paused for only the span of two breaths, chest heaving, but it was just enough time for me to realize that I had no chance. I was going to die.

I'd been such a fool. Such an arrogant fool, thinking that war was anything like sparring with cousins who loved me. I would never get the chance to apologize to my abba for not listening to his wisdom and instead running headfirst into battle with palms clapped firmly over my ears. I would never beg forgiveness of my ima for breaking her heart, never jump into a spring-fed pool with Elidor or teach the littlest ones to swim.

And Shalem . . . I would leave my cousin alone in a cave, wondering why I did not return at sunset.

The Ammonite widened his bloody grin at the resignation he saw in my eyes and lifted his khopesh high in both hands, readying to deliver the blow that would usher me into the arms of my ancestors.

Then Gavi came from nowhere, a battle cry pouring from his mouth and his crimson-coated sword flashing. The Ammonite crumpled, his gut slashed open, and he dropped into the dirt in a heap, his guts soaking the ground with gore.

I blinked at the horrific sight, ears ringing for a hazy moment before my body convulsed forward and my stomach wrenched, spilling its entire contents on the ground while I coughed and choked.

Gavi grabbed me by the shoulder strap of my armor, tugging hard. "Get up, Avi! Get up! Forget this and move!"

I shook my head. "I can't. . . . I can't. . . ."

My cousin crouched to scream in my face. "Stand up, now! Fight! Or you will die!"

I looked past him, my bones numb with cold and my lungs screaming.

Zevi was a few paces away, fending off two Ammonites at once. He looked like one of the heroes I'd imagined in the stories of ancient men of valor. Gavi had just saved my life with one decisive blow of the sword he'd made with his own hands. And I was nothing but a quivering, vomiting mess.

Gavi growled through his teeth, shaking me one more time. "Idiot. You should not have come."

Then he was gone, off to fight someone else and leaving me to my own folly.

Somehow, though, his fury had snapped me out of my haze. After sucking in painful gulps of air tinged with both smoke and the coppery scent of blood, I heeded his advice and pushed to my feet. I wiped the sick from my mouth with one shaking hand, gripping the dagger I somehow still held, white-knuckled, in the other. The sounds of battle were already waning, and I saw no enemies around me, other than the ones already engaged with my cousins and other Hebrews not far away. I spun slowly, taking in the savagery that surrounded me on all sides: the dead man at my feet, the burning or toppled tents, the agonized screams of the broken bodies that littered the ground, and those whose eyes stared sightlessly at the heavens above. Nothing but destruction and torment lay before me.

And my father was right. None of it was glorious.

12

My hands were caked in blood.

I rubbed them together beneath the icy water, using sand and pebbles from the streambed to scrub at my skin. If only it were deep enough to wash away the horrors I'd just witnessed.

Gavi knelt beside me, scooping fresh water into his palms to drink, then plunged his entire head into the stream before sitting back on his haunches. Water sluiced down his face and dripped from his shoulder-length brown waves before he shook his head like a dog and turned to grin at me. "Refreshing, isn't it?"

A thick stripe of crimson slashed across his face, instantly taking me back to the moment he'd gutted that Ammonite. I'd never be able to repay him for saving my life. Nor would I ever forget the moment I thought I had truly breathed my last.

Gavi slicked his hair back from his forehead, looking far older than his years, as if the battle had stripped away the final vestiges of childhood that had clung to him. Engaging the Ammonites had brought him to life in a way I'd never seen before. For all his usual caution, he'd become almost reckless in his dogged pursuit of the enemy.

One thing was for certain: Gavi was made to be a warrior, and he knew it full well. I, however, was not. I'd been next to useless in battle and suspected I'd never fully recover from all I'd witnessed.

What remained of Nahash's army had scattered like rats well before the sun slid to its zenith, our sheer numbers overwhelming them in less time than it had taken us to march from Bezek. But it had taken hours to round up injured and fallen Hebrews, to collect Ammonite weapons, and to drag the multitude of enemy dead to piles that would more than likely burn all night long and well into tomorrow.

I blinked, clearing away the images. There would be time to think on all of this later, to stew in my regrets for ever having set my foot on the path to Yavesh. But now it was time to find Shay so we could turn our faces toward home. The sun would be going down soon, and I refused to let him think I'd forgotten my promise.

I scrubbed my face and stood, seeking out Zevi. He sat on a fallen tree trunk, eyes trained on the eastern horizon. He'd been nearly silent after the battle, and I sensed that no matter how proficient—how truly magnificent—he had been today, memories of the raid he'd been taken captive in as a boy must have caught up with him.

Gavi, on the other hand, had not stopped rehashing every moment of the conflict aloud, his voice rising with every account of his own heroics during the assault. And although I was truly grateful for his skill and fearlessness, I wished away my ability to recall every sight, every smell, and every sound of what I'd experienced today. The stories I'd been so eager to recount were far too gruesome and far too disturbing to share with Shay or my younger siblings. If I could erase them from my mind, I would.

"How far away is this cave?" Gavi asked, intruding on my musings. "Zevi and I need to get back before the armies break camp and move west."

The two of them had been among the first volunteers when Saul's men announced the king planned to chase what remained of Nahash's forces back to Rabbah and rescue any Hebrews who had been taken as prisoners of war along the way. Neither had asked me if I planned to join them but they had insisted on accompanying me back to where I'd hidden Shay just in case any stray Ammonites were lurking about. This time, I took no offense at the assumption I would be returning to Naioth with our young cousin. Any delusions I'd entertained of being a warrior had died on the battlefield, along with my pride.

I'd kept myself alive today, but only because Nahash's men had been vastly outnumbered. After Gavi killed the first Ammonite to save me, I'd only engaged with two others. One I'd managed to wrestle to the ground and disarm, then choke to unconsciousness, and the other had been pierced by a stray arrow to the neck just as he'd lunged toward me. And then it had just been . . . over. The satisfaction I'd anticipated to feel in victory was hollow at best.

Now drained of everything except the determination to fetch Shalem and set our sandals toward home before the sun went down, I gestured to the slope across the stream. "Up on that ridge."

"That's fairly close to the road," said Gavi, hand shading his eyes from the glare of late afternoon sunlight to peer at the ridge. "Are you sure he was well hidden?"

"Who is out here searching caves?" I snapped, weary to the center of my bones. "He's fine."

Gavi lifted his palms in surrender. "Lead the way."

With no apology for my outburst, I crossed the stream and the two of us trudged up the hill toward the cave, leaving Zevi behind to stew in his own grim thoughts.

"Shay?" I called out as I neared the entrance. "We're back."

I waited, listening for the rustle of Shalem's body sliding out of the opening but was greeted with only silence. Confused, I crouched down and repeated my call directly into the mouth of the cave. Only the shallow echo of my voice returned to me from within. Unease slithered through me.

"Shay, answer me," I said, bending down to peer into the shadowed recesses. "Are you asleep in there?"

We'd walked so long with little rest for the last two nights that it was entirely possible he was deep in slumber. However, I'd never known Shalem to be the kind of sleeper who could not be roused easily. My pulse kicked up, a flash of something frigid seeping through my veins.

"Why isn't he answering?" Gavi asked.

I ignored him and dropped to my belly. Using my forearms like before, I dragged myself into the cave. The space was cool and dimly lit by the threads of sunshine that stole past the entrance, but instead of Shay curled up within the limestone chamber, I found only the packs I'd left with him and a dark patch of something soaked into the dirt where it looked as though he'd been lying.

"Avi?" Gavi pressed from behind me. "What is going on?"

I sucked in a shaky breath, and then another shallower one, my heartbeat pounding so loudly that it had to be reverberating around the tiny space where I'd left my cousin—my fifteen-year-old cousin—all alone so I could go pretend to be a soldier. My eyes scanned the space again and again, but no matter how hard I peered into the alcove, he was just . . . gone.

I'd thought my limbs had been numb after leaving that bloody battlefield, but now they were nothing but pure ice as I reached out and placed my hand on the spot on the floor, a prayer of "please, please, please" barely whispering from my stiff lips. When I smelled my fingertips and found only the rich scent of mud—not the metallic tang of blood—my breath whooshed out in a painful rush. I grabbed the straps of the packs and slithered back outside, dragging them with me, along with a terror I'd not felt even as I faced the white-haired Ammonite this morning. I emerged into the sunlight, my stomach just as hollow as the empty cave.

"Well?" Gavi's eyes dropped to the packs in my hand, then narrowed on me. "Where is he?"

I swallowed hard, my eyes darting about the hillside, then traveling over the valley, seeking out a thatch of black hair, a dark green tunic, something—*anything*—that would lead me to Shalem. But all I could see was brush, trees, rocks, and weeds. Nothing of the boy who'd innocently thanked me for standing up for him before

I turned my back and walked away, leaving him in the wilderness. Alone. So very, very alone.

"I don't know," I croaked out, dropping the packs on the ground. "He's . . . gone."

"Gone?" Gavi's face contorted, arms splayed out. "Gone where?"

My chest ached as I shook my head and dug my fingers into my hair. "I don't know. The only thing in there were the packs and a wet spot on the floor. I think maybe the waterskin spilled. It's not there."

"Did he go down to the stream?" A surge of hope blazed high, and I turned to head down the rocky slope toward the water. If Shalem had indeed left the cave for something to drink, he would not have gone far. He was young, but he was not foolish. If anything, he was one of the cleverest people I'd ever known.

"He shouldn't have gone anywhere," Gavi said as he followed. His superior tone made my hackles rise. "Which is why I made it clear he was to stay put until we returned."

"Didn't listen, did he?" Gavi muttered at my back. "The little fool is probably wandering around lost. We don't have time to scour the countryside."

Irritated at his lack of concern, I snapped, "He probably just went upstream a short way. We'll break up and find him. Or should we just let our cousin wander out here by himself?" I didn't care how annoyed Gavi was, we had to find Shalem. And when we did, I would not let the boy out of my sight until he was safe in his mother's arms.

"Avidan! Gavriel!" Zevi's voice floated up from somewhere down below. "Come here. Now!" The frantic edge in our older cousin's voice made my heart triple its speed. I'd never heard Zevi so panicked.

Without a word between us, Gavi and I ran, skidding down the rocky slope, causing a dusty cascade of pebbles and stones all around. Zevi stood at the bottom of the cliff just beneath the cave, his expression bleak and his face ashen. Dangling from his hand was the missing waterskin.

As we approached, Zevi held up the vessel, which was shredded and spattered with blood.

A haze of disbelief descended as I grabbed the bag to examine it, hoping the tattered remains held a clue to Shalem's whereabouts. Nausea flamed at the back of my throat. "Where is he?"

Zevi gestured to the ground nearby, where a scattering of overlapping paw prints were pressed into the soil, each four-toed impression tipped with wicked claw marks. "Hyenas."

The word nearly brought me to my knees. *No. No. No. It can't be. Not Shay.*

"I *knew* this would happen." Acid dripped from Zevi's tongue. "I should never have let myself be persuaded by the two of you. What will I tell Hodiya and Iyov?"

Scrambling for an explanation to contradict the ruined and bloodstained waterskin in my hands, I spun around, scanning the area as my heart pounded out an erratic beat. "But where is he?"

"He couldn't survive an attack like that." His tone turned bleak. "He's gone."

My lungs screamed, and I couldn't get a full gulp of air. I clutched at the neck of my bloodied leather breastplate, trying in vain to give myself room to breathe. "But wouldn't there be something—" I lost the fight against a crack in my voice—"left behind?"

"I think he fell from the ridge," said Gavi, a few paces away. "Look. There's more blood here."

In a daze, I went to where Gavi pointed to a rocky area near the foot of the short cliff. My stomach lurched at the crimson slick streaked over a flat stone, and I let my eyes travel upward. The distance from where we stood and the cave entrance was about nine cubits. A fall from that height would cause severe injury without a doubt. But still—there was no body, no clothing, nothing at all to prove Shalem's life had ended here.

"I don't think—" I began.

"No. You don't think," snapped Zevi from beside me. "You never do, Avi. You do whatever you please without regard for the consequences. I told you to go home with him and you refused. Now look what has happened!"

My face went hot, my defenses flaring. "Gavi could have taken him. I'm not the only one who refused to go."

Gavi scoffed. "You weren't even supposed to fight, Avi. You had no business out there on that battlefield."

It didn't matter that it was true; it was the last thing I needed to hear. Something inside me sharpened, and I advanced on him. "Say. That. Again."

Gavi's eyes flashed pure venom. "If not for me, you'd be dead too."

"Stop!" Zevi jammed his body between us, pushing us apart. I stumbled back, shocked at the force he'd used, chest heaving. "What good is it to fight each other? He's gone. There's nothing to be done now."

I turned my gaze on him, horrified that he'd simply tossed any hope for Shay's survival on the dung heap. "You don't know he is dead. There's no body."

Gavi splayed a hand toward the paw prints back near the stream. "Do you think a pack of hyenas took him in and offered him a meal, Avidan? No. He *was* the meal. There is no surviving such an attack."

I nearly heaved up my guts again at the ghastly picture he painted but managed to control my gorge. "If that was true, the ground would be soaked with blood. He's got to be around here somewhere. We have to keep looking."

"There's no use," he said. "Hyenas are relentless, especially a pack this size."

"Even if that were true—and I don't believe it is—he would deserve a proper burial. We should keep looking."

"All we would find are pieces," Gavi said. "We need to return or the army will leave without us."

"Let them! Our cousin is out here by himself, probably wounded and terrified!"

"You heard the commanders before we left, Avi. Anyone who helps pursue the remaining Ammonites will be rewarded. I'm not missing the chance to prove myself. Perhaps even have Yonatan take notice."

My jaw went slack. "You would choose chasing glory over finding Shay?"

"Look around you." He flung his arms wide. "Those animals could have dragged his remains in any direction. Where would we even begin?"

"Well, I promised not to leave him alone," I said, resolve hardening. "If I have to scour every square cubit of this wilderness, I'm finding him."

"I came to fight for our people. I won't toss that aside to go search for pieces of a dead boy."

I flinched at his callous statement. I knew Gavi loved Shalem—knew it in my bones. He'd always been the first to protect him whenever our adventures as boys went awry, and he doted on him just as much as the rest of us. So why he would give up so easily when there was even a small indication our cousin was still alive was truly bewildering. And beyond disappointing.

"Zevi? You'll help me, won't you?" I pressed, praying that he might knock some sense into Gavi.

My oldest cousin's gaze tracked back and forth between the two of us before it dropped to the destroyed waterskin in my hand. The grief and resignation on his face stripped me of any hope he would take my side.

Releasing a long, slow breath, he shook his head. "As much as I wish it were not true, Gavi is right. There's nothing to be done for Shay now. Take it from me, even if we by some stroke of fortune found his remains in this vast territory . . . there are some things you can never wash from your mind. We have a duty to the living, Avidan. There are entire towns in need of rescue. People who've been enslaved to the Ammonites. We must answer the call of our king."

At his final betrayal, bitterness coated my insides like sticky tar. He'd already been commended publicly by one of Yonatan's men for bravery on the battlefield, but it seemed even that was not enough to slake his thirst for military acclaim.

"Fine, then." I lifted my right palm, displaying the crosswise mark at the base of my thumb, the one that matched theirs. "I'll find our cousin alone."

"You can't just wander around out here by yourself," said Zevi, grabbing for my arm.

"Watch me." I shrugged off his hold, pushed past Gavi, and strode back toward the stream. If Shay had survived whatever happened here—and I had to believe he did—then he would have gone straight to the water. It was as good a place to start as any.

"Avi!" Zevi called out. "I don't want to have to deliver terrible news to your parents as well. Go home."

I ignored him and kept my pace steady. Once Zevi made up his mind, it was nearly impossible to sway him, but I half expected Gavi to appear at my side any moment, repentant and prepared to turn over every rock in the wilderness to find our young and vulnerable cousin.

However, when I chanced a look back over my shoulder, they were both gone. I stumbled, gutted that they'd actually chosen their swords over their kin.

I hesitated for a moment. Had I made yet another foolish decision? What if Zevi and Gavi were right and I was chasing the wind?

But Shalem's young face, wide-eyed with fear before he'd crawled into that cave, formed in my mind. It was my fault that he'd come here. Zevi had absolutely been right that I'd been wrong not to turn back to Naioth the moment Shalem appeared on the road to Bezek. And for what? So I could tell a story someday about my supposed heroics on the battlefield?

I scoffed. So much for proving I wasn't a coward. I'd put my cousin in danger to make myself feel like a man. That was not bravery. It was pure selfishness. If I'd listened to my father in the first place, Shalem would be safe at home, not lost in the wilderness on the other side of the river.

He was only a boy, terrified of wild animals, and I'd left him by himself to fend off an entire pack of some of the most vicious predators in the Land. He was bleeding and alone. I refused to let him down again, no matter how easily Zevi and Gavi had given up hope.

When I reached the stream, I shaded my eyes with my hand, searching first to the east and then to the west, seeing nothing but waist-high reeds and acacias perched on the banks, bowing over the water. My guess was that he would have set out to find Zevi, Gavi, and me, so I turned to my left, heading eastward along the stream, picking my way along the muddy bank with my eyes on the ground. When I'd gone a hundred paces and saw nothing but my own footprints, I turned back and retraced them until I'd come to my starting point and headed west.

"Please, Yahweh," I whispered. "Help me."

The plea came almost unbidden from my lips, making me feel foolish for talking to empty air, but I'd spent a lifetime hearing my father speak of Yahweh's nature—the One Who Hears, he called him. Although I'd never put voice to the questions I had about things he seemed so convinced of, I'd also never spent much time meditating on the ways I'd been taught since infancy.

Samuel and the priests recalled stories of Avraham, Yaakov, and Mosheh calling out to Elohim and receiving answers, yet I was anything but a hero of faith. In fact, I'd all but rejected my own Levitical heritage when I ignored the law to run off and fight for Saul. Why would Yahweh bother listening to such an ignorant fool?

However, as I continued to search, the story of Hagar and her pleas in the wilderness on behalf of her son, Ishmael, came to mind. If anyone deserved rescue by the One Who Hears, it was tenderhearted and innocent Shalem, so I set aside my doubts and pleaded for answers. When they came only a short time later, I almost could not believe my eyes.

I dropped to a knee to inspect a patch of mud. Fresh sandal prints marred the ground, ending at the water's edge. My heartbeat kicked into a gallop. *These have to be Shay's footprints.*

But as I inspected the imprints closer, I could see that there were two different shapes pressed into the mud. Perhaps one was my cousin, since it was a little smaller, but the other was my own size. Had someone come along and found him bleeding? Taken him somewhere to tend his wounds?

After plowing through the knee-high water and tracking the prints up the bank and toward the trade road, I stood blinking at the empty wagon-rutted path that stretched endlessly in both directions. There were fresh hoofprints on the edge of the road, perhaps from a mule or a small horse going eastward, but I had no idea whether that meant Shalem had been taken away in a wagon, or if it was merely a coincidence and my cousins were right that I was pursuing a ghost.

Perhaps I should heed Zevi, head west toward home. But how would I ever face Iyov if I did not try to search for his son? How would I look Hodiya in the eye if I did not do everything in my power to bring her precious boy home?

As I turned one way and then the other, my mind a tangle of indecision, something white in the middle of the road about ten paces to the east caught my eye. A kick of almost painful anticipation jolted in my chest as I headed that way.

I swallowed hard against the emotion that burned at the back of my throat as I crouched to pick up the object. A white seashell lay in the palm of my hand, something wildly out of place a world away from the Great Sea in the west.

Many years ago, Zevi had given a shell just like this one to Shalem as a reminder to be courageous. He'd carried it all the way from Ashdod, where the Philistines lived by the sea. On its gently rippled surface, there had been a repeating pattern of long rough grooves, and on the smooth, pink underside a crude portrait of a dog, carved there by a lonely, frightened boy with a shard of glass.

I took in a long, shaky inhale and turned it over. A sob I could not contain burst from my throat. I turned my back to the setting sun and set a brisk pace that would make even Zevi proud. Although I was so far beyond exhaustion, I would walk until there was no light left to see and then keep going until this shell was tucked back into my cousin's palm.

I'd already failed him once. I would not do it again.

13

Keziah

I did my best to ignore my hunger pains as Sarru and I wound through the forested hills south of Kamon, avoiding the main trade road. After so many exhausting hours navigating steep slopes and nearly impassible valleys astride, I finally was forced to seek out something to fill my empty belly. I certainly could not make it all the way to the valley of Pisgah without food, and Sarru's coat was slicked with sweat from our difficult trek. We both needed a rest, water, and sustenance, so when we crested a rocky ridge to find a village perched above the crossing of two wide trade roads, I decided to set aside my fear of discovery for both our sakes. Surely the circuitous and difficult route I'd taken had kept anyone from home from tracking us this far. And besides, between my disguise and the thick dust that coated my face and hands, I was certain no one would recognize me as the daughter of the wealthiest man in Kamon.

In a shallow gorge cradled between two hills, I tied Sarru beneath a sprawling acacia, grateful for the abundance of yellow blooms that nearly touched the ground, hiding him from view. Entering a town full of strangers was dangerous enough—I certainly could not ride in on a costly warhorse, dressed like a beggar. His distinctive markings alone would be far too recognizable if some-one happened to search for me here. Sarru was all I had left in the world now, and I refused to put him in jeopardy. I swallowed back the searing reminder that Imati was gone, and that it was my fault.

"I'll be back as soon as I can," I told my horse, with a kiss to his dusty muzzle. He huffed a disinterested farewell and dipped his head to nibble at a clump of spindly weeds as I brushed aside the dense foliage and slipped out from under the acacia.

My knees trembled as I followed the path in the village, which held no more than twenty homes nestled into the side of the hill, some of them so ancient they looked to predate Hebrew presence in the region. Many of the towns scattered around our territories had been either abandoned by or captured from the Canaanites and Amorites who once ruled these lands. Even the small temple at Kamon had been constructed by Canaanites who'd left behind both religious implements and idols we worshipped to this day, their ancient presence a lasting testament to their power and a point of pride for my father.

Imati had done her best to make me appear like a boy by shear-ing off my hair and smearing me in grime, but there was no guar-antee I would not give myself away with some feminine gesture or even the timbre of my voice. So as I followed the pathway toward the busy marketplace at the center of the village, I concentrated on keeping my head down and lengthening my stride, reminding myself to speak as little as possible and adjust my tone.

The market, such as it was, left much to be desired. Unlike Kamon, where the center of town was a well-organized collection of stalls, this village had only a few rickety tables laden with a variety of commodities: leather goods, wooden tools, and stacks of roughly woven fabrics. The rest of the merchants assembled here were either farmers with produce heaped in baskets on handcarts or villagers with meager wares spread out on blankets in front of their homes. Despite its small size, the marketplace was full of local customers bartering for their daily needs and travelers, evi-dent by the dusty camels or mules that trudged along in their wake.

Determined to remain as forgettable as possible, I avoided the areas with the most activity and aimed for the edge of the market, where the least desirable goods were on display. Just past a potter's stall that boasted little more than a couple of lopsided pots, four boys who looked to be around thirteen or fourteen were studying a small collection of roughly made tools on a long oak table. One of the boys lifted a flint knife, examining the deer-horn handle in the sunlight. The merchant snapped at him to put it down unless he had something to trade for it. The boy replied with a curse and carelessly dropped the knife back on the table, where it clattered against the other tools. His friends laughed and took turns shoving more implements to the ground behind the table.

"Get out of here, Rayed," said the merchant, as he bent to retrieve his goods, "and take your worthless friends with you. Unless you want me to tell your father about those dates I just saw you steal from one of the farmers."

Rayed simply laughed at the man and called him a foul name before striding away with his beastly companions in his wake, like a king with his retinue. I breathed easier when the four troublemakers walked in the opposite direction.

At the far edge of the market, I came across a woman sitting on the ground, a small array of colorful produce surrounding her on a blanket, and an infant perched on her lap, clutching a root vegetable gnawed beyond recognition. My empty belly shouted for joy at the smell emanating from a basket of fresh bread by the woman's knee.

"Shalom, young man." The woman's kind smile made my heart ache, even as I gave thanks to Asherah that she'd fallen for my disguise. The baby looked up at me with enormous brown eyes, gifted me a toothless, drooling grin, and lifted the mangled root up to me. I held back my urge to coo over the sweet little one and instead focused on pitching my voice low before I responded.

The yellow apples on her blanket caused my mouth to water. I could practically taste their sweet crispness on my parched tongue. Mounds of purple grapes called to me as well, along with each of the brightly colored vegetables, some varieties I'd never even seen before. As hungry as I was, I wished I could take it all, but I could only carry what would fit in my palms. "An apple and two loaves of bread, please."

"And what do you have to trade for those?" She shaded her eyes against the harsh sunlight as she peered up at me, then frowned, likely noticing my empty hands. Most of the customers trading here carried sacks of grain or other goods to barter with the merchants and farmers.

Cursing myself for not having payment at the ready, I stole a quick look to my right and my left before reaching into the neck of my tunic and drawing out the little purse Imati had given me. My amulet slipped out at the same time, and I quickly tucked it back inside my tunic before I pushed two fingers into the top of the bag to stretch out the drawstrings and pulled one of the metal pieces through the gap. I startled when I realized they were not copper, as I'd expected. Instead, a glimmering silver piece sat in my palm, winking at me as the truth of its origins hit me between the eyes.

This was one of the twelve embossed pieces of silver from my mother's wedding headdress, which Imati must have dismantled in order to help me flee. Grief for both women bloomed heavy in my chest, but I could do nothing now but accept the gift as necessary for my survival.

"Is this enough?" I'd never before purchased anything at a market, and I had no idea of the actual trading value of the silver.

The woman's eyes flared when she saw what was in my palm, her reaction making it clear that its value was far greater than I'd even guessed. "That it would be . . ." She lowered her voice, glancing about furtively. "And quite a bit more. I cannot take so much for only bread and fruit."

"Please. I have nothing else to trade."

"I . . ." Her mouth hung open as she looked between me and the shekel in my palm. "It is far too much, young man. You could buy everything I have here and so much more. A shekel of pure silver like that would be worth an entire month of labor. At least let me fill a basket for you." She shifted the baby onto the blanket, then twisted to reach for an empty basket on the ground behind her.

I shook my head. I had no time to argue with her and could not bring attention to myself by hefting a basket of food through town. "Then I pray it will bless you and your child. Please. Just the bread and apple."

"Are you certain?" Her voice was incredulous.

I nodded.

The tears glittering in her eyes as she selected three flat loaves of bread for me and searched through the apples on her blanket for the very best one told me that this lone shekel would indeed be a blessing to her household.

"May the gods be gracious to you." I gave her a small smile as I accepted the food and handed over the silver piece.

She wrapped her fingers around the shekel and pulled it tight to her chest, hand shaking. "Because of you, they already have been. You cannot know what a gift this is. My husband was injured while cutting firewood last week and we are not certain how long his leg will take to heal."

Warmth filled my chest at the sincere gratitude, but I'd already been away from Sarru far too long so I could not linger. I offered the women a parting shalom and steered myself out of the market, stuffing my mouth full of bread as I followed the path back up toward the gorge. I would share the apple with Sarru when I made it back to his hiding place. They were his favorite.

I passed a group of young women returning from some water source nearby with full jugs balanced on their heads but kept my gaze averted as they passed, and to my great relief, they ignored me completely. A thrill of victory shot through me as I realized that I'd successfully passed myself off as a boy today. Imati would be so proud.

The thought of my maid—no, my *mother*—hiding under my wedding veil to protect me and then suffering my fate dashed icy water over my giddiness, the food in my mouth suddenly tasting of dust. I swallowed down the dry lump, along with the burn of tears. I'd spent all day trying to reconcile what the girl by the stream had revealed about her fate. If only Imati had come with me, instead of staying behind—

Just as I crested the shoulder of the hill, an arm came around my throat, jerking me to a brutal stop.

"And where do you think you are going?" said a voice that sounded eerily familiar. Dread pulsed through my limbs and the bread I'd eaten threatened to come back up as three of the boys from the marketplace swarmed around me. Rayed, the one who had cursed at the merchant, tightened his hold on my neck. "What? Not going to share?"

Fingers shaking, I lifted the apple in the air. He slapped it out of my hand. "Not that."

He swiped my legs out from under me, and I crumpled to the ground with a sharp cry. The other boys laughed as Rayed threw his weight on me, his hand smashing my face into the dirt. I struggled, gasping as my cheek scraped against the rough terrain.

"I'll take this," he said, reaching for something at my neck.

Mind spinning with the realization that my little purse had slipped out of my neckline in the struggle, I somehow grabbed the leather pouch before he could get it over my head or break the cord, holding tight with every bit of strength I had. Rayed pulled harder, choking me as he twisted the cord, but the remains of my mother's headdress were all I had to survive. I refused to relinquish it.

"Let go!" he bellowed, spittle spraying my face. He kneed me in the back, spewing curses that made the ones he'd leveled at the merchant sound like endearments.

Terror and anger roiled in my gut as I scrambled my feet against the ground, trying to slither out of his hold. He may be a couple of years younger than I was, but he was stronger by far. I would lose this fight, no matter how hard I struggled.

"Get the silver away from him," he ordered his friends. One of the other boys attempted to pry my fingertips off the purse, but I held on tighter, my knuckles going white and my teeth gritted.

"Don't be a fool," said Rayed. "Give it up, or I'll smash your skull."

As wicked as the boy seemed to be, I did not doubt he would follow through with his threat, so I kicked back with my leg, having nothing to lose. From the shout of pain and the way he jerked his arm, I'd managed to hit his most tender place.

"Now you are *dead*," he snarled, the menace in his voice causing all the hair of my neck to rise. With a grunt, he flipped me over and plowed a fist into my jaw. I bit my tongue, blood filling my mouth. Dazed and with my ears ringing I barely felt the bag slip from my neck.

"Got it," shouted one of my other attackers. "Take his necklace too!"

No! They'd already taken the silver. The amulet was all I had left. I rolled onto my belly, trapping the amulet beneath my chest and the hard ground. The cold stone dug into my breastbone as I tried to cover my face while my assailants resorted to kicking me over and over, shouting vile threats.

I'd made a horrible, horrible mistake. Not only had Imati died for nothing, but when these blackhearted boys discovered I was a woman, I suspected my life was not the only thing I would lose.

14

Avidan

I blinked my bleary eyes, convinced they were lying. But no, there on the ridge above a crossroads stood a village. I scrubbed my face with both hands, daunted by the short ascent after so many hours of walking on very little sleep. I'd attempted to sleep in a bed of weeds that had been surprisingly soft, but even though I'd only had a few hours rest on the way to Bezek and a few more before the march to Yavesh, my mind had refused to give my body respite.

Images of a bloodied and terrified Shalem fending off those hyenas hounded me every time I let my eyelids drop closed. I *had* to find him. I'd made a promise to not leave him behind.

So although it felt like there were boulders tied to my ankles, I trudged up the slope toward the village. It was fairly small by all accounts, but its proximity to the crossing of the road I'd been traveling and the much larger one that flowed north and south indicated that there might at least be a sizable marketplace in which to make quiet inquiries about my cousin. I could only pray that whoever had found Shay had stopped here, because from here they could have traveled in any direction, and I had no way to determine which. If I was fortunate, they'd even left Shalem here with someone to tend to his wounds. If I was really fortunate, by the time the sun went down tomorrow, the two of us would be halfway home.

At the well just outside the village, three young women took turns dipping their large jugs in the water. One of them spotted me about thirty paces out and with a startled cry gestured to her companions. Before I could call out reassurances, all three of them had left their jugs on the edge of the well and fled in a swirl of colorful skirts and dust.

So much for quiet inquiries. By the time I made it to the marketplace, everyone in the town would know a stranger was coming.

Looking down at myself, it was clear why the young women had been so frightened. I was still clad in armor. And the beautiful leather breastplate Gavi had crafted so carefully, piece by tiny piece, was stained with blood and gore. Even the gray tunic beneath was spattered with evidence of the battle. But I had no way of carrying the armor, so for now it must remain strapped to my body.

After taking the liberty of slaking my thirst from one of the jugs left behind, I scooped some of the water into my palms and quickly scrubbed my face clean of blood and dust. I headed toward the familiar sounds of a marketplace, passing by a number of townspeople on the way. However, just like the three young women, none allowed me to get close and either scurried in the opposite direction as I approached or ducked into their homes with a slam of doors.

The market was small compared to the one in Ramah, but there were at least fifteen stalls set up around the square, and a variety of permanent shops showcased an array of goods. Sitting at the crux of two trade roads must be lucrative, since they would benefit from traders streaming in from four directions instead of two.

It felt as though every eye was on me as I approached a cobbler with an assortment of footwear displayed proudly on his table. The artisan was engrossed in his work, his bone needle moving through the leather with swift efficiency as he pieced together a pair of boots that would come halfway up a man's calf.

"Shalom," I said, giving him what I hoped was a benign smile, although I was so weary I wasn't certain my mouth could hold the expression long.

"Shalom," he echoed but did not look away from his nimble fingers.

"I've come from the battlefield with the Ammonites," I said, "seeking my young cousin who went missing."

The cobbler jerked his chin up to look at me, eyes wide and mouth agape as he took in my gruesome armor. But at least he did not run away.

"He's about this tall." I held my palm up to my shoulder. "With curly black hair and a streak of silver about here." I pointed to my right temple. "It's also likely he's been injured. Have you seen a wagon carrying a boy like that?"

The man shook his head. "Wagons cannot make it up the steep path into this village. Most traders carry goods on their shoulders or strapped to pack animals. There have been a number of traders through here today, but the coming storm has most heading for shelter." He pointed at the gathering dark clouds in the east. "None of those who came through had a boy with them that I could see. But I've been focused on restitching these boots all morning." He scratched his chin with his needle, gaze roving around the market for a moment, then used it to gesture across the way at a man with various herbs and root vegetables on his table. "I'd ask Gamel. He's always watching the comings and goings around here. A suspicious sort, you know?"

I thanked the man and followed his advice, but Gamel was just as wary as the cobbler had suggested and merely shook his head at me, eyes narrowed as if my questions were a ruse to steal his radishes.

I moved on to the next shop, then the potter, the spice trader, the fabric merchant, but none had any information. By the time I had made it to the opposite end of the market, I figured whoever had picked up Shay either passed by this town or hid my cousin in their cart before coming here.

A commotion at the blacksmith's shop caught my attention. Four boys were messing with the man's wares. He chased them away with a threat, but not before they called him some foul names and knocked his tools on the ground. Surprised at their brazenness, I strode over to help him pick up the assortment of tools and knives the little troublemakers had thrown into the dirt.

"Thank you," the man said, then muttered under his breath. "Those four are the scourge of this town."

"They could use some discipline," I said, thinking that my own father would have had me working my fingers to the bone in the blacksmith shop if I'd done such a thing.

"Their parents are even worse, if you can imagine that," said the blacksmith. "Canaanites, you know. Or at least half-breeds. They live outside town somewhere and come through every couple of months just to terrorize us. There's not much we can do."

I set the tools back on his table, wondering why the elders did nothing about the disruption in their town. "What about the—"

I paused, all thoughts of rude boys wiped away as my hand reached for a knife on the table. The blade had been fashioned from flint, its handle carved from a rack of antlers Gavi found on the forest floor nearly a decade ago.

My lungs constricted, and my pulse began to race. "This knife . . . Where is the boy who had it?"

The man furrowed his brow. "No boy," he said. "A trader offered that for a quick repair to a handle of a copper pot. Took me all of a quarter of an hour."

"Who was he? What did he look like?" I pressed, my hand shaking. "What goods was he trading?"

The blacksmith scratched his head. "Can't say I remember much. Hebrew, I think. Although with a strange accent, so maybe not. Dark hair, perhaps a hand or two shorter than yourself?" He shrugged. "I was distracted because my little sons have been ill this morning and my wife is upset—"

"Which way did he go?" I interrupted. "Was he alone? Please, I have to know. The man has my injured cousin with him."

The blacksmith's expression softened. "Wish I knew more."

It was next to nothing to go on, but the knife in front of me was everything. It was Shalem's. One he carried on his belt at all times. I had a matching one back under my bed in Naioth. And Gavi and Zevi each possessed one as well.

The flint knives had been Gavi's first successful attempts at weapons, and he gave them to us as a token of our friendship bond. The tip of my own had carved the mark of our brotherhood on the palm of my hand. This one had done the same for Shay. I *had* to have it.

However, all I had in my possession were odds and ends in my satchel, the bloodied armor on my body, and of course . . . I pulled out my bronze dagger. Gavi would murder me for even considering trading it away. But the flint knife was proof that the people who had my cousin had been here. It was his most prized possession, even more cherished than the shell Zevi had given him. I could not leave it here.

"I will give you this for the knife," I said, offering the bewildered blacksmith my dagger.

He put up his palms, shaking his head. "No. That trade is not a fair one."

"This knife is my cousin's," I said. "He had it on him when I last saw him."

Understanding floated across his features as he allowed me to press my dagger into his hand and examined it. "This is finely made."

"Crafted by the same hand," I said, "only the artisan learned a few things over the years since he made this one." I slipped Shalem's knife into my sheath. Although it was not nearly as long as the dagger, its bulk caused it to fit well in the leather holster.

"I can't in good conscience make such an uneven trade," he said before I could turn away. "Please, take something else with you."

Most everything on the table was a farm implement, things that might be used as a weapon. But I picked up a lump of iron, which could be used to spark a flame against the flint. "This will do."

He gave me a nod. "May you find your cousin soon."

I thanked him and walked on, my hopes renewed. But my inquiries at the next stalls yielded nothing else of use. Even if they did answer my questions, no one had seen a boy like my description. The trader who brought the knife to the blacksmith must have left Shalem down in his wagon. As I paused to consider whether to keep questioning the townspeople or head back down to the crossroads, someone tugged at my sleeve.

"Shalom," said a young woman with a drooling baby on her hip. "I heard you were looking for a boy?"

My gut fluttered. "Yes. Have you seen him?" I repeated the description of my cousin.

"Possibly," she said, "although the sun was in my face while we spoke. I don't know if there was a silver streak in his hair or not. He purchased some food and then went up that way." She gave a little flick of her wrist, indicating that the boy had gone past the village and where the skirts of the two hills came together.

My heartbeat whooshed in my ears. "When? When was this?"

"A little over a quarter of an hour, maybe?"

"Was he injured? Bleeding?"

"Not that I could see, but, as I said, it was difficult to see his face. All I know is that he was so kind to me. And generous."

That did sound like Shalem. In the worst of circumstances, he offered nothing but compassion to others. There was a reason all of us adored the boy. Even if we'd teased him about his mother's obvious favoritism, I'd secretly wondered if that streak of silver on his temple did in fact prove there was something otherworldly about my young cousin.

I thanked the woman and turned to follow her direction. It *had* to be Shalem. What were the chances I would come across his knife in the middle of a market, after all?

I'd not gone more than ten paces past the edge of the village when I heard shouting up ahead, past the tree line. I stepped up my pace, my weary limbs powered by nothing more than wild hope and the last dredges of my determination.

Up ahead, the four boys from the blacksmith were waling on a black-haired boy on the ground, their young mouths full of foul insults and their greedy hands attempting to turn him over.

Shay!

A thrill of cool relief mixed with hot rage shot through my bones, burning away all my exhaustion and giving me a boost of energy I did not know I had left.

"Leave him alone!" I bellowed, running toward them at full speed.

Stunned by my shout, the boys ceased their assault and spun around.

For once I was glad I was covered in blood and gore. The sight of me coming at them had them paralyzed with fear. I grabbed for the tallest one, since he looked to be the leader of this gang, and shook him by the neck like a dog. I slipped Shay's knife from the sheath and pressed it to the boy's throat. I bent to look the ruffian in the eye and glared, my words edged with fury.

"Run," I said through gritted teeth, pushing the point of Shalem's knife into his skin. "Or I'll add your blood to the Ammonite filth on my armor."

The Canaanite boy's eyes were wide as moons as he trembled in fear, and he suddenly looked far younger than I'd guessed him to be. Perhaps only about thirteen or so. Far too young to be so vicious and plenty old enough to know better.

I released his tunic, and he sped away, he and his cowardly group scattering like the roaches they were. With my eyes still on their retreating backs, I put out a hand to help my cousin up from the ground. "It's a good thing I got here in time, Shay, or they might have—"

My words ground to a halt the moment my gaze collided with that of the boy still cowering on the ground. The eyes that met mine were not honey-gold with a thin scar on the right brow. They were a rich, deep brown, and wide with terror.

This was not my cousin at all but a stranger. Before I could even untangle my thoughts enough to ask if he was hurt, the boy pushed to his feet, turned his back on me, and ran.

15

Stunned, disappointed, and my blood still rushing with left-over anger from dealing with the ruffians, I watched the boy disappear into a gorge that split the hills, limping as he fled. My instinct was to chase after and see if he needed help. But my cousin was still lost. I had a promise to fulfill and could not turn aside from my mission for the sake of a stranger. He'd find his way home to his own parents eventually and be well cared for.

Shay had no one but me out here.

Panic gripped my guts in a tight fist as I dug my fingers into my hair with a moan and surveyed the dimming landscape around me. The storm the cobbler had spoken of was coming in fast from the southwest, the wall of dark clouds already covering what was left of the sun. The moment the rain hit, the cross-roads below would become a slog of mud, and I still had no idea which way to go. Shay could have been taken north toward Damascus, south toward Moabite territory, east toward Rab-bah where Saul and my cousins were headed, or even back west toward the Jordan.

I was only a day into my search for Shay, and I'd already failed him. I'd lost his trail completely and was so far beyond exhausted that my vision was beginning to blur and I could barely recall which direction was north and which was south. I needed sleep and to find a place to wait out the storm.

Then I could think about my next steps. Decide which way to go. Because I had proof in my hand that Shay hadn't been dragged off to some hyena den.

A sudden surge of anger welled up.

Why had he left that cave in the first place? I didn't care how thirsty he'd been, it had been foolish to emerge before we returned. We would already be most of the way home if he had listened to me.

And if Zevi and Gavi had cared at all about Shalem, they would not have turned their backs and walked away. I turned my hand over to glare at the blood-brother mark on my skin. Did it mean anything to them?

I dropped my hand and let my shoulders sag, finding myself wondering about the boy who'd run off to lick his wounds. The storm was almost on us. Was he wise enough to get himself home before it unleashed a torrent? If he was a fool like Shay, probably not.

A trickle of unease slid down my back. That cloud above us was heavy with rain. What if the wadi filled up and a flash flood washed the boy away? I'd heard of entire trading caravans being swept into oblivion by quick-gathering rivers in such places.

He may be a stranger, but he was still all by himself. The least I could do was tell him to get himself home where he belonged. Then I could find a spot to rest. Think about what to do.

Hoping to beat the storm cloud, I sped up the dirt path made smooth by decades of villagers fetching water from one of the springs that carved meandering streams into the rocky hillsides around this village. I could see no trace of the boy among the rocks and thick vegetation that filled the small valley.

But before I could turn away to search out a place to sleep, I heard someone crying. I followed the muffled sobs to a wide-spread acacia tree growing up the hillside above the gorge, its wide canopy tilted so that its long, flowered branches draped to the ground.

I'd found him. And the place he'd found to hide was high enough that he'd be safe from a flash flood. But still, he needed to go home. His parents would be worried sick.

Just like Iyov and Hodiya would be. Another wave of guilt washed over me. I'd left their child by himself in the wilderness, vulnerable and terrified. He may be fifteen, but he was just as innocent as Elidor. What if it had been my little brother lost and alone? My parents would never recover.

Not wanting to frighten the boy any further or embarrass him by forcing him to reveal his tears to a stranger, I crept up to peer through the thick foliage. To my shock, he was not alone at all. His forehead was pressed against the long neck of an enormous black horse with four white-and-black speckled legs, one that must stand at least fifteen hands high.

"What will we do? It's all gone." Another sob burst from the boy's lips, his shoulders shaking as his fingers tangled into the horse's mane. "I don't care if I have to dress like a boy for the rest of my life. I won't go back."

The whispered words continued, but my mind had shuddered to a halt. The boy I had saved from those ruffians was a *girl*?

I must've made some small noise of surprise because the horse suddenly jerked his head in my direction, and the girl snapped her attention toward me as well. The terror on her dirt-and-blood-smeared face caused my chest to squeeze. What a horrifying sight I must be in my battle gear, fresh from war. Besides that, I was a head and shoulders taller than she was and much more resembled my Philistine ancestors than my Hebrew ones.

Something told me it would be best to allow her to continue the ruse for now, if only to afford her a small measure of comfort.

On a rumbling peal of thunder, the clouds overhead opened, forcing me to take shelter under the canopy of leaves or endure a drenching. I kept my hands splayed out, displaying my empty palms, but she shied away, pressing her back against the horse with her wide eyes latched on me.

"I have no intention of hurting you, my friend. I only want to make sure you are all right. Are you hurt?"

Her lips trembled, and she sniffed. Outside the protection of the tree branches, the rain was pouring in earnest, raindrops pattering on the thick leaves. Now that I knew she was a girl, the feminine features were obvious—her nose smaller than Shay's and slightly upturned, the cheeks more rounded, and the lips plump on a narrow mouth. But it was also clear why I'd fallen for her disguise. With her curls trimmed haphazardly at her ears and her tunic oversized and shapeless, she'd easily pass for a boy. The question was, *why* was she dressed this way?

Her cheek was bruised and swollen, her bottom lip split, and she must have bitten her tongue, since blood coated her teeth, yet she shrugged like none of it mattered. "I'll survive," she said, then cleared her throat and lowered her tone. "Nothing broken."

I imagined her entire body was sore and bruised after the vicious kicks those boys had inflicted on her.

"Why were they after you?" I pressed.

She hesitated, perhaps wondering if she could trust me with her explanation. "To take my purse."

"They robbed you?" Heat tingled in my veins. The brazen thieves had set upon her in the light of day, taking advantage of her slight stature. Whether they knew she was female or not, it had been an evil act.

She nodded.

"Of how much?"

"Everything." Her voice cracked, and something deep inside me squeezed painfully at the despair in her expression, and I wished I hadn't let the little beasts go before paying them a lesson.

"They should be held accountable. Go on home now and tell your parents. They should demand retribution."

She pressed her lips together and tilted her chin, seeming to take stock of me before she spoke again. "I am . . . only traveling through."

Shocked, I stared at her, slack-jawed. "By *yourself?*"

She nodded, her fingers still gripping the horse's mane like a tether. This girl was out here alone, with nothing but a stallion to keep her company, and now with no purse?

A thousand questions flooded my mind, but another clap of thunder boomed overhead, followed by a flash of lightning that lit the sky like midday. A small gasp came from her lips as she peered through the branches.

"Looks like we may be here a while. Mind if I have a seat?" I gestured to the ground near my feet but at least five long paces away from where she stood with her horse. No need to make her more nervous than she already was by crowding her in the small space, but my limbs were almost numb with exhaustion.

She frowned at me, her gaze dropping to the blood smeared across my armor.

"Ammonites," I explained with a grimace. "I came from across the river with King Saul's army." I scrubbed at the evidence of carnage on my leather breastplate, wishing I had something more than my battle garb to wear. I'd need to burn the once-gray tunic beneath the armor. I was anything but ritually clean now, so I was glad my father could not see me. I let out a sigh, shaking my head, and muttered to myself, "Not that I was in any way useful during that battle. . . ."

"The King of Israel is on *this* side of the river?"

Even though we spoke the same language, her words were tilted oddly, reminding me that we came from not only different sides of the Jordan but tribes that had been separated for hundreds of years.

"He is. A city southwest of here was under siege by the Ammonites. We came to their rescue." The words sounded noble, and I could not argue that it had been a righteous deed to come to the aid of our brethren. But it did not stop flashes of yesterday's bloodshed from barraging my mind.

"So Yavesh is safe?"

I flinched as her question jerked me out of one of my more gruesome memories, surprised that she knew about the attack.

I pinched my eyes shut for a moment, breathing deeply before nodding.

"The battle was over before midday. Saul's army is pursuing those who retreated."

The girl watched me carefully. "You did not go with the army?"

I took her question as invitation to remain, so I slid my pack off my back and onto the ground, then folded down in the rain-speckled dirt. My muscles twitched, and I could not hold back a groan of relief. "One of my cousins went missing during the battle. I followed clues here to this village."

"You didn't find him?"

I shook my head.

"What will you do?"

"Keep looking. He's only fifteen. I can't leave him out here alone. I thought you were . . ."

"You thought it was your cousin being beaten instead of me," she finished.

Another clap of thunder caused the horse to dance. The girl murmured quiet reassurances to him, stroking his side in a soothing rhythm until he calmed. She was so slight, reminding me of my aunt Miri, who barely reached my collarbone, and I wondered whether she was truly able to command such a formidable animal. A horse with legs that long must be able to cover an extraordinary amount of ground in a short time.

And time was something I had in short supply. Shalem could be anywhere by now, and the longer I tarried here, the farther away he could be moving. An idea popped into my mind, one that would not only give me a faster mode of transport but would also mean I could keep an eye on this vulnerable girl for a while longer.

"Where are you headed?" I asked.

She paused her murmurings, eyes narrowed on me. "South."

There was no way of knowing whether the traders who had Shay had gone north or south, but I had to choose a direction. "What if we can help each other? Looking for my cousin would be much faster if I were riding instead of walking."

Her expression turned flinty, her jaw setting. "You can't have my horse."

I huffed a rueful laugh. "I've never even mounted a horse before. But perhaps we could ride together?"

She was quiet, considering my proposal. "I'm going to the valley of Pisgah, just north of Har Nebo."

My brows flew high. "Isn't that near Moabite territory?"

The stories of Mosheh atop the mountain of Nebo and the struggles between Israel and the Moabites during the wilderness wanderings were familiar stories to me.

Her chin lifted, and she stared as if challenging me to argue her destination. "Why would you want to travel with me anyhow?"

I chose my words carefully. "You have nothing left to trade for food, am I right?"

She did not respond, her lips pinched tight.

"People like those boys who robbed you would think twice about bothering you if you're with me." I was certainly not the warrior I appeared to be in this armor, but my presence would at least deter those who might mean her harm along the way.

She turned away, stroking the horse's face as she considered my argument, then squared her shoulders and glared at me. "What makes you think I can't take care of myself?"

Her show of bravery was impressive after what she'd just endured. "Nothing at all. But it won't hurt to work together to find food and shelter."

She pursed her mouth, still regarding me with a suspicious gaze. I did not blame her. In fact, I was glad for her caution. A girl had no business traveling this rough country on her own. If I could search for Shay a little faster while ensuring she was protected along the way, we both would benefit.

"To show you that I mean you no harm . . ." I slipped Shalem's knife from my belt and held it out to her by the blade. "You can hold on to this tonight."

She stared at me for a long time before slowly approaching.

Eyes pinned to me, she took the knife and then swiftly retreated to settle down against the trunk of the tree with it in her lap. It looked as though I had gained both a companion and a means of travel.

Perhaps tomorrow I could convince her to trust me enough to reveal the truth about her identity. But if not, I would let her continue the deception for as long as she needed to feel safe.

16

Keziah

The warrior twitched and shuddered in his sleep all night long. I kept his knife clutched in my lap and my eyes latched on him until I was certain he was unconscious, then finally allowed myself to doze. But sometime in the middle of the night, I was jerked awake by moaning and mumbling. At first, I feared I was under attack again, but in the sparse moonlight I saw the man was still flat on his back. He sounded almost panicked as he called out someone's name, then let out a sound that could only be described as mournful before going still again.

When he'd first appeared in my hiding place, I thought he was there to finish the job those horrible boys had started. But even though he'd been stoic and outfitted like a soldier in bloodied armor, he'd spoken gently to me and surprised me by not only offering to travel with me but even giving me a means of protection against himself.

He was a stranger, and one who'd been terrifying when he'd come to my defense back near the village, but also a man who was deeply troubled and, I sensed, truly afraid for this cousin he was searching for.

Yesterday's beating had made it abundantly clear I could not make this journey alone. There were too many unknown dangers and now I didn't even have anything to trade for food or necessities. So when he asked to travel with me, it had not taken me long to decide that it was worth the risk.

I could not explain why I trusted him, especially after my own father had betrayed me, but I'd relaxed my white-knuckled grip on the stone knife and let myself sleep on and off until dawn, only waking whenever the man made more of those heartbreaking noises.

Both of us had roused at daybreak and made the decision to get on the road as soon as possible. The rain had long ceased but the ground was still soaked. Sarru's once-shining coat would be slathered in mud before long, although that might be for the best. A little filth would make my prized warhorse appear like any other beast of burden on the trade road.

As the man approached us now, preparing to mount up behind me, I held tight to Sarru's reins, forcing him to keep still and stroking his withers as I murmured reassurances.

"You'll put your foot in that loop hanging from the saddle," I told him, "then pull yourself up and throw your other leg over his back. Move slowly so you do not spook him."

I did not mention that I'd been the only person to ever ride Sarru. Nor that he'd tolerated the stable hands' ministrations to his coat and hooves but never allowed anyone else to mount him. The warrior was nervous enough as it was, his body twitching when Sarru snorted at him and shook out his mane aggressively.

Man and beast eyed each other for a few more tense moments before the warrior seemed to screw up enough courage to come a little closer, his expression wary. Sarru huffed, dancing for a moment, and I put up a staying hand until I brought him back under control.

"Let him get used to you as you approach," I said, smoothing my hand over my horse's mane. "His name is Sarru. Talk to him in a quiet voice."

To my surprise, he heeded my advice. "All right, Sarru. My

name is Avidan," he said, his low voice taking on a soothing cadence. "I'd appreciate if you would allow me to join your master up there on your back. Or at least don't trample me to death on my first try."

He must have seen my mouth twitch with amusement. "You said to talk to him," he accused.

I pressed my lips together, composing myself before speaking. "He's under control now. Try again."

He blew out a breath and came near. Then, fitting his foot into the loop, he vaulted himself atop the saddle behind me with surprising ease.

It was disconcerting having such a tall and imposing stranger so near to me. Even if he had no idea that I was a woman, the intimacy made my face feel warm and as if I didn't quite fit in my own skin. I closed my eyes and took a long, deep breath, trying to quiet my racing heart.

Once I was satisfied Avidan was seated securely behind me, I clicked a forward command to Sarru and steered him away from the gorge. At first, Avidan did not touch me, keeping his palms on his thighs, but when the path pitched steeply upward, he made a startled noise and grabbed my hips for balance.

"My apologies." He released me quickly, his voice sounding pinched. Although the sensation of his long fingers wrapping around my waist had caused a buzz of nerves, Sarru would sense if the two of us were unsettled, so I determined to ignore the feeling.

"Relax," I said. "If you squeeze your knees, Sarru might mistake the gesture and take off at a run."

"I'd rather not fall off this beast and dash my head open within the first hour."

"You'll get comfortable after a while. And so will he."

Veering away from the village, I directed Sarru toward the trade road and pointed him toward the southern horizon. We passed over the crossroads before the sun was even four fingers above the distant hills, and I set us at a fairly easy pace, not wanting my horse to tire too early in the day, especially since he was carrying extra weight.

"I've told you both my name," Avidan said. "But I have yet to learn yours."

"Kez—" I began, before cutting myself off. Why had I not thought to conjure something more boyish? I refused to look back at him for fear he'd see the lie written on my grimy face.

"So tell me, Kez," he said, after a long bout of silence, "why are you headed to the valley of Pisgah?"

His question stirred up thoughts of Imati, her sacrifice, and what horrible things Vadim may have done to her. The unfairness of knowing the truth about her and losing her all in one day was too much to dwell on for now, so my answer came out on a clipped rasp.

"My mother's clan lives there."

"So you are of the tribe of Reuben?"

I shrugged one shoulder. "All I know is that they're a small clan that remained by the mountain where Mosheh died when Israel moved on to conquer the Land."

He paused, as if waiting for me to expound on the clan I knew so little about. "And your father?"

"He is of Manasseh." I refused to speak anything more about the man.

He must have sensed my reticence since he asked no further questions. We let silence settle between us, and I was surprised at how comfortable it was between two people who'd just met. However, after an hour or so, Avidan seemed to have had enough of the quiet.

"I am not a warrior." His proclamation came from nowhere, his voice overly loud.

Startled, I jerked my neck around to stare at him. "The blood on your armor says otherwise."

His smile was rueful. "I should not even be wearing it in the first place. I am a Levite."

"You are a priest?"

I had only met one of the holy men—a toothless, ancient lunatic who'd come through our town during one of our moon festivals many years ago. He remained clear in my mind because, as the traditional offerings were being made to the gods, he'd seen the Asherah pole outside our little temple and began screaming. He cursed the priestesses, calling them horrid names and threatening to summon fire from the heavens.

I'd been terrified, hiding behind my mother's skirts, but she'd reassured me that the man was simply full of evil spirits. When no flames came down from the clouds and the old man was dragged away by my father's guards, his powerlessness was evident. However, Avidan looked nothing like the wild-eyed man with spittle drooling down his beard.

"Aren't the Levites extinct?" I asked.

"Extinct?"

"Yes, married into other clans and such?"

I'd heard that hundreds of years ago they'd held cities on this side of the river, even if their center of worship had been in some ancient tent far away. But most towns had their own temples now and their own appointed priests and priestesses—ones who did not limit themselves to the notion of worshiping only one god but made room for other gods and goddesses to revere.

"Not all of them have disappeared," he said with a note of sadness in his voice. "I grew up in a community full of Levites, in a school of sorts for prophets and musicians who serve the Most High. It was founded by Samuel himself."

"Who is that?"

"You've never heard of Samuel of Ramah?" He sounded bewildered by my ignorance.

"Is he a Levite too?"

Instead of answering, he suddenly lifted one of his large hands to gesture at a wagon off in the distance, dust billowing around its wheels in the breeze. "There! That could be the traders who have my cousin! We have to stop them!"

Desperation crackled in his words, bringing to mind the restless torment I witnessed while he slept. Ordering him to hold on, I kicked Sarru into a gallop. With a gasp, Avidan wrapped his arms around me, and I did my best to ignore the sensation of his long limbs encircling my waist and focused instead on catching up to the wagon ahead.

Sarru reveled in the stretch of his long legs, his huge body soaring over the terrain as if he had wings attached to his heels. It had been a week since I'd let him break into an exhilarating run like this, and both of us huffed in disappointment when we too quickly approached the wagon and I was forced to pull back on the reins to slow him down.

We bypassed the wagon and its team of plodding oxen, along with its two occupants, and I spun Sarru around about ten paces ahead of them, forcing the team to a halt.

"Do you have a wounded boy with you?" Avidan called out. "Found near Yavesh?"

"No," said the driver of the team, eyes wide as he took us in. "It's only my brother and me."

"You are certain?" Avidan pressed.

"You're welcome to take a look," said the trader, gesturing back toward the overflowing wagon bed. "The only thing back there is lumber and sacks of barley we are driving to the market in the next village."

I lifted my brows at Avidan. "Shall I get closer?"

He nodded, so I circled Sarru slowly around the wagon. As the man had said, it was full of nothing but timber and small bags of grain. There was no room for anyone among the contents of the bed, even a young boy.

"Have you seen any other travelers this morning? Ones who might have a boy with them who looks similar to my friend here?" He put his hand on my shoulder, and I held my breath until he released me. "He's around the same age, fifteen or so. No beard and a silver streak in his black hair."

"I'm nearly seventeen," I muttered, so only Avidan could hear.

"I'm sorry, but no," said the man. "We've seen no one at all today on this road. The king's army came through two days ago, and I think most everyone is staying close to their homes until the region is free of Ammonites."

I could practically taste the disappointment in the air as Avidan thanked the men and apologized for delaying their journey. Strangely enough, I found myself disappointed as well that we'd not found this cousin he so worried about and wondered how the boy had gotten lost in the first place. But by the stiff set of his body on the saddle behind me as he gazed off into the distance, I sensed Avidan might not be of a mind to answer the questions that burned on my tongue. So I turned Sarru southward again, urged him to a fast walk, and left the man to his thoughts.

By the time the sun was high in the sky, Sarru's coat was slick with sweat, and all three of us were desperate for a drink. So when Avidan spotted a sparkle of sunlight glinting off water in the distance, I turned off the road and toward the promise of quenching our thirst.

Once we reached the spring cascading out of a crack between boulders in the side of an embankment, I slipped off Sarru and held him still for Avidan to do so as well. I forced my face to remain blank as he walked with labored movements and quiet groans, his unaccustomed body protesting the long ride.

"You'll adjust," I said, nearly forgetting to lower my tone in my amusement. "All new riders are sore for a while."

"Is that your experience too?" He hissed when some fresh ache assailed him as he crouched to cup a palm into the spring.

"I've ridden horses since before I could walk."

He paused to look over his shoulder at me. "Have you?"

Of course he was surprised. I was dressed as a slave, not the child of a wealthy chieftain. We were far enough away now that I could reveal a hint of my origins, so I told him I came from a household that bred horses and about Sarru's illustrious bloodlines.

"So you took this animal from its owners?"

"Of course not. Sarru is mine!" I retorted, before I thought better of it. He arched his brows, questioning my overwrought response.

Too late I realized my mistake. Either I reveal myself as the runaway child of a rich man or let him think me a thief. To stall my response, I stepped into the spring and bent to allow the cool rush to stream over my cupped hands before bringing the water to my mouth. I could feel Avidan's eyes on my back the entire time. How could I explain without revealing my identity?

I cleared my throat, deepening my voice as I chose my words carefully. "My father made an ill-advised alliance with a powerful chieftain of a neighboring city, one that put me and others in danger. Someone discovered a plot against me by this man, and I was forced to flee, disguised as a slave."

I tugged on the neck of my sleeveless tunic, which was nearly as covered in mud and dust as my horse.

"I did not steal Sarru. He has been mine since the night he was born. He answers only to me. In fact, I'm more than a little surprised he allowed you on his back. He's never so much as allowed one of the stable hands to sit astride."

"I'll take that as a compliment—" His words cut off abruptly. Before I could turn to find out what he was staring at with wide eyes, he grabbed me by the arm and pulled me behind him, putting himself between me and whatever danger had crept up on us.

Trembling at the urgency in his movements, I peered out from behind his back.

Four men stood glaring at us from about fifteen paces away, all with loaded slings in one hand and daggers in the other.

The eldest one took one menacing step forward. But it was not his threatening posture, his weapons, or even his fierce expression that had me holding back a gasp. It was the strip of linen that barely covered the swollen, weeping wound in the place of his missing right eye.

Avidan

The old shepherd stared at me impassively with his one good eye. "What business do you have on our land?"

It was not hard to guess who'd inflicted the damage on him and another of his companions—Nahash, the Ammonite king, had threatened the very same punishment against Yavesh. And yet no one had come to the rescue of these men.

My gaze went over their heads to the small cluster of homes near the top of the next hill. Five of the humble dwellings had been burned, their roofs caved in. Somehow the last one remained standing, but its stone walls were charred. These people had lost far more than their sight.

"Why are you on our land?" called out the white-bearded man who I assumed to be the patriarch of the clan.

"We are only travelers passing through," I replied with a respectful bow of my head. "We mean no harm, I assure you. Only stopped for some water after a hard ride."

"Just two of you traveling alone?" His gaze was still wary, but he tucked his sling back into his belt, as did the others.

"Indeed," I replied, on a rush of relief. "We are searching for my young cousin, who is likely traveling with some traders. Have you seen any wagons come this way?"

"Not many these past few days," said another man, his craggy features similar enough to the elder that I guessed he was the man's son. "Not since Saul's army came through anyhow."

"You saw the army?" I'd been so focused on finding Shay that I'd not even considered that I might be following the footsteps of Saul's forces, and among them, Zevi and Gavriel, as they marched southeast toward Rabbah in Ammonite territory.

"That we did. Spoke to a couple of the king's commanders, even. They assured us the Ammonite threat is gone and that our new king will make certain it does not rise again any time soon." A bold promise from a king without a standing army, or even full support from a large part of his nation.

"May it go from his mouth to the ears of the Most High," I replied, with a hand to my heart.

"In that we are of one accord," said the elder, his stance softening further at my proclamation. "My name is Ohel, and this is my son, Raham, and his sons, Tam and Naar."

The two young men nodded their chins at us, and I took the introduction as a sign that they'd decided we were no threat. "I am Avidan. And this is my friend, Kez."

"We welcome you to Emeq," said Ohel. "Such as it is, after what the Ammonites destroyed."

"It will take years to rebuild our flock," said Raham, "but now that we have a king to keep our enemies at bay, we'll be able to do so in peace and security. Something we have not enjoyed in decades."

Confused, I looked around at the assembly of woolly brown heads spread over the lush hillside, ripping up choice grasses. There must be at least a couple hundred scattered about in bunches. "Did they take some of your animals?"

"Indeed," said Ohel. "A great horde came through. Slaughtered two-thirds of our flock where they stood in the fields." He paused, seeming to collect himself. "Every ram, ewe, and lamb sacrificed to the appetites of those brutes. When we protested the injustice, they did this." He gestured to the bandage over his eye.

"Their king reveled in the torture," said Raham. "And his men cheered our agony. Then they burned our homes. We barely managed to save the one left standing. Thankfully, one of my grandsons saw them coming up the road and got the women and children to a cave up in the hills. It could have been much worse. There was nothing of worth in those men at all." He spat on the ground. "They were animals. The only reason any sheep remain is because Tam and Naar had taken a third of them up to the stream in a hidden wadi for water earlier in the day. Otherwise we would have nothing left."

"I hope they do not return," said Tam, rubbing his right eye as if considering the loss of it.

"We don't have to worry anymore, son," said Raham. "The king himself promised once they were finished toppling Rabbah, he would send men here to help us rebuild our homes."

I knew that Saul had ordered the army to liberate the territories Nahash had taken, but a campaign to overthrow the Ammonite stronghold could take months. How would an army made up of volunteers who'd left in the middle of the harvest be sustained through such a long, drawn-out war? As a new king without even a throne to sit upon and fractured support from his people, Saul's resources were slim.

But who was I to question any of it? I was not a king, not a commander like Yonatan, not even a soldier like my cousins—a fact I was more than able to acknowledge now. I could not imagine a lifetime of bloody battles like the one I'd seen. The face of that first Ammonite Gavi had killed flashed in my mind again, making my gorge rise. I swallowed it down and reminded myself that he and his comrades had taken the eyes of these men and consumed their livelihood without remorse.

"We certainly took down Nahash's army swiftly up at Yavesh," I said. "I pray that the rest of Saul's campaign is just as quick and you see your homes rebuilt soon."

"You were at Yavesh?" asked Raham, his gaze dropping to my armor. "Under Saul?"

Ignoring the way my stomach curdled, I nodded.

His eyes lit. "He is a great man, isn't he? I'd heard Israel had a new king but did not expect him to be so impressive, especially after the elders of our tribe said he would care nothing for those of us on this side of the river, tending only to his own."

"You met him personally?"

He nodded "Both he and his son, Yonatan. And a more striking pair of warriors I've never seen. They are so tall, aren't they? Even taller than you!"

"That they are."

Kez turned to me, her eyes flaring. "You've met them as well?"

"No. Yonatan spoke to our company just before the battle, and I saw Saul once, from a distance, on the day he was chosen as king."

"You were *there* that day?" Raham's words were tinged with something that bordered on reverence.

"I was not supposed to be. But yes, my cousins and I watched as the lots were cast."

"What was it like?" asked Tam. "Seeing the king chosen?"

"I imagine it was much like when Yaakov gave Yosef that colorful robe in full sight of his jealous brothers."

"Who is this Yaakov and Yosef?" Tam asked with a curious tilt of his chin.

I paused, staring at the boy. Had his elders not told him of our ancestors? The patriarchs' histories were so ingrained in my childhood that they seemed almost like old friends.

"You've not heard of Yaakov and his twelve sons?" I cast a quick glance at Ohel, hoping it did not seem too obviously disapproving. However, both Ohel and Raham seem just as baffled by the mention of those counted as heroes among our people.

"Yaakov is the father of the tribes of Israel," I said, making certain my tone was not in any way condescending. "Of Gad and Manasseh and Reuben, the sons from whom the people on this side of the river descended."

"Oh yes. We are of the tribe of Gad," said Ohel, with a note of pride. "And I do seem to remember hearing about his father when I was a young boy, but I had forgotten his name. Didn't his brother trade his birthright for a sword?"

I tried not to gape at the man; the tale of Yaakov and Esau had been one of my favorites as a boy. "He traded it for a bowl of stew," I replied, my stomach snarling at the memory of my own mother's delicious red lentil stew. "But yes, that is the same man."

Ohel nodded and grinned, his gap-toothed smile showing just how pleased he was with himself for remembering something from his childhood.

"A bowl of stew?" cried Tam. "Why would he be so foolish?"

His intense curiosity sparked an idea. Kez and I had eaten nothing more than a few half-desiccated berries near the roadside. I was going on two days now with no food and had no idea when Kez had last eaten a meal. But more than once I'd traded my siblings a story for their help with my chores and had even been bribed a time or two to spin an exciting tale with Shay's portions of Miri's famous stuffed dates.

"Well, now . . . people are known to do foolish things to fill their bellies." I patted my stomach, hoping these shepherds heeded the ancient traditions of hospitality. "I'd be more than happy to tell you the story, but we must be moving along. We will need to seek out our own meal."

"No! Don't go!" said Naar, darting forward. "I want to hear the story."

"Please do remain," said Raham. "We'd be grateful to have you share our evening meal with us."

"We certainly do not want to impose," I said.

Raham waved his palm at me. "It is far from an imposition to have one of the king's men at our fire."

After the way I'd performed on the battlefield, I wasn't certain I should be called such, but I held my tongue.

"We'd love to hear a story or two," said Ohel. "It sounds as though you know some of the ancient ones—ones we seem to have forgotten. And it's been a long while since I've heard a good tale."

"I told you a story about those three geese and the speckled rock just the other day, Saba," protested Naar with a frown.

"I meant a story we have not heard thirty times before. . . ." The old man gave me a sly wink as his grandson huffed in offense.

I glanced to Kez, who'd moved to stand beside me during the conversation, wondering if she was comfortable with the idea of remaining. She gave a me a quick little nod, as if she'd already divined my thoughts and was eager to accept the invitation. If her stomach was half as empty as my own, there was no reason not to pause here for a while and accept a meal. Trading a story for something to fuel our bodies for the journey ahead was the easiest decision I'd made since I'd left home.

"I would be more than happy to share a story or two. And honored to break bread with you all."

The men led us through the pastures and up near the burned-out homes, where we were joined by three wives, two sisters, and an assortment of children, all of whom eagerly gathered around the campfire for a boisterous meal. Once our bellies were full nearly to bursting with lamb stew and freshly baked bread, I began to weave the ancient story of Yaakov and Esau—both fathers of nations—beginning with the way they'd wrestled against each other even before birth and the famous bowl of stew that cemented their lifelong feud.

Much pleading for more stories followed the first, and although I was hoarse by the time Kez and I settled near the fire, having easily acquiesced to Raham's insistence that we remain overnight, I'd recounted most of the history of Yaakov's sons as well, along with that special robe that bestowed uncommon authority and favor on his second youngest.

Once Ohel and Raham left to watch over their flocks in the moonlight and the rest of the family had taken to their beds, Kez and I lay on our backs with our eyes on the stars overhead. Exhausted from the long walk, Sarru was on his side nearby, breathing deep and even.

"I have never heard those stories either," she said softly, forgetting to maintain her false identity with a low tone. The sound of her undisguised voice was sweet as honeycomb stolen from a hive.

I looked away from the brilliant stars to study her profile against the firelight. "You haven't?"

The knowledge that she was not nearly as young as I had guessed had been slightly unsettling. As did the realization that the slender waist I'd been holding on to to keep myself from being thrown off the horse had not been that of a girl but a woman nearly my own age. It made the mystery of her origins and her flight south all the more intriguing.

She shook her head, licking her lips as she kept her eyes on the black sky.

"What stories do your people tell during convocations?"

"Which ones?"

"The festivals commanded by Yahweh—Pesach, Shavuot, Yom Teruah, Yom Kippur."

"We celebrate Pesach," she said with a little frown, "to remember Yahweh's vengeance on Egypt and to praise his consort for another new season of rebirth. But the rest of those days I've never heard of. Are they moon festivals?"

Ignoring her question, I stared at her in disbelief. "His consort?"

She furrowed her brow, her hand going to the center of her chest, as if to cover something. "Asherah. Mother of the Gods."

I was stunned speechless. This young woman believed Yahweh had a *wife*? I'd heard of Asherah before, listened to Samuel himself rail against the pagan practice of raising wooden poles in her honor. Why would Hebrews bow their knees to a foreign god? From the sound of it, they even worshiped her as equal with the Eternal One.

It seemed the separation between the Hebrews to the west of the Jordan and those on the east side had caused more than simple fractures between brethren. It had made many of them forget who they were and where they'd come from in the first place.

No wonder there was such friction between us. It was almost as if we were a completely separate people after all this time.

"We've had a long day. We both need rest," I said, not knowing what to say that would not offend her. We were still strangers, after all, and she'd been gracious to let me ride south on Sarru, not pausing for even a moment when I insisted we chase after those traders in pursuit of my cousin. "Perhaps I can tell you more about the history of our people tomorrow as we travel."

She turned her face back toward the heavens, settling her head back on her folded arms. "I'd like that," she murmured softly, yawning. "I'd like that very much."

Keziah

I was fairly certain Raham's wife knew I was a woman. She'd kept giving me surreptitious looks over the fire last night during Avidan's stories. This morning, after she'd insisted Avidan and I fill his pack with enough fresh baked bread and dried meat to last us several days, along with a full waterskin, she'd taken me aside and made a point of asking whether I was certain I had everything I needed. The way she'd dropped her voice and pinned me with a somber gaze told me she'd been asking about my traveling companion more than anything.

When I smiled, telling her that I was prepared, she reached out to stroke my cheek. "I believe you are, child. But know that if you ever need refuge, you are welcome here with us." I could no more control the tears that sprang to my eyes than I could direct the clouds in the sky. Between her family's kindness and that of the man who'd come to my rescue and placed himself between me and danger without hesitation, it almost felt as though something—or someone—was orchestrating my every move.

The shepherd's wife might wonder whether I trusted Avidan, but there was no longer a doubt in my mind about his intentions or his trustworthiness. I enjoyed watching his sweet interactions with the shepherds' children during the meal and listening to the mellifluous tone of his voice as he told story after story over the fire—each one filled with so much detail that I felt as if I was there with Yaakov, deceiving his blind father with goat hide on his arms, sweating as he slaved under the sun for fourteen years for love of his Rachel, and then with Yosef, shivering in the bottom of the pit as he screamed fruitlessly for brothers who'd left him for dead. I'd wanted Avidan to continue talking forever, filling my mind with the vivid pictures he drew with words.

What surprised me even more than his skill for weaving stories with such a passion was how he spoke of Yahweh. Anything I'd ever heard of the God our ancient ancestors worshipped made him sound terrifying, a deity who meted out justice with horrifying plagues and demanded perfect obedience and absolute holiness. And yet Avidan spoke of Yahweh like he was a benevolent deity who loved his people, who spoke to Yaakov in a dream about the beautiful future that lay ahead, who guided him, blessed him, and caused him to flourish in spite of his many weaknesses. I'd been astounded when Yosef had cried out to Yahweh, trusted him in each circumstance, and then *forgave* his brothers for the cold-blooded crime of selling him for the price of a slave.

I found myself hungry for more stories of my ancestors and the ancient ways that Avidan's family still held to. Perhaps I should make room for worship of the God of my fathers alongside my beautiful goddess after all.

So, as soon as Avidan and I were back on the road, I asked him to tell me more about the festivals he'd spoken of last night. With the rhythmic cadence of Sarru's hooves clipping along in the background, he told me of the *moedim*—the appointed times of celebration, remembrance, sacrifice, solemnity, and joy that our people had been told to observe hundreds of years ago. During the long hours of riding, he only stopped speaking long enough to question two more traders and one large family traveling to visit relatives along the way—with no luck—then launched back into his stories without pause.

I'd been so wrapped up in the descriptions of the meaningful and rich traditions his family enjoyed and the way he spoke of his parents, siblings, and extended family with such adoration that I could not help but scream with my full voice when something swooped at me with a piercing shriek, nearly colliding with my head. With a flutter of wings, the terrible creature darted back up into one of the oak trees that lined the road.

"Are you all right? That kestrel must be protecting its nest," Avidan said, his grip on my waist tightening.

My breaths coming fast one upon another, I shook my head with vehemence. "I hate birds."

Demeliah, one of my father's wives, kept a huge gray bird with a red tail that she kept chained to a pole in the house. Imported from Egypt, the thing spent its days squawking endlessly, mimicking words at all hours of the day and night, and sharpening its horrid beak like a knife. When I was about seven years old, it had gotten loose of its chain and chased me through the house, pecking at the back of my head until one of the servants had caught it. I'd been frightened of anything with wings since then.

So, when the kestrel swooped down once again, screeching and nearly getting its talons tangled in my hair, I did not think. I kicked Sarru's sides and sent him into a gallop, desperate to be away from the feathered demon.

"Kez!" Avidan locked his arms around my waist like two iron bands, leaning so that his voice was directly in my ear. "Slow down! I'm going to fall!"

I ignored him. I would not have my eyes pecked out. The road pitched sharply upward, and Sarru took the ascent full speed, huffing his pleasure at being let loose again.

"Stop!" Avidan shouted. "The bird is long gone. I'm sliding off!"

Although I acknowledged the truth of his statement, I did not pull back on the reins until we were at the top of the hill, and even then only to slow the horse to a quick trot.

"What was that? You nearly killed me! Over a bird!"

With as panicked as I was, I did not temper my words. "You survived a battle three days ago. I don't think a short gallop will end your life."

He shifted behind me, his body jostling mine in the saddle. "Perhaps not, but my backside feels like it's been through its own war." He shifted again, and I glared at him over my shoulder.

"What are you doing back there?"

"It feels like I'm sitting on a pile of rocks."

"You'll adjust to the position eventually."

"No," he said. "There is something inside the padding, something hard. I can't ride like this any longer. Let's find some shade to rest in and see what it is."

"I'm sure it's just Sarru's hip bones you're feeling."

"It's not, I assure you. And if it's uncomfortable for me, it probably is for him too. I already add more weight to his burden. He should not be subjected to rocks grinding into his back."

Surprised by the compassion Avidan showed for my horse, I looked for a place to stop but continued glancing up at the sky to watch for that vicious winged beast. We'd traveled away from its nest, but I did not trust that it had given up its pursuit.

Spotting an abandoned home just off the road up ahead, I steered Sarru into the shade of the mudbrick wall, which was slowly crumbling into dust beneath the hot sun. Tossing my foot over Sarru's neck, I slid off my horse, landing safely in the soft weeds, then waited as Avidan none too gracefully dismounted, his feet hitting the ground with a thud and an uncomfortable grunt bursting from his mouth.

"Sarru needs water."

Avidan slipped the strap of the sheep's bladder Raham's wife had given us over his head and held it out to me but did not let go when I reached for it. "How about this? I won't tease you over the bird if you don't tease me over my sore backside."

I looked into his green eyes, the same color as the cypress trees that cast long shadows over the empty house, and realized with a start that there was a hint of amusement in the arch of his brows. Regardless of his appearance as a blood-soaked warrior back in the village, the times when he retreated into silence when I guessed he was worrying over his cousin and the way he seemed to be fighting something or someone in his sleep told me that Avidan was a man who cared deeply for those he loved. For a moment, I wondered what it would be like at the center of such devotion.

His stories, and the enthralling way he told them, revealed a depth of soul that called me in a way I'd never experienced before. Even more, when I spoke, he truly listened to me. Even if he thought I was a boy and I did my best to avoid answering personal questions, I'd still never had any man look me in the eye and act as though my thoughts held any weight.

I'd been so grateful for the opportunity to sit across the fire from him last night as he spoke to the shepherds. To have the freedom to study his face the way I'd wanted to from almost the first moment I've seen him hovering over me with concern back in that village.

I'd also been grateful for the camouflage of my false identity so that whenever he'd caught me staring as he'd done more than a few times last night, he could not guess that it was because I was fascinated with *him* and not just his tales.

His unique features, his voice, his patience with the many questions from the shepherds and their children, his uncommon skill with words . . . all of it combined caused my belly to flutter and my lips to seize up whenever he met my gaze like he was doing now. I was so engrossed in the surprising connection I felt with a man I'd met only two days before, I nearly forgot to answer his proposition.

"My fear of birds is rooted in a very real, very terrifying attack," I said, pausing with a sober expression to let my words soak in before letting a tiny smile curve my lips. "You simply have a tender rump."

He barked a short laugh, and I busied myself with the waterskin so Avidan did not notice the way my face flushed with pleasure at how I'd broken his stoic demeanor with my little dig. If I was not more careful, he'd figure out my secret just by taking note of the ridiculous blush on my cheeks. And although I was firmly convinced he meant me no harm, there was no way to know how he would react to the truth of who I actually was.

"I was right," he said as I poured out a palmful of water for my horse to drink. "There is something back here between the layers of padding."

He slid his long fingers into the gap he'd found in the leather. "Whatever it is must've shifted when we took off at a run, or else I would have felt it earlier."

I lifted Sarru's front leg to check his hoof for rocks and other signs of stress to the tendons and joints. He didn't seem to be limping—even with the additional weight of a very large man— but after that run, I did not want to take any chances.

When Avidan spoke again, his words were layered with a thick coating of suspicion. "I think, my friend, that you have something to tell me. The truth, if you please."

I halted my ministrations, dropping Sarru's hoof, but did not look back at Avidan for fear he would see the alarm on my face. My mind scrambled for every conversation we'd had, seeking out times when I might have given my gender away with a word, expression, or gesture.

"There was no need for me to tell stories for our meal, was there?"

Confused, I pushed to standing and turned to face him. "What do you mean?"

Avidan held a woven bag in his hands, one that nearly overflowed his large palm. If that had been hidden inside the saddle, no wonder he'd noticed something there. I was surprised he'd not discovered it earlier. "You mean to tell me you had no idea what was hidden inside the saddle?"

I blinked at him, bewildered, and shook my head.

He held out the bag, its leather ties dangling free, and I came forward to peer inside, my eyes going wide as I understood exactly why he'd been so baffled. Sarru's saddle contained a hoard of treasure. Strings of colorful stones, gold rings, copper cuffs, and silver bracelets. I felt the blood drain from my face. I'd seen those exact pieces before—it was the same fortune Vadim had given to my father on the day they'd signed the ketubah. How had it ended up hidden in my horse's saddle?

Before I could conjure any sort of intelligent response to Avidan's demand for truth, the reverberation of pounding hooves on the road yanked our attention away from the treasure in his hands. He and I looked at each other, brows lifted. It was not just one set of hooves thundering along, but many. A group of horses was coming toward us at full speed. All the hair on the back of my neck rose to attention. There were few explanations for why men on horseback would be hurtling toward us and none of them good.

Without a word, I whirled around, grabbing Sarru's reins to tug him behind me as I ran to hide behind the ramshackle house, praying that whoever was coming would not bother to stop and explore the abandoned dwelling.

Avidan followed, and the two of us crouched in the long grass behind the house, our backs to the disintegrating wall. I held my breath as the relentless hoofbeats descended on us. It could be anyone: my father's men, Vadim's, Saul's commanders, or even some faceless enemy. No matter what, I refused to be dragged back to Kamon and forced into the bed of the man who'd killed Imati. I gripped my amulet and whispered a chanting plea to Asherah that we would be invisible. Then, for good measure, I let fly a prayer to the one Avidan had last night called the God Who Hears.

When the thunder of hoofbeats passed by, not even slowing as they sped by our hiding place, I released my long-held breath, my bones going liquid as I slumped forward, landing on my knees.

Sarru nudged me with his nose, questioning whether I was all right, and I scratched his cheek in answer.

"Well, my *friend*," said Avidan, his tone nearly as sharp as it had been when he'd run off the boys who'd robbed me, "it is time for answers. Real ones this time."

19

Avidan

"Were those men after you?"

With the way she'd reacted to the riders barreling down on us, darting behind the old house with her horse as though it had been a whole flock of kestrels, there was no way I would let her get away with denying she was on the run.

She let out a long breath, not meeting my eye as she ran a hand up and down Sarru's neck in a soothing motion. Whether it was to comfort him or herself, I wasn't certain.

"It's possible," she admitted.

I lifted the bag of treasures. "Because of this?"

She pressed her lips together. "Perhaps."

"Kez. Look at me."

Reluctantly she did so, turning her deep brown eyes my way. I forced myself to ignore the twinge of . . . something . . . I felt whenever she faced me straight on.

"Why was all of this in the saddle?"

"I don't know. I had no idea anything was sewn into it."

"You said this was your horse. Did you lie?"

"No! He is *mine*. I raised him from birth, fed him by hand

after his mother died. I did *not* steal him. I swear it by the moon and the stars."

I closed my eyes, pinching the bridge of my nose in frustration. "Kez. Just tell me the truth. Who is after you? And why? I need to know what we are facing."

She slumped against her horse, pressing her face into his mane and breathing deeply. I'd noticed she did that whenever she needed to find a measure of calm. It reminded me of the way my littlest sister, Sari, chewed on the blanket our grandmother Yoela had made her whenever she was in need of comfort.

"I told you, my father made an agreement with a chieftain from a larger city—"

"Which one?"

"Beit Arbel."

I was shocked she'd actually given me the name of the place after being so evasive before now.

"A wedding celebration was taking place the night I ran away. I used the confusion of the preparations to cover my flight so no one would notice. I also had someone help me by creating a distraction. When I arrived at the stables, Sarru was already outfitted with the saddle. I think these things were part of the *mohar* exchanged between my father and the groom."

"How would a bride's wedding gifts end up in your saddle?"

She gazed down at her hands. "I have no idea."

"So whoever is after you is looking for this?" I shook the bag, the metal inside jingling. "Or are they after *you*?"

"It must be the treasure. I am of no worth to anyone in my town. Not anymore."

An odd thing to say, especially for someone who claimed to be from a household of standing.

"We need to go," she said, chewing her lip as she continued to avoid my eyes. "Your cousin could be just up ahead of us."

"Perhaps it is best if we veer southwest for a while," I said, resigned to my decision. "Remain in sight of the road but far enough away that we won't be seen by passersby."

"From what Raham says, there are no more major Hebrew towns until past the crossroads. Those who lived in the area before fled years ago when the Ammonites became more aggressive, so it is unlikely I'd find any trace of my cousin around here even if he was taken south on the King's Highway. If we continue that direction, we will eventually cross the Jericho trade route. He said our destination is not far from there."

"It will take longer to stay off the road," she said. "The terrain will be difficult."

"Agreed. And we have two rivers to cross along the way. But if we are to avoid whoever is after you, we should keep out of sight."

"What about your cousin?" Curiously enough, she sounded nearly as concerned about Shay as I did.

"As I said, we will keep close to the road, just not on it unless we have to. Whenever we come to a town, I'll go in alone to ask about Shay. You and Sarru will hide until I return."

"Why?" asked Kez.

"So they don't recognize you and this beast," I said, patting Sarru's side. He huffed at me and then dropped his head back to the patch of weeds he was devouring. The horse truly seemed to be tolerating me more each day, even if I did have the sense that he would gladly throw me off his back if his mistress told him to.

"No. Not that. Why are you bothering with me? I've only caused you trouble. And if they come after us—"

"Then you'll need protection. You and I made a deal, Kez. I said I would get you to your mother's clan. And I already have covered far more ground in this search than I would have on only two legs. Perhaps your mother's people can even help me with information and supplies before I continue on to look for Shalem."

The longer I went without a clue as to which way my cousin had been taken, the stronger the urge was to press on. I would deliver Kez safely to Har Nebo and then I would walk all the way to Damascus if I had to. I would never be able to face Shay's parents if I did not turn over every stone in the search for their son.

I could not fathom how Zevi and Gavi could have walked away

so easily. Their failure to live up to the pact we'd made as boys was something I could not reconcile with the loyal cousins I'd grown up with. I doubted I would ever understand or forgive such betrayal.

Kez's expression was one of complete bewilderment as she gave me a little shake of her head. "I've never met anyone like you, Avidan."

And I'd never met anyone like her. I had plenty of strong and capable women in my life, my aunts Shoshana and Miri, my grandmother Yoela, and especially Eliora—my own mother—but there was something inspiring about Kez's courageous determination to find her mother's family in a faraway place she'd never seen before. It was getting harder and harder not to call her out on her steadily unraveling disguise as a boy. Especially after she'd let slip that she had been fleeing a wedding and just happened to have bridal gifts hidden in her saddle. But I'd vowed to give her the freedom to tell me the truth in her own time, so I would continue to bite my tongue. For now.

Once we were back up on Sarru and traveling again, Kez asked me for another story. "I've heard of Mosheh, and you told of the shepherds of Yaakov and his sons. But who came before them?"

"How far back would you like me to go?"

"The beginning. I want to hear it all."

Anticipation welled up. When I'd told the stories of our ancestors at the fire last night, not only had the shepherds and their families been both fascinated and entertained, but there had been something exhilarating about unrolling the stories of our ancestors for fellow Hebrews who'd never heard them. I was overcome by a feeling of awe that I had been the one to reveal the ancient past to people who had mostly forgotten where they came from, who'd been so far removed from our center of worship that even the celebrations of our festivals had become foreign. And Kez seemed almost ravenous to know more about those who'd come before us.

So, as I told her the story of Adam and Chavah in the Garden and how their decision to eat the fruit of the knowledge of good and evil cut them off from fellowship with Elohim, I let myself truly lean into the telling. Not a simple relay of words I'd memo-rized when I was only a small boy, but giving each thought weight through plentiful descriptions, varied inflections in my voice, and even fluid hand gestures to explain how, because of their pride and desire to be like gods, our first ancestors had broken communion with the One who'd made them. Kez was silent as I spoke, her face turned in the direction of our travel, but I could tell she hung on every word that came out of my mouth. And when I was finished, she paused for a long while before turning to face me.

"I have heard stories of the gods creating this world before but never like that."

"Which have you heard?"

"The priestesses talk of Tiamat, the goddess of the ocean, mingling with Apsu of the freshwaters and how they gave birth to all the other gods. Their children warred against one another, and the strongest one emerged as the creator who made man to serve the gods. To feed them and labor for them and worship at their feet. I have never heard of Yahweh creating a beautiful garden for man's pleasure. Or walking with him in the evening simply to enjoy his company."

The way the Hebrews on this side of the river had abandoned the heritage of our forefathers, inviting in gods from the nations around us was disturbing. My father had never shied away from telling me how the Canaanites worshipped their bloodthirsty gods through perverse rituals, even offering up their own children in fiery ceremonies. And although she'd openly confessed to revering one of those very same goddesses, I could not imagine this sweet young woman condoning such a thing.

She fidgeted with something at her neck again. "Yahweh has always frightened me."

"Why?"

"The priestesses in Kamon describe him as terrifying, a god who ruthlessly punishes those who do not obey his commands. Did he not destroy the world in a great flood?"

"He did," I said. "But he also provided a way for Noach and

his family to be saved from that flood. And he told Noach to warn people for over one hundred years to change their ways before the rains came." I'd never thought of Yahweh as anything other than a deity worthy of respect and awe, so her confusion about his character was foreign.

"He is just and powerful, but he is also a God of steadfast love. A God of mercy and kindness who has called our people to share in his goodness and be a light to the nations." I'd heard those words a hundred times from my abba, but somehow as I spoke them now, I felt them sink beneath my skin and settle into my bones.

For as much as I loathed participating in all the musical performances that the rest of my family reveled in, I could not deny that the things of Yahweh had been deeply ingrained in me through endless repetitions of my father's songs and those of the other Levitical musicians in Naioth. If Kez had grown up like I had, among people who kept our sacred histories alive through song, she would not be so confused about Yahweh.

It would seem I not only had apologies to make to my father about my insistence on running off to fight a war despite his warnings, but I would also have to acknowledge that his music had had a far greater impact on me than I ever realized.

20

Keziah

With as thirsty as all three of us were after another full day traveling through the hilly region of Gilead, it took no time at all to decide that we should follow the distant sound of crashing water, even though it took us farther from the trade road.

When a waterfall came into sight, I caught my breath. I'd never seen anything so beautiful. Rushing streams cascaded down from a dizzying height, meandering down three tiers of rocky cliffs before emptying into a deep, roiling pool below. Rainbows danced through the air on the cool spray, dazzling my eyes as I took in the sunlit glade we'd stumbled upon.

"It's paradise," I said in a reverential whisper. "Like the garden Yahweh designed for Adam and Chavah in your story."

Avidan swung his leg over Sarru's rump and slid off his back, something that was coming increasingly easier to him each day. "That it is. And it's the perfect place to give my aching hindquarters a rest." He patted Sarru's neck. "No offense meant, my friend."

My horse snorted and flared his nostrils at Avidan. Yet it was not an aggressive gesture but closer to affectionate annoyance. My traveling companion must have noticed the shift in his attitude because he spent a few more moments scratching the knots between Sarru's ears where he liked it most. It made my heart squeeze with pleasure that the two of them had made peace.

Although Avidan was still fairly stoic and had not stopped striving against something awful in his dreams at night, a small measure of light would seep through from time to time, as if the cracks in his outer shell were getting wider by the hour. I longed to see a full and genuine smile on his lips, the severe lines of his intriguing face transform into open amusement, and those lovely forest-green eyes glitter with mirth.

He may still be dressed as a warrior with his leather armor and possess an imposing height and build, but I felt nothing but safe in his presence. And just a touch enamored. Which only made the guilt over my continued pretense weigh heavier on my soul.

And yet, for some reason, it had actually become harder to tell him the longer the ruse went on. Perhaps because I knew that once everything was revealed, the easiness between us over these past couple of days might come to an end.

He was a man and I was a woman and there were strict traditional boundaries between the two. He might not even want to ride so close to me on Sarru's back if he knew. My own father and brothers did not even eat at the same table as myself and the other women of the household most days and usually remained in their own wing of the villa. I hated to think of a wall going up between us just when I'd come to feel more comfortable with Avidan than with any other man I'd met before, either inside or outside of my family.

When I returned from taking a moment of privacy in the bushes, which he blessedly did not seem to find odd, Avidan had already led Sarru to the pool, where the stallion seemed to be drinking his weight in fresh, cool water. But the man himself was nowhere to be seen.

I took off my well-worn sandals, then stepped into the shallow edge of the pool and bent to cup some of the clear water in my hands. The waterfall must have originated from some deep underground spring because the water was cold and sweet. Once my thirst was slaked, I waded out a little farther, up to my knees, and tipped my head back to enjoy the warmth of the sun on my face after the last few days of gray sky.

An enormous splash made my eyes pop open, and my pulse stuttered as I searched the churning surface of the pool for whatever had stirred the waters. When Avidan's golden-brown head bobbed to the surface and he blew out a loud breath, I let out a relieved laugh.

"You nearly scared me out of my skin," I called out.

He swam closer, his long arms pulling the water with practiced grace. "My apologies. But I could not help myself. The pool is so clear and deep that the rocks up there called my name." He gestured to the first tier of ledges above his head. My eyes went wide as I took in their height.

"You jumped from up *there*?"

"I do it all the time with my brother Elidor. There's a spring-fed pool similar to this one not too far from my home in Naioth, although the drop is not nearly as far."

I shook my head, astounded.

He drifted a little closer in the water, keeping his arms moving as his soaking wet hair glimmered in the sunlight and rivulets of water sluiced down his face to drip from his beard. "You want to try?"

"By the heavens, no," I said, taking a few steps backward. "I don't even know how to swim."

"Don't you?" His tone was the lightest I'd ever heard it. Perhaps his spontaneous dive into the pool had washed a bit of the melancholy away. "Would you like to learn?"

My mouth dropped open. "You want to teach me to swim?"

"Why not? I've done the same for most of my younger siblings and even for my cousin Shay. . . ." His voice drifted off and he glanced away.

Shay. That was the name he kept calling out during his nightmares. That must be the boy we were searching for. Although I was almost desperate to ask him more about what had happened during that battle, I could not bear to see the heaviness come back over him. So I pushed aside the fear the idea of venturing out into the deep provoked.

"All right, Avidan. Teach me to swim."

He spun about to face me, and to my satisfaction, a beautiful smile curved on his lips. A real one, full of delight. "Yes?"

I nodded, and he encouraged me to wade out of the shallows. Although my heartbeat protested noisily, I obeyed until only my shoulders remained above the surface. I shivered, my body suddenly feeling the chill of the water, but when I realized that Avidan had moved much closer, within arm's length, a tide of warmth came over me. He reached out a hand, green eyes locked on mine, and without hesitation I slipped my own into his palm.

"Call me Avi," he said, giving my hand a slight squeeze underwater. "All my friends do."

I could not help the grin that followed as I repeated the nickname aloud. To be counted among his friends made something new flourish deep inside me. I'd never truly had a real friend, unless I counted my horse, and certainly had never known a man who cared anything for me besides my worth as a bride.

Before I could react to his implicit declaration of friendship between us, he tugged me off my feet. I floundered for a moment, my head nearly going under. Avi whirled around, wrapped his long fingers around my forearms, and urged me to kick my feet. His hold kept me from drowning, and his patient and encouraging words kept me calm.

For the next half hour, he instructed me on how to stay afloat on my own, how to propel myself through the water with my legs and arms, and how to breathe carefully so I did not suck water into my lungs. The only thing I refused to do was float on my back, because there would be no way to conceal the curves of my body in that position. But there were times I lost focus on his directions because I got caught up in the feel of his strong hands maneuvering me through the water and the forest-like depths of his entrancing eyes as he spoke.

When he noticed I was tiring, he helped me back to the shallows, but before I could figure out how to emerge from the water and hide my body at the same time, he'd already swum away, heading for the far side of the pool near the base of the waterfall.

After turning my back to him, squeezing some of the water out of my sodden tunic, and situating it so the fabric no longer clung to me, I settled myself on a large, flat boulder nearby and sat in the sun, watching Avidan climb out of the pool and up to the ledge before diving back in again. I cheered his splash this time, and he came up grinning, then repeated his jump, from the second tier this time. It was so high that just the thought of him flying through the air made my stomach wobble.

But he emerged after his jump with another heart-stopping smile and made his way toward the boulder, where my threadbare tunic was already mostly dry.

He climbed atop my perch and lay down not too far from me, still breathing heavily from his last jump. "That was exhilarating."

"I'll take your word for it," I said, my eyes fluttering closed as the sunlight soaked into my skin, making me drowsy. He was so close that if I reached out, I could slide my hand into his. The thought was as thrilling as it was terrifying.

"It's my fault he's missing," said Avidan, after a long but companionable silence.

My eyes flew open and all fatigue melted away in light of his statement, but I said nothing as I waited for him to continue.

"I should never have stepped foot on that battlefield," he said, eyes turned to the heavens above us, "but I was too stubborn and prideful to listen to reason. And when I had the chance to turn back and make certain Shalem was safe at home, I chose my own path. While I was off nearly getting hacked to pieces because I was not in any way prepared for war, he disappeared."

He told me about the empty cave and the hyenas and the clues he'd found in a shell and the very same knife he'd loaned me that first night. The realization that he'd offered up something so precious to him so I would feel safe caused my heart to thud painfully. He was so good. So kind. I hated that he was downtrodden and ridden with guilt.

"And as angry as I am at Zevi and Gavriel," he continued, "for not coming with me to search for him and betraying the oath we made as boys to always protect and defend one another, I am ultimately to blame."

I had no words of wisdom to offer because I felt the same way about Imati. If it were not for me, she would still be alive. In fact, my very existence had kept her enslaved for over half her life. But I could not speak those things aloud without revealing myself, so I tried to reassure him instead.

"We will find him, Avi. If your God is as all-knowing and powerful as you say he is, then he can lead you to him, can't he?"

He turned to look into my eyes, staring so intently that the space between us began to vibrate with something I'd never felt before. Then he blinked, breaking the connection, and gave me a sweet smile that warmed my insides.

"That is true," he said. "I should probably listen a little better to my own stories."

"That you should." I settled again with my arms crossed behind my head and aimlessly searched the endless blue sky for a moment. "Perhaps before we get back on Sarru you can tell me another one. Maybe we will both learn something."

"I could," he murmured, "but I'd rather hear one from you."

"Me?" I turned to gawk at him in bewilderment.

"I've done a lot of the talking over the past couple of days. I think it's your turn." Something sly came into his expression.

"What do you . . ." I stuttered. "What . . . sort of story do you want to hear?"

He turned his gaze to the one wispy cloud that was gliding overhead, his tone nonchalant. "Start with the one about the young woman who ran away from her own wedding with the bridal gifts hidden in her horse's saddle."

21

Avidan

Kez bolted to a sitting position on the boulder, brown eyes wide and one hand reaching for the short curls at the back of her neck. "How did you know?"

I'd seen her do this before when she didn't know I was watching, fingers mindlessly searching for what I assumed to be missing hair length. It never failed to conjure up a picture of what those lustrous black curls might have looked like while tumbling down her back and the way they would frame her delicate features.

Now that she was free of the dust and mud that had clung to her for the past three days and with her wet hair slicked back, her gender was even more pronounced. The gentle sweep of her high cheekbones, the deep pink of her lips, and the smoothness of her olive skin could no longer be hidden behind unruly curls and a threadbare disguise. I'd nearly kicked myself for suggesting that I teach her to swim once I'd realized it meant such intimate proximity. It had been all I could do to not stare at the woman who was becoming increasingly fascinating to me.

"I heard you talking to Sarru under the tree outside the village before you noticed me," I admitted.

She let out a little gasp. "You've known this *whole* time?"

Her shock caused a small niggle of guilt for forcing her to keep up the ruse for so long. "I wanted you to feel safe. Even if that meant entertaining your pretense."

She ran both hands through her hair this time, and the pinched expression on her face made my chest squeeze tight.

"You are safe with me, Kez," I said. "I would never hurt you. You know that, don't you?"

She answered without hesitation. "I do."

Her quick response was a relief. "Good. But why do you look so worried?"

"If you figured out I was a woman within the first hour of meeting me, how will I convince anyone else?" She tugged at her awful tunic with a groan. "I was supposed to look like a slave boy."

I squelched my amusement at her frustration. "If I had not overheard you talking to your horse about being dressed as a boy, I would not have known. At least not right away."

She let out a huff of indignation.

"But perhaps from now on . . . you should let me do the talking whenever we encounter others."

"Why?"

"Because that voice you have been using fools no one."

Her cheeks flushed pink, so I said nothing about the way she walked with an effortless grace that was even more obvious than the contrived deepening of her soft voice.

"Kez isn't your real name either, is it?"

She gave me a shy smile. "It's Keziah."

"Glad to meet you, Keziah." I gave her a little bow of my head. "I am Avidan ben Ronen from Naioth in Benjamite territory. Although my father is a Levite and my mother was born Philistine."

Her mouth gaped a little. "You are part Philistine?"

"I am. But that is a story for another time. First, I need you to tell me the whole truth about why you are fleeing your home and why you are being chased by men on horseback."

After another quick flush of her cheeks, she told me of her maid's revelation on the evening of her wedding to a violent lecher, how the two of them managed to get her out of town, and how the woman named Imati had sent her off with a purse full of silver taken from her mother's wedding headdress.

My anger at the boys who'd beaten her and stolen from her flared to life again, because it had not only been silver they'd taken but something priceless to her. However, it was nothing compared to the fury that sparked to life after hearing that her father had traded his precious daughter to a man who had bruised her, threatened her, and meant to use her before passing her off to another savage. Warrior or not, I had the strong urge to relieve both men of their worthless heads.

When she then told me Imati had been killed after donning Keziah's wedding gown and veils, I understood the woman in front of me a little better. No wonder she contained so much courage within her small frame. The woman who'd given birth to her had been woven from the same strong threads.

When she went quiet, I pressed on. "So the men on horseback . . ."

"Probably Vadim's men. He is not the sort to let such a slight against his honor go unanswered. Of course, it's also possible those men were headed elsewhere. But I cannot take the chance. I won't go back there, not after what happened to Imati."

She paused, swallowing hard as tears glittered in her beautiful brown eyes. "She did not deserve to die like that. And I will never forgive my father for allowing it."

Again, I was struck with thoughts of what her life would have been like had Keziah been raised in Naioth. Fathers arranged marriages for their children all the time there, just as anywhere, but all the families I knew personally valued their daughters. Wanted the best for them and chose husbands who would be devoted to them and who honored the Torah and its unique protections for women and children. A Hebrew who would treat his beautiful and tenderhearted daughter as nothing more than chattel was a man who was a curse to his own family.

Gratitude for my own abba and the way he led our family with such honor and steadfastness welled up, and my throat went tight as I thought of how much I had wronged him with my rebellious actions. When had I forgotten how desperately I'd once wanted to walk in his admirable footsteps as a boy?

I would start again now by making certain Keziah was delivered safely to her mother's family, even if the thought of leaving her behind had begun to sting a little. Then I would find my cousin and bring him home—or die trying.

"Are you dry enough?" I asked reluctantly. "We should probably be moving on."

She nodded, but her gaze traveled over the quiet glade, the majestic waterfall, and the deep blue pool that had washed away what I hoped was the last of the secrets between us. She looked almost as regretful as I was to leave the quiet beauty of this place.

But as we remounted Sarru and wound our way farther south through the forested hills and toward the river I knew we must soon cross, I felt more at peace than I had since I'd walked away from my home. Perhaps it was that I'd unburdened myself a little to Keziah or because she'd finally trusted me with the truth, but maybe it was that a bit of the serenity from that lovely place lingered on our skin and in the air between us.

Whatever it was, I hoped it would last because I was weary of the empty caves and bloodstained battlefields that filled my restless nights.

The glitter of sunlight off water in the distance announced that we'd reached the Jabbok River. Narrower than I'd anticipated but running swiftly downhill toward where it would empty into the Jordan, this stretch of river would be difficult to cross.

"How well does Sarru swim?" I asked when we came to the edge of the water.

"I don't know," she replied. "I've never taken him into a river. Especially not one like that."

"We should find a wider point to ford where the water isn't so fast," I said. "Perhaps back toward the trade road there is a place where the rest of the travelers cross. A bridge of some sort."

She pressed her lips together, contemplating. "You might be right. Wagons and animals have to cross somewhere, don't you think?"

"They have to. Otherwise the road between Damascus and Egypt would be impassible. Then again," I said, my hand over my eyes to shade the sunlight refracting off the surface of the river, "there is a possibility that the men who are chasing you will be waiting there for you, knowing you must cross somewhere. I don't think we should take the chance."

"What do we do, then?"

I leaned forward to take stock of our choices. The river was not nearly as high as the Jordan had been when I'd crossed with my cousins, but it was narrower, so the current looked to be strong here. Perhaps our best course would be to head west and seek out a wider stretch where there might be a shallower place to ford.

Distracted as I mulled over which way to go, I'd not been holding on tightly when Sarru jolted sideways with a sharp whinny, and I nearly toppled from the saddle just as two men appeared on his right side, daggers drawn.

Although I was both dazed with shock and livid with myself for failing Keziah by not being more aware of our surroundings, I immediately recognized the familiar design of their armor and the drawl of their words as they demanded we get off the horse.

Ammonites.

One latched on to Sarru's bridle, and the other one lunged at me. I kicked out, knocking his arm back, but did not dislodge his weapon. Keziah slammed her heels into Sarru's sides, and the stallion darted forward, his hindquarters dancing to the left as I squeezed my knees tight against his body. But the Ammonite's grip on the horse's bridle kept us from breaking free.

The one nearest me let out a curse and surged again with a swing of his long blade. I kicked again but even as my foot connected with his jaw, he sliced my thigh with the tip of his dagger. Pain shot through my leg, but I had no time to care how deep the wound was because Keziah kicked Sarru again while screaming at him to run and bravely leveling a blow of her own foot at the Ammonite who held Sarru's head.

Thankfully, the horse with warrior bloodlines proved to be far stronger and far too terrified to let his captor win so easily. He bolted forward, dragging the one who held his bridle, heading straight for the river. However, the man refused to let go, and I could do little more than hold on to Keziah. Even if I pulled my knife from my belt, it would do no good. My arm was long, but the blade was not. All I would do if I tried to reach the Ammonite would be to throw us both off-balance.

Panic gripped my gut. I'd been so useless in the fight for Yavesh that Gavi had been forced to come to my rescue. But it was not simply my own life I had to preserve now—it was Keziah's too.

When an idea of how to distract the Ammonites came to me, I had no time to second-guess it, nor to count the cost. I'd faced these men in battle and knew their ruthlessness. Not to mention I'd seen the way their king had treated Ohel and Raham. Not only did I value both my eyes, but I knew for certain what would happen to Keziah if these men discovered she was a woman, and I would die before I saw that happen to her.

Holding on to Keziah with one arm and squeezing my knees tight, I jammed my hand into the pack over my shoulder, snaking my fingers past the remaining food the shepherds had blessed us with, and grabbed the woven bag inside. I yanked it out and swung it in the air; equal parts heartsick and relieved when some of the colorful strings of beads along with rings and silver bracelets slipped out of the opening I'd only loosely cinched together.

"Take it!" I bellowed and launched the bag into the air, gratified when the remainder of the treasure sprayed in every direction and rained on the riverbank in a glittering shower. Aghast, both Ammonites watched the costly treasures land haphazardly on the rocky shore.

"Go, Keziah!" I yelled and slid my other arm back around her waist, locking us tight together. And this time when Sarru surged forward, the Ammonite let go, his attention on the wealth strewn across the ground behind us.

Sarru splashed headlong into the river, his neck straining forward as his torso heaved with giant, labored breaths. He plunged into the water without hesitation and took three long strides before the water was up to his belly. The slope of the riverbank must be even steeper than I anticipated. Within moments, the stallion was scrambling for purchase and then, without warning, a current caught us, sweeping him completely off his feet.

Sarru screamed, his head tossing back and forth as he struggled to find footing and the river pushed us out to its center. When Sarru tilted sideways, Keziah and I were dumped from his back and came to the surface, sputtering. I called to her and reached out, but the river refused to relent and pulled us apart, carrying her lighter frame and Sarru's struggling one farther downriver and yanking me into an eddy that swirled me about and sent me toward a large boulder near the opposite shore. Kicking to free myself from the vortex, I headed for Keziah. She'd gotten a grip on Sarru's bridle as the horse fought to keep his nose in the air and remain above water.

The current was so strong that the two of them sped along as if they weighed no more than pebbles. Keziah called for me, the terror in her voice clawing at my heart.

Up ahead, a couple of trees had fallen into the water, forming a tangled wall of limbs partway across the river. Keziah and Sarru were headed directly into the barricade, and all I could imagine was her being impaled on one of the shattered branches. I stroked harder, kicking my legs with every bit of strength I had left, but I was forced to watch helplessly as both of them crashed into the trees.

Keziah cried out, whether in pain or fear I had no idea, but I felt the plea at the center of my bones. Redoubling my efforts, I dug into the water with renewed vigor born of desperation, but just as I came within a couple of paces of her floundering form, the water pushed her under the tree. My gut clenched as I reached out, searching under the surface and nearly crying out with relief when I caught her tunic and dragged her toward me. She breached the surface, gasping, still gripping one of Sarru's reins in white-knuckled resolve. The horse struggled, kicking as he too fought against the unforgiving wall of trees and the river's determination to swallow him.

"Sarru!" Keziah screamed. "Help him!"

"I need to get you out first!"

"No! I'm fine. His saddle is stuck on a branch. He'll drown! Please! He's all I have!"

One look at her red eyes and the devastation on her face and I was reaching for the knife at my belt, relieved when my hand found the pommel. Through some miracle, Shay's knife had remained firmly tucked in its place throughout my fight with the river.

"Hold on to one of the branches so you don't get pulled under," I said, then moved toward the horse, who was lunging over and over, searching for purchase on the ground as he wrestled against the tree's hold on him.

I reached for Sarru's nose, trying to stroke his face in a calming motion. "Whoa! You're all right, my friend."

His eyes wheeled, his nose bobbing up and down and neck muscles straining, but to my surprise, he stopped screaming.

Fighting against the suction of the water rushing under the tree trunk, I moved down his body and felt for the belly strap of the saddle.

"Be calm, Sarru. I'll get you loose." I struggled to keep my tone soothing, even if panic was clogged in my throat. Although I feared he might kick me in the head out of blind hysteria, I began to saw at the braided leather with Shay's knife.

However, the longer I worked at the sodden strap, the more I sensed Sarru was running out of strength, his fight lessening moment by moment. If either one of us gave up now, he would be sucked under the tree and drown. I was surprised at just how upset

I was at the thought, and not just for Keziah's sake. Somehow I'd gotten attached to the animal myself over the past few days as well.

My hand slipped as I tugged against the leather belly strap, and I nearly lost my grip on Shay's knife. Then, to my horror, Sarru let out a huff that sounded far too much like resignation, his legs stopped their frantic kicking, and his head went fully under the water.

"No, Sarru!" Keziah screamed and the torment in her voice was enough to crush my heart into a thousand pieces.

Would I ever stop letting down the people I cared about most?

Keziah

Both of them disappeared, pulled under the surface by the unforgiving river.

Agonized cries burst from my mouth. This could not be happening. The man had already saved me once, had allowed his search for his precious cousin to be detoured because of me, and had now put his own life in danger for my horse. If he drowned because of me, I would never be able to forgive myself.

Through my tears, I stared at the surface of the foaming water, begging my goddess and the entire array of heavenly beings for mercy, for help, for a miracle. But all that I could see was the swirl of the current against the tangle of tree branches. No man with a head of golden-brown hair and an elusive grin, no beautiful warhorse. My knees wobbled and collapsed as numbness set in and one word echoed in my head. *No, no, no, no . . .*

But the moment I hit the sand in a brokenhearted heap of sorrow, an idea cut through my haze—if my gods cared nothing for Avi, then perhaps I should appeal to his own. Desperate enough to plead with the terrifying deity on his behalf, I kept my eyes on the water and fervently begged the One Who Hears to rescue the Levite warrior.

"Keziah!" came a voice from somewhere above the noisy rush of the water—one that had somehow become infinitely dear to me in only four days.

I twisted around, heart galloping as I searched the river for Avi's form, then when he shouted my name again, closer this time, I came to my feet, whirling around to see a drenched Avidan, with a trickle of blood trailing down his leg, coming toward me on the narrow beach. At his back, my sweet Sarru ambled along, muscles quivering.

A shout of relieved exultation flew from my mouth as I ran toward them, closing the twenty paces of distance between us without care for my tear-blurred vision or the wet sand that filled my sandals and scraped at my tender soles.

Without thought, I barreled into Avi, throwing my arms around his waist and sobbing into his chest. When he reacted not by pushing me away but wrapping his long arm around my back, I pressed my face against his sodden tunic and let all the fear, doubt, grief, and hurt pour out in a torrent of tears and garbled words about how thankful I was that he was alive and how I'd not thought the two of them could survive.

Avidan murmured assurances, his hold on me firm and comforting, and then to my astonishment, he wrapped his other arm around me, pulling me closer as I felt the distinctive press of his lips against the top of my head. This kind man was embracing me in a way I'd never experienced. Not from my father, my brothers, or even from my mother that I could recall.

I clung to him and wondered how it was that he'd stumbled into my life when I needed him most. It was almost as though some unseen hand had gently shepherded us on to the same path.

When finally my tears were spent, realization that I'd practically assaulted him in my elation began to trickle in, causing my cheeks to warm. Perhaps, in my addled state of relief, I'd only imagined the kiss against my hair.

I stepped back and relinquished my hold, reluctantly turning my eyes up to the forest-green ones that I'd thought I might never see again. Yet, he was not looking down on me with annoyance but instead with an expression I could only describe as relief mixed with a small amount of wonder.

"Are you all right?" he asked.

"Me? You are the one who nearly drowned."

His cheek quirked. "True. But I thought perhaps you had as well."

I shook my head. "I was able to pull myself close enough to the shore by using the branches that I could get free of the current."

"So my swimming lessons were helpful after all?"

Shivering now, I blinked at him and the glimmer of amusement in those deep green eyes, astounded he was able to jest after such an ordeal. "How did you get free? I saw you both go under and feared you were trapped beneath the trees."

He let out a sigh. "As did I. But when Sarru went under, I dove and cut through the rest of his belly strap. Once he was loose, the force of the water pushed us through a wide gap in the branches, and on the other side of the trees, the river spat us back out again. Took me a few moments to get my bearings again, so we were swept downriver, but we landed on a shallow spot. Thankfully, both of us managed to emerge without broken limbs and only a few scrapes."

I looked past Avi to Sarru, who was also shivering and appeared nearly as exhausted as the man who'd saved him. I went to him and pressed my face against his long neck, tangling my fingers into the wet strands of his long black mane. He snorted and bobbed his nose, and I let a few more tears flow as I thanked the heavens for his life.

Or perhaps I should thank Yahweh.

"We should get away from the river," Avi said. "Those Ammonites may be distracted for now with the bridal gifts, and we've been swept downstream quite a distance, but I don't want to take any chances that they will swim across and come after us. And we need to warm our bodies, so movement would be best."

Reluctantly, I let go of Sarru's neck and wiped my face, nodding, and grabbed my horse's reins to follow Avi on a meandering path away from the river. When we'd gone far enough away from the Jabbok and deep enough into the forest that he felt we were relatively safe, he asked if I needed a rest.

I shook my head. "I'm all right. We should probably find a large rock or something so we can mount up." I was skilled at pulling myself onto Sarru, even without the beautiful saddle and the loop of leather that I normally used, but Avi had never done so.

He'd not spent half his lifetime flying through the countryside, wind in his hair, on the back of this warhorse with the tender heart of a beloved pet. And yet he'd put his own life in jeopardy for him.

I spun to face him, another wash of tears brimming over. "Thank you, Avi. For saving him."

"I'm just glad he's not hurt." In what seemed an unconscious motion, he pressed a hand to his thigh, where his tunic was still stained with blood from the wound the Ammonite had inflicted there.

With a gasp, I stepped toward him. "You are bleeding!"

He waved a dismissive hand through the air. "The injury is shallow. It stings, but it has already stopped bleeding. It's nothing."

"It is not nothing. You saved me, twice. And now you've rescued Sarru as well. How can I ever thank you?" My voice broke.

He studied my face for a long time. "That you are safe is all I can ask for."

Again, I was forced to ask myself why this man was so different from the ones in Kamon. Perhaps he was innately honorable, but he'd also known that I was a woman all along and spoke to me like I was his equal. Was it simply the way he'd been raised? To be so generous and protective?

Once we found a place to mount, we decided to head directly south, along an offshoot of the Jabbok that led us to a narrow trade road and through the mountainous region filled with deep valleys and steep inclines. As we wound vaguely southeast along a tiny stream, Avidan told me more of his family and how his

Philistine mother and uncle had come to be joined to the Hebrews, and about his three cousins and the bond between them.

When he recalled stories about their adventures together as boys, I began to ache for his loss. It was clear that Zevi, Gavi, and Shalem were as close as brothers and that Avi was grieving not only the disappearance of Shay but the breach of trust he'd placed in the others. His heart must be shattered in a thousand pieces. If only I could bind it up and heal the man who'd done so much for me.

During the next couple of days, we encountered a number of hamlets up in the hills, where Avi questioned anyone he could about whether they'd seen a boy with a silver streak in his hair riding along with traders. One elderly couple traveling north on a weary mule said they'd seen a caravan of three wagons headed south on the King's Highway a few days ago and thought perhaps they had seen a boy Shalem's age riding in the back of one but hadn't gotten close enough to be able to describe him.

Even though it was not a definitive answer, the sliver of hope breathed new energy into Avidan, brushing away some of the melancholy that had settled back into his demeanor since the Ammonites had attacked. I had the sense he'd been blaming himself for not anticipating the ambush, but all I could think was that had I been alone, I'd surely have been violated and killed. I'd never be able to fully convey my gratitude and was so relieved I did not have to lie to him anymore.

At most places we stopped, it was fairly easy to find people interested in Avidan's stories, and he returned to our hiding places with plenty of food. We were astonished to learn that our path was similar to the army of Saul as they had pressed toward Rabbah, and we came across many who were quick to heap praise on the new king for liberating their towns, some speaking of him as nearly divine. However, the farther south we traveled, the less effusive such praise became.

In one community, Avidan was told that the army had come through like a horde of locusts, stripping their bountiful vineyards nearly clean and offering little more than a scant handful of silver and a promise of compensation once Rabbah was taken from the Ammonites.

One of the vintners said he'd been told that Saul's men had indeed chased the remnant of Nahash's army back to Rabbah but had for some reason stopped short of advancing on the Ammonite stronghold and instead veered southwest toward the Jordan River. That left the vintner and his neighbors not only with nothing in their fields to sustain their families but also with a hornet's nest of enemies stirred up only a short distance away.

"We were told this king would deliver us, but instead he left us even more vulnerable than before," the man spat. "I should have known not to put any trust in a Benjamite."

The morning of the third day after we'd escaped the Jabbok River, we came upon a walled city. As had become our tradition, I stopped Sarru outside of the town, meaning to find a place to hide while Avi went in alone to ask about Shay. But to my surprise, he told me to keep going.

"So far, I've heard nothing about anyone looking for a woman on a horse," he said. "We are far enough from your town that I don't think you are at risk. Whoever those men were on horseback are long gone. Besides, this is a larger city. We should be able to blend in fairly easily."

After being forced to wait in hiding for so many hours over the past two days, I took no time at all to dig my heels into Sarru and lead us toward the walled city. Once we neared the gates, we dismounted. Two guards stood on each side, eyeing us with suspicion as we approached. When one brusquely asked what our business was in the city, Avidan informed the guard that we only meant to seek out food and possible shelter for the night.

"See that your time in Yazer is peaceful," said the guard. "Or you'll be asked to leave. We've no tolerance for those who stir up trouble."

"We have no intention of causing trouble," Avidan said. "Only passing through on our way south."

Once we left the gates and the guards behind us, Avidan led us toward the center of town. "I have heard of Yazer," he said. "It is one of the forty-eight cities allotted to Levites by Yehoshua when we first came into the Land of Promise."

Immediately I felt my hackles rise, thinking again of the Levite who'd come to our town with his frightening antics. But I reminded myself that Avidan's family was Levite as well, and everything he'd told me made them sound almost too good to be true.

A group of three young boys suddenly stood in our path with their eyes locked on Sarru, all with slings dangling from their right hands. I stumbled to a stop, belly clenching. They were similar in age to the ones who'd robbed me. So smoothly I barely noticed the move, Avidan shifted his body forward, partially shielding me from them.

"That is a beautiful animal," said one boy. "He's huge."

"That he is," replied Avi, his tone wary.

"Are you that traveling storyteller?" asked another.

Avi's back stiffened. "You've heard of me?"

"Some traders came through two days ago and said they've never heard stories like yours," said the first boy. "Will you tell us one?"

"Oh, yes, please," said the smallest of them. A few passersby stopped to gawk as the boys' pleas grew louder.

"I'd be happy to share," Avi said, apparently satisfied that the boys meant no harm. "Any requests?"

"A battle!"

"Giants!"

"Sword fights!"

Avidan tilted his head, tapping at his bearded chin for a moment. "I think I know just the story. Have you heard the one about the man who bested three thousand Philistines with only the jawbone of an ass?"

With mouths gaping, the boys shook their heads in tandem.

"Then by all means, let's find some shade," Avi said with a flourish of his hand. "I must tell it, but it's far too hot to sit in the sun!"

The boys led us through the center of town, past a well-appointed temple with a large Asherah pole and a line of suppliants carrying votives or animals for sacrifice. The familiar sharp smell of incense and blood wafted through the air, making my stomach turn.

Once our little parade reached a group of three palms that cast a wide swath of shade, I tied Sarru to one of the trunks and was surprised when a young woman came toward me with a wide-mouth pot of water for my horse. The people of this town were far more welcoming than the first one I'd entered alone.

The three boys sat on the ground in front of Avidan, their eyes bright as they waited for him to begin his tale. About ten additional onlookers of various ages had joined us along the way, some standing nearby and some taking a seat beside the boys. It seemed word of Avi's talents had indeed traveled ahead of us. He settled into a relaxed pose, arms crossed behind his back, one that I'd come to recognize as the stance he used to begin stories.

"Long ago, many years after the death of Yehoshua, there lived a man of Zorah, born of the Danite clan, named Manoah. To her great disappointment, Manoah's wife was barren. One day, while she was grieving her childlessness, the Angel of Adonai appeared to her. 'You are barren now,' he said. 'But you shall conceive and bear a son. Therefore, from this moment, drink no wine or strong drink and eat nothing unclean. No razor shall touch his head for he shall be a Nazirite to Yahweh from the womb and he shall begin to save Israel from the hand of the Philistines . . .'"

As Avi told the story of the man named Samson with extraordinary strength who defeated so many of the Philistines and whose gift from Yahweh became his own demise, I could not take my eyes off him. Every entrancing lift and fall of his deep voice commanded those gathered to not miss a word. His green eyes sparkled with delight as he pretended to hold the jawbone in the air and then swung it wide with such fervor that the boys in front of him flinched. He spoke as if he'd actually experienced the events he described, the characters good friends he'd known his entire life.

The crowd had grown as he talked, every one of them completely enveloped in the world he crafted; their minds, like mine, replete with colorful descriptions of places we'd never seen and enemies we'd never faced. Avi's expressive tone grew even more animated as he described the way Delilah, the wicked woman Samson so desired, began to work her wiles on the man whose pride—not the loss of his long hair—was his greatest weakness. Once the temple at Gaza had been destroyed and the dust settled around the broken hero, Avidan lowered his voice, inviting his audience to follow him to the somber ending of the man whose death was both a victory and a tragedy. The crowd was left in breathless silence until the youngest of the boys lifted his high-pitched voice.

"That was a good story, but there weren't any giants!"

Spell broken, the crowd laughed, and Avidan gave the boy a warm smile. "Well, no. Samson was extraordinarily strong, but he was not a giant, was he?"

He paused to think, again stroking his beard in contemplation. "What about if I tell you how Yehoshua bested King Og of Bashan—a man who was so tall that his iron bedstead was nine cubits long and four cubits wide?"

"Yes!" shouted the boys.

So, without hesitation, Avi launched into the story.

I'd heard of Og before, having grown up not all that far away from Edrei, but never with the kind of enveloping detail Avidan provided. He spoke of the city with walls that seemed to reach to the sky and that lay atop a complicated maze of tunnels carved out of the limestone beneath, of crawling alongside his fellow Hebrews in those dim tunnels in a bid to sneak into the stronghold.

Each moment was filled with vivid descriptions that made me see Avi there, wielding a sword against the giant king as they battled to the death, almost as clearly as I saw him standing before me.

When Avidan finished his story and indicated it was time for us to go hunt down some food and drink, the entire assembly protested, and within minutes, we had our hands full of bread, stew, and barley beer. Another basket of fruit sat at my feet, given to us by two young women who looked to be temple workers. Their beguiling grins, lashes fluttering like butterflies, and pointedly alluring behavior toward Avi set my own teeth on edge.

The boys begged for another story of battle and glory, and I thought I saw Avidan wince at the suggestion, but he began the tale of a young Samuel and how Yahweh spoke to him. How astonished the high priest Eli was when he realized that the child had been hearing the voice of the Most High. And how the disobedience of that priest and his horrible sons led to the loss of the golden box that contained the Ten Words written down by Mosheh to the Philistines. He told of how the Philistines took the precious ark to their cities, parading it before cheering crowds, and how his own father and mother were caught up in both the return of the object and its near theft as well. He told of how Samuel had led Israel with wisdom for most of his life and how even in battle the shofet had always listened to Yahweh's voice.

Just as his story was coming to a close, I noticed an older man off to the side of the gathering, arms folded over his chest and a deep frown on his face. Alongside him were two others with similar expressions, and all three were wearing identical embroidered robes that seemed to denote some authority. They put their heads together, whispering among themselves until Avidan spoke his final word.

The first man then strode forward, his long robes flapping behind him like a flock of blackbirds. "I think we've had enough fantastical stories for one day," he said, his words themselves sounding quite genial but the underlying meaning obviously full of disdain.

"On you go," he said to the people who'd gathered around Avi and me, as if every one of them was a small child who'd wandered away from a household chore. "There's nothing to be gained from having your ears tickled by such nonsense." He wiggled his fingers, shooing them off like stray cats.

Stunned, we watched as one by one the crowd obeyed his command. Even the young boys who'd been so enthralled turned their backs and slumped off. Beside me, Avi had gone still as stone.

The man approached, his frown somehow even more pronounced.

"It's time for you two to be moving along as well," he said.

"My cousin and I are simply passing through," said Avi, shocking me by labeling me as family. "We hoped to find some shelter here tonight."

"There's nothing more here for you," he said as he pointed at the basket of fruit. "Take what you have now and go."

"Have we offended in some way?" asked Avidan. "I am a fellow Levite."

The man pursed his lips, looking my companion up and down, his gaze locking on Avi's battered armor. "Levites do not fight battles, and they do not look like you."

Avi's jaw worked back and forth as a flare of anger shot through me. This man knew nothing of him or his family. How dare he make assumptions based on his appearance?

"I have no issue with stories of valor like our glorious victory over Og of Bashan, but I will not tolerate such nonsense being taught to my people about that *deceiver* receiving direction from the Most High. As if a man could hear the voice of a deity with human ears. That is nothing but a lie to prop up an illegitimate claim of leadership."

There was such vitriol in the man's words as he seethed with hatred for Samuel. Perhaps he *was* just like the rabid man who'd barged into my town so long ago— only his hatred was directed toward one of his own kind.

"I understand there have been fractures between those on the east and west sides of the Jordan," said Avi, speaking slowly to overcome the shock I'd seen on his face. "But surely we can agree that now we have a king who will unite us as one nation."

"This is a Levite city, young man. We have held this stronghold since Yehoshua gave it to us four hundred years ago and maintained order among its residents without interference from anyone on the other side of the river. We've certainly no need for a *king*, who, I've been told, was too cowardly to advance on Rabbah after making promises to do so. And neither do we have any use for illegitimate high priests or self-proclaimed prophets with made-up stories about voices from the sky. Now, as I said before, it's time for you both to move along."

He turned his back, dismissing us without ceremony, but then he whirled around with a haughty expression on his face. "And by the way, I don't know what you did to the girl who was riding that horse." He pointed at Sarru. "But if my guards do not report that you've left this city within the next quarter of an hour, I'll not hesitate to send a messenger after the men who came through searching for her."

23

Avidan

Only one man had the courage to talk to us on our way out of Yazer.

However, even though the sandal-maker responded to my inquiries about Shalem, telling me he'd seen no such boy, and then curtly responded to my request for directions to Har Nebo by telling me it was just south of the Heshbon River, he quickly dropped his attention back to the leather he was braiding, dismissing Keziah and me just as thoroughly as the elder who'd banished us.

I was still in shock that the Levite elder had been so hostile, especially in light of the hospitality the people of his city had shown us. I'd been so enveloped in storytelling that I'd not even noticed the group of elders off to the side of the gathering. My blood had practically been singing with elation as the crowd grew until there was no more room, their attention riveted on me as I spoke of people and places they'd never heard about before. The words had poured from my mouth without much forethought, as if drawn from a natural wellspring deep inside me.

The longer I spoke, and the more the people begged for more, the deeper my conviction grew that it was what I had been born to do. Just as my father had been born to compose and play music, and my cousins were born to lift their swords against the enemies of Israel, I was meant to tell the stories that filled my head day and night. I did not know what it all meant, but I knew that nothing had ever felt as satisfying as watching the people in Yazer feast on my words.

Therefore, the Levites' anger about my telling stories of our ancestors, ones that had been faithfully documented, collected, and preserved by Samuel and the priestly scribes in Naioth, was baffling. And beyond frustrating. It was clear that sharing how Yahweh had manifested himself to Israel through the priesthood and the leaders he'd raised up since we entered the Land of Promise threatened their control over the people of Yazer.

The temple we'd passed on the way through the city made it clear that even if this city was once a place of worship only to the Most High under the guardianship and direction of faithful Levites, those who held the seats of power now were anything but Torah-abiding.

The gaudy Asherah pole stood unapologetically in front of their temple. There were a variety of niches built into the city walls holding various idols—Molech, Chemosh, Ra, and even one with many horns and eyes marked YHWH. The stink of smoke from within the sanctuary had made my head swim strangely, and the women who'd approached me with barely any clothing on their figures were quite obviously temple prostitutes.

No wonder my Torah-based storytelling had offended them. If this place was worshipping other gods alongside the One True God, perhaps even making their own children pass through the flames like the pagans around us did, then they'd twisted the truth until it was unrecognizable.

These people were so confused, so bound up in lies told to them by men who should know better, that I felt an irrational urge to turn back to Yazer and teach them the entirety of the Torah from beginning to end—even if it meant delaying both Keziah's reunion with her mother's family and my search for Shay.

"How much longer?" Keziah asked, pulling me out of the strange, guilt-inducing thought. It was fruitless anyhow, as we would not be allowed back through the gates of Yazer again. And I'd wasted my chance to question more people there about Shay because I'd been wrapped up in telling stories.

"The sandal-maker said it would only be a few hours on horseback. However, it may take us some time to find your mother's clan."

"Imati told me her village was near a large spring that is the source of a stream."

"Did she give you any further directions?"

"That is all I know." Her voice warbled, and she took a moment to compose herself before speaking again. "What will I even say to these people when I do find them, Avi? Imati is gone. They don't have any obligation to me. I am but a child born of her slavery and have nothing to offer them. What if they send me away?"

"They won't—"

She spoke over me, panic rising in her voice. "But what if they do?" Her body trembled. "I have nowhere else to go."

I'd done my best to maintain respectful boundaries for the last couple of days, leaving a small gap between us as we rode on Sarru, even though I could still feel how perfectly she fit in my arms after she'd crashed into me like a tidal wave on the beach. But the sound of the sob she muffled behind a hand made my chest ache.

I leaned forward and gently wrapped my hands around hers where they held Sarru's reins. Slowly, I pulled back on the leather cords just as I'd seen her do many times over these past days, and the horse ambled to a stop.

"Keziah," I said. "Look at me."

With red-rimmed eyes, she complied.

"I didn't know Imati. But she must've had a good reason to send you to her people. She loved you, didn't she?"

She sniffed and nodded. "I believe she did, or she would not have sacrificed herself in that way."

"Then she must have been certain her people would embrace you or she wouldn't have told you to flee with Sarru."

"She didn't count on me getting robbed of the silver she gave me on the first day."

"She was desperate enough for your freedom that she felt the risk was worth it. And from what you've told me of Vadim, she was right to do so."

There was nothing on the earth that would cause my father to sacrifice one of my sisters in such a way. My father may not be a born warrior, but I knew without question that he would fight to the death for any one of us. This woman deserved nothing less.

"But it's been many years since Imati was taken from her village," she continued. "What if they don't even remember her? She didn't know if any of her family even survived the raid. I could have come all this way for nothing."

"We will deal with those questions as they come, Keziah." I squeezed her hands. "I told you yesterday how my uncle disappeared for ten years into Philistia and how heartbroken my mother and her family were for all that time."

She nodded.

"And I will assure you that if he had not returned and instead a child of his had somehow found his or her way to our door, there still would've been rejoicing."

"Not every family is like yours." The wistfulness in her voice told me she was envious of my upbringing. Which was understandable after the things she'd told me about her father and the hints of deep loneliness she'd unwittingly revealed along our journey.

"I don't know what will happen with these people, Keziah. But I am your friend, and I will not abandon you. I will not move on until I know for certain you are safe—and happy."

A pang of something sharp hit me square in the chest as I thought of leaving Keziah. It may only have been days since we'd met, but I'd become accustomed to her quiet presence and the sweet sound of her voice—especially now that she'd stopped trying to sound like a boy. Her bright curiosity as she asked me question after question about our ancestors was intoxicating. I needed to continue on and find Shay, but walking away from Keziah would be far more difficult than I'd ever have guessed. I'd never found myself drawn to a woman like this before.

Her luminous eyes held mine captive in a way that made me wonder whether she might be having similar thoughts. I let my gaze roam her face. The scrape on her cheekbone had healed, the bruise on her chin now more yellow than blue, and the cut in her lip was barely noticeable. All I could see now was how full and soft her mouth was as she stared back at me. It did not matter that Keziah was still dressed as a boy. Her innate beauty far over-powered the disguise, pulling me toward her with nearly as much intensity as the river that had nearly drowned us.

"Thank you, Avi," she said before I could succumb to the sur-prisingly strong urge to press my lips to hers. "I don't know how I ended up crossing paths with someone so good and kind, but I will always be grateful that I did."

She turned back around and clicked her tongue at Sarru, moving us away from whatever strange moment had just passed between us and toward the place where, as soon as we found her mother's clan, we would part ways for good.

An unexpected thrill went through me as I took in the Abiram mountain range rising up from the valley floor with an air of quiet majesty. I'd heard the story of Mosheh's mysterious death many times, how he'd addressed the people and then climbed this peak to spend his final moments with Yahweh. Har Nebo had always seemed like some mythical far-off place of fire and smoke. There were no swirling mists or burning bushes to mark the place where Mosheh's bones lay, and the only thing that set the sacred moun-tain apart from the others around it was its superior height. Yet, from this day on, whenever I told the story of Israel's great leader and prophet of the Most High, I would be able to describe this place from my own memory.

We easily found the wide stream Imati had described in the valley of Pisgah that lay on the northern side of the mountain, but the farther we traveled along the edge of that stream, the more I could feel the tension build in Keziah's body. For all my earlier assurances that her mother's people would not reject her, I could understand why she was afraid. These people may be of her blood, but there was no guarantee they would welcome her—or even that we would find them.

"It will be all right," I said, squeezing her waist gently. "I will not leave until you tell me to go. I promise."

She turned to me with a sheen of tears in her eyes. "Thank you."

A group of mudbrick houses came into view through the thick foliage, and I heard Keziah's breath catch. For some strange reason, as we approached the village, I found my own nerves vibrating. For her sake, I hoped her mother's people would give her a home among them, but I also could not help wondering what it would be like to take her back to Naioth instead. I had no doubt that my mother would be delighted if I reappeared with a woman. Even though I was only eighteen and would not be expected to take a wife for a few more years at least, I'd heard her not-so-subtle comments about how eager she was for grandchildren.

We came out of the trees, and I realized that the place was very quiet. Too quiet. Although there were at least twelve dwellings in the clearing that straddled both sides of the stream, there was no movement around them. No women calling out as they tended their homes. No men working at their trades. No children darting about, laughing, playing games. No sounds of animal life either, except for birdcalls up in the trees. All was silent and still.

Keziah turned to me, her face pale. "Where are they?"

I shook my head, just as bewildered. But as Sarru carried us into the village, the reason was made far too clear.

Although most of the mudbrick homes still stood intact, every door and window was ringed with the char of smoke damage.

Roofs had caved in, swallowing up whatever fire had not consumed. Shattered pots, splintered looms, and a host of burned and weathered household items lay scattered about on the ground. The remains of household gardens sprouted only overgrown weeds. But nowhere among the destruction lay any bodies. Only the sun-bleached skulls and bones of a few goats that looked to have been hastily butchered. Most likely consumed by whomever had raided this village.

"They're gone," Keziah murmured.

I had nothing to say that would offer any comfort. This place had been her hope for refuge, yet it held nothing but silence and the ghostly remains of the people who'd once filled this village with life.

Keziah did not pull back on the reins, so Sarru continued moving forward, plucking out a careful path through what was left of the village. All too soon we faced the spring where thin streams of water trickled over a wide, flat-topped cliff and into a small pool below. Sarru stepped up to the edge and dropped his head for a drink while Keziah stared wordlessly up at the spring.

Then her head too dropped forward, her shoulders shaking as she wept silently. Everything in me screamed to wrap my arms around her, to calm and comfort her, but I did not want to step over a line without her invitation. So instead I placed my hand on her shoulder and squeezed.

"I'm here, Keziah. I will not leave you."

"What will I do?" she choked out. "Where do I go?"

That vision of myself returning home with Keziah alongside me nudged its way into my mind again, but before I could open my mouth to say that my family would welcome her with open arms, the distant whinny of a horse jerked my attention to the top of the cliff ahead of us. Sarru too had heard the sound. He danced sideways, ears pinned back as he searched for its source.

A stranger on horseback looked down from the ridge above the spring. He pointed at us, calling out something indecipherable over the noise of the water. And then he was joined by a few others who took one look at us before kicking their mounts into a run as they headed toward the sloping path down the ridge that would lead directly to us.

Without a word, Keziah dug her heels into Sarru's sides. The horse bolted at her urging, his powerful body surging forward as she whirled him around and headed southwest, toward the mountain.

"Where are we going?" I barked out as I gripped her waist tighter.

"I don't know," she said. "But I recognize one of the men as Vadim's. They found me."

I held on to Keziah with all my strength as she drove the horse faster and faster until the trees whipped by. No wonder Sarru's breeding had been so highly prized. His long stride and massive strength was unparalleled, and the woman who commanded him with unwavering focus was like none other. I may be the one wearing armor, but on the back of her horse, Keziah had the confidence of a warrior.

A break in the hills appeared off to our left, and Keziah turned Sarru toward the gap, somehow setting him into an even faster pace that caused the entire world to blur as we thundered along. I could not hear our pursuers over the tattoo of his hooves on the ground, and I did not look over my shoulder to count them for fear of setting us off-balance. Keziah took us up a slope, Sarru snorting as he strained to ascend but his speed barely slowing. We breached the top of the hill and began descending on the southern side of the mountain, passing through a small herd of mountain goats that startled and scattered. I took a chance and looked behind us, relieved to find that our pursuers had not yet caught up.

"What do we do? Hide?" she called back to me.

"Let's put more distance between us and them before we even try," I said. "They've come this far and have been waiting to ambush you at the village. I don't think they'll give up any time soon."

She nodded her agreement and took Sarru around a blind bend, but a man astride a dusty golden camel was suddenly in our path.

Keziah yanked on the reins so quickly that Sarru reared and with a cry of dismay, she leaned forward to throw her arms around his neck. Feeling myself sliding on his sweat-slicked back, I tried to clamp on to his heaving sides with my knees, but Sarru stood on his rear legs and twisted his body sideways. I flew off the horse, landing in the weeds. The impact knocked the wind from my chest, and I gasped, my lungs screaming for air. And then just as quickly as it had been snatched away, air rushed back into my body, and I sucked in a painful but beautiful breath.

"Avi!" Keziah cried as she leapt from Sarru's back. As I'd been fighting to breathe, she'd gotten control of him. And then she was on her knees, hovering over me, her hands cradling my face. "Avi, are you all right? Are you hurt? I'm so sorry."

For a moment I allowed myself the luxury of staring into her beautiful brown eyes, in awe that this woman I'd only met days ago was so concerned for me that she appeared on the edge of hysteria. The thought filled my lungs with something nearly as life-giving as the breath I had just been struggling to catch before.

"I'm all right," I said, wanting to soothe her. I did not mention that my chest ached as though I'd been trampled by a herd of oxen, and I could already feel the places where bruises would form on my shoulder blades.

A large figure suddenly blotted out the sun, casting a long shadow over the two of us. I pushed up to my elbows as a man glared down at us from his high perch on the camel, an arrow nocked and pointed directly at my head. Within moments, we were surrounded by at least ten other men on camelback, their own arrows aimed at us.

Whatever danger we had escaped from Vadim's men had just multiplied. Keziah pressed in closer to me, her breathing quick and her hands trembling where she still gripped my face.

A flicker of movement in the distance caught my eye. The men who'd been pursuing us came around the bend, but upon seeing the group on camels surrounding us, they quickly turned their mounts around to retreat the way they came.

"Should we follow them, Naveed?" one of our captors asked.

The man he addressed watched as Vadim's men disappeared from sight. "No. I don't think they'll bother with us." Then he looked down at me again, his arrowhead still pointed at my face. "As for these two, we'd best take them to Qadir. He'll know what to do with them."

24

Keziah

The men tied Sarru's reins to the saddle of one of their camels. My horse huffed his displease at the proximity to the giant beasts, his ears pinned back, but the leader tugged his chin down with a firm yank and whispered something into Sarru's ear. Astonishingly, my stallion calmed and followed along with no further argument.

I clung to his mane as we set off and was glad for the reassuring weight of Avi's arms around my waist as we were led by our captors through a dizzying maze of canyons to the south side of the mountain. I gave myself permission to lean back into Avi, grateful for his steadying presence as the men who surrounded us joked back and forth about what they planned to do with their prisoners.

"Perhaps we should take the horse and leave them behind," said one of the men.

"The boy should be worth something," said another. "I don't know about the warrior who can't keep his seat."

They all laughed, and my blood curdled at the ease with which they jested about selling us as slaves. But surrounded as we were by well-armed men and camels on every side, there was nothing we could do but wait for our fate to be revealed. It was entirely likely that these were the same people who'd destroyed Imati's village, and if so, I doubted they would have any mercy on the two of us.

Each of the camels carried four enormous waterskins tied to their saddles, soaking wet and bulging with liquid. The size of the animals, along with their ability to carry such extraordinary amounts of cargo, astounded me.

We entered a narrow pass into a valley. Up on the ridge above us, a few men stood on the rocky outcropping, eyes on us and rams' horns strapped across their chests. Beside them, a signal fire burned, the smoke wafting lazily into the sky, most likely having just relayed that strangers were near. Each one of them was thick-muscled and weather-worn from a lifetime of battling the elements. We had no chance of escape.

My pulse thrummed as we moved farther into the valley, my breaths coming shorter and shorter as I tried to keep from imagining what they might do when they discovered I was a woman.

At my back, Avi murmured, "Breathe, Keziah. I will not let anything happen to you."

The promise was not one he could fulfill, not when we were so far outnumbered, but I appreciated his assurances all the same and took a small measure of comfort from the sound of his voice near my ear. If only my father would have betrothed me to a man like Avi instead . . .

A herd of black-and-brown goats meandered about, taking advantage of the spindly vegetation. They startled as our group came through, scattering with bleats of annoyance before ambling off to gnaw at the next patch of luscious weeds. When the path tapered, the men who'd been traveling on either side of us fell back, giving us a view of a number of tents pitched in the valley. Each one was made from woven goat hair, black with a pattern of brown and red stripes. Several of the tents had their sides rolled up or stretched into a canopy. Some were only one room, but others looked to house more than just one generation. In and around every one of those tents, curious eyes stared at us.

I'd expected these men to take us back to an encampment of

some sort, but not one with so many people. A few of the women were seated at looms, constructing that distinctive striped pattern I'd noticed on the tents. They paused their work as we passed by, their hands still on the threads and loom weights dangling in the air. Another group of women had been working together to stretch hides across wooden frames as they prepared to hang them over a fire to dry. And just beyond them, a group of children halted a game of hitting a goat bladder on the ground with sticks to watch us pass, their rounded eyes full of interest and their mostly naked bodies dark from constant sun.

None of the people in this valley looked at all threatening. Simply . . . curious.

Even the men who'd captured us had lost their veneer of menace. Naveed, the leader who'd first come upon us, sat tall in his saddle with a satisfied expression on his face, greeting the gawkers with remarks about how he'd not even had to release one arrow to secure his prisoners, boasting like he'd dragged back an entire unit of enemy combatants and not one barely armed soldier and a bedraggled girl dressed as a boy.

Our little caravan finally halted in front of a large tent perched higher on the hillside than any others. An older man, one with plenty of silver shooting through his black curls, sat on a low stool, a half-constructed bow in his hands and a little boy seated on his knee.

He stood when he saw Avi and me, pushing the boy behind his back with a scowl on his face. Then he set the bow aside and told the boy to go into the tent.

"What's this, Naveed?" he asked.

"Found them near the mountain, Qadir," Naveed replied. "Leading those horsemen our way."

Naveed demanded we dismount as Qadir approached, his black eyes keen on us. This man was without a doubt the chief of this clan, his bearing surprisingly regal as he lifted his thick-bearded chin. "Who are you? And why were you leading those men to our door?"

"We come in shalom to this region, my lord," said Avi, his tone respectful. Submissive, even. "And we were chased by those men directly into the path of your companions. We mean only to pass through."

Qadir's brows arched high as he looked between the two of us. Behind him, the tent flap parted slightly, and two female faces appeared in the gap, an older woman with silver hair and a golden ring in her nose and a younger woman who flinched when she took in the sight of a strange horse and two captives. Their curious gazes passed over Avi and landed on me. They put their heads together, whispering, and I shifted on my feet, uncomfortable with the scrutiny.

"Your speech sounds foreign, and you look like no Hebrew I've ever seen," said the chief, his eyes narrowed. "Where do you hail from?"

"My friend Kez here is from the north, and I am from the other side of the river." Avi gestured to the west, where the sun was just beginning to fade on the horizon.

"Are you? From what tribe?"

Avi paused, but only for a moment, and I wondered what story he was conjuring up. "Levite," he said, surprising me by revealing the truth. "But I live with my family in Benjamite territory."

Qadir's expression went hard. "And yet here you are, at our mountain, leading men who have been hanging about for days right to our encampment. Endangering our women and children."

Those men had been here for *days*? How had they known my destination? I'd assumed the horsemen had followed sightings of us as we traveled, but if they knew where I was headed, someone must have tortured that answer out of Imati before she died. My stomach lurched at the thought of her suffering even worse than I had imagined.

"I vow to you that we did not mean to lead those men to you. We did not know anyone lived in this area," said Avi.

"Then why are you lurking around our mountain?"

Avi looked to me, silently asking permission to reveal the truth.

I nodded, resigned to the idea that convincing these people of our innocence meant we must be honest. Perhaps they could give us insight into what had happened to Imati's people, or if they had had something to do with the destruction.

Instead of answering the chief's question, Avi asked one of his own. "We saw an abandoned village near the headwaters of the stream. What happened there?"

The chief's expression remained impassive. "Moabites. They came and burned it. Again. Killed many. So the villagers left. The Moabites were too relentless in their quest to take back land they call theirs. It is not worth rebuilding homes that will simply be burned over and over."

The last of my hopes faded away with his words. Imati's people were gone and with them my only hope for finding a place to belong. I was now without a home, a family, or even a destination. I swallowed against the glut of hot tears building in my throat as the older of the two women came out of the tent and moved toward us.

"What are you doing, Ima?" Qadir demanded as the woman stepped closer. He put out an arm to block her from approaching.

The woman ignored him, pushing his arm away, and came closer to me, her ebony eyes keenly focused on my face.

"Who are you, girl?" she demanded. I sucked in a breath. How had she seen so easily through my disguise when I had not uttered a word? "What do you want with the people of that village?" Her commanding tone broke through my haze, startling an answer out of me.

"My mother was born there. Lived by that stream until she was stolen during a raid."

The woman appeared stricken, her dark skin paling. "Who?" she pressed. "Who is she?"

"Her name was Imati," I replied, "of the Rehavite clan. She sacrificed her life so I could take refuge with them."

A noise came from the mouth of the other woman, a cry of grief if I'd ever heard one, and she fell to her knees, ululating. Murmurs rose all around us, expressions of shock on most of the faces around us. Sarru danced as the sounds of mourning poured from the younger woman's mouth.

"I knew it," said the old woman. "You look just like her." And then her arms were around me, pulling me close, her grip nearly suffocating as she embraced me. "Welcome home, granddaughter."

25

Avidan

F or such a big man you certainly have a weak stomach," said Naveed when I turned away as he yanked the gory entrails from the ibex he'd shot with his bow.

I'd hunted game before, of course, with my father or cousins, and had even taken part in the butchering, but when the arrows met their mark today, the bloody aftermath swept me back to the battle with the Ammonites, and I simply could not watch the men field dress their kills. Perhaps I never would again.

But to Naveed I simply said, "I've never been too keen on entrails."

The man laughed, all of his earlier suspicion of me having been wiped away by the revelation that Keziah was the daughter of the long-lost Imati. My traveling companion had been almost immediately whisked away by the women of this clan to sleep in one of their tents, and even before I'd managed to see her this morning, I'd been commandeered by the men to come along on a hunt. Apparently, a homecoming celebration in Keziah's honor was being planned for tonight.

As we climbed their sacred mountain, I learned that this clan was directly related to Mosheh himself through his grandson

Rehaviah. They had remained behind after the great leader's death when the rest of Israel had moved on, determined to be the guardians of their forefather's burial site, even if the ever-expanding tribe had split into a number of different clans over the years.

This group had set aside their tents and built a village near the prolific spring, generation after generation living in the shadow of the mountain they considered holy. However, they had been repeatedly invaded by both Moabites from the south and Ammonites to the east. After that final attack, when Imati's father, the chief, was killed trying to defend his people, Qadir, as his successor, had made the decision to pack up whatever and whoever was left and return to the nomadic lifestyle of their distant ancestors.

Following the rains, the seasonal pastures, and living off what meager offerings the land provided, the Rehavites under Qadir's leadership traveled far and wide each year but always returned to this mountain during the rainy season to take advantage of the green slopes and to remember Mosheh. If we had arrived a few weeks later, they would already have moved on to their next encampment and we would have missed them completely.

During the long climb, I also recounted our journey to the men, who were greatly amused by my description of Keziah's flimsy pretense as a boy, furious at how I found her being beaten, and grateful for my willingness to escort her here.

As I waited for them to prepare their kills for transport to the camp, I turned my face toward the west, wondering if Yahweh had shown Mosheh all of the Land of Promise from this very vantage point or somewhere else nearby. The green and brown hills across the Jordan Valley spread in every direction, their beauty breathtaking. I could only imagine the devastation Mosheh must have endured when he was told by Yahweh that this was the closest he would ever come to Canaan and that his sandals would never step over the river he'd spent a lifetime longing to cross.

Somewhere over there, my family waited for me, not knowing where I was or whether I was even alive. But they would have to endure the unknown for a little longer, because I refused to face them without my cousin in tow.

My eyes searched the endless distance all around, where somewhere out there Shay still breathed. He had to, or I would never forgive myself. If this was indeed the place Yahweh had spoken to Mosheh, I took the chance that he could perhaps hear me better on this high peak.

"Please," I whispered, "help me bring him home."

Qadir came up to stand beside me, his own gaze tracking the distant landscape.

"Tell me more about this boy you are looking for," he said. "How is it that he disappeared?"

The familiar wash of shame came over me, but I told Keziah's uncle of the battle and how the place I'd hidden our tagalong cousin had led to his injury and disappearance.

"So, you are the All-Knowing One, then?"

I stared at him in confusion.

"You say that it is all your doing that Shalem is lost, but perhaps there are reasons for it that you do not understand. Think of our blessed father, Mosheh. Did he not think he'd destroyed everything when he was exiled to Midian after killing the Egyptian overseer? And look, even so, Yahweh came to him there, showed his glory in the burning bush. Gave him the power to cause miracles in Pharaoh's presence. That time of exile was what was best for him. He was already a great general in Egypt. But this is when he learned to be a shepherd—a skill he would need to guide our ancestors in the wilderness."

"It is not best for Shay, who is only fifteen years old, to be taken away from his family. To be lost and wounded among strangers. Perhaps even—" I swallowed hard, loath to even voice the thought aloud. "Perhaps even enslaved."

He shrugged. "In the kingdom to come, we may understand all. But for now, our eyes are blind to the ways of the Ancient One, are they not? Only Yahweh knows the end from the beginning. You, my new friend, do not."

Just as my father would do, Qadir went quiet, allowing me to chew on his words for a good long while. He was right that I had no idea why this all had happened, and I could not regret meeting Keziah, but I could not accept that anything good could come of losing my cousin. Of whatever pain and fear he was enduring.

"My son tells me that you came across the river with a king to battle against the Ammonites."

"I did."

"Are the Ammonites truly defeated?" the chief asked.

"From what I have heard, Saul's forces chased the remnant of Nahash's forces back to Rabbah, but he did not take their city."

Qadir made a noise in the back of his throat. "So they will return, stronger and angrier."

This was exactly what the vintner had said as well. "They might," I conceded.

"And you say this man was chosen as king by Yahweh?"

"I saw the lots cast by Samuel himself."

"I don't know who this Samuel is, but I don't trust a king who would be so unwise with his enemies."

"Unwise in what way? He was victorious. Nahash was put to the sword before the battle's end."

He shrugged. "It seems to me this new king might have taken a larger bite than he can swallow. My father, when he was alive, used to say that it is never wise for a man to run ahead of his own camel."

"And what does that mean?"

"One must always count the cost before setting his foot to a path, or he might end up getting trampled. He also said it was foolish to pick a fight with a viper in its own hole. My father always sought the guidance of Elohim before making any decision, no matter how small or seemingly insignificant. And he always put his people before himself. It is why he died on the night my sister was taken from us. He refused to hide. He fought until his last breath to ensure that our casualties were as few as possible. My two older brothers followed his example, to their own deaths. But because of their sacrifice, the rest of us did not perish."

From memory, my father's words arose, spilling out of my mouth in a whisper. "The voice of the Ancient One to light his every step . . ."

"What is that?" asked Qadir.

"It is from a song my father wrote many years ago. I've never thought much of what it meant until just now." I cleared my throat. "'The anointed one shall abide by the counsel of the Most High, The voice of the Ancient One to light his every step.'"

The chief hummed his approval. "Your father sounds quite wise. Perhaps this king of yours should seek *his* counsel instead of his own."

"Are you of the opinion, then, that Israel should not have asked for a king to stand strong against the nations around us?"

He shrugged. "I will leave those concerns up to Yahweh himself. I care only that I lead my own people in the manner in which my father did—like a shepherd whose task was to guard his sheep, even at the cost of his own life. This was part of the legacy inherited from Mosheh, the greatest of leaders, who never aspired to be king over the people, even though in many ways he filled that role. His strong leadership was perfectly balanced with his humility, and although he was certainly not perfect, he *never* forgot who sat on the throne of the heavens. It is his example this Saul should pattern himself after, not the kings of Egypt and Babylon."

He paused, his gaze roving over the distant hills across the river. "You know," he said, "it is not only Mosheh who heard the Voice atop this mountain peak."

I startled, furrowing my brow as I studied Qadir's thoughtful expression. "It's not?"

He shook his head. "Have you heard of the seer called Baalam? The man whose own donkey rebuked him?"

"Of course. He was hired by the king of the Moabites to curse Israel, but Yahweh caused him to proclaim blessings instead."

"You *do* know the ancient stories well, my friend. My niece told me how you provided for her with your skill with words. She says you have the gift of explaining our histories with great passion, and that she has learned much from you."

I knew Keziah enjoyed my stories, but to hear that she'd praised my talent to Qadir caused a rush of honey-sweet warmth to flood my chest. How I would miss her dark eyes fixed on me, making me wish things were different. . . . I shook the futile thought away. I'd fulfilled my vow and brought her to her people.

"I am glad to hear that Keziah has found some value in my tales, and although I have learned many stories of our people from Samuel and the other prophets in Naioth, my father has sung a song about the reluctant prophecy of Baalam for as long as I can remember."

"Ah." He pressed a flat palm to his chest, a sign of respect. "Then you learned your art from him."

"No. . . . I am not a musician. I am a storyteller." The designation felt right coming from my mouth.

"Is it not the same thing?" He lifted his brows, but before I could respond, he continued on, stroking his beard with one hand as he gestured toward the springs. "Did your father's song recount the prophecy that flowed from Baalam's mouth, about the One who was to come? 'A star will come from Yaakov, a scepter will arise from Israel . . .'"

He let his words hang in the stillness, so I added, "'He will crush the foreheads of Moab and the skulls of the sons of Seth. Edom will be conquered—his enemies will conquer Seir, but Israel will triumph.'"

Together, we spoke the rest of the oracle. "'One from Yaakov will rule and destroy the city's survivors.'"

Could this ancient prophecy, spoken from this very mountain, be speaking of King Saul? I'd heard the Levitical apprentices say there were witnesses to Saul himself prophesying soon after he'd been anointed by Samuel. But did that mean he was this star to arise from Israel? How would we know that Saul or one of his descendants was the One of whom Mosheh spoke of as well?

I suddenly had a very strong impression that even if I knew many of the ancient stories, I had so much left to learn. As much as I'd felt burdened for the people of Yazer, and indeed all the Hebrews on this side of the river who had forgotten the ancient ways and the truth about Yahweh, I had not even completed my Levitical training before I ran off like a boy with a stick-sword facing down giants. I'd taken my sacred responsibilities to my people and my God far too lightly.

As I looked out over the Land given to my fathers by the Creator himself, something new stirred in my breast: a whisper of inevitability, perhaps, or a brush of something heaven-breathed that I had no name for. But as I followed Qadir and Naveed back down the mountain, I knew something had changed inside me. I just had to discern what it meant for the future.

Once we returned from the hunt and delivered the carcasses of the ibex to the women who were busy preparing the meal, Mailah—one of Keziah's aunts—handed me a fresh tunic.

"Muddy garments stained with blood are not welcome at my table," she admonished, then gave me a pot of water and directed me to her tent to change. Although the red and blue striped tunic wasn't quite long enough to reach my knees, the sleeveless garment was wide enough in the shoulders. I thanked her for her kindness, glad to be rid of the ruined clothing I'd worn all this time and grateful to wash the dust and filth of my travels from my body. When I emerged from the tent, I felt nearly as refreshed as I had after the waterfall.

Uncertain of where to go, I ambled through the camp, seeking out Qadir or another of Keziah's uncles to offer my help. The chatter amongst the clan was bright as the men tended their animals, women stirred pots over fires, and children flitted about with armloads of scavenged firewood, pillows for the gathering, or baskets of food. Everyone had a part, it seemed, in the celebration of Keziah's homecoming, just like during celebrations with my own family back in Naioth.

I wondered whether Zevi and Gavriel had returned to the village already and informed my parents that I'd remained behind to look for Shay. Each day I remained on this side of the river was another they would be forced to wonder where I'd gone. For as much as I feared for Shay out there all alone, my mother and father would do the same for me. I missed them—missed everyone in Naioth—but I could not completely regret all that had come to pass since I'd run off to fight for the king. Without my journey here and my search for my cousin, I would not know Keziah. I would not have had that oddly sacred experience atop Mosheh's mountain.

Thinking of moving on without Keziah beside me caused a sharp pain to throb under my ribs—as if something vital had come loose, threatening to tear away. And yet, I had no choice. I had to keep searching for Shay. Keziah's place was with her family, just like mine was on the other side of the river.

Sarru was tied up a short distance away from the camels, his muscles twitching and tail swishing as he shifted from hoof to hoof, uneasy with the proximity of the enormous animals. I took a few moments to scratch between his ears, thanking him for permitting me to ride, and received a nuzzle of his hairy chin and a hot gust of breath against my ear. The two of us had come to an accord, it seemed. I realized I might miss the great beast nearly as much as I would his mistress.

Large groups of women were busy at work preparing the meal, and I wondered how Keziah fared with the women of her mother's clan. She'd appeared a bit overwhelmed as they all gathered around her last night, chattering and asking a thousand questions, but seemed happy nonetheless as she was whisked away in their care. It had seemed strange to not wake with her beside me this morning, her smile outshining the dawn as she mounted Sarru to take the next leg of our journey. There'd been a hollow spot in my chest since we'd parted last night to sleep in different tents, and I suspected it would only grow larger once I took my leave of her clan.

Unable to catch sight of her short black curls anywhere among the busy women and feeling useless in all the bustle of preparations, I stood in the shade of a tent nearby and waited, watching a mother direct her two young sons to slow their feet as they carried small pots of stew to the gathering place, her commanding but affectionate tone making me miss my own ima.

A young woman approached, likely one of Keziah's many cousins that I could not keep straight. Her skirts flapped about in a stiff breeze that had swept off the mountain, and she held a wine jug in her hand. The bangles on her wrist jingled as she neared, the turquoise beads on the long tail of the head scarf that trailed over her shoulder glinting merrily in the late afternoon sunshine. Her bare feet and hands were decorated with the swirling patterns all the women of this clan wore, and her thickly kohl-rimmed eyes met mine as she offered me a clay cup. Her henna-dark lips tipped up with a welcoming smile.

"My thanks," I said as she poured a measure of wine into the cup. "Your hospitality honors me. Do you know what happened to Keziah? I haven't seen her since this morning." I peered past the girl to search yet again for her familiar form.

Laughter jerked my attention back to the young woman in front of me. I knew that sound as well as I knew my own voice.

"*Keziah?*"

She grinned up at me, amused by my surprise. "You don't recognize your traveling companion?"

Stunned by the change in her appearance, I stared, taking in the way the green and black kohl made her eyes appear even larger, how the silver ring in her nose accentuated the delicate slope and how the color of her lips drew my eyes to their fullness. A black scarf twisted around her head into a turban, its tail trailing over her shoulder to her waist, giving the illusion of long hair over the soft curls that framed her face.

She held one side of her skirt out to the side, the fabric made of a similar weave to the tunic I wore, although hers was a riot of many interlacing colors and its fit lent shape to enticing curves

I'd never let myself linger on before. I frowned at the thought, strangely missing the shapeless gray tunic and her unkempt curls. This new Keziah was far too unsettling, causing my chest to ache with something I refused to put into words. I was leaving. She was safe here with her mother's family. I had fulfilled my vow to her, and now I must fulfill the one I'd made to Shalem.

"I had no choice but to submit to their ministrations," she said, tugging at the neckline of her dress, then swiping her palm over her skirt. "They refused to let me look like a boy any longer." She wrapped one arm around her waist, fidgeting with the blue beads that dangled from the edge of her headscarf.

Another breeze wrapped around us, fluttering the curls around her face and stirring the fragrance of desert flowers from her skin. Without thinking, I breathed deeply of the exotic scent.

"You look . . ." *Beautiful. Lovely. Exquisite.*

She blinked up at me, a dimple on her cheek twitching as she waited for me to land on the right word.

I stalled, clearing my throat. I took a drink of the sweet date wine, using the moment to scramble about for something to say.

". . . Not like a boy anymore," I stuttered, my pulse whooshing in my ears, and I immediately chastised myself for my thick tongue. Her obvious discomfort with her new clothing melted away, and she let out a small bubble of laughter at my awkward compliment. For someone who claimed to have the gift of words, all mine seemed to have fled.

I pulled at the neck of my tunic, face burning. The truth was, it did not matter what she looked like in these new clothes. I'd found her enthralling even in her slave garment and her beautiful face smudged with dirt. She was kind. Intelligent. Witty. And so very brave. And in two days' time, I would be leaving her behind for good.

The second drink of the date wine was nowhere near as enjoyable as the first. My stomach had suddenly gone sour.

"We lift our voices to you, Elohim, God of our father Mosheh, in thanksgiving for the return of our daughter Keziah and for the blessing of her presence among us. We humbly praise you for the many gifts you have bestowed upon your servants. . . ."

Standing before the assembly, Qadir's large hands were raised as he recited the prayer of gratitude to the heavens. He was not just the leader of this clan but its high priest as well.

We'd already feasted on the ibex we'd hunted this morning, the meat spiced with herbs I'd never tasted before that gave it a lightly sweet but spicy flavor I could not get enough of. The roast was served with a thick sauce made from the flowers of an acacia tree, alongside date honey swirled into soft goat cheese, and dough baked in decadent pools of fresh butter and milk.

Now that the meal had been consumed, another round of date wine was poured into our cups as the large bowls we'd shared food from were removed. A group of musicians, made up of four drummers, three reed pipers, and a boy with a tambourine, began to play. The lively tune inspired a circle of dancers, both male and female, to perform what I was told was a traditional dance handed down from generation to generation. It involved a volleying chant between the two sexes, full of teasing, and ended with a loud yodeling call by the men as the women pretended to attack. The expression of false fear on their bearded faces caused fits of laughter all around, especially from the children.

Across from me, Keziah sat between two cousins who'd latched on to her from nearly the first moment she had been revealed as family. The nose ring she wore flashed in the firelight as she swayed to the rhythm of the drums, and the bangles on her wrists twinkled as she clapped along to the beat. I could not take my eyes away from her. Perhaps sensing my gaze, she turned and gave me a smile far sweeter than the date wine she'd offered me earlier, making me wish that she was beside me now, whispering into my ear instead of her cousin's.

"Beautiful, no?" said Naveed. "Just as her mother was."

"No," I replied, flustered. "I mean . . . I never met Imati, but yes, Keziah is lovely."

"She will make someone a good wife."

My throat closed up, and I had to swallow twice to push out my words. "Will she be forced to marry? After what her father did, selling her to protect his town, I hate to see her pressed into a similar situation." I hated to think of her married at all but had no right to complain.

"Qadir will not force her into anything," he said. "That is not the way among us. But I think it will take little time for offers to be made." He gestured to a couple of young men seated nearby and sure enough their eyes were on my Keziah.

No. She was not mine. She could not be. But that did not stop the blood from speeding hot and fast in my veins and emotion I'd never felt before rise to the top like curdled cream. I recognized the jealousy for what it was but forcefully pushed it down.

"You must promise me she will be well cared for, Naveed. She's endured so much and been neglected by those who should have loved her best. She deserves to be treated with tenderness."

He met my eyes. "I vow it. She will be cared for just as if she were Imati herself. But . . . my friend, perhaps it is you who desires to care for her in this way?"

Shocked that my feelings were so evident, I swallowed again, my attention still on Keziah, who had been dragged out to the center of the gathering by her cousins. They were teaching her a dance that challenged participants to squat lower and lower as the drumbeat softened and then jump back upright the moment the horns bleated a jaunty tune.

I'd vowed to leave her only when I was assured of her safety and happiness, and she would have both here with her mother's people. As gut-wrenching as it was to leave her, I had to. Taking her with me would only put her in danger. I could not be selfish like I'd been with Shalem. She needed to stay here where she was protected and I would know she was not in harm's way—just like I should have done with my cousin.

"My goal was to bring her to her people and then to find my cousin," I said. "She belongs here, not with me."

From across the fire, Keziah's gaze met mine once again. The lie I'd just told lay on my tongue like a mouthful of thick and sticky black tar, and I had to look away.

26

Keziah

My cousins Numa and Meital let loose with a few shrill calls, their trilling summoning the goats that had wandered out of the campsite and were grazing on some of the lush grasses in a dry wadi. The girls found a low, flat rock and spread a paste of smashed dates and roasted barley across its surface, then selected a couple of does and gently guided them to the treat, letting them indulge while the girls squatted beside them.

"First," said Numa, "you'll grab her legs like this." She pulled the goat's ankle upward so the animal balanced on three legs. "And then hold on to the teat like so." She moved her fingers expertly, the milk spurting into a waiting bowl.

"What if she kicks me?" I was not certain I trusted the little goat that had been eyeing me warily as she licked the barley-date mash.

"Just be confident and talk quietly to her. She has a very full bag since she's nursing twins, so she will be glad for the relief."

Wanting to please Numa and knowing that living among the Rehavites would mean taking part in their daily chores, I squatted beside my cousin and followed her guidance, but my every attempt was a failure.

The initial excitement I'd felt when I realized the Rehavites were Imati's family had begun to wane just a little. Without question they'd accepted my claim and immediately swept me up in changing my clothing, painting my eyes, and asking a thousand questions about Imati. And yet with as kind as they were, I could not help but wish that Imati herself were here beside me.

But there would be no sweet reunion for her. She would never feel the warmth of her mother's embrace after so many years or feel tears of gratitude slide down her cheeks. She'd had so many things stolen from her, but from the little I knew of her, it was her family she grieved the most. I felt like an imposter accepting the love she should have received upon her return.

And as much as I wanted to feel content here with Imati's people, with those whose blood ran in my veins, it was Avi who made me feel at ease, who made me feel strong, capable, and cared for. The past two mornings I'd awakened in my aunt's tent without him by my side and felt as though something precious had been stripped away.

It was far too easy to imagine leaving here with him, continuing on together as we searched for his cousin, burrowing into his strong embrace whenever I felt lonely or frightened, maybe someday even bearing his child . . .

And yet, I'd overheard him talking with Naveed and Qadir during the celebration last night about which trade roads were the most heavily traveled and about possible connections they might have to inquire about his cousin, along with the very gracious offer to take him by camel to Heshbon. There was no mention of my going with him. There wouldn't be, because he'd always meant to leave me behind.

I flinched as the goat pulled her leg from my grasp and knocked over the bowl, spilling the precious liquid into the dirt. Defeated and dreading the moment Avi walked away for good, I dropped my head forward.

"Don't fret," said Numa, rubbing her palm between my shoulder blades. "It'll get easier with time."

I was fairly certain it would not.

"Avidan!" Meital directed a cheerful grin over my shoulder. "It looks as though our brothers have been showing off their camels' speed."

My heartbeat stuttered as I turned to find Avi coming toward us, covered nearly head to toe in thick dust. Even his golden-brown hair was painted the dusty color of the vast wilderness that surrounded the mountain.

I forced a smile. "Even *I* wasn't that dirty when I was a boy."

His lips twitched with reluctant amusement. "Rasul insisted on racing back from the spring, even though I was riding behind him. And since I'd been wet from washing in the stream, the dirt clung to me. Now I need another bath." He ran his fingers through his hair and then shook his head, a puff of dust swirling around him. I could not help but laugh at his disgruntled expression.

His eyes lit with amusement as well but sobered just as quickly. "May I speak with you, Keziah?"

"Of course. My cousins have been teaching me how to milk the goats, but I've yet to succeed. It'll go faster without me." I stood and dusted off my skirt.

"You'll get the knack for it," said Meital. "We will make a Rehavite of you yet." She gave me a reassuring wink.

Avidan and I walked together in silence, but this was not the sweet and companionable silence we'd enjoyed for so many hours while traveling on Sarru's back. There was a strain between us now, a sense that things were changing, and I hated it. I longed for the easy way between us, back before I knew that he'd seen past my disguise. Or for the intimacy I'd felt dancing in the air between us at the waterfall after I'd admitted the truth to him. Even though we'd only spent a little over a week together, he'd become so much more to me than a friend along our journey.

"I'm leaving," he said without preamble, halting in the path to face me. "Earlier than I planned."

Agony streaked through me, surprising me with its intensity. "When?"

"Right away."

I sucked in a painful breath. I'd been trying to prepare myself for his departure, knowing it was inevitable, but *now*? I could barely contain the instinct to plead with him for just a few more days. Or forever.

"Qadir's son, Omar, and some other men have trade to conduct in Heshbon, but they want to visit friends of theirs on the way. They want me to . . ." He paused, scraping his sandal over a pebble on the ground. "They want me to share stories with the group."

Imati's people had been enthralled by Avi's stories last night. When the dancing had stopped, he'd told how Yahweh had made the sun stand still so the Hebrews could win over their enemies, and then spoke of a battle at a place called Mitzpah when Yahweh caused a great earthquake to nearly swallow up the Philistine chariots, giving the Hebrews a great victory and protecting the sacred Ark from destruction. When my family had pleaded for more tales, he spoke of a battle led by a man named Gideon who, with only three hundred men and a clever ruse, had bested the vast Midianite army.

Both Naveed and Qadir had been full of questions for Avi about these events. They seem astounded to hear that Yahweh was still interceding for the tribes of Yaakov, especially in such miraculous ways. They'd been so separated from the rest of Israel and its priesthood that they assumed all miracles died with Mosheh. And even after hearing so many of Avi's stories during our travels, I could not help but be surprised as well. I'd certainly never witnessed anything supernatural in the temple of Asherah.

In fact, from what Avi had said last night, worship of Canaanite gods, like Ba'al, Molech, and even my own goddess, were forbidden for the people of Israel. The way he'd spoken of the true prophets of Yahweh destroying the Asherah poles and razing the high places that I'd always thought were holy and sacred had made my stomach go sour.

Had I been giving my worship to something evil? And if so, that meant my good and kind mother had done so as well. I wasn't certain I could reconcile such a thing, but ever since last night, the amulet at my neck had seemed to hang with an odd weight.

Avi said that Yahweh not only created the earth for the delight of humankind, but he also took pleasure in communing with his people, forgiving even the most egregious of sins, and protecting and providing for those he'd chosen as his *am segula*, his beloved people. I was a descendant of both Mosheh and Manasseh, and I had cried out to the God of my fathers on Avi's behalf, but until I'd met Avi, I'd never thought of Yahweh as anything more than the fearsome husband of my goddess. How could I serve something so unfathomable? So incomprehensible?

A thousand questions swirled in my heart and mind, but now that Avi was leaving, who would I even ask to explain them? All I could do was swallow them down and pretend, for his sake, to be glad for him to be able to pursue his cousin without me. I'd done enough to delay his search.

"So, you'll travel to Heshbon?" I asked, pushing past the burn in my throat. "I thought you planned to go north instead."

"Omar says that anyone traveling south on the King's Highway, either to the land of Midian or down toward Egypt, travels through Heshbon. If I hear nothing from his contacts there, I'll know to go back north."

I nodded, knowing this course was a wise one but loathing it all the same. "I'm glad you've found someone to travel with."

"I'd far rather ride Sarru," he said with a gentle smile. "My backside had at least gotten accustomed to sitting astride. I always feel like I'm going to slide off one of those camels and break my neck. I thought Rasul and Zakir were going to kill me today when they were racing like demons back from the stream."

I laughed, envisioning a white-faced Avi holding on to my cousin like his life depended on it. "Sarru will miss you."

"Will he?"

"He will." I paused, turning to face him. "But he knows you need to go find your cousin."

His gaze turned soft. "I'm glad he understands. I could not live with myself if I did not do all I can to bring Shalem home."

"It's one of the reasons Sarru knew you were a good and trust-worthy man from the start."

"I will miss him too," said Avi, his eyes traveling over my face slowly, as if he were memorizing what he saw. "He has been the best of traveling companions."

I smiled at him, going teary. "He would agree. Even if he still thinks you have a tender backside."

He laughed, tipping his head back, and my heart swelled pain-fully at the sound. Nothing was as beautiful as Avi's full-throated laugh. It was impossible not to respond with my own. A few tears escaped, and I wiped them away quickly, hoping he would assume they were tears of amusement and not because I was being torn in two.

When our laughter died away, his gaze traveled over the camp that was my new home, at least until the tribe moved on to find more fertile pastures.

"Are you . . . content here?" he asked, his voice low.

I swallowed against the ache in my throat. *I'm content when I am with you,* I wanted to say, but now was not the time to throw myself at his feet and beg that he take me with him. Now was the time to repay him for his kindness and protection by being grate-ful that I was safe with Imati's family and letting him go—even if it felt like my insides were being shredded to pieces. How could I say good-bye to the man who had somehow stolen my heart?

"I'm glad to be with my family," I said, hoping he would not hear the anguish in my voice. "It's all new and this lifestyle will be challenging, but these people seem to truly care for me." I gestured back to my cousins, who were making a shoddy attempt at hiding that they were watching the two of us.

"I care . . ." He paused, looking into the distance and rubbing his beard. My pulse thrummed as I waited for whatever words he was searching for. "I care about your safety, and I feel confident these people will protect you well. They've been patrolling the area for the past two days and have seen nothing of the men who were chasing you. I think they've given up, thinking you and me captured. Besides, I don't think they'll come after you with all these warriors on camels around."

Foolish disappointment welled up. Of course his first and only concern was for my safety. I forced another smile. "Yes, I feel quite safe here. You don't need to worry about me anymore."

"Not sure that is possible," he murmured.

Is he trying to undo me?

Everything in me cried out to rush forward and throw myself into his arms, but I could not be so selfish. I'd caused enough destruction by leaving Imati to suffer in my stead. I would not put my desires above Avi's love for his cousin. He was too honorable, his need to protect me too much of a distraction from his purpose. So instead, I took a step backward, ignoring the sensation of something deep inside tearing at the physical separation.

I willed my voice to not break, even if my heart was in pieces. "Thank you for everything. I would not have found Imati's people without you. You may not count yourself a warrior, but you will always be one of the mighty ones to me."

I took one last look at the man who'd made me feel seen, and cherished, for the first time in my life, then I turned and walked away because if there was anything I'd learned from Avi's stories of Yahweh, it was that love was nothing without sacrifice.

27

A grinning Rasul released the cluster of dates from what seemed to me a precarious perch near the top of the tree, the bundle raining fruit onto the blankets spread below as it crashed to the ground. A cheer went up from the youngest of my little cousins as they surged forward to snatch up sweet handfuls while Tannir and Gassan, the oldest of my boy cousins, shimmied up the other date palms.

The Rehavite mothers chastised some of the older children for not waiting their turn, but not for sampling the fruit, since there was plenty for all. This desert oasis contained a large natural grove of date palms, most holding at least nine or ten full clusters of dates that were so ripe the air all around was tinged with sweetness.

While the sticky-cheeked children playfully argued over who'd found the biggest date and the boys hacked down more clusters, the women began shaking and plucking dates from stems, tossing them into sacks that would be carried back to camp on camelback. The bounty would be spread in the sun to ripen further and then made into honey, traded, or cooked into stews and other meals.

Unable to resist, I popped one into my own mouth and groaned in pleasure. No wonder the children had been vibrating with excitement as they waited for the treasures to fall from the sky. I threw myself into the job, ignoring the stickiness of my hands while I worked alongside my aunts and cousins, grateful for the distraction.

Avidan had been gone since yesterday. The hours we'd spent together on Sarru now seemed even more precious than they had before and far too fleeting. What I would not give to have his voice in my ear, recounting stories of the ancients and escapades with his cousins. Or to feel his rich laughter vibrate against my back as he gently teased me and the warm reassurance of his arms around my waist.

But it was no use wishing for the impossible. He was gone and would not be coming back. He had a duty to his cousin, one he must fulfill or he would not be the honorable man I'd come to know. But still, it had been nearly impossible to keep my sandals planted in the sand instead of running after him as he rode away behind Omar.

I shook my head, trying to chase away thoughts that made my chest ache and instead focus on plucking the juicy dates one by one from their stems.

"Can I ride Sarru now?" came a small voice at my shoulder. I looked up to find Suyah, one of my little cousins, staring at me with pleading eyes. I could not help but be surprised again at how much this girl and I looked alike, just how the resemblance between myself and Imati would have been unmistakable had I paid closer attention.

Another pang of sadness speared me. I had no doubt Imati would have adored this little girl. She'd missed so much in the years since being taken—births and deaths, marriages and celebrations, joys and sorrows. All for my sake.

I tamped down the guilt and smiled at the sweet child. "If your mother gives her permission, you can ride back to camp with me."

She clapped her hands and then knelt to help me, anything to hasten her ride. Hobbled nearby with one of the Rehavites' altered saddles strapped to his back, Sarru was happily nibbling the lush grasses growing in abundance around this spring-fed oasis, even though he still was skittish around the camels nearby.

I was so absorbed in the chatter between the women around me and the laughter and calls of the boys in the trees that I did not hear the thunder until it was too late.

A swirl of dust, thrown up by myriad hooves, encircled us so quickly that none of us had any time to react before we were surrounded. I coughed, choking on the sand-filled air, and blinked hard to clear my eyes of the stinging barrage. Suyah clung to me, trembling.

Although I was disoriented by both the screams of the children and the whirlwind of dust, horses, and veiled riders spiraling around us with swords glinting in the sunlight, I had no doubt of the cause. My presence among the Rehavites had not been a blessing at all, but a curse.

Vadim's men had found me.

One of their number moved his horse closer to me as the rest continued their menacing circle, preventing the boys in the trees from coming to our defense. The women and children huddled together, eyes wide, many with tears dripping down their cheeks.

"Hello, Keziah," said a voice I instantly recognized even through the scarf he wore over his mouth. "Your father is very worried about you."

"Nabal?"

My father's cousin and closest confidant tipped his head to me, gray eyes gleaming with twisted delight. "I've been sent to take you home, where you belong."

"Please, let these people go," I said, pressing Suyah behind me. "They are innocent. They've done nothing but give a stranger shelter. Do not harm them."

Nabal threw his leg over his horse and leapt to the ground with the ease of an experienced horseman. Striding toward me, he withdrew a dagger from his belt. "Well now, I think that will depend on you, my lovely cousin."

With my pulse pounding in my ears, I shuffled backward while trying to extricate myself from Suyah's clutches, but the little girl was so terrified her grip only tightened on my skirts.

"Take me, Nabal. I am who you want." I shook my head vehemently as he came close, but there was nothing I could do as he grabbed for Suyah and yanked her away.

"Please! No!" I shouted as the girl wailed in terror. The women cried out, and her mother screeched her daughter's name. "Don't hurt her!"

Without apology, Nabal put his dagger against the child's neck. He leaned closer to me and dropped his voice. "If you want to keep her and the rest of these savages alive, you have one choice. Get on my horse and take me to my reward."

"Your what?"

"You have what is mine and I want it back."

I blinked at him in confusion as he pinned me with a glare that reminded me of that kestrel diving toward my face. "Don't mistake me for a fool, girl. All that was inside that saddle is *mine*."

Those stolen bridal gifts had been meant for Nabal?

"Yours?" I sputtered. "But how?"

"That's none of your concern. Take me to it. *Now*."

He had no way of knowing I was no longer in possession of the jewels, and I had little doubt that he would slaughter all of us if I told him it was gone.

"It's not here," I said, swallowing hard against the burn in my throat. I was taking a huge chance, and my life would probably be forfeit when he discovered my deceit, but I had to protect Imati's family.

She'd given her life for mine and now it was my turn.

"I found the wedding gifts in the saddle," I said, "but I was being pursued by Ammonites. I buried them beneath a tree in case I was overtaken."

Nabal's glare narrowed. "Where?"

Knowing I had to make the lie convincing, I kept my gaze steady on him and my expression blank. "Back at the Jabbok River."

Fury swept over his face, and he shook Suyah, who let out a horrifying yelp. "You fool!"

"Please!" I threw my useless hands in the air. "Let her go. I know right where it is. I'll take you. I swear it."

He pressed the dagger harder against her neck. "Where?"

"A certain tree on the riverbank. It's distinctive. I hid it well so I could come back later."

He let out a snarl of frustration. "It had *better* be there or you will regret it."

I would never regret protecting these kind people. And I was beyond grateful that Avi had left when he did, because if he'd been with me today, I was certain his life would already have ended.

"Get the stallion," Nabal called out to the other men. Then he leaned in close again, his stale breath wafting in my face. "You say nothing about where we are going to the others, or I'll deliver you back to Vadim without a tongue. Am I understood?"

Insides trembling, I nodded. Then looked on helplessly as Nabal roughly handed Suyah up to one of the other riders while another man attempted to tie my frantic horse to his saddle. Sarru tossed his head, whinnying and eyes wheeling in fear, but Vadim's brute jerked the reins hard, forcing him to comply.

Nabal raised his voice, loud enough that Rasul and the other boys pinned near the trees by one of the riders could hear. "Anyone follows and the little one dies."

The moment both of us were situated atop his horse, he spun us, mercilessly kicking his animal into a dead run as we left the ululating Rehavites behind in a storm of dust and grief.

Once we were well away from the oasis, Nabal slowed his mount to a trot. "You've been foolish, little girl," he hissed in my ear. "Trying to run and hide. Your father is beside himself."

"My father sold me to a murderer. I had no choice."

He scoffed. "And who is it that you think Vadim has killed?"

"His first wife," I said, "for nothing more than birthing a daughter. And then he killed Imati for helping me."

Nabal barked a laugh, something I'd never heard before from the usually soft-spoken man. "I don't know anything about his first wife, but a man can do with his property what he wishes."

Sickness rolled through me at his callousness.

"As for that slave woman—" his lip curled in distaste—"she's not dead. Even if she should be."

My jaw went slack as I blinked at him in bewilderment. "But . . . I was told that a servant died the night she posed as me in my wedding garb."

"That was one of Vadim's slaves. The fool had been seen talking with her earlier that day and admitted to being a part of the conspiracy to defraud his master of his bride."

Joy rushed through my veins. *Imati still lived?*

However, a sickening thought swiftly overtook my relief. These men had known exactly where I'd fled to. Had they tortured the location out of her? "How did you know where I would go?"

He let out an amused huff. "As soon as I realized that woman had helped you run, I knew where you were. After all, I am the one who bought her in the first place."

I felt the revelation like a javelin to the chest. "*You?*"

He shrugged. "I was traveling to Heshbon, taking horses to a buyer there, and came across a group of Moabites leading slaves up to Damascus. The others were half dead and of no use to me. But Imati was beautiful, even as a child. I knew she'd fetch a great price. If only I'd been wise enough to not bring her back to Kamon first. Your grandfather was still chief then, and he insisted I give her to Chava as a wedding present. I could've gotten a fortune for her at one of the Canaanite temples or sold her myself to any number of willing customers."

My stomach churned at his bloodless explanation. No wonder I'd always sensed that Nabal despised me—he'd felt cheated of the profit he could have made off Imati's body all these years. And I, as her offspring, was only of value to him until there was restitution in the form of those bridal gifts in his greedy hands. How did my father not see that his cousin, the man he trusted implicitly, was so malicious and conniving?

"Perhaps I'll even take her off your father's hands, once he tires of having her locked away," he mused. "She'll still fetch a fair price." He pulled his horse to a halt. "Now," he said. "Do I have any reason to think that you will try to escape?"

I shook my head. I would lead these men as far away from the Rehavites as I could before revealing the truth.

"Good." He called to the man carrying Suyah, instructing him to put her down.

Once on the ground, my little cousin stood shaking from head to toe as she looked up at me with huge, watery eyes. It was all I could do to remain in place, desperate as I was to jump down and comfort her.

"Listen to me," he said to the child, his tone menacing. "You'll stay here behind these rocks." He gestured with his dagger to a group of boulders nearby. "And you will count your fingers and toes a hundred times before you start walking back. Or I will kill Keziah." He pressed the dagger into my ribs. "Understand?"

Suyah nodded, a river of tears flowing down her cheeks.

"Good girl," he said with mocking condescension. Then he grabbed my chin and forced me to look into his dead gray eyes. "And you don't bother trying anything foolish, or I will come back here and slit that girl's throat."

My pulsed thrashed as he smiled with malevolence. "I never forget a face. Ever."

28

Avidan

I'd never seen anything in my life like the city of Heshbon. Located near a crossroad on the King's Highway and perched atop one of the many verdant green hills that filled this region, the city was canopied by a thick mist as we approached, its high walls a reminder of the ancient King Sihon who had built it. And yet its valuable and strategic position also brought to mind the ancient Hebrews who had, under Yehoshua, toppled the famed king of the Amorites and captured the vast territory he'd wrested from the Moabites decades before.

A series of wide pools lay beside the road leading up to the city gates, so clear that one could see all the way to their rocky depths and catch the glimmer of silvery fish darting about far below the surface. An assortment of people lined their edges, collecting water, watering animals, or dropping baited lines or nets to catch their meals. How the landlocked pools were even stocked with fish with the Heshbon River a distance away was a mystery.

Zakir offered to remain behind with the camels by one of the pools to give them a chance to drink their fill and nibble at the ample grasses at the edge. Once the beasts were hobbled and se-cure, he settled on the ground nearby, his back against a rock and his arms folded behind his head. "Make certain you bring me back some of those stuffed figs from the stall beside the temple," he said with a wink. "I'll be hungry after guarding the camels so diligently."

His cousin Estal playfully toed him in the backside. "When are you not hungry, Zakir? You're a bottomless pit."

Zakir grabbed Estal's ankle and tugged, nearly pulling him over. They began scuffling and trading harmless insults. Their antics brought Zevi and Gavriel to mind. No matter that I was still wounded by their abandonment, I missed them too. I doubted the three of us would ever again play around together the way Keziah's cousins did. Because even if I did find Shay, the horrors of that battle had set fire to whatever remained of the innocence of our youth.

Once Omar commanded the two to cease their idiocy, we made our way into the city, where the impressive walls kept watch over a vast marketplace, bigger than any I'd ever seen. Even though rain continued to drizzle on the teeming masses of traders, travelers, and merchants, the market buzzed with life. Somewhere here, among all this chaos, could be the clue that led me to Shay. I should have felt invigorated now that my search for my cousin had recommenced, especially after the detour to Har Nebo, but instead I could not get the dream I'd had the last two nights out of my head.

Since Yavesh, I'd not slept a night without being on the battlefield in my dreams. The blood. The sightless eyes. The smell . . . All of it was so real that at times I woke choking on the stench of burial fires. And each time I'd opened my eyes before we found the Rehavites, I'd seen Keziah an arm's length away, breathing softly and evenly, and somehow her comforting spirit—even in repose—had calmed me enough to sleep again.

Not only had the last two night's dreams been different, but when I'd awakened, breathless and aching for her soothing presence, I had nothing to keep me company except the endless black sky above, vivid memories of the terrifying dream, and my growing regrets for leaving her behind.

Even now as I followed Omar and the others through the marketplace, the dream played like a vision in my head, drowning out the chatter of commerce around me.

Keziah and I had been on Sarru's back, the warm sun on our shoulders, laughing about something when a great bird, some huge black thing, swooped down, just as the kestrel had. It tangled its mighty claws in her hair, then ripped her off the horse and out of my reach before lifting into the sky as I screamed her name over and over.

I'd awakened both nights certain I'd made the wrong decision to leave her, my body screaming to turn around and return to the mountain, to make certain she was safe and claim her for myself. And yet, how could I tell the men who'd escorted me to Heshbon that I'd changed my mind or that I did not trust their kinsmen to keep Keziah from harm? The indecision plagued me hour upon hour as we bumped along on camelback, and I'd kept my lips sealed, but even so, I could not shake the foreboding.

With well-wishes that I might find evidence of my cousin, Omar and the others took their leave of me, their arms laden with bags full of cheese, fine wool made by the Rehavite women in their unique patterns, ibex horns, and wild honey they'd harvested from a remote cave high on the mountain. These goods they hoped to trade for grain, which was one of the supplies they could not procure by themselves in the wilderness.

I forced myself to push aside my worries over Keziah and meandered through the market, inquiring of as many people as I could whether they'd seen a boy with a silver streak in his hair. I received little more than disinterested shrugs, shaking heads, and lewd offers from prostitutes.

From Samuel's teaching, I recognized Heshbon as yet another Levitical town designated by Yehoshua. But nothing about this place harkened back to its ancient roots. Indeed, there was such a variety of people with all hues of skin tones and nearly as many languages that it hardly seemed Hebrew at all. A result, I guessed, of the countless decades it sat on the King's Highway and the thousands upon thousands of people who streamed through its gates every year. More than a few had settled here, it seemed.

I did not see one priest or Levite, and neither were there any indications that Yahweh was worshipped here at all. Instead, like Yazer, there were plenty of merchant tables with idols and altars to various gods and goddesses throughout the city. And just as when I was in Yazer, I felt an inexplicably heavy burden for the Hebrews within Heshbon's walls. Did they even know who the God was who brought their ancestors out from Egypt and into this good land?

Although most of the market stalls had canopies strung over their wares, rain dripped off my hair and down my neck. It did not matter. Like everyone else, I was drenched. Here, the exchange of goods did not cease for the rain. Neither did the trade of rumors, since I heard more than a few talking about King Saul and his "timid army" who'd been too afraid to go all the way to Rabbah and finish off what remained of the Ammonites.

In fact, I learned that Saul and his men had already retreated back to the west side of the Jordan. Perhaps Zevi and Gavi were already back home in Naioth, telling our family how completely I'd failed them all.

After hours of finding no trace of my cousin, I was forced to admit that he must have gone north with the traders after all. Perhaps to Damascus or further into Mesopotamia.

I hunched my shoulders against the rain and walked back toward the pools. As much as I wished I could return with the Rehavites and claim the piece of my heart that was missing, I should instead find a caravan going north and continue my search.

The camels were folded on the ground, chewing their cud, eyes closed against the rain. Zakir was nearby, talking with two boys about his age as they pulled a small net from the water.

When he caught sight of me, he waved, gesturing excitedly for me to hurry toward him. "Avi!" he shouted when I was within twenty paces. "I think I know where your cousin might be! Hurry!"

I jogged the rest of the distance and met the three young men beside the pool. When I arrived, breathless, I realized Zakir's new friends were twins, both tall and lanky but much younger than I'd guessed.

"Tell him," said Zakir to his companions. "Tell him what you told me."

"When your friend here told us you were looking for a boy traveling with some traders, I remembered something. It was about, oh . . . What do you say, Simi? Four days ago?"

His twin nodded, and my heart began to pound.

"Yes, I remember," said the boy. "Because it was before this rain started up. Anyway, we were fishing like we do every day, and there was a large caravan here, headed east. I remember that because they were driving a herd of mules to Babylon. I've never seen so many mules in my life, of all colors and sizes. Don't know how they made those stubborn things move—"

I interrupted, sensing that the boy had forgotten the original path of this conversation. "So my cousin is going east?"

"No. The caravan was, but we saw this boy, standing at the edge of this very pool. He was just staring at the water for the longest time. I asked him if he wanted to use our nets to fish, but he didn't even answer. I thought perhaps he didn't speak our language or there was something wrong with his ears because he only glanced at us for a moment and then just kept staring at the water. It was the oddest thing—"

"He was with some traders. Phoenicians, perhaps?" interjected his twin, likely used to cutting in on his verbose brother.

"What did he look like? Did he have a silver streak in his hair?"

The first boy shrugged. "Not sure. His head was covered. But his face was scratched up."

"Didn't you say your cousin was attacked by animals?" Zakir interjected, his tone pitched high with excitement. "The scratches would make sense."

I gestured to the place above my right eye where Shay had bled so profusely back in our childhood, the first time I'd failed him. "Was there a scar on his eyebrow?"

He nodded. "Like it had been sliced through with a knife. He had this odd, faraway look in his eyes too. Like he wasn't sure his feet were even on the ground."

My pulse went wild. It *had* to be Shalem. The scar was too distinctive, and if he'd fallen from the ridge like we guessed then perhaps his head was still a bit muddled. I'd seen one man after the victory at Yavesh who'd been struck by a blow to the head with an Ammonite mace. The poor man had babbled drooling nonsense as his kinsmen carried him off the battlefield. I hoped whatever had happened to Shay had not damaged his keen mind permanently. "Where were they heading?"

"South? Perhaps. Or maybe southeast? We didn't think to ask."

My mind raced. My cousin had been in this very place less than a week ago. There were countless destinations south of here and who knew how many roads branched off of the main one along the way, but at least I'd not been far off course because of my detour with Keziah. If anything, it was fortunate I'd come here with her cousins or I'd more than likely have missed coming across these two boys. Perhaps a divine hand had even guided me to this very place and at the perfect time.

"I need to follow after him," I said. "Do you know of anyone who is going that way today?"

The boys did indeed know of a group heading through Moabite territory, and promised to take me to their leader as soon as I parted ways with the Rehavites.

Perhaps Shay and I would be making our way back home soon.

Omar and the others returned shortly, and I filled them in on what I had learned about my cousin.

"Thank you," I said to Omar, "for bringing me here. I would have missed him completely otherwise."

"It is our pleasure, my friend," he replied. "We have enjoyed getting to know you. You are always welcome in our tents. And do not fear for Keziah. We will take good care of her."

My throat went tight as I nodded my thanks. Now that I had an actual lead on where Shalem might be, I had to let go of her.

Trust that her kinsmen would keep her safe and refuse to let the images of that giant bird carrying her into the heavens cling to me. She was where she needed to be, for now. Perhaps someday, after I'd delivered my cousin back to his parents, I could return to the mountain and see if she—

The ground shook, startling me out of my hopeful musings, and both Omar and I turned to find a line of camels racing toward us. Rasul, one of Keziah's cousins, was in the lead of a group of Rehavites, which included Naveed, who'd remained back at the mountain camp. The young man halted his animal a few paces away and vaulted from his perch, breathing hard and looking just as sweaty and dust-covered as his camel. They must have raced all the way to Heshbon.

"She's gone," he said without preamble.

My blood went ice cold. It could only be Keziah he spoke of.

"What do you mean? Gone where?"

He shook his head, his eyes full of remorse as he relayed the story of the ambush at the oasis and Keziah's abduction. "I'm so sorry, Avidan. The patrols had seen nothing of those horsemen for days. We should have been more on our guard. Had lookouts. They attacked while Gassan, Tannir, and I were up in the trees, and they surrounded the women before we could react, then took Keziah and Suyah with them."

And I never should have left her behind in the first place. No wonder I'd been hounded by that dream. "When did this happen?"

"Yesterday afternoon," he said. "We searched all around the mountain and the valley. We found little Suyah, who said the bad men took Keziah north. But it rained hard last night, so any hoof-prints we could have followed were washed away. We set out for here at dawn, hoping you might know where they took her. One of the women said she mentioned the Jabbok River."

"The Jabbok?"

He shrugged. "Something about a missing reward Keziah buried by a tree?"

With a groan, I dug my fingers into my hair. What had she done? Why would she lie to these men about the treasure we'd left on the riverbank?

Sickness roiled in my stomach as I stared into the distance. "I know where they've taken her."

Of course I could leave the pursuit of Keziah to her family. Direct them to the place we'd crossed the Jabbok and trust they would do their best to find her, but I had vowed to keep her safe. To not leave her alone.

And yet, finally, after so much searching, I had proof Shay was alive and knew which direction to pursue him.

If I'd been cleaved in two back on the battlefield, I could not feel more divided. Nearly every time I had made a decision lately, I'd failed or caused destruction. Either way, I would be leaving someone behind. Leaving them to an uncertain fate. And I could not stomach the thought of either Keziah or Shay suffering because of my lack of wisdom.

However, I did know of One whose entire being was wisdom itself. The One who had known Keziah and Shalem before their first breaths. The One who watched over their every step—and my own as well, even when I rebelliously chose my own way.

I closed my eyes, ignoring the sound of the crowd around the pools, the huffs of the impatient camels, and the urgency I could feel coming off the Rehavites like rolls of thunder, and pleaded with the God Who Sees for the answer to where I should go, and for the first time trusted that he would direct me to the right path.

As if the chief of the Rehavites himself was standing before me, I suddenly heard Qadir's admonition from the top of the mountain in my mind. *"Perhaps that time of exile was what was best for him . . . Only Yahweh knows the end from the beginning."*

Like a warm tide lapping at my shins, growing ever stronger, came a rising flood of peace like I'd never known before, and a conviction washed over me that I could not ignore.

Shalem may be young but at fifteen he was, by our traditions, a man. One whose path may be unknown to me but indeed not to Adonai. He was alive, I felt it in my bones. And, from what the twins said, he did not seem to be in any imminent danger.

Keziah, however, was a vulnerable young woman, alone and with men whose intentions were anything but honorable. I never should've left her behind in the first place. She was far too precious. When I found her, I would never leave her again.

Firm in my decision, I opened my eyes and sought out Omar.

I gestured to the camels. "I've seen how fast those things can run, but how far can they go without stopping? The Jabbok is at least a day's ride from here."

Omar traded weighty glances with Naveed before giving me a fatherly nod that communicated their collective satisfaction with my unspoken decision. "Let's put them to the test, shall we?"

29

Keziah

The last time I'd approached the Jabbok River, I was seated on my stallion with Avi at my back, his reassuring warmth surrounding me and his low voice telling me of the steadfast love of Yahweh for his people. The day had been bright and the sound of the flowing water cheerful as it rushed toward the Jordan River Valley.

But this time clouds hung low in the sky, turning the river to iron gray, and I was being led by the arm toward the riverbank by my father's cousin, dreading the outcome of my lie. I could only hope that I'd taken Nabal so far away from the Rehavite camp that he would not bother to return once he'd cut me down. Perhaps, if I was truly fortunate, he'd only beat me and return me to Vadim.

The other men waited for us twenty paces away with the horses, where Nabal had instructed me to dismount. But the looks that passed around the group made it clear they were suspicious about why we'd left the King's Highway after crossing the stone bridge over the Jabbok and turned west to follow the river's course for a couple of hours. They were all just as twitchy and restless as their mounts, but none of them questioned Nabal's authority.

I'd heard one mutter something about collecting his reward and fleetingly wondered if Vadim had promised something for the return of his rebel bride or if my father actually cared about his wayward daughter. Either way, any promised reward had to be far less than the glittering trove stashed in that saddle. My father's cousin would be merciless.

Nabal yanked at my arm, causing me to stumble as we approached the water's edge. This was the exact place Avi and I had plunged into the rushing river to escape the Ammonites, I was sure of it.

"Well?" Nabal pressed, pinching his fingers into my skin. "Where is it?"

I took a deep breath and thought of Avi's face as he tilted his head back to laugh, of his beautiful voice telling stories, and the way he'd watched me while I'd danced the other night under the stars. I thought of sweet little Suyah and the Rehavites who'd been so kind to me, and I did not regret my deception.

"Rabbah, I would assume," I said.

"What?" he barked, his face going a shade of mottled red I'd never seen before. "You said it was here under a tree."

"Yes, it was. But that is because my travel companion threw it at the Ammonites so they would leave us alone. It's gone."

He cursed, calling me the filthiest names I'd ever heard, and then shook me until everything became a blur. "That was mine!" he bellowed. "*My* reward for putting up with my *fool* of a cousin all these years! *My* reward for brokering the deal *you* destroyed by running off!" More filth spewed from his mouth as my mind sifted through his admissions.

I'd assumed it had been Imati who'd had the wedding gifts hidden beneath the saddle as another way of providing for me, but they must have been there because Nabal stole them from my father's treasury. And if he'd hidden his spoils on Sarru's back, did that mean Vadim had promised him my horse as well, since he'd been included in the dowry?

Between Nabal shaking me like a rabbit in a dog's teeth and

my spinning thoughts, I did not see the other men surrounding us until one of them tried to pull me out of Nabal's hold.

"Let go!" he shouted at Nabal. "She's worth nothing dead. You're going to break her neck!"

"I'll do worse than that!" my father's cousin bellowed, his eyes seeming to bulge from his florid face. Just as the other man freed me from his grip, Nabal's fist slammed into the side of my face so hard my head whipped back against the man's shoulder. Everything went dark.

It was well before dawn, and I remained shivering on the sand where I'd fallen, my eye swollen shut and the side of my face from my forehead to my jaw throbbing and tender. None of the men had spoken to me as they prepared camp, hobbling the horses nearby and then lying on the sand around me on all sides. But neither did they talk much to one another. There was a distinct undercurrent of mistrust toward Nabal as they decided who would take the first watch and settled into sleep. One of them was now on guard, seated on a log with his back to me and his eyes roving the blackness.

Nabal slept nearby with his head pillowed on his folded-up cloak. He'd not even given me a glance since I'd come to. With as murderous as his expression had been, I was surprised he hadn't tried to hit me again, even once the other men got involved. Something they said while I was unconscious must have gotten through. Perhaps I would survive after all, at least long enough to endure whatever punishment Vadim had in store for me.

I was not certain whether I could believe Nabal was telling the truth about Imati being alive. But if she was, I hoped that I might have just a brief moment to tell her about this journey she'd sent me on. Without her, I never would have found the Rehavites. Never known what it was like to love a man like I did Avi or hear stories that so profoundly changed the way I saw the God of my ancestors.

No longer did I fear the one who had crushed Egypt. I now understood how he offered mercy and protection to those who called on his name, guidance to those who sought his wisdom, and steadfast love to all of humankind from the very beginning. And if Yahweh heard the cries of Hagar the Egyptian, Rahab the Canaanite, and Eliora the Philistine, then surely he would hear me—a descendent of Mosheh himself—wouldn't he?

And yet I still felt unworthy to ask anything on my own behalf. I'd only lifted such prayers to the goddess I wore around my neck. The necklace I'd once cherished now seemed nothing more than a piece of stone carved by human hands, not a powerful talisman or connection to a heavenly deity. In fact, as I lay listening to the shush of the Jabbok hurrying along toward its union with the Jordan, the gentle sounds of the horses breathing in the cool predawn air, and a lone night bird singing his farewell to the last of the stars, it felt like a burden instead of a precious heirloom from my mother.

In all of Avi's stories about the God who created everything, who chose our people as a special treasure among the nations, and who offered grace after grace in his Torah, there was never a mention of a wife. Never an indication that Yahweh had any need of a consort or indeed whether there was any among the gods and goddesses who could ever be his equal. As I searched the vast heavens, brilliant with myriad stars, I decided I could no longer worship any god but the one whose Word alone breathed all life into existence.

Grateful that the darkness would hide my movements, I slowly reached inside my neckline and slipped the amulet over my head, the first time I'd taken it off since my mother had died.

I wrapped my fingers around it one last time, a good-bye not to the idol but to the woman I'd called Ima. Chava may not have given birth to me, but I'd loved her and knew she'd loved me.

Using the edge of the talisman, I dug a small hole in the sand beside me, laid the necklace inside, covered it, and patted the mound down for good measure. The action felt strangely freeing.

Perhaps the leather strap that held the goddess around my neck had not been simply a decoration but a tether.

My task complete, I lay still again, watching the sky turn from black to deepest sapphire, and lifted a prayer to the one Avi called the God Who Hears.

Help him find who he seeks, I pled. *And usher him safely back to the ones who love him. And if it be your will, let me live to praise your name.*

From somewhere close by, one of the horses nickered and was answered by another, sounding agitated. But although I held my breath and listened intently, I heard nothing but the sounds of impending dawn.

Then a gasp broke through the stillness, and I turned my head toward the sound. The man who'd been on watch was gasping for air. His body jerked forward, and he landed face down in the sand, just as a second moan of distress came from another man closer to the river. Even in the dim light I could clearly see the outline of an arrow shaft protruding from his neck.

His body twitched and then went still. Nabal and the rest of the men were on their feet, daggers in hand and searching the lingering blackness beyond our makeshift camp for whoever had attacked. I curled into a ball, trying to make myself as small as possible. I had nowhere to go except to the river, and I'd already nearly drowned in the Jabbok. I knew its currents and hidden rocks were treacherous.

"Where are they?" Nabal snapped. "How many are there?"

"Don't know," said another man, posture stiff and eyes on the black tree line past the beach. "The arrows came from different directions. I think we are surrounded. Could be two, could be twenty."

A shout came from the brush to the south of us from somewhere within that blackness, and the men turned toward the sound. At the same time, two indistinguishable figures surged toward us, one from the east and one from the west, arrows nocked on bows.

Arrows flew, but Vadim's men spun away, managing to dodge

the missiles. A few more shadowy figures emerged from the trees as the first men dropped their bows and withdrew daggers, never letting up their stride. Dawn had not yet broken over the distant hills, and even though the sky had lightened, I could not make out what sort of enemy had appeared, nor how many were converging on us. Surely the Ammonites who had chased Avi and me were not still in the area?

I did not wait to find out. Sarru was hobbled with the other horses about fifteen paces away near the water. Since my captors were now occupied with their attackers, I did not hesitate to run for him.

With practiced motions, I untied his hobble and then I swiftly did the same for the other horses as well, hoping they would spook and run. From the corner of my eye, I saw one of the attackers go down in the sand, struck in the chest by a blow from Nabal.

Pulse racing, I yelled and flailed my arms, which made the horses scatter in all directions. Nabal bellowed for me to stay put, barreling toward me, and I grabbed hold of Sarru's reins and vaulted into the saddle. Before I spun him around to flee, one of the attackers grabbed the back of Nabal's tunic and whirled him around, throwing my father's cousin off-balance even as he swiped his dagger toward the man.

At this moment, the sun broke over the horizon and a shaft of sunlight pierced the gloom, finally illuminating the melee on the beach. Naveed, Omar, Rasul, and a few other Rehavites were fighting what remained of Vadim's men, and standing opposite Nabal, with a dagger in hand, was the man I loved.

His name flew from my mouth before I could think better of it. Avi's attention went to me for the briefest of moments, but it was just long enough for Nabal to take advantage and knock him backward, his weapon positioned directly at Avi's throat.

My entire world narrowed down to the tip of that dagger.

Nabal snatched Avi's weapon and pressed it to his ribs—one wrong move and either his throat or heart would be pierced through.

"No, Nabal! Please don't hurt him!" I shouted, bringing Sarru closer as the rest of the men continued to struggle on the beach.

"Stay back," Nabal said. "Or I'll kill him."

"Please. It's me you want. Let him go."

"I want my reward," he sneered. "But you robbed me of what was my due."

"We had no choice," I said. "The Ammonites would've killed us and taken it anyhow. There's nothing to do about it now. If I had a cache of gold to give you, I would."

"*Someone* will pay for what I lost. I'll start with him and then I'm coming for you." He pressed the dagger farther into Avi's skin, making him hiss in pain.

An idea occurred to me. One that made me both violently ill and vastly relieved because I *did* have something of worth to offer Nabal, something far more valuable than gold. Something that would make him as rich as my father someday, which is what I suspected had been his true goal. The words shredded my throat as they emerged, but I spoke them anyhow.

"Take Sarru," I said, my eyes still pinned to the place Nabal held the blade to Avi's throat, a line of crimson trickling down his precious neck.

"Keziah, no!" Avi rasped, but I ignored him.

"You know that he is priceless as a stud, Nabal. People bring their mares from all over the region to breed with him. I cannot replace the bridal gifts, but I can offer you the means to build a fortune that will far surpass it. But you have to let Avi go. Otherwise, you'll never see either one of us again. You have no mount to chase me." I gestured toward the empty beach behind me. At least I'd succeeded in letting the rest of the horses free.

Nabal let out a curse as he saw the truth of his situation. He had only one choice that made any sense and it was not killing Avi. The Rehavites had already nearly bested the rest of Vadim's men anyhow. It was his only chance to flee.

"Go and find a new place to breed him. Build your own wealth. Because I don't think Vadim will forgive your failure to retrieve his *property*"—I gestured to myself—"or the loss of so many of his men."

I kept my gaze steady on him. His eyes flicked to Rasul, who was standing a few paces away, bow in hand and an arrow nocked, even though his tunic was bloody and he looked pale as death. Nabal had to know that if he hurt Avi, my cousin would finish him.

"Get off the horse," he snapped.

I could not help the tears that slipped down my face as I swung my leg over Sarru's back for the last time. I slid down his side, landing on the sand, then went to wrap my arm around his muzzle as I had thousands of times before. My horse leaned into me, his warmth and familiar smell making my heart bleed as he huffed in my ear.

"I'm sorry. Thank you for being my friend," I whispered, then kissed his velvet cheek one more time.

"Release Avidan," I said, as I slowly led Sarru toward Nabal. "Then I will hand you the reins."

His eyes darted back and forth between me, the horse, and Rasul. As I approached, I lifted a staying palm to my cousin, worried that if he let an arrow fly it might hit Sarru or Avi, and I would not risk either of them. As soon as I was within reach, Nabal released Avi to grab for the reins and darted away with a confused Sarru in tow.

Shaking, I watched Nabal attempt to mount my beautiful stallion. Sarru skittered sideways, head bobbing and making a shrill call at the stranger trying to climb onto his back. Nabal snarled curses at Sarru and yanked the reins hard, then roughly maneuvered himself astride.

Then with a violent kick to poor Sarru's sides, he galloped off toward the King's Highway. Before I could catch my breath or blink away the hot tears that blurred my last glimpse of what was once my only friend in the world, they had disappeared into the glare of the sunrise breaking over the distant hills.

A sob broke free, and my knees buckled, but before I hit the sand, strong arms enveloped me. One of Avi's hands tangled in my curls as he held me so close that I could feel his heartbeat pounding in my ear, his other hand brushing a soothing path up and down my back. Somehow, I felt both shattered to pieces and completely whole in one moment.

Finally, I looked up to find his green eyes brilliant with tears.

"You came for me," I whispered.

His gaze traveled over my face, dropped to my lips for a heart-stopping moment, and then lifted to mine again. "I promised I would never leave you alone."

"Will Rasul be all right?" I asked Avi when he finally settled beside me on the beach where I'd been staring into the flames of the fire.

He scrubbed his hands to warm them. He'd washed blood from his skin in the frigid river after helping the others deal with the bodies of Vadim's men. "He'll be fine. One of the men cauterized the wound."

I winced at the thought of scalding metal meeting tender flesh. "No wonder he moaned so loud."

"He's very brave. I'm certain I would have made a lot more noise."

I leaned into him, laying my cheek against his arm. "I cannot believe Zakir is gone. Because of me."

The young man had been the only one of the Rehavites to fall, although there were a few minor injuries besides Rasul's. I'd wept as I watched Omar wrap his nephew in a blanket and the men dig a grave in a flat area beneath the trees.

"It is not your fault, Keziah," he said, wrapping his long arms around me. "Zakir chose to come to your rescue. He knew the risks. We all did. And he died valiantly in service of his family."

I pressed my face into the reassuring warmth of his chest and sniffed back tears. "I am still shocked that the Rehavites came all this way for me. That *you* left off the search for Shalem for my sake."

"You are a daughter of this clan, just as much as Imati was. And it is far past time for me to submit my life—and Shay's—to the wisdom of the Eternal One," he said, his deep voice rumbling against my ear. "He would not be lost in the first place if I had honored both the Torah and my father. I can only be grateful Yahweh used my folly to bring me to you."

I pulled back to gaze up at him, astounded at the adoration I heard in his voice. "But you need to—"

"I *need* to be with you, Keziah." He curved his hands around my face, and I savored the feel of his rough palms on my skin. "Don't you understand?" he whispered, then leaned forward to place the gentlest of kisses on my bruised cheek. "I am yours. Always." He kissed my other cheek, allowing his lips to linger for a few heady moments.

Then he gathered me into his arms again and held me tight. "I never should have left you in the first place. Should have turned around when even in my dreams I could hear you calling my name. The farther I traveled from your side, the deeper the chasm inside me grew."

My chin trembled as I burrowed into him like I'd wanted to do since the waterfall. "I wasn't sure the pain of missing you would ever go away."

Another kiss landed on my hair as he stroked my back. "Then I propose that from now on, we remain together, no matter where Adonai leads us."

I could think of nothing I wanted more, except I doubted he would be thrilled at where I wanted to go from here. Reluctantly, I looked up into his eyes, lifting a silent prayer to Yahweh that Avi's love ran deep enough to grant my request.

"I have to go back to Kamon."

He stared down at me for a few breathless moments, brows furrowed. "Why?"

"I think Imati might be alive," I blurted. "And if she is, I must help her get free."

"My aunt is alive?" Omar's voice at my back startled me into pulling out of Avi's embrace, my cheeks going warm at being caught tangled together.

But Omar simply waited for me to explain, arms folded over his chest, while the rest of the Rehavites gathered around us.

I cleared my throat. "Nabal—the man who took me—said it was not she who was killed that night. It was another slave who'd helped her plan my flight from Kamon. She's imprisoned somewhere in my father's house. I have to help her escape."

"You aren't going anywhere near Kamon," said Avi. "They are obviously still looking for you. If anyone is going to find Imati, it's me."

"Or me," said Omar and Naveed in tandem.

I shook my head, astounded that they would even consider this. "I'm the only one who knows how to get into that house and knows where she might be kept. None of you could get inside the villa walls without notice, anyhow."

"Well, if there is even a chance Imati is alive, we aren't going back to the mountain without her," said Omar, the authority of a future tribe leader ringing in his voice. "We've already lost one family member today. So, I guess we'll need to plan."

30

Avidan

Dressed in a borrowed tunic with a tattered scarf around her head and with one side of her face black and blue, Keziah looked nothing like the Rehavite beauty she'd been at the mountain. Once again, she was the battered boy she'd been when I met her and, like a dutiful slave, walked behind me with her eyes on the ground.

I, however, strode toward Kamon with all the confidence of a masterful traveling storyteller, whose imminent arrival had been whispered about for the past three days. The fact that those whispers had been set into motion by none other than our shepherd friends from Emeq was a blessing I never could have anticipated when we concocted our plans back on the beach.

However, Raham and his boys had been eager to help us when we showed up in their valley, with a group of Rehavites and their camels in tow, and had even gathered a few others to spread rumors in the marketplace.

Omar, Naveed, and the other Rehavites were already here, posing as travelers lounging about at the tavern and waiting for night to fall, while Keziah and I laid the foundations for the next steps of our scheme.

Three men met us on the last stretch of road up to Kamon, ones I was certain by the look of them were some of Vadim's. I arranged a wide grin on my face and lifted a palm of greeting as I neared. "Shalom, my friends!"

They stared at me with varying degrees of suspicion as I approached, and the eldest among them stepped into my path. "What's your business here?"

"Nothing of importance. Only passing through. Perhaps will do a little trade while I'm here."

The man looked me up and down, focusing on my empty hands. "And what do you have to trade?"

I let my knowing grin spread slowly. "Something worth far more than a purse full of silver, I assure you. I trade in *stories*."

He met my declaration with laughter and a wave of dismissal. "Take your tales elsewhere, storyteller!"

"Wait, Gedor," said one of the others, grabbing the man's sleeve. "I think I've heard of this traveling storyteller. They say he's like no other. It's almost as though he can put images directly into your mind with his words."

I had to stifle a groan. It sounded as though the shepherds had taken it upon themselves to exaggerate my skills. I'd have to give a worthy performance.

"I've heard of him too," said the third guard, his eyes round. "I want to hear one."

The eldest one took another scrutinizing look at me. "All right," he conceded with a smug expression. "Go ahead and tell us one of these stories. If you can impress us, then perhaps I'll let you in. If not, be on your way."

"It would be my pleasure," I said, then adjusted my posture, folding my arms and lifting my eyes to the sky as if contemplating what tale I would spin. In truth, I'd conjured it up last night, knowing just what sort of men I needed to make an impression on. I'd apologized to Keziah in advance.

Swallowing down repugnance at my own upcoming words, I launched into a detailed and fairly debauched story about five

276

brothers and their travels to Egypt, which included an accidental association with a pack of thieves and murderers and ended with a visit to one of the most famous brothels in Avaris. Soon, the three men were laughing and elbowing one another at the most repulsive parts, fully enraptured by my every word.

By the time my distasteful story came to a close, my skin was crawling, and I felt as though I needed to scrub my tongue with sand. I'd have to plead Keziah's forgiveness again later and reassure her that such filth would never cross my lips again.

But it worked even better than I'd hoped. Within only a short while, Gedor himself was leading the two of us up the path through town, certain his commander would be fully entertained by one of my stories.

Chancing one quick glance behind me as we passed through the gates of the villa, I caught Keziah's eye, a last silent check of her readiness before the next step in our plan was set into motion. She gave me a little nod of confirmation and bent to fix the strap of a sandal that was not untied at all. When I took another peek behind me, she'd already slipped off into the deepening shadows. *So much boundless courage contained within one small woman.*

Although my heart quaked with fear for her, she was right that her knowledge of this villa was our best weapon. If her mother was here, she would find her location, gauge the difficulty of her release, and then meet Omar and the others at the tavern to pass on the information. Whereas I, with my arsenal of stories, was responsible for the diversion.

The guard led us into the courtyard, where a group of men were gathered for a meal. He took me straight to Vadim in the seat of honor. Menachem, the man I assumed was Keziah's father by the look of his expensive garb, was relegated to a place nearly halfway down the table, a well-earned expression of shame on his face.

Standing before the ruthless man my Keziah was to have married, his piggish eyes like two vacuous pits, my anger toward her father flared hot. How could he be so spineless? So cavalier with his precious daughter?

Curiosity piqued by Gedor's raving over my brilliant tales, Vadim offered me a place at Menachem's table, along with a cup of his fine wine. For Keziah's sake, I swallowed down my wrath at both repugnant men to throw myself into my ruse, regaling them with stories of battles, full of exaggerated details conjured from both my imagination and my own terrible memories of Yavesh.

The more they drank, the louder Vadim's men became, their raucous laughter at my descriptions of torture grating on my nerves. Only Menachem and a younger man, whom Vadim had offhandedly introduced as Lotan, his youngest son, remained impassive. Keziah's father looked as though he would rather be anywhere but at his own table, and Lotan drank cup after cup of wine, looking miserable and bored.

Once the sun had fully set, I prayed that Keziah had been given enough time to search out Imati, then I feigned giving in to the group's plea for yet another tale before launching into the one I actually wanted to tell.

My part in this rescue plan was not to charge in and cut down the enemies of the woman I loved. But as I lay beside her on the ground in our camp last night on the shepherds' land, with the flicker of firelight caressing her precious, bruised face, I'd been strongly convicted that I *could* fight for her with my words. I could wield truth against men whose evil desires and selfish motives had put her in harm's way. And I would pray that Yahweh might somehow use my efforts to protect her in a way I could not, just as I trusted he would watch over Shalem, wherever he was, and perhaps even guide him home someday.

Hoping that he would notice my pointed stare in his direction, I waited for Keziah's father to look straight at me and then held his eyes as I began.

"There was a man of old—perhaps you've heard his name? His history is as familiar as your own. This man lived in the land of Ur, where towers stretched to the heavens in glorious magnificence and the array of gods worshipped at their peaks numbered as many as the stars in the sky.

"This man was born to a craftsman, whose vast wealth came from skill in depicting those many gods in vivid relief with stone and wood and precious gems. But this man, who was called by the name Avram, found no wisdom among the carvings on his father's market table and no peace from raising supplications to deaf gods. Instead, Avram sought the voice of the Ancient One worshipped by his great-grandfather, who regaled him with tales of the fallen ones of old, of the floodwaters that covered the earth, and the vessel upon which a remnant of life was saved by the mercy of the God above all gods."

I paused for only a moment, gratified that although my audience was confused by the shifting tone of my stories, I still held their attention.

"When the Voice he had been seeking in the stillness urged him to embark on a journey to an unknown land, Avram broke with his father and his father's gods and obeyed, setting his sandals toward the unknown, firm in his conviction that the Voice had the answers to every question he could imagine.

"However, along the way he forgot to heed the Voice and found himself in Egypt, where Pharaoh coveted his wealth. In an act of pure cowardice, and to preserve both his riches and his own neck, he sacrificed what should've been most precious—his beautiful wife—offering her to the king of Egypt with a half-truth about who she was to him. The deception nearly cost him everything. He barely escaped Egypt with his life, and with the woman Elohim had given him to cherish and protect—the one who would someday be the mother of nations."

A host of bewildered expressions met my survey of the table, but I did not care because this story and the next were for one man.

"Sometime later, Avram and his nephew parted ways, dividing the land between them. Avram took the hill country to the west, but his nephew, Lot, chose the more fertile area to the east, where five great cities stood, known for every sort of vice one can imagine."

At this description, some of my listeners perked up, thinking I would expand on the repugnant things these ancient cities celebrated.

"For many years, Avram's nephew lived in one of those decadent cities, his wealth expanding day by day, his reputation as a man of power and influence soaring, as the echo of the Voice his uncle revered grew fainter and fainter. Until, that is, Elohim sent two of his special messengers to inform Lot that the city he lived in and those around it were to be destroyed. Not by sword or chariot but by fire from heaven itself.

"Suddenly, a horde of repugnant men surrounded Lot's house, beating on the doors and windows and insisting he send out the messengers so they could assault them in the most heinous of ways."

Eyes flared at the direction my story had taken, but I kept my gaze trained on Keziah's father.

"And what did Avram's nephew do? Did he call on the Most High to rescue his family and his otherworldly guests? No. Lot was a coward, just like Avram had been in Egypt. He caved to his fears and offered up what should have been most precious to him."

I paused and hardened my gaze on Menachem. Then I infused my words with every bit of disgust I held for his contemptible actions.

"His *daughters*."

To my satisfaction, Menachem flinched, his jaw dropping slightly, and even though the sun had set and only the flicker of the lamps on the table illuminated his face, he seemed to pale.

"If the messengers had not struck the men of that horrible city blind, Lot would have allowed his beautiful daughters to be torn to pieces because he valued his *own* comfort and security above the ones entrusted to his care. What followed was beyond imagining, a cataclysm without rival, a curse on the Land that remains to this day, and generations of fear, hatred, and bloodshed. All because of one man's cowardly decisions and refusal to bow his knee to the true King of the Universe."

I let the accusation hang in the air, still refusing to release Menachem from my pointed glare. The man deserved to squirm, deserved to swim in an ocean of shame.

But at the same time, I felt the weight of my own words. Because had I not tried to be my own king as well? Had I not placed my own selfish desires above my sacred duties to Yahweh? I too had much to repent for, both to my earthly father and the one who'd created me, a son of Levi, to fight for his people with the truth. For without that truth, and the clear understanding of both their identity and their God, how would Israel stave off the many enemies that crouched at our door? Unless we turned our faces fully toward Yahweh, we would continue to bow our knees to worthless idols and open the gates to the Enemy himself.

Realizing I'd been silent far too long while caught up in self-revelation and my audience was regarding me with increasing confusion, I made a show of emptying my wine cup in one gulp and releasing a satisfied belch. It was my job to keep Vadim and his men occupied for as long as possible so Keziah could find Imati and the Rehavites could retrieve her. So, until the signal was given that they'd been successful in their rescue attempts and I could take my leave of these unworthy men who'd used Keziah for their own selfish gain, I would swallow down my revulsion and keep them entertained.

"Now, my friends," I said, with as much flourish as I could muster, "have you ever heard of the Champion of Ashdod, who mercilessly crushed rivals both on the fighting grounds and off?"

I paused to cast a questioning look around the table, encouraged that the gleam of interest had once again sparked in Vadim's eyes, even if Lotan was now fully passed out on the table, looking as though he'd drunk more than all his father's lackeys combined.

However, Menachem remained preoccupied, his gaze cast down and a frown on his weary face. Perhaps my subtle chastisement had affected him after all.

I leaned forward, tone laden with the promise of an enticing tale, and grinned at my rapt audience. "Then let me tell you of the Philistine worshipped as a god among men, whom women lusted after and whose bare-knuckled matches were the stuff of legend. The one they called Demon Eyes . . ."

Keziah

The sandals Imati had given me the last time I'd been in this house scuffled on the stone steps that led to the upper level, the papyrus fibers no longer abrasive against my soles but perfectly molded to my feet after so many days of wear.

It had been surprisingly easy to steal through the shadowed outer courtyard of my father's villa, around the back of the stables that I refused to look at for the sake of my broken heart, and then into the house itself.

I'd barely even needed the jug of water I carried as a reason for a young slave to be entering the master's house. Although there'd been a few of Vadim's men about, most were either occupied with drink and dice games or, in the case of one reckless fellow with a tuft of greasy hair protruding from under his bronze helmet, snoring against the wall not far from the back entrance he should be guarding. The rest must be listening to Avi's stories in the inner courtyard.

In fact, I had not recognized any of my father's household servants at all when I'd swiped the water jug from the kitchen, and I wondered if Vadim had replaced those who'd been loyal to our family for so many years. Perhaps he'd even used Imati's deception as an excuse for doing so.

Whatever the reason, it made breaking into my own home far easier, and for that I was immensely grateful. I'd already searched the two lower levels, which were mostly cast in darkness, holding my breath as I slipped from empty room to empty room but finding nothing more than eerie silence and echoes of my lonely childhood. I did not even see evidence of my older brothers and wondered if they were part of the revelry below.

A chorus of drunken laughter wafted up from the inner courtyard and the sound caused me to relax a small measure. Avi must have them enthralled. Although I was too afraid to lean over the parapet to catch a glimpse of him and could not hear his words clearly, the familiar cadence of his voice rising and falling reassured me that Vadim and his men were plenty distracted for now.

Assuming Imati was not being held within the chambers of either of my father's wives, I stepped carefully past their darkened doorways, hoping they and their younger children were already sound asleep. I briefly wondered if Demeliah and Belah had taken to their rooms early to avoid the wine-soaked ruckus. Even so, their chambers seemed oddly silent.

At each vacant room I encountered, my hopes dwindled further. Had Nabal lied about Imati's survival? Or had my father locked her up somewhere else—the servants' quarters, perhaps? Or even in the stables?

There was only one more place to look on this level: my own chamber in the very top corner of the house. With no expectations that I would find anything there, I reached for the handle of the place that had been my sanctuary for so many years.

Instead of the well-worn acacia wood latch I knew by feel, links of cold metal met my palm. The door to the room I'd once shared with my mother, Chava, was chained shut. A surge of anticipation flooded through me, and my hand trembled as I pressed it against the locked door. Could it be that my father had imprisoned Imati *here*, in my room, while I was gone?

I startled as the men below groaned nearly in chorus, caught up in the details of whatever tale Avi was spinning. I needed to stick to my task before Avi lost his hold on Vadim's interest.

In days' past, I would have reached for my amulet in this moment, muttered a prayer to my goddess, and hoped my worship and offerings had been enough to garner her protection. But now it was the One Who Hears—the God of my fathers—to whom I whispered a wholehearted plea. An answering calm came over me before I'd even finished the supplication, and I took a strong and steadying breath.

Then I quietly tapped at my own door and waited with my pulse racing.

All was silent from behind the solid wood.

Hoot and whistles down in the courtyard sounded out, along with chants of "Demon Eyes!" and then more raucous laughter. Even more listeners had joined the gathering, and Avi had them all spellbound.

Using the din to my advantage, I knocked on the door just a bit louder, then waited, my stomach in knots.

"Yes?" came a voice from inside, one that I knew just as well as my own. My eyes blurred, and relief sluiced through my veins. Nabal had not lied, in this at least.

Imati *was* alive!

I pressed my face close to the crack of the door. "Imati," I rasped, "it's me. Keziah."

"Keziah?" came the surprised response. "No! Why are you back here?"

"I'll tell you everything later, but right now we need to get you out of this room."

A pause, then her voice came a little closer, as if she too had her mouth pressed to the sliver of space between the heavy door and its frame. "How? They only unchain the door when they bring me food twice a day."

"Who has the key?"

"One of the guards."

"Which one?"

"I don't know his name, only that he has an odd color of hair. Like the plume of a hoopoe."

Could it really be so simple? The sleeping man I'd slipped past beside the back entrance had hair the exact shade of rust that topped the distinctive bird.

If I could lift the key from him without notice, Imati and I could very well escape the villa together before Avi even began another story. The Rehavites would not even need to put themselves at risk by entering the compound.

Before I could second-guess my decision, I told Imati I would be back and ignored her frantic whispers begging me to wait. Then I stole past my father's wives' chambers on light feet, descended the stairs at double the speed I normally did, and made my way through the dark house to the back entrance.

There, with his back still propped against the doorframe, was the guard with the red hair, mouth wide open as he slept.

With no time to think, I bent to check his belt pouch for any sign of a key, but it held only the crumbled remains of a stale meat pie and a pair of knucklebone dice. He stirred and mumbled something, blowing out putrid breath that had me clapping a hand over my nose.

But he did not wake.

I leaned in closer and nearly went weak-kneed with relief when I noticed the four-pronged piece of metal dangling from a cord around his thick neck.

I pulled out the flint knife Avi insisted I carry from my belt, the very one of Shalem's he'd loaned me that first night, and with one quick flick of my wrist, the key to Imati's chains was in my hand.

Pulse going wild, I flew through the house, up the stairs again, and back to the door of my room. With shaking hands, I jammed the key into the iron lock, fighting with the mechanism for a few heart-stopping moments before it clanked open. I untangled the short chain from the latch, tossed it into a dark corner, and pushed open the door.

And then I was in the arms of the woman who'd chosen my life over hers—twice—both of us trembling as we embraced.

"You foolish girl," she said, pressing a kiss to my temple. "Why are you here? I sent you away to save you."

"Because you are my mother, Imati. And because Yahweh provided a way."

She let out a strangled sob and pulled me tight. The smell of almond blossoms on her warm skin gave me a small measure of calm, even though my blood was still racing from taking the stairs two at a time.

In that moment of bone-deep relief and overwhelming gratitude, a memory bloomed from somewhere deep inside me: Imati, kneeling beside my bed when I was delirious with a childhood fever that had kept me in its grips for days, and that same sweet fragrance lingering in the air as she whispered a prayer of protection. Yet it had not, as I had then assumed, been a prayer to one of the gods the people of Kamon worshipped, but the one her *own* revered—the One Who Heals. Yahweh, God Most High.

From the very first moment of my flight from Kamon, I'd felt as though something unexplainable had brought Avi and me together, had guided us to the kind shepherds, reached into the raging river to hold open a gap for Avi and Sarru between those deadly tree branches, and used Vadim's men to chase us directly into the arms of the Rehavites.

And now I knew for certain what it was: the God of the Universe answering the secret prayers of a devoted mother for her child.

The moment of clarity for just how boundless Yahweh's steadfast love was for me was so awe-inspiring, I nearly fell to my knees in worship. But there would be time enough for Imati and me to praise the Holy One together. A lifetime, perhaps.

As long as the two of us got out of this villa alive.

"We need to go," I said, concerned that the sounds of enjoyment and chatter in the courtyard had dampened a bit during our reunion. "Avi may be losing their attention, and Omar will be wondering where I am."

"Avi?" Her ebony eyes gleamed in the dim reflection of the torchlight from out in the courtyard. "Omar?"

I huffed a laugh. "It is a very long story, one that you will not believe. First, let's get out of this villa, then I will tell you all about my journey to Har Nebo and back."

A gruff voice from the doorway cut off her surprised gasp. "No. First, you can explain what you are doing inside this room."

The guard marched both of us down the stairway, through the house, and out to the inner courtyard at the tip of his sword.

I should have stuck to the plan and run for the Rehavites as soon as I'd found Imati. My impatience and inattention had cost both of us our freedom. And potentially our lives.

The man pressed his weapon into my back, and I jolted against the sting of its point digging between my shoulder blades. "Step faster, boy."

Thanks to the dim light, he'd not recognized me as a woman, but I feared my disguise would not hold much longer. Pushed into the glare of the torches, I saw the man who'd fathered me at the table in the center of the courtyard.

My brothers, Azan and Bram, were not among the many men gathered in the courtyard, as I expected. But all present were watching the guard herd Imati and me toward Vadim. The only exception was Lotan, who looked to have been bested by wine this evening, his cheek pressed to the table and drool trickling from his mouth as he slumbered.

I felt Avi's horrified stare before I even saw him, seated across the table with Vadim's men surrounding him on all sides. I had the distinct feeling that he was very close to throwing himself out of the chair and barreling toward me, so I gave a very subtle shake of my head before I turned my eyes away. There was no use in all three of us being taken captive. For the moment, he was the only one able to get away and alert the Rehavites to our situation.

The usurper of Kamon lounged at the head of the gathering, nodding his head at something one of his men was saying as he indulged from a platter of rich food supplied by farmers whose fertile lands he'd overtaken by sheer manipulation.

"Found this boy trying to break the slave woman out of the room, my lord," the guard said, poking me again with his sword. "Sneaky one there. Swiped the key off Hamor, who is snoring away his turn at watch."

Although every part of me was screaming to run, I refused to react, keeping my head down and eyes low. There was nothing to be done now but trust that the God who'd answered prayers made on my behalf long before I acknowledged his goodness was watching over us now.

"I'll deal with Hamor later," Vadim snapped. "Go take his place and leave these two to me."

The guard retreated as Vadim hefted himself from his chair. "What business do you have with this slave, boy?"

I reacted to his encroaching nearness the same way I had during our initial meeting, my skin crawling with revulsion. But I said nothing. As Avi had pointed out, my voice was a clear giveaway that I was a woman.

"Why don't you let me deal with this, Vadim?" My father rose from the table and came around to stand beside the man he'd allowed to steal his authority. "I'm the one who had the maid locked up in the first place. I'll make certain the boy is punished for trying to help her escape."

Vadim grunted. "I shouldn't have let you talk me into sparing her life, Menachem. She shamed me in front of the entire town with her deceit. She deserves the lash, at the very least."

"And as I told you, my wayward daughter is a talented manipulator. There's no way this ignorant slave planned that escape. She's little more than a desert savage, anyhow. She merely obeyed her crafty mistress when she was ordered to trade places, and then suffered the outcome. My daughter obviously did not think enough about her maid to care what happened after she ran off."

The more my father slandered me and insulted Imati, the more confused I became. None of what he was saying made sense. He may not have spent much time in my company over these past years, but he knew I was in no way manipulative or scheming, and neither would anyone call Imati an ignorant savage. She was quiet but well-spoken and articulate.

A tiny thread of hope began to wind itself around my heart. My father *had* to have recognized me. Was he planning something? Did he mean to protect us from Vadim's wrath by some scheme of his own?

"You promised me a bride, Menachem. And all I got was this slave beneath a wedding veil."

"And have I not made restitution for my daughter's folly?" said my father, slowly moving to the side, as if to draw Vadim's attention away. "I've gifted you five more of my horses. Given you and your men the use of my entire villa, even going so far as to remove my whole family to an inn while your men prepared for the coming invasion. And I sent my own cousin, the man I trust most, to find Keziah. I have no doubt he and your men will return shortly with the girl in tow and claim the reward I promised."

Vadim grunted. "I should let the Ammonites burn this place. Other than the horses, Kamon is worth far less than I was led to believe."

Lies you believed from Nabal, I wanted to blurt out. He said he'd been the one to negotiate my marriage in the first place and that he'd been promised the bridal gifts as payment. He'd enticed Vadim to come here under the guise of protecting Kamon, with the ultimate goal of taking my father's wealth and power for himself. A takeover he could not have accomplished on his own.

A curse for the man who'd caused so much destruction and heartache for the sake of his own greed boiled in my blood. *By the name of the Most High, wherever he is, may Nabal find the just end he deserves.*

"Keziah?"

The moment my name echoed across the courtyard, my

gaze unwittingly snapped to its source. Vadim's son Lotan peered across the table at me with bleary eyes. Of all the moments for him to awaken from his inebriated stupor and recognize me, it had to be when he was not in charge of his faculties.

Vadim jerked his attention from his fool of a son to my bruised visage, his eyes narrowing on me like some great predator. My father had gone white-faced only a few paces away, his expression full of horror, and Avi was on his feet, chest heaving and looking ready to leap to my defense.

But it was Imati's hand sliding into mine that kept me standing tall before the man who would have owned me body and soul had she not put herself in my place.

"Well," said Vadim, with an oddly pleasant chuckle, "if it is not my sweet little bride." He put his fingers under my chin, jerking it up so he could run his greedy eyes over my bruised face. "Battered and dressed as a boy, no less. Where have you been, my darling?"

I took a deep breath. The Keziah who'd silently endured this man's abuse beneath the betrothal table and submitted to his veil, the one who'd been too afraid to speak in her own defense to the father who'd betrayed her trust, and the one who'd run from Kamon thinking she had been alone her whole life, had returned a different woman.

The woman I was now knew for certain that she was loved— had *always* been loved, both by Imati and by the Eternal God she served.

Vadim was only a man. And the God I now served was infinitely more powerful. So, instead of pleading with him to spare my life, I squared my shoulders and stared the snake in his eyes. If Avi could speak truth with boldness, then so would I.

"After years of being ignored and isolated in this household," I said, as I faced down the bear of a man who could crush my skull in his hands if he chose, "my father sold me to a murderer, and I had no choice but to run. But I am no longer afraid of you, Vadim. Because over these past two weeks, I have learned of a power that far surpasses yours, no matter how many towns you overthrow or how much gold and silver you amass by treachery, lies, and deceit. And when you die surrounded by your ill-gotten gains, your name and memory will crumble into obscurity. But as the true and eternal king of Israel, Yahweh's name will be glorious for all of time."

At the provocation, Vadim snapped. With a snarl of fury, he slapped my bruised cheek, throwing me off my feet and to the ground. Then, as he spewed a litany of foul curses at me while my head rang like a silver bell and my cheek throbbed anew, a number of things happened at once.

Releasing an unmistakable battle cry, Avi vaulted over the table with a pilfered sword in his hand. With a gasp of horror, Imati wrapped her arms around me, and my father—the same man who'd traded me for the sake of his own little kingdom—threw his own body between us and Vadim.

My father's unexpected move startled Vadim, keeping his attention away from the Levite warrior barreling toward us. Although a couple of Vadim's men made drunken attempts to grab for him, Avi easily slipped past them, so great was his determination to get to me.

Too quickly, Vadim turned to find Avi nearly upon him, and with a roar, he unsheathed his own sword to meet Avi's with a jarring clang that seemed to echo in the pit of my stomach.

The two of them clashed iron swords once again, and Vadim's men stood by, blinking in confusion, uncertain whether to intervene or watch the fight play out. Vadim was bulkier than his opponent by far, but with astounding flexibility and quickness, Avi was able to deliver a blow to Vadim's shoulder that caused him to drop his weapon.

The older man cursed as blood spilled down his arm but recovered far too quickly and swept Avi's right leg out from under him. Vadim followed him to the ground, pinning him under his weight. Blood streamed from his lips, staining his teeth crimson as he grabbed Avi's jaw in one hand and slipped a wickedly serrated knife from his belt with the other.

"Say good-bye to your tongue, Storyteller," he spat, trying to pry Avi's mouth open with his fingers. "You've told your last tale."

"Avi! No—!" I struggled to my feet, fighting Imati's protective hold on me, but a chorus of startled shouts drew my attention to the chaos that had broken out in the courtyard around us.

A bevy of arrows winged through the air, piercing three of Vadim's men through nearly all at once. Wild, tremulous calls emanated from the shadowed parapets atop the house in every direction, and from doors on either end, Rehavites poured into the courtyard, faces painted in terrifying charcoal smudges and daggers flashing in the torchlight.

The distraction gave Avi the opening he needed. With a swift and brutal twist of his body that I could not comprehend, he maneuvered himself into a dominant position above the brute. Vadim lashed out once more with his knife, but the arrow that pierced his forearm was faster, and he dropped the blade.

Vadim bellowed and struggled against Avi's weight. But before he could manage to wrestle himself free, Avi snatched up the serrated knife and plunged it into the man's neck. Mouth wide open as he struggled for air, Vadim's eyes rolled back into his head, and his body went still.

When I finally peeled my shocked gaze away, I glanced up to find Omar ten paces away, another arrow nocked to finish Vadim if Avi's blow hadn't done the job.

Only a few of Vadim's men remained standing in the center of the courtyard but more had just entered the fray when a loud cry of "Halt!" burst from the mouth of none other than Lotan. Looking both sober and horrified, he shouted the word again and again until all of his father's men stood frozen.

"No more!" The young man waved his arms. "No more! This is madness. We are *brothers*."

"But your father—" one soldier began.

"Is dead," Lotan stated, pointing at the body on the ground. "He is dead, and as his son, I am your leader until we return to Beit Arbel and you are released into the service of my eldest brother, his heir."

The men traded uncertain glances amongst themselves.

"Or I could just let these warriors finish off the lot of you," he said, gesturing to the Rehavites, who stood with arrows nocked and pointed at their heads. "It would serve you right for doing the bidding of that monster." He jerked his chin toward his father's corpse.

Slowly, weapons retreated into sheaths, those who survived choosing to heed the authority of Vadim's young son over falling to a Rehavite arrow.

Lotan ordered the men to leave the villa and to gather the rest of the company outside Kamon. "We will leave this place within the hour. And carry *nothing* in our hands that was not brought from Beit Arbel."

Then he turned toward my father. "My brother is a good man, nothing like our father. I am certain once he hears of this tragedy, he will insist on restitution for the damage Vadim caused."

As if too stunned to speak, my father only nodded.

Then Lotan met my eyes, and the guilt in his expression was overwhelming. "I beg your forgiveness. I thought you were dead. I was so stunned when I came out of my drunken stupor that I thought I was dreaming of you in disguise. I was not in control of my mouth."

I shook my head, grateful he'd not revealed my identity on purpose after all. "Go in peace, Lotan."

With his shoulders low, the young man turned away, and I prayed that he would indeed find peace. And that without Vadim ruling over it with an iron fist, Beit Arbel might heal as well.

Imati squeezed my hand, her incredulous gaze on the Rehavites. "Is that . . . ?"

With a smile, I nodded. Released by the confirmation, Imati ran to reunite with her family, tears streaming as men who'd been only children when she was kidnapped embraced her with joyful whoops.

My father, however, remained in place with his back to me. But before I could decide what to say, or whether to speak to him at all, I was swept completely off my feet and wrapped into the long arms of my love.

Avi pressed his bearded face into my neck, breathing me in and kissing my skin. "My Keziah," he murmured, pressing his lips against my ear, "I thought I'd truly lost you for good this time."

"Don't you remember," I said, winding my arms around his neck and ignoring the many curious stares around us, "you and I made an agreement. We remain together."

32

Imati's skilled fingers threaded through my hair, the strokes soothing as she twisted the short locks into tiny braids interwoven with copper and carnelian beads.

"I so wish I'd not had to cut your beautiful hair." She pressed one warm palm to my shoulder, seeking my eyes in the mirror. "If I'd thought of any other way . . ."

I lifted my own hand to cover hers. "We've already been through this. It will grow back. Besides, my hair was a small price to pay for my life and the gifts I have been given."

She bent to place her chin atop the crown of my head, our similar features lined up in the reflection. "There is no greater gift for me than you, my precious girl. And the knowledge that you now walk with El Shaddai."

I swallowed down the sting of emotion in my throat. It would not do to ruin the kohl rimming my eyes before my wedding.

The tent flap flew open, and a whirlwind of aunts and older cousins stormed in, exclaiming over my hairstyle and cosmetics. Although they'd given Imati and me some time alone while she helped me start dressing for the day, the women of our family had obviously waited long enough to join the preparations.

Within moments, I was surrounded, every woman voicing her own opinion about patterns as they marveled over the henna on my hands and feet. A few of them added their own sparkling rings, necklaces, and bangles to the colorful Rehavite wedding garments I'd chosen to wear today, along with my well-worn papyrus sandals. I'd declined to give them back to Imati after my return, and at my insistence, Imati's calloused feet were now encased in soft kidskin leather.

I'd also flatly refused to wear a veil.

It had been three weeks since the men from Beit Arbel had retreated from Kamon, and in that time, the Rehavites had taken their place. My father, in one of his many acts of remorseful restitution, had publicly set Imati free and invited her people to the valley, giving them the choicest land for their herds to graze. It was more than likely they would remain only for a season or two before making their yearly pilgrimage to the sacred mountain in the wilderness. But Qadir himself had hinted that he was ready to plant roots again and perhaps even build homes on this fertile soil so that generations to come would no longer have to scratch a meager existence from the desert.

The entire tribe, well-practiced in swiftly packing up their belongings on camelback, had arrived a few days ago, and now their black and red tents fluttered in the cool breeze not far from the stream where I'd hidden after my flight from the villa, while their herds of dusty goats indulged in supple grasses on its banks.

I'd also formed a fledgling friendship with Lena, the girl who'd warned me to run from that very place, since the day I'd gone to her home with a basket of gifts for her family in gratitude for her kindness. Little did she know that the blessing she'd spoken over me before I'd fled the valley would have so much significance in the days to come.

Once the women were satisfied that I was sufficiently prepared for my bridegroom, they took turns kissing my cheeks before exiting the tent, leaving my heart full to overflowing for the ocean of love Yahweh had submerged me in over these past weeks.

Soon, only myself, Imati, and her mother remained in the quiet tent, the two of them standing near the entrance, arms around each other's waists. Seeing Imati reunited with her own mother with shouts of joy was a memory I would cherish for the rest of my days.

"Your father would like a moment with you," said my grandmother in the low and distinct rasp I'd come to adore. "But first, come." She gestured me closer, that gold ring in her nose twinkling into a ray of sunlight from the tent flap. "We will pray a blessing over you, daughter."

I knelt before them, and with their hands layered atop my head, my mother and grandmother spoke words of benediction over me, over Avi, and our future children. They asked that Yahweh consecrate our marriage unto himself and that the words of truth we held high and the outcome of our faithfulness would echo for a thousand generations.

By the time they were finished, I could not speak, so great was the intensity of my love for them and for the God who'd brought us all back together beneath his banner.

As a result, the kohl around my eyes had to be redone after all before they left the room and my father sheepishly took their place.

We'd made peace, he and I, once he'd come to me with repentance on his lips and shame on his face. Although I'd offered my forgiveness for his betrayal, I knew that the sweet relationship we'd had when I was a child would never be fully mended after all that had transpired. And neither would I accept the lovely red-spotted mare he'd offered to replace my stallion. Nothing could take Sarru's place in my heart. I felt I would never again want to mount another horse, so deep was the pain of missing him.

"This was Chava's," said my father, holding out a thick copper bracelet studded with lapis gems that glittered like stars in his hand. "She would want you to wear it today." He blinked, a sheen of emotion in his weary eyes. "She may not have carried you in her body, but she adored you, Keziah. She would be proud of the strong and kindhearted woman you have become."

Grateful to have a token of the first mother I'd known, I accepted the gift, sliding the cool metal over my wrist, then dipped my chin with a nod of thanks.

My father had already submitted to a new town council, appointed by tribal nassim at the request of Bram and Azan. I'd been shocked to discover that they had left Kamon a few days after I had to plead with the elders of Manasseh for help when they'd been unable to convince our father of Vadim's lies. They'd returned to find Kamon already free, thanks to the Rehavites, and our father more than willing to turn his own seat of authority over to Bram.

Avi's bold words had convicted my father so deeply that I was certain he would never again be the same. And I could only pray that the Voice of the Ancient would continue to transform his heart, just as it had mine.

He stretched out his hand to me. "Are you ready to see your bridegroom?"

"I am." On a deep breath, I slid my own into his grasp, giving it a little squeeze to reassure him that even after everything, he was still my abba.

With a smile, he pulled back the tent flap and led me out into the bright sunshine, where my love waited on a bench a few paces away, dressed in finery that I'd never seen before. One leg twitched up and down, and his long fingers tugged the golden-brown curls on his neck.

I'd not seen the poor man so nervous since the first time he tried to mount my horse.

The moment he saw me, he leapt to his feet, and then after a long pause where he did nothing but drink me in head to foot, a heart-stopping smile curved over his face.

Keeping his forest-colored eyes latched on mine, he came forward to wordlessly accept the offer of my hand from my father. Once our fingers were entwined together, my bridegroom leaned in to whisper in my ear, the feel of his soft breath on my skin triggering a ripple of heat and gooseflesh.

"There is no one in this world more beautiful than you, my bride," he said, then pressed his lips against the tender flesh beneath my earlobe, causing another shiver. "But I've known that since we swam beneath rainbows at the waterfall."

Before I could respond to his sweet revelation, the Rehavites began to gather around, preparing to usher us in a joyful parade up the road to Kamon and to the villa, where a bevy of cooks and servants who'd been restored to their positions had prepared the grandest feast our town had ever seen. It would be a celebration not only of the union between Avi and me, but of both sides of my heritage coming together as one to witness the new covenant dedicated to the Holy One of Israel.

My cheeks ached from smiling. But between the endless dances to the rapturous music from the Rehavites, the countless blessings from family, shepherds, and the people of Kamon who credited the two of us with their rescue, and the many stolen kisses from my husband, there was so much joy in my heart that I did not care.

Wrapped up in Avi's long arms, the two of us looked on as Meital and Numa, along with my other cousins, danced. Holding the ends of vibrant ribbons in their hands, the girls twirled around and around until the song ended in a giggling tangle of colorful skirts.

Avi's laughter vibrated against my back, and I pressed closer, content to remain in this perfect place for all of eternity.

"When do I get you all to myself?" he muttered low, hand smoothing over my hip as the reed pipes started up once again.

I swiveled around to face him. It was already such a thrill to call this good-hearted man my husband, it was hard to believe that after this night we would be one. Free to find pleasure in our physical oneness but also in the ever-deepening intimacy of a friendship that had begun in the most unlikely of ways.

"Want to sneak away?" I said with a sly grin.

His eyes flared. "*Yes.*"

I tipped my head toward the courtyard gate, brows lifted. "I'll go first. Meet me behind the stables."

Giving him no time to react to my bold suggestion, I slipped out of his arms and darted toward the shadows that lay outside the brilliant circle of torchlight, knowing he would not wait long to follow.

Every day with Avi had been an adventure so far, in both joyous and hard times, but I could not wait to see what surprises Yahweh had in store for us as we walked through life together. Even though the path we would be taking within a few days would lead us away from my home and across the river to his, Avi had promised me that one day we would seek Yahweh's guidance about returning to this side of the river.

The burden he now carried in his chest for the people of Eastern Manasseh, Gad, and Reuben was growing stronger by the day, a weight he felt increasingly certain was a calling to remind those who had forgotten their special heritage about the God who'd chosen them for a unique purpose.

Caught up in my anticipation of both this night with Avi and the thousands more to come, I slammed full force into a man's broad chest as I turned the corner toward my father's stables.

Two hands grabbed my shoulders, preventing me from tumbling to the ground. "Haven't you run away enough, cousin?"

I blinked up at a windblown Rasul, no longer looking pale and weak after Nabal had nearly gutted him on the beach.

"You're here!" I threw my arms around my cousin. "I thought you and the others would not arrive for days!"

"We could not miss your wedding." He squeezed me tightly. "What good is a celebration without your most handsome and talented favorite cousin, anyhow?"

I laughed and slapped a playful palm to his shoulder. I'd never admit aloud that he was indeed my favorite, or I would never hear the end of it. And I would never forget that it was he who insisted on riding to Heshbon to find Avi before coming north to save me on that beach—even though he barely knew me at the time.

"Avi!" he called out as my husband joined us. The two men greeted each other with an affectionate embrace that caused my throat to tighten.

Avi missed Zevi and Gavi equally as much as he remained hurt and angry at their abandonment of both him and Shalem. Even though my own cousins could never replace the lifelong bond he'd shared with his own, I was grateful that new friendships had blossomed.

"I've brought the two of you a wedding gift." Rasul flourished a palm toward the darkness behind him.

"What sort of gift?" I lifted my chin to peer at him. The young man was full of mischief, and I did not trust the gleam in his eyes.

"Follow me," he said, with a jerk of his head. "It's with Naveed. The camels are tied up just outside the villa walls."

Although I was disappointed that our secret meeting behind the stables had been waylaid, Avi and I followed Rasul through the outer courtyard, hands entwined as he began to tell a story of how one of the younger boys had fallen into one of the pools along the journey and had to be rescued by his older brothers.

"Avi will have to teach the boy to swim before we leave for Naioth," I said, giving the back of Avi's hand a swift and secret kiss behind Rasul's back. "There's no better teacher."

"We found him there," said Rasul, his tone shifting slightly as we passed through the gates and toward the southern corner of the villa walls. "He's in rough shape after what he's been through. That's why I came to fetch you. He's not in any mood to join a celebration."

"Who are you talking about?" I asked. "The boy who fell in the water?"

"No. Your wedding gift. Sure, we wanted to join the wedding celebration, but he's the real reason why we hurried north with barely a rest. I knew you were crossing the river soon and would not want to leave him behind."

A thrum of excitement began to build in my veins, and I looked up at Avi with wide eyes. Had Rasul and the others actually found Shalem? The prospect was far too thrilling to even wrap my mind around. And yet I recalled as we lay beneath the stars how Avi had told me he was convinced the God Who Sees had Shalem firmly in the palm of his hand.

I could not wait to meet the boy Avi spoke of with such adoration and see the face of my husband when he was reunited with someone he considered a brother.

My husband said nothing as we approached the place the camels had been tied, but his breaths were coming faster, and his fingers tightened around mine.

Two familiar golden beasts stood chewing their cud a few paces away, while Naveed and Gassan worked together to unload the heavy packs strapped to their sides.

But there was no sign of Avi's cousin, or anyone else near the camels. I glanced around in confusion. Had Rasul been playing some awful trick on us?

Then Avi gasped as one of the dusty giants stepped to the side, and everything inside me went incredibly still. I was terrified to move. Terrified that if I blinked my eyes the mirage in front of me would vanish.

"How?" I choked out in a whisper. "How?"

"We saw him tied to a trader's wagon in Heshbon. He refused to let anyone close to him, kicking and biting and lashing out. In fact, we had to throw that scarf over his head just so we could get him to come with us."

"How did he even get there?" asked Avi incredulously, his strong arm the only thing holding me upright.

As if he was just as stunned by the sight before us, Rasul blew out a shuddering breath. "Apparently, he was found in a dry wadi just south of Heshbon, along the King's Highway, attached to a corpse with a broken neck. The poor beast was just standing there, nearly half-dead himself, with the decomposing body dangling by the leg from the loop below his saddle. If he hadn't been found that day, he would have died of thirst."

At this revelation, a sob burst free. I pulled myself from Avi's gentle hold and bolted toward a beautiful black stallion with white legs standing between two enormous camels, a thick brown scarf wrapped carefully around his precious head and over his eyes.

With shaking hands, I reached for him, cooing words of love

and reassurance. He startled at first, dancing to the side, huffing and snorting, but I held tight, stroking his velvet jaw and talking to him gently as I worked at the knot until the fabric fell away from his beloved face.

He sniffed, taking in a quick breath against my hair. As tears of wonderment at the measureless grace of Yahweh rolled down my face, he placed his whiskery muzzle against my cheek, releasing what could only be described as a sigh.

Sarru had come home.

Avidan

GILGAL, ISRAEL

Tugging Sarru to a stop at a crossroads, Keziah stared slack-jawed at the mass of people, tents, and animals spread over the surrounding hills and valleys. "Why are they all here?" I shook my head, equally bewildered.

After we'd forded the Jordan near the town of Adam, we'd followed the trade road that ran along the west bank of the river heading for Jericho, meaning to find the route I had taken up to Bezek with my cousins nearly two months before. But as we approached the valley of Gilgal, we'd been shocked to discover that some sort of gathering was taking place in what had been the very first camp for the Hebrews upon their arrival in Canaan so long ago.

The site was not only ancient, but sacred. And judging by the white-clad priests milling around the flat hilltop, where twelve enormous standing stones marked the beginnings of our nation and an enormous tent fluttered in the breeze, something of great significance was happening here.

"Perhaps we should veer east and try to skirt this horde closer to the river," Keziah suggested, stroking her horse's neck in a soothing rhythm.

Sarru had calmed a great deal since he'd been returned to his mistress but was still prone to startling at loud noises and shying from strangers. I had no idea what Nabal had done to him in the days after the skirmish on the beach, but Sarru's already fragile trust, especially with men, had been damaged. It had taken two full days to convince him to let me come near, and Keziah still had to block him from nipping at me whenever I mounted up behind her.

Hopefully, like me, whatever nightmares he had been reliving would ease in coming days. For both of us, it was Keziah's presence that brought the most peace. Sleeping with her in my arms had done much to chase away the bedeviling images in my dreams, but there were still nights I woke myself by calling out in horror, and only my wife's gentle kisses and quiet words could soothe the lingering torment.

Before I could decide whether Keziah's plan to loop around the crowd and head toward Jericho was our best option in all this chaos, a sudden burst of music pulled my attention back toward Gilgal. Although we were a good distance away, I could see a large group of men in white garments gathered near the gates, their voices lifted in song and accompanied by an array of instruments. They began a melody and then cut off the notes after a few moments to begin all over again, practicing for whatever convocation was to come.

Whenever there were Levitical musicians preparing for an assembly, it was more than likely my father was nearby.

"Turn Sarru west," I said, gesturing toward the hill. "It looks as though you might be meeting a few of my family members today."

Her large brown eyes went impossibly round. "They are *here?*"

"My father is one of the leaders of the Levitical choirs. I suspect he may be directing those singers."

She took a deep breath and then blew it out loudly. "I'd hoped not to meet your family while I was covered in travel dust and horsehair."

I tugged her close, bending to press a lingering kiss to her sweet mouth. "They'll adore you, dirt and all. Just like I do."

She let me tease her lips for another few moments before pushing me away with her palms. "You are incorrigible, Avi ben Ronen," she said, turning Sarru's nose west on to the narrow road that led toward Gilgal and the plume of smoke curling up from an altar in the distance.

The mention of my father's name sparked a moment of sobering clarity. If he was indeed here today, then I must be prepared. Not only did I have so much to apologize for and so much recompense to offer, but unless my cousins had returned to Naioth in my absence, I would be the one to bring the terrible news about Shalem.

The rest of the ride toward Gilgal was spent mulling over what to say, my dread increasing with each fall of Sarru's hooves. Thankfully, my wife knew me well enough now to let me stew in silence. But somewhere along the way, she reached to intertwine her fingers with mine in a wordless show of support.

Yahweh had blessed me indeed.

When we were still a good distance away from the choir, they once again stopped singing to allow the instruments to play and then replay a few lines of a melody I knew well. The song was one my father had written many years ago that extolled the characteristics of a good and noble king—the same one containing the refrain that had come to mind as I spoke with Qadir atop Har Nebo.

The anointed one shall abide by the counsel of the Most High, The voice of the Ancient One to light his every step.

The confirmation that I'd indeed found Ronen ben Avidan in this confusion of people had my blood rushing and my palms sweating. But when I heard my name excitedly shouted from somewhere among the milling crowd, it was not the voice of my father but that of my younger brother, Elidor.

He waved frantically, running toward us. "Avi! Avi!"

I swung my leg over Sarru's rump and leapt from his back, then threw my arms wide as Elidor crashed into me with a sob.

"You're back!" he choked out, clinging to me. "You are alive!"

"I am." I kissed his curly-haired head. "And so thankful you found me."

He pulled back to look up at me, huge tears rolling down his cheeks. "Where have you been? Abba and Ima have been so worried for you. Gavi and Zevi returned for a couple days after the battle, but you stayed over the river. Why? How come you didn't come back too?"

"I am so sorry, brother. I never should have left in the first place." I bent to look him straight in the eye as I delivered the first of many apologies. "And I *never* should have left you with the burden of telling our parents I'd run off. Please, Elidor, forgive my carelessness. It was cowardly and wrong."

His brows furrowed. "I'm not mad, Avi. I just wanted you to come home. You said we'd go to the pool and jump from the rocks, remember?"

Grateful for his sweet and merciful nature, I laughed, pressing a kiss to his temple. "That I did. And when we get back to Naioth, I will made good on my promise."

He beamed up at me with my mother's eyes, joy and relief in his expression. "Did you really go fight for the king?"

I winced at the innocent excitement in his voice. "I did."

"Abba was really angry," he said, frowning. "I did what you asked and waited until almost sundown to tell them you went with Gavi and Zevi. But he left anyway."

"Left? What do you mean?"

"He followed you," said Elidor. "All the way to Bezek. But he was too late. The army had already crossed over the river."

I blinked at him, stunned. "Abba tried to come after me?"

"That I did."

I jerked my chin up to find my father approaching, his pure white Levitical garments gleaming in the bright sunlight and his expression thunderous. The closer he came, the more my chest felt as though it was being pressed between two enormous boulders, carved from equal measures regret and elation.

"Abba," I breathed out, bracing myself for the moment my father raised his voice in fury for the very first time, and knowing I deserved every word of chastisement. I may be a man outwardly, and a married one now at that, but inside I felt as young as Elidor, a little boy terrified of his father's well-earned wrath.

What I was not prepared for was the way he threw his arms around me with a loud, broken cry of relief, and although I was a good handspan taller than my father, I curled into the unexpected embrace.

"Avidan," he said, his voice shaking. "My son. Thank you. Thank you, Adonai, Most High. Thank you for hearing my prayers."

He held me close for a few more moments, weeping unashamedly. Then he reached up to place his hands on either side of my face and kissed both my own wet cheeks.

"Abba," I began, "I must beg your forgiveness—"

He shook his head as he released me. "I want to hear what you have to say, Avidan, but this conversation will take a good long while, and the king's coronation will begin soon. They've already begun the sacrifices. I went for a walk with Elidor to clear my head for a few moments, but I need to get back to the choir."

"Saul is being crowned here today?"

"He is. His decisive victory over the Ammonites proved Yahweh's hand is upon him. Now that all of the tribes are finally in accord about his kingship, this assembly was called so the people can see him anointed with their own eyes. Samuel himself was the one to suggest it."

I let out a weighty sigh. When I'd left home, with my head full of wrongful notions and a heart full of rebellion, I'd believed Saul had been chosen because Yahweh had appointed him the savior of Israel, the one to rescue us from our oppressors and usher in a lasting kingdom of peace and prosperity. I'd upheld him as nearly divine himself, a man whose impressive form and fearlessness on the battlefield would bring the nations to their knees.

And yet the longer Keziah and I had traveled across the Jordan, the more dismayed I'd been to see that although he chased the Ammonite remnant back to Rabbah and returned the territory they'd stolen into Hebrew hands, he'd also left a mess behind the wake of his army. Destroyed fields. Hungry bellies. Empty purses. And a rising tide of resentment among the people across the river.

But it had been the morning we returned to the valley of Emeq that I'd truly become disillusioned with Saul of Gibeah. Because although I'd learned in Heshbon that the campaign against the Ammonites had concluded, the shepherds' charred homes were still in ruins and the promise he'd made to help them rebuild abandoned. The sacrifice the loyal men had given of their own flesh had already been forgotten.

It was the Rehavites who'd taken it upon themselves to come to the aid of those who'd not hesitated to join the rescue of their kinswoman. It would not be long before Ohel's clan slept in rebuilt homes, while their flocks slowly recovered from the damage wrought by both a ruthless enemy and a fickle king.

With insight born of my recent experiences and Qadir's wise observations, I could not help but compare Saul to Samuel who, like Mosheh, never lifted himself up as king over Israel but still led the tribal armies to victory because he never failed to seek the guidance and blessing of Adonai first. It was an example of humble service I was determined to emulate with every step of my life.

I would still respect Saul as the leader chosen by Yahweh, but I would remember that he was still a man, with the weaknesses inherent in all mortal flesh.

"Your mother will be relieved to see you, son," said my father. "Elidor can lead you to our camp. You and I will talk once the ceremony has concluded."

I could not wait to embrace my beautiful mother and repent

310

for knowingly hurting her in the very same way her brother had done. But first, I had to admit the worst of my crimes to my father.

"Abba . . ." I paused, the confession rising like broken glass in my throat. "I lost him. I lost Shalem."

Seeming unsurprised, he bowed his head, eyes cast down as I told him of the search for my cousin and that even though I'd found evidence of his survival in Heshbon, I'd had to abandon the pursuit.

He lifted his gaze. "What took you off course?"

In answer, I turned to seek out Keziah, who was patiently answering Elidor's many questions about the black-and-white stallion currently holding his fascination.

Catching her eye, I gestured for her to join us. Coming forward with an obvious expression of trepidation, she accepted the hand I reached out to her. I wrapped an arm around her slender shoulders and tugged her close to my side, hoping to reassure her.

"Abba, this is my wife, Keziah."

His brow arched high as he looked between the two of us. "Your *wife*?"

I nodded. "I have quite the story to tell."

"It appears so, son." And then my abba nudged me aside to reach for Keziah. He placed gentle palms on her cheeks, just as he had done to me, and kissed her forehead. "Welcome, daughter."

Two tears streaked down her dusty face as my father released her, and an overwhelming wave of love for both of them swelled in my chest. I could only hope to be as honorable and full of mercy and compassion as my abba. One day.

"Go find your mother, son. Bringing this lovely girl to her will go a long way toward her acceptance of your apologies. We will talk more when I return." He clapped a palm to my shoulder, giving it a strong squeeze that communicated, once again, his gratitude for my return. "And when we are back in Naioth, you and I will go speak to Iyov and Hodiya together."

It was hours before the coronation began, following a slew of sacrifices accompanied by song after song from my father's choir. Keziah and I had enjoyed a tear-filled reunion with my mother and the rest of my siblings, who begged for detailed stories about our journey until the sun perched above Jericho, setting the orange hills around the ancient city aflame.

The multitude around us remained hushed as the triumphant notes of the final song flowed from the mouths of hundreds of Levitical singers, echoing through the valley. Pride filled my soul. Even if future generations forgot the name of Ronen ben Avidan, there were scores of men and women who'd been taught to sing or play an instrument at his feet—some who would perform for kings. Some who may sing praises before a rebuilt Mishkan in our lifetime. And some who would write songs remembered for millennia.

When a chorus of silver trumpets blared a command for the crowd to come to attention, our family stood with myriad Hebrews around us. With Keziah tucked into my side beside a skittish warhorse, we watched as Saul knelt before Samuel the Seer on the distant platform, and the kingship he'd been charged with, back on the day my cousins and I had spied on the casting of lots, was confirmed before all the people.

Once the king was anointed by the prophet and a golden crown placed upon his head, Saul ben Kish stood to receive the cheers and shouts of thousands, stretching to his full and impressive height. He'd indeed proved himself an effective high commander of the armies of Israel, and it was apparent from his regal posture that he no longer had difficulty accepting the adulation of his people. But my focus was not on the newly reconfirmed King of Israel. It was on the elderly prophet I'd known all my life.

Samuel's eyes were not on the man basking in the praise of the people at his side. Instead, his gaze roved over the vast sea of Hebrews spread out before him. Although I was not close enough to examine the expression on his well-lined face, his rigid posture told me that something was amiss.

Without preamble, he threw his arms wide and called out in a loud voice, one that seemed to reverberate almost supernaturally throughout the valley. "Behold, I have obeyed your voice. I have made a king over you!"

Almost immediately, the celebratory noise of the multitude withered, and every eye shifted from Saul to Samuel.

Ignoring the king's shocked expression, the revered prophet began to address the people of Israel for what I guessed may be the very last time, boldly charging the multitude to bring forth evidence of any misdeeds he might be accused of throughout his long tenure as prophet and judge over Israel.

When no one responded to the challenge, Samuel explained the history of our people in succinct terms, from Mosheh's calling to the conquest of the land by Yehoshua. Then he reminded us of all the times Israel had turned her back on Yahweh, the enemies who'd been allowed to oppress her because of such rebellion, and the *shoftim*—like Gideon, D'vorah, and Samson—Adonai had raised up to rescue his wayward bride because of his steadfast love for her.

Then, with a startling jolt, the old prophet lifted a gnarled finger to point at the man he'd just crowned king. His tone turned ominous as he delivered a stark warning: If we—and the king we'd begged for—feared and obeyed Adonai, then things would go well for the sons of Yaakov. But if we sank into rebellion again, the hand of the Eternal One would be against Israel and the man upon her throne.

Gooseflesh sprang up all over my body as the same God who'd brought Egypt to its knees promised similar destruction if we defied him.

With his hands spread toward the heavens, Samuel then called for thunder and rain as incontrovertible proof that the admonishment he'd just delivered came from the King of the Universe himself.

So swiftly that it did not seem real, the sky went dark and a massive swirl of storm clouds appeared above us, its long tail hovering above the enormous tent atop Gilgal that I realized must contain the Ark itself. I tightened my hold on Keziah as screams went up all over the valley and a gust of violent wind tore through the camps, ripping tent pegs from the ground and toppling handcarts.

Headscarves and cloaks went flying as mothers and fathers grabbed for their children, using their own bodies as shields while the storm above us spilled like greenish-black ink over the distant hills. Thunder shook the heavens, and a torrent of rain and hail came down on us. From all around, cries for mercy rang out, paired with groveling confessions, repentance for demanding a king, and pleas for Samuel to beg Yahweh to spare our lives for the sake of his own glorious name.

Sarru screamed, bucking and kicking out with his front hooves. But even though her body shook within the iron circle of my arms, my brave wife held tightly to his reins, chanting soothing words to her horse as the otherworldly storm raged on. With terror pumping through my veins, I curved my body around hers and let a prayer for mercy flow from my own lips. Surely the Most High did not mean to kill all of us right here, did he? Not when Keziah and I had just begun our life together?

Then, as if the Ancient One had heard my one plea among millions, the storm was instantly snuffed out. The circling clouds dissipated, rolling harmlessly off into the distance, leaving a sea of windblown, rain-soaked, and bewildered Hebrews staring at the impossibly blue sky above.

After a short stretch of stunned silence, broken only by the lingering cries of terrified children, every single man, woman, and child in the valley of Gilgal—from the king's fearless warriors to the priests and Levites and musicians—fell to their knees in worship. Not for the man wearing a crown of gold who'd already disappeared from the coronation platform, and not for the old prophet with the long braid of silver who wore weariness like a mantle across his shoulders, but for the One True King whose majesty was without equal.

As I bent my own stubborn knees before the Most High, I vowed to never stop telling of how Keziah and I pressed our faces into the dirt this day, lifting thanks to Yahweh and praising his Holy Name for sparing us in his great mercy. For the rest of my days, my mouth would boldly bear witness to his incomprehensible power and the unending, steadfast love he had for a people who did not deserve such grace.

It was a story I had a feeling was only just beginning.

EPILOGUE

ONE MONTH LATER

Once a nondescript village among hundreds of others in Israelite territory, Gibeah was now, by virtue of King Saul's residence, the center of everything. Crews of men were already clearing land and laying the foundation of what would be a royal fortress atop the hill.

I directed Sarru toward one such crew trudging up the curving path that led to the low summit, their backs laden with baskets of rocks, to ask after my cousins. Although no one knew where Gavi was, I was told Zevi was among the men clearing trees from the construction site, something I should have guessed from the start.

Although it was not a difficult journey from Naioth to Gibeah, only a few hours' walk southeast, Keziah had insisted I ride Sarru. She'd said that, according to our agreement, we were not to be apart for even one night. And since the stallion had finally learned to trust me again, I did not argue. The only times I'd been away from her since we arrived in Naioth had been my daily training sessions with the Levite teachers, or whenever my sisters dragged her into my mother's extensive gardens, desperate to spend time with their new sister. Not only were they enthralled by her skill as a horsewoman, her intriguing accent, and her foreign clothing, Shiron had already begged Ima to cut her hair short to emulate her. While Keziah had been flattered, she'd assured Shiron that her long golden-brown hair was exquisite and that she was actually quite eager for her black curls to grow back.

I, for one, did not care whether her tresses went to her knees or if she shaved her head completely bald. She was mine and I was hers and that was all that mattered. Therefore, I was eager to get this confrontation over with and then head back to Naioth before sunset, where I could hold my wife in my arms in the tiny room I used to share with Elidor and Koli. With my father's help, I would soon begin building a small extension at the back of our home, a place where Keziah and I would grow our own little family.

But first, I needed to pass on what I knew of Shalem to my cousins.

Although his loss still pressed into tender places at the center of my soul and the sharp edges of guilt had not entirely dulled, I was certain from the many hours I'd spent on my knees asking for Yahweh's direction that it was not my place to continue the search. I had been given both a clear purpose and a precious wife, neither of which I could neglect, even for my cousin's sake. Whenever fear took hold and I imagined the worst for him, I reminded myself of Qadir's words—*"only Yahweh knows the end from the beginning"*—and took comfort in the knowledge that there was no place upon the earth where Shalem could be hidden from the God Who Sees.

A shout rang out ahead as Sarru and I crested the hill, followed by an echoing crack, and then the reverberating thud of timber slamming to the ground. My eldest cousin stood with his back to me, dressed only in the rough kilt of a laborer, gesturing to a couple of young men in a way that led me to think he was not only a part of this crew but in charge of it.

Keeping clear of the teams of men chopping away at the mighty oaks, I steered Sarru away from the fall zone and within twenty paces of my cousin before one of his charges noticed me. His gesture caused Zevi to cast a quick glance over his shoulder. Then, with his jaw slightly slack, he took a second look at who was approaching on horseback. However, he swiftly wiped the surprise from his expression and finished instructing the men before sauntering toward us. I dismounted and led Sarru by the reins to meet him halfway, murmuring calming words to the twitching warhorse.

"You are back," Zevi said evenly, as if I'd not been gone for months.

I folded my arms over my chest, realizing that even though I had made peace with Yahweh over Shalem, I still held a fair amount of anger toward our cousins. "I am."

"I'm glad to see you are well. Your parents must be relieved."

I nodded. "They were kind to forgive me for following after you."

His brows lifted in surprise.

But I had no interest in discussing my folly. "Where is Gavi? We need to talk about Shay."

He scratched his chin, momentarily distracted by something going on behind me. Another tree fell, the vibration of it shaking my bones. But even if I was furious with Zevi, I trusted he would keep me from danger. Sarru danced for a moment, unsettled by the noise, so I held tight to his bridle, stroking his nose until he relaxed.

"That's quite an animal." Zevi took in the warhorse's impressive height. "Where did he come from?"

"He belongs to Keziah, my wife."

"Your what?"

"You're *married*?" Gavi's interruption cut off my explanation.

Our younger cousin came to stand beside Zevi, his bare torso equally as covered with sweat and dust as Zevi's. One of the men I'd asked about Gavi earlier must've sent him.

"How did that come about?" he pressed.

"I met her during my search for Shay." I hoped the mention of my reasons for staying behind might stir guilt in him, but he was too distracted by the idea of my having a wife.

"She's from across the river?"

"She is, from north of Yavesh, although her mother hails from a nomadic desert tribe on the edge of Moabite territory."

"And what did your parents have to say about you bringing home a bride?"

"They adore her," I said. "But I am—"

"Can't believe you are tied down already," Gavi interrupted. "You won't find me binding myself to a woman anytime soon, especially when there are so many lovely ones to peruse." His grin bordered on lewd as he waggled his brows suggestively.

My resentment began to simmer. "Do you want to hear what I discovered about our cousin, or shall I leave you to build your king's empire?"

Gavi bristled at my vitriolic tone. "He's your king too. I seem to recall you lying in order to fight for him."

Sarru butted me with his muzzle, and I took a moment to scratch the knots between his ears, tempering the heat in my blood. "And I was wrong to do so. As you pointed out, I had no business on that battlefield."

He folded his arms over his chest, a look of surprise on his face at the admission.

"But if I had not run off with you," I continued, "I would not have my wife, and she is worth everything."

Gavi's expression softened. "So it's like that, is it, cousin?"

"I have work to do, Avi," Zevi broke in. "What do you have to tell us?"

In response, I took out the stone knife and held it toward him. He reached out to accept it, brow furrowed in confusion. "Why are you giving me this?"

"It's Shalem's," I said. "I found it on a market table in a village about four hours' walk from that cave."

Zevi flinched, as if the blade had cut into his skin.

"It looks like his," said Gavi, leaning over to inspect the knife. "I hadn't yet learned how to set the tang when I made those first blades for the four of us, and I cracked this one. See?" He reached to slide a finger along one side. "I filled the split with bitumen before I stained the wood. The ones I made for you, me, and Zevi don't have that imperfection. But what does this prove?"

"He's alive, Gavi. Traveling with the traders who sold it."

He scoffed. "They sold a knife they found on the ground, Avi. That means nothing."

I shook my head. Then, careful to not get carried away with the details of my time across the Jordan, I explained what had happened from the time I'd parted ways with them until I met the boys at the fish pools in Heshbon.

"So they did not actually see a streak in the boy's hair?" asked Gavi.

"No, but the scratches on his face and the scar—"

"Prove nothing," he said with a shake of his head. "How many people in this world have scars on their faces and hands? He's gone, Avi. Killed by hyenas. Whoever sold the knife either scavenged it from his body or found it out there in the wilderness. You have to let go of this."

"How can you discount the evidence that he is still alive, Gavi? These are not just coincidences. These are real clues, real sightings of our innocent fifteen-year-old cousin being taken who knows where by strangers." I swallowed hard, giving voice to my worst fears. "For all we know, these people are slavers. Don't you even care about Shay?"

"Of course I do!" he shouted. He squeezed his eyes shut for a moment but by the time they opened, he seemed back in possession of himself. "Of course I love him. And maybe you are right that he is alive, Avi. But what are we supposed to do? Shirk our military duties to go search the entire earth? That southern wilderness stretches on endlessly in all directions. He is one boy in a vast unknown."

"He is," I said. "But his location is not a mystery to Yahweh."

Zevi had been silent for the exchange between Gavi and me, but now he spoke up, his voice like gravel. "I hope you did not give Iyov and Hodiya false hope."

I shook my head. With my father beside me, I had told Shalem's parents about my search. I apologized for my part in his disappearance and for not turning back when I was given the opportunity on the road to Bezek. Although Iyov had been forgiving and was grateful that I'd tried my best to find his boy, Hodiya could barely stand to look at me. Her suffering was palpable, which was why I'd kept the possible sighting in Heshbon to myself.

"He may be lost to us for now, but I believe Yahweh will bring him home someday. I came to tell you what I know and ask you both to look for him as you travel with the army."

Zevi swiped a palm over his dust-covered beard. "I have a mountain of timber to clear and a crew waiting. I need to go."

"Wait, Zevi," I said before he could turn away. Then I slipped the token I'd found in the dirt of the trade road from the pouch at my belt and held it out to him. He blinked at the shell three times, his face going pale.

Then, without meeting my eyes, he turned and strode off. I opened my mouth to protest, but he was already ten paces away, Shay's knife still clutched in his hand.

Wordlessly, Gavi and I watched him go.

"He hasn't been the same since Yavesh." Gavi shook his head, his hand smoothing over a new scar that traveled the length of his bicep. "I thought maybe after finally taking out his anger on the Ammonites he'd relax. But he's even more of a stubborn jackass than before."

From the awful dreams that still dogged me and the blood-soaked memories that sometimes reared up without warning, I too had been changed by Yavesh. And I knew without asking, and by the new hauntedness in his eyes, that Gavi had been affected as well. Only the One Who Heals could mend wounds that lay so far below the ones on our skin.

I jerked my chin toward Zevi and his crew of woodcutters. "He in charge now?"

"He commands twenty men. And with his experience felling timber, he's leading the effort to clear the entire area. It won't be long before he is in charge of a hundred men or more."

"And you?"

He scoffed. "Who would put me in charge? I'm just happy to do my part. I think most of them guess that I'm not yet twenty, but they don't care. They need swords, so right now they are accepting anyone who volunteers as Saul builds his own army. Hopefully I'll soon get the chance to remind Yonatan of my skill with crafting weapons. He's been occupied with spying for his father since we returned from Yavesh."

"So you aren't going home?"

"No."

"Have you told your mother?"

He shrugged. "She knows my first duty is to the king." His gaze drifted toward the building site as if, like me, he was imagining how the fortress would look at completion.

"Were you at Gilgal during the coronation?" I asked.

A tight-lipped nod was my answer.

"Then you saw that storm, Gavi. Saul is only a man. One who has already made some wrong decisions."

His shoulders twitched. "He wears the crown. That's all I know. And Yonatan will be next to do so, and he is one of the most honorable men I've ever met. Israel will be great one day, Avi. Like Egypt or Aram or Babylon. And I will be part of it. So no . . . I won't be going back to Naioth." He pointed to the encampment down at the bottom of the hill. "This is my home now."

He started to turn away but paused, meeting my eyes again. "Zevi has always been the leader of the four of us, you know. If Shalem is alive—and I still am not convinced he is—then that means Zevi probably blames himself for failing him. For leaving him behind." He sighed, his sober expression making him look twice his age. "Either way, we probably should have stayed and helped you search. We could have caught up with the army later."

I nodded acknowledgment of his sideways apology. There was no use continuing to wear a path in dirt that lay behind us. What was done was done. "I would do it all over again—alone—for Keziah."

The solemn look melted from his face, and he reached to grasp my forearm. "My blessings, brother, for your marriage. And I am glad you made it home alive."

I returned the gesture, wrapping my hand around his elbow in a tight grip that I hoped would convey more than my feeble words could express. "I wish you well, Gavi. Be safe."

With a quick nod, he turned and walked away with sure strides, the boy I'd known almost completely swallowed up in the warrior he was becoming.

I wasn't sure how long it would be before I saw him and Zevi again, or if we would ever be as close as we'd been as children, but just as I'd learned to do with Shalem, I would trust Yahweh had a plan for each of us, even though I would never fully understand the mysteries of His ways on this side of the kingdom to come.

Connilyn Cossette is a Christy Award– and Carol Award–winning author whose books have been found on ECPA and CBA bestseller lists. When she is not engulfed in the happy chaos of homeschooling two teenagers, devouring books whole, or avoiding housework, she can be found digging into the rich ancient world of the Bible to discover gems of grace that point to Jesus and weaving them into an immersive fiction experience. She and her husband currently call a little town south of Dallas, Texas, their home. Connect with her at ConnilynCossette.com.

AUTHOR NOTE

When I began working on this first book in THE KING'S MEN series two years ago, I was blissfully unaware of what was in store for me in the months to follow. I was merely excited to dig into a new era, that of the Kings, and thrilled when I decided not to start from scratch with an entirely new cast of characters but instead to spin off THE COVENANT HOUSE series.

I chose this route for two reasons. First, because the timing fit so perfectly with the years of King Saul's early reign, and second, because I selfishly did not want to let go of Eliora and Lukio's family. So, when the idea sparked to take the four little boys from *Between the Wild Branches* on an adventure with King Saul, I could not have been more thrilled.

There is a tendency, in my opinion, to kind of gloss over the years Saul of Gibeah sat on the throne of Israel. We see him as little more than the "bad guy" who tried to kill our beloved David and who frittered away his divine blessing and destroyed his promised legacy. And yet, for all his faults and all his weaknesses, Saul was still the man chosen specifically by God to unite Israel beneath one banner and to defend his people from their enemies. He received the outpouring of the Holy Spirit and then lost himself in madness. He triumphed in some battles and failed in others. He made wise decisions and reckless, impulsive ones. He fell prey to his own vanity and greed but also laid foundations for the glorious future of Israel.

Therefore, I decided it would be fascinating to slow time down a little during these years of major transition for Israel and explore what could have been happening among the sons of Yaakov (Jacob) as Saul built a kingdom from scratch. There was no standing army, beautiful palace, or royal dynasty in place. Israel had been only a loose federation of tribes for hundreds of years up until this point, longer than the United States of America has been a country. The tribes had been doing things their own way while they dug deeper roots into the Land of Promise, evolving and expanding as tribal entities while being influenced by the pagan people who lived in and around their territories. They fought bitter civil wars as they struggled over boundaries and power and resources, and either completely forgot their special identity as the set-apart people of Yahweh, or mixed idolatrous worship practices with that of the One True God and called it holy.

I began to see many modern parallels to those of us who have been grafted into Abraham's family but who are so divided by tribalism, by cultural misunderstandings, by confusion about the nature of our God, by ignorance about the foundations of our faith, and by just plain old sinful rebellion that our true identity as the chosen and holy people of Yahweh has gotten muddled along the way.

Some of us are, like Avidan, so focused on following our own path and so caught up in the things of this world that we cannot hear the Voice of the Ancient anymore. And some of us are like Keziah, so confused and bound up in our precious idolatries that we don't even know how to seek out the still, small voice in the first place. And some of us are like Saul, appointed to do great things for Yahweh but so entangled in our own desires that the Voice grows fainter and fainter with every passing day, and we squander our time on earth building our own kingdom instead of His.

So I pray that this story, which was by far my most difficult to write because of the storms I weathered over the past couple of years, will encourage and challenge you to be a warrior for Truth. No matter if that is through music or storytelling, art or technology, teaching children or discipling adults, tending to physical needs or battling on your knees in the spiritual realms. Because if we continue to forfeit our sacred calling to wage war against the Enemy, he will continue to make inroads in our countries, our churches, and our homes.

From the very beginning of my cancer diagnosis, I needed the comfort of my Good Shepherd, so I bathed myself in the Psalms. And as I did so, two words kept popping up over and over. They were so noticeably repetitive that I began to underline them as I read and even went back to the first chapter so I could catch every single mention. It did not take long before each time I underlined these words while I read, I could hear them being spoken directly to me. *Steadfast love. Steadfast love. Steadfast love.* In Psalm 136 alone, the phrase is used twenty-six times. It was a constant reminder that even in the valley of the shadow of death, he was and is and always will be beside me.

Being the curious girl I am, I had to search out these words in the original language and found that *steadfast love* is derived from the root *chesed* (Strongs #H2616), which means loving-kindness and mercy. From deeper research, I discovered chesed is also related to the idea of an everlasting, covenantal commitment. The Lord describes himself in Exodus 34 as a God who is "abounding in steadfast love."

What a beautiful story we have to tell, don't we? It's the one about the steadfast love of a Creator who did not have any lack in himself but designed us for his pleasure in his very own image. The steadfast love of a God who would sacrifice his own Son so we could be adopted as his own children. The steadfast love of a Savior who traded the glories of heaven for a bloody cross so we could walk beside him in paradise someday. And the steadfast love of a Father who invites us to crawl into his arms, lean in close, and hear his own heartbeat as he carries us through the darkest valleys.

These last two years have been by far the deepest valleys I have walked, but I cannot describe the depth of peace I experienced because of that steadfast love. And I am so grateful that I have been given more years on this beautiful earth to continue to tell the story of his endless mercy and faithful loving-kindness.

Thank you for giving me the chance to do so by reading my stories.

And thank you, Nicole Deese, for your own faithfulness to me over these past two years, especially. You are not just a writing partner but a soul sister whose constant encouragement kept me going on the toughest of days.

And a million thanks go to Tammy Gray, because without you, my brilliant, bold, and caring friend, this book would have been 18,000 more words of meandering boringness leading to an unsatisfying (and fairly confusing) ending. My readers thank you as well, I'm sure, for helping me to transform the chemo-brain version into this one.

More love goes to Amy Matayo and Christy Barritt, the last two members of our precious Plotters Society. Your creative insight never fails to spark unexpected ideas and interesting new story trails to explore.

Thank you to my editors, Jessica and Jennifer, for your unending patience during this mess of a writing season, and for all at BHP who've supported and encouraged me along the way.

Thank you to my precious husband and family for your own steadfast love for me through everything. My beautiful daughter Corrie, especially. You served your mama with such unparalleled devotion over these long months. Without your help, I could not have possibly been able to finish this book during endless treatments and surgeries. You are a treasure, my sweet chickadee.

And to my mama, who has been walking her own deep valley over this past year and yet continues to cling to her Savior day by day. Your legacy of boundless curiosity and thirst for Truth lives on every page of my books.

Soli Deo Gloria.

Sign Up for Connilyn's Newsletter

Keep up to date with Connilyn's latest news on book releases and events by signing up for her email list at the link below.

FOLLOW CONNILYN ON SOCIAL MEDIA

Connilyn Cossette   @connilyncossetteauthor   @connicossette

ConnilynCossette.com

You May Also Like . . .

Determined to bring the Ark of the Covenant to a proper resting place, Levite musician Ronen never expected that Eliora, the Philistine girl he rescued years ago, would be part of the family he's to deceive. As his attempts to charm her lead in unexpected directions, they question their loyalties when their beliefs about the Ark and themselves are shaken.

To Dwell among Cedars by Connilyn Cossette
THE COVENANT HOUSE #1
connilyncossette.com

After a heartbreaking end to her friendship with Lukio, Shoshana thought she'd never see him again. But when, years later, she is captured in a Philistine raid and enslaved, she is surprised to find Lukio is now a famous and brutal fighter. With deadly secrets and unbreakable vows standing between them, finding a way to freedom may cost them everything.

Between the Wild Branches by Connilyn Cossette
THE COVENANT HOUSE #2
connilyncossette.com

Three Philippians whose lives were changed by Paul—a jailer, a formerly demon-possessed enslaved girl, and the woman referred to as Lydia—find their fates intertwined. In the face of great sacrifice, will they find the strength to do all that justice demands of them?

The Woman from Lydia by Angela Hunt
THE EMISSARIES #1
angelahuntbooks.com

◊ BETHANYHOUSE